# ACCLAIM

*Remain In Light* is a wonderfully dark, somber mystery steeped in Parisian culture as well as American know-how, creating its own little world you'll be glad to inhabit.
—*Out In Print*

*Remain In Light* is a complex book with very real characters. It harkens back to the work of Hemingway and Fitzgerald, leaving the Champs-Élysées and prowling the back streets of Paris. The plot is full of twists and turns, dark corners and alleyways of both Paris and the human psyche. If you're looking for a light, fluffy read, look elsewhere. If you're looking for a book you can sink your teeth into, re-read and find things you missed the first time, then I highly recommend *Remain In Light*.
—Rochelle Weber, *Rock Bound and Rock Crazy*

I'm in love with the characters in *Remain In Light*, the good, the bad, the duplicitous. Collin Kelley has created a group of people real enough to be in the next room. The intrigue and connections are unforgettable, and the feel of Paris rings true enough to slip into a guidebook.
—Jessica Handler, *Invisible Sisters: A memoir*

# REMAIN IN LIGHT

*a novel*

## COLLIN KELLEY

SIBLING RIVALRY PRESS
ALEXANDER, ARKANSAS
WWW.SIBLINGRIVALRYPRESS.COM

OTHER WORKS

Remain In Light

Copyright © 2013 by Collin Kelley

Cover art, *Gargoyle at Notre-Dame*, by Alex Nikada

Author photograph courtesy of Krystyna Fitzgerald-Morris

Cover design by Elizabeth Holmes

Sibling Rivalry Press, LLC
13913 Magnolia Glen Drive
Alexander, AR 72002

info@siblingrivalrypress.com

www.siblingrivalrypress.com

ISBN: 978-1-937420-54-3

First Sibling Rivalry Press Edition, November 2013

*for*
Donna Kile

# REMAIN IN LIGHT

Thus it is that certain persons always reappear in one's life to herald one's pleasures or one's griefs.

—Marcel Proust,
*Time Regained*

It's a poor sort of memory that only works backwards.

—The White Queen,
*Through the Looking-Glass*

*January, 1997*

David,

*I know you're never coming back to Paris. It's been more than a year since I left the key to my apartment so you could find the poems I wrote for you and the statue of Venus de Milo. I don't know if you ever went there. You may not even receive this letter. Maybe your father will intercept it and throw it in the garbage.*

*I am living with Irène, editing manuscripts for a publishing house and trying to move on with my life. Irène is my best friend, sister and second mother all rolled into one. You only got to spend a little time with her, and that's a shame. She gives me unconditional love and support, has given me a home. She would have done the same for you.*

*I've been dating a guy who runs a bookstore on the Left Bank. He's nice and wants to take our relationship to the next level, but I still think about you. I keep hoping you're going to show up here on rue Rampon and we can pick up where we left off. Remember how happy we were those last days in Paris—walking along the Seine, making love, planning our future?*

*If you didn't love me, that was one thing, but to deny who you are because your father threatened to cut you off is crazy. You're an adult,* and to let someone else dictate your happiness makes no sense to me. But you've made your decision and I have to live with that.

I told you once that I believe nothing is random. There is chaos all around us, but if you pay attention, listen closely, patterns begin to emerge. I call it synchronicity, but others call it fate, or destiny or divine intervention. I believe we were fated to meet, but perhaps we weren't meant to be together.

I guess I'm writing this letter as a form of closure, whether you read it or not. I just needed to put the words down. I want to be happy, so I'm saying goodbye to you.

Martin

P.S. I still have a scar on my forehead from the bomb.

# Prologue: Time Ticks

Hands in motion. Fingers fly over letters and numbers, type out a message, a brief history of self, of time, of need and directionless desire. The screen bathes those hands in bruised light, flickers on a face in the darkness. A face grown two years older, forehead scarred by a bomb blast often hidden by blonde bangs and more tiny lines around the eyes behind glasses. There is an unmistakable tattoo on the left hand between the thumb and index finger: two interlocking crosses, equal but opposite.

Here is how the monster is kept at bay: he surfs through pornography, lurid images and chatrooms, searches for the lowest common denominator. There's a picture of a beautiful young boy, only eighteen, on one side of the screen and an open dialogue box on the other. *17 Rue Ferrandi*, the boy types. *I am Thierry. What is your name?*

He types back: *Martin*.

He leaves the apartment on rue Rampon silently,

makes sure not to wake his roommate. But she is awake. She hears the almost imperceptible click as the laptop switches off; his feet pad down the hardwood floor of the hallway. Then there's the other click, the one that makes her mouth go dry with dread and disappointment. It's the sound as the door softly opens and closes, a maneuver only she hears. Even the cat at the foot of her bed, with preternatural senses, sleeps through his leaving. These late night disappearances happen at least twice a week, and they've been going on for months. Every time he leaves, it's still a surprise, as if it's happening for the first time. She gets out of bed and opens the doors to the balcony.

It is late summer, the tourists have gone home, the city is quiet, but there is expectancy in the air, something or someone she cannot name. She feels it as intensely as when Martin Paige's arrival was imminent just two short years ago. It is early morning; Venus is visible overhead. It rivals the moon for the sky. Irène Laureux leans on the balcony, the tattoo on her pale left hand in sharp relief against the metal railing even in the weak light. Equal but opposite—the same ink she shares with Martin. Irène looks up, summons the inevitable with words that have served her well in the past: *Paris, Paris, Paris.*

# 1 the Tunnel

The first night it happened, Irène thought Martin was just going for a walk because he was unable to sleep. The clock ticked on her bedside table, a quarter past two in the morning on a Tuesday. The next morning over breakfast, before their work began, she asked him casually and he played it off the same way: It was simply a walk to clear his head. Then it happened twice more, and then so frequently she lost count.

On the last Sunday in August, she decided to wait up for him. She sat in the darkness of the living room, a sliver of moon sending weak light through the French doors that led onto the balcony. It was after four in the morning when Martin returned.

At the sound of a key in the lock and the door opening, she lit her cigarette, so that the match illuminated the room in a red glow, revealed the shocked look on Martin's face, the visible twitch of his body recoiling in surprise.

"Irène . . ." he said, trying to suppress the shock at being discovered.

"Are you having trouble sleeping, Martin?" she asked gently. "I can give you one of my pills."

He faltered for a moment. "Yes, maybe that would help."

Irène opened her cigarette case and pulled out a Gauloises. "Smoke with me." The cigarette sat in her palm like a peace offering. The glow from the one dangling between her lips lit her beautiful face. In the two years since they met, she continued to age gracefully. There were more lines, the dark circles under her eyes were perhaps just a bit darker, the downturn of her mouth a bit more pronounced. She cut her still-blonde hair shorter, to simplify her life. Sixty-nine years old. The red glow also revealed the tattoo on her hand, equal but opposite, the binding link. Reflecting hands, she called them.

Martin sat on the couch next to her and took the cigarette and the offered match. He smelled of sex. She was not so old that she had forgotten the scent. She noted his mussed hair, the sheen of sweat on his forehead, the rumpled state of his clothes. Irène looked away, stared at the statue of Winged Victory resting on a pedestal near the front door. Two years ago she had placed it there, after dispatching Venus de Milo to Martin in America as a call to return to Paris.

*You must change your life.*

Martin had returned to rue Rampon, alone but hopeful. He had left the statue behind in his empty Memphis apartment for David McLaren to find along with a manuscript of poems and a box of matches. *Tuck it away or turn it to ash, but you must set its worth.*

In his mind, Martin could see David putting the poems into the kitchen sink and setting them on fire. Rinsing the ashes down the drain and waving away the smoke. Maybe he had smashed the statue of Venus, left it behind for the next tenants to find. What else could have happened? It had been two years and there had been nothing but silence from America. He only knew that David had gone away to college in another state. One year passed, then another. The hurt began to heal; the memories could be stashed behind the white-hot door in his brain and some semblance of life returned. At the age of twenty-four, Martin met someone else. Someone older, thirty-four to be exact, who found Martin charming and offered love unconditionally. Irène believed this, too, was fate at work. The apartment across the hall had been vacant for more than a year, then just before Martin arrived in the summer of 1995, had been purchased. Finally, someone moved in. Irène and Martin had been leaving the apartment to go to the market, and there he was. Dark curly hair, well built in a sweater and tight jeans. He had an English accent. Irène had done all the talking while the man and Martin nervously eyed each other.

"I'm Euan McEvoy," he had said, and even Irène felt a flush of heat in her face.

"My name is Irène Laureux and this is my friend Martin Paige," she said, and surprised them all by kissing Euan on both cheeks.

"Did you see the way he was looking at you?" Irène said excitedly on the street. "I was entertaining naughty thoughts myself. Just think, after all this time, someone moves in and it is your new boyfriend."

"Woah, just a second," Martin said. "Don't even try to play matchmaker. He may not even be gay."

Irène snorted. "Oh, Martin, even my, what do you call it, my *gaydar* was going off."

By 1997, Martin and Euan were sleeping with each other, essentially dating, but Martin resisted the term "boyfriend."

When Euan asked him to move across the hall into his apartment, Martin politely declined and said he wanted to keep it casual. Euan was often out of town buying books for Anglophile, the store he had opened on the Left Bank, and working with various charities in London. When he was away, Martin found himself in front of the laptop seeking other arms, boys who reminded him of things past. Boys who had that intensity and uncertainty that drew Martin like a moth to a flame.

And so it was on that last day of August in 1997 that Irène confronted Martin about his late night roaming.

"It worries me that you are out so late," she said.

"There was some kind of accident at the Pont de l'Alma tunnel. I was stuck in traffic in a taxi," Martin said.

"That's not what I mean," she said, blowing a ring of smoke at the ceiling. "You know what I mean."

"Just leave it alone," he said. "It's my life."

She leaned forward so he could see her face. "But why? I just want to know why. Euan is in love with you, and you give him false hope."

"I've been very plain with Euan about my feelings," Martin said.

"You toy with him. Just last week when he was here for dinner, you were cuddled up to him and staring into his eyes."

"I like him. And we are sleeping with each other, so I can be affectionate without . . ."

"You're using him because it's convenient."

"That's your word, not mine," Martin said, crushing his cigarette out in the ashtray. "Let's not fight about this."

"You should make a clean break then. If you don't love him, then don't toy with him. It's no different than what David did to you." She instantly regretted the words.

For a moment, Martin said nothing. He looked at the floor

and shook his head. "And no different from what Jean-Louis did to you."

Irène took the mention of her husband's betrayal in stride. It was true. Almost thirty years ago, in the tumult of the 1968 student and worker riots, her beloved Jean-Louis had been unfaithful. He had been drawn into an affair with a radical student named Frederick Dubois. Together they had fought at the barricades, but Frederick had escaped and her husband had died under mysterious circumstances. Officially, Jean-Louis was murdered, possibly by agents of then-Prime Minister Charles de Gaulle, who was trying to crush the student rebellion. Or perhaps he had taken his own life. Irène believed that Frederick knew the answers. Her search for Frederick, urged on by Martin, continued. But Frederick was as elusive in 1997 as he had been in 1968. She and Martin had spent most of the past year tracking Frederick Dubois, but the efforts were fruitless. A private detective was now on the trail, but had reached nothing but dead ends.

"Why keep making the same mistakes?" Irène asked, taking Martin's hand. "Why not be honest?"

"About what? That I fuck around with other guys? That's none of his business. I don't ask him what he does on his trips back to London."

"You know he's not sleeping with anyone else. He's smitten with you."

"I wish I could be in love with him," Martin said. "I really do. But I'm not. To pretend otherwise would be really dishonest."

Irène sighed heavily. "Fine."

"Sorry to disappoint you," Martin said, getting up from the couch and going into the kitchen.

"I'm not, I'm just . . ." she called.

"Disappointed."

The phone rang. It was almost five in the morning, and Martin came out of the kitchen and looked at Irène. They both looked at the telephone that sat between the two desks pushed together where they edited manuscripts for the publishing house. Late night calls were always a harbinger of bad things. Martin picked up the receiver. It was Euan on the line, calling from England. Even from across the room, Irène could hear Euan's voice. He was crying.

"Turn on the television," Martin said to Irène.

They both watched the screen. There was an image of a black Mercedes twisted in the Pont de l'Alma tunnel surrounded by police and emergency personnel. The camera pulled back to reveal hundreds of people near the mouth of the tunnel, standing on the bridge above. Then the scene shifted to an ambulance pulling up outside the Pitié-Salpêtrière Hospital. Martin let the phone slide away from his ear. A sound caught in Irène's throat. Salpêtrière, where they had taken Jean-Louis to be identified, where David had been taken after the bombing of the metro that left the scar on Martin's forehead. Then an announcer's voice in French: "It is confirmed that Princess Diana has died."

Tears rolled down Irène's cheeks and she covered her face. Martin spoke softly to Euan, who had met Diana and idolized her. The pain in his voice moved Martin to tears. Martin and Irène would sit up until long past dawn watching the news, until she fell asleep on the sofa and Martin sobbed under a scalding hot shower that could not cleanse the feelings of guilt and loss that bubbled to the surface that morning.

# 2 Mid-Life Crisis

The night of Princess Diana's car accident, Diane Jacobs sat in the kitchen of her parents' Memphis home getting very drunk. It was after two in the morning and she had woken from a dream about sitting on Irène's balcony with Martin, sipping wine as the sun set over Paris. Pleasant enough, but it left her gasping for air, as if a noose was tightening around her neck.

From the moment she left Martin standing on the roof of the Bel Air Hotel that summer night in 1995 after bringing him and David together, she had been on the road not only less traveled, but also completely unmapped. She had stepped on a train at Gare Lazare en route to Poland to see the concentration camp where her father had been imprisoned during World War II and never looked back to her old life as a high school teacher. Being completely untethered, to come and go as she pleased, was both liberating and frightening. She was completely on her own, free to set her own timetable and pack up and go at her leisure. The fact that she was now back in her parents' house and going back to teaching in a week's time was soul crushing.

Diane had blown through her savings until her bank account was nearly empty. In Spain, she realized she would have to go back to America and get some kind of job. Would have to face her disapproving parents, who had been storing her furniture and belongings while she "threw her life away with both hands," as her mother so gently put it.

"What's happened to you?" her mother pleaded over the phone when Diane called from Amsterdam during Hanukkah in 1995. "You have lost your mind. Do you know there's a letter here from the Shelby County Department of Education saying they have suspended your teaching license? I've told the rabbi everything and he says you need to come back and go to synagogue. Let him counsel you. Don't go to one of those public places and tell all your personal business. That's for the goyim."

"Mother, you desperately need Jewish Anonymous. When dad starts going to synagogue again, let me know and I'll think about it."

"You are killing me, you know this. You know your father never goes to synagogue."

"Exactly. I have to go, Mom, the flophouse I'm staying in is being raided," Diane said and rang off as her mother continued to scream.

Diane, who had never wanted to leave America in the first place, found herself not wanting to return. She finally understood Martin's need to escape the constraints and expectations that society there placed on everyone. In Europe, she could be a penniless drifter and no one gave it a second thought. In America, and especially in Memphis, she was a divorced, cracked up, failure of a human being. Damaged goods. Rumors flew about what had happened in Paris, about why, after she had safely seen home most of the children she chaperoned that summer, she had gotten back on a plane and returned to Paris. The talk circulated back to her mother, who wanted to know if she had gotten pregnant by one of her students. There were even rumors that she and David McLaren had a torrid affair in Europe. When her mother suggested this during another phone call, Diane had laughed until she began choking on her own spit.

"Your name is being dragged through the mud," her mother said. "Everyone said that McLaren boy stayed in Europe, too. What are people supposed to think? It's crazy, Diane, crazy."

"Mom, David McLaren doesn't bat for my team. If you get my drift."

"I have no idea what you're talking about. You've lost your mind."

In Spain, Diane went to a cyber café, got online and contacted an old friend from college who was a principal at a small private school in Memphis. Diane gave a not-exactly-truthful account of her last year, and mentioned that her teaching certificate had lapsed. Her old friend hired her anyway and said she could take evening and weekend courses to get recertified. It was a private school full of rich, smart kids. She would only have to teach literature to four classes each day and the pay was comparable to her income from the Shelby County Public School System that had previously employed her. Diane had vowed not to teach again, but she had to be practical.

The first night back in Memphis, sleeping in her old room, she seriously contemplated suicide. She was forty-four years old and living with her parents. Her mother was equal parts delighted and horrified by her daughter's return.

"What were you thinking?" her mother kvetched, pacing

the kitchen floor. "Why can't you just keep a job? Everybody has to work, whether they like it or not."

"You didn't work," Diane said, face buried in her hands.

"Don't you say that to me. I worked my fingers to the bone raising you and keeping this house up for you and your father while he worked day and night. Who do you think cooked your food and mended your clothes and changed your sheets? It was me, and don't you forget it."

"No chance of that."

"At least you'll be here for Hanukkah."

And, on August 31, 1997, it appeared Diane would be in Memphis for Hanukkah and for every other holiday to follow. She drained her glass and listened to her mother snoring upstairs.

"She can't be quiet even in her sleep," Diane's father said, startling her. He was standing at the kitchen doorway in his ratty old bathrobe. Diane laughed under her breath and relaxed. "What are you drinking?" he asked.

"Jack Daniels."

Her father got a drinking glass out of the drying rack and sat down across from her at the table. He pushed the glass toward Diane and she filled it halfway.

"Don't be a Jew," he said, and Diane filled it almost to the rim.

He took a long sip of the whiskey and his face flushed almost immediately. A smile played across his face as the warmth of the alcohol settled in. His wife's snores grew momentarily louder then subsided.

"She has sleep apnea and won't do anything about it," he said. "The doctor said it might kill her."

"Why don't I detect any concern in your voice?"

He shrugged. "She's a grown woman. She's been told. If she chooses not to get treatment, who am I to say anything?"

Diane raised her glass. "To sleep apnea," she said and tapped her glass against her dad's before they drank.

They both listened to the sounds of the house: the hum of the refrigerator, a plop of water from the sink faucet, the air conditioner turning off and on. Her mother's snores were comical in their depth and tonal quality, but eventually she rolled over and there was quiet from that corner of the dwelling.

Diane watched her dad drink and enjoy the silence. Every one of his seventy-two years showed on his face and body. The tattoo from the concentration camp peeked from beneath his sleeve. He and Diane rarely had private talks. The last had been when she was divorcing her husband six years ago. They generally spoke in passing or shared little jokes about her mother, but it was always small talk.

"I think I'm in trouble, Dad," she said, breaking the silence.

He looked up at her and put the nearly empty glass on the table. "Don't worry about money."

"It's more than money . . . ." she trailed off. "I think I'm having a mid-life crisis. It's stupid as hell, but I don't know what else to call it. I'm just not happy here. Not here specifically, but just in America. I saw a lot of Europe, Dad. I saw Poland and the camp. I just don't know what to do with myself. I'm so restless I feel like I'm burning up inside."

The old man nodded, but did not speak. He hated talking about the past. He had only told one or two stories about his time at the camp as a teenager and those were just about specific friends he had made there. Friends who had all died before the liberation. That much she knew. During her visit to the camp, Diane saw a blown up black and white photograph that had been taken by a soldier who helped liberate the prison. It was of the survivors, and her father, skeletal and haunted, had been among them. His clothes were tattered rags and he wore no shoes. She would not have recognized him at all except for the eyes. Even near death in 1945 and now as an old man, they were huge and luminous. Those eyes stared at her now.

"You'll go back to Europe then? To Martin and his friend?"

"I think so."

"They are good friends. They will help you be happy again. You should go."

"Maybe if I teach for a year, I can save up enough to get settled."

Her father snorted. "I mean go now. Why do you wanna wait a year?"

"Uh, I'm broke. I'm living in your house."

"Can Martin find you a job over there?"

"He said he could, but . . ."

"I'll write you a check. You can pay me back once you get settled."

Diane wept openly, something she never did. Her father took her hand across the table and held it. "I hope those are tears of happiness," he said quietly.

She nodded. "Are you sure, Dad? I won't go without your blessing."

"I give you my blessing on one condition."

Diane wiped her eyes with both hands. "Name it."

"I want you to go to my village and put stones on my parents' graves. I'll tell you how to get there. I still remember."

Diane's eyes welled up again. "Of course."

He gripped her hand tightly and fought back his own emotions. "I want them to know we are still here. That despite it all, our family is still alive. We carry on."

Father and daughter finished the bottle of whiskey, until they were tipsy and telling jokes. They were still up when her mother came downstairs to make breakfast, berating them for being alcoholics. Diane kissed her father good night at his door and went into her room. She lay down on her bed for a minute then rolled over and picked up the phone. She dialed Irène's number in Paris. A sleepy sounding Martin answered the phone.

"Are you still asleep? It's almost two there, isn't it? You lazy Frenchies."

"We were up late watching the news."

"I've got some breaking news for you. I'm coming to Paris." There was silence from Martin's end. "Oookay, don't get too excited."

"You haven't heard have you?"

At that same moment, she heard her mother let out a little shriek from downstairs. "Oh, my god, Princess Diana is dead!" her mother shouted.

# 3 Missing

The day after Labor Day, Diane was on her way to the bank to cash the check her father had slipped to her. She had expected a couple thousand to tide her over, and felt woozy when she opened the envelope and saw the number ten followed by three zeroes. She didn't notice the car that followed her from her parents' house to the bank and then to Wal-Mart, where Diane was going to buy new underwear and other necessities for Paris. She had yet to tell Martin and Irène that her visit to Paris might be permanent.

Diane pushed a shopping cart down the aisles in a daze, trying to ignore the out of control children who blocked her path and their Stepford Wife, suburban mothers who were either glazed over or so perky that she wanted to slap the white trash out of them. What if Martin and Irène didn't want her in Paris? What if she couldn't get a job? Or find an affordable apartment? A wave of panic made her stomach cramp. Diane caught a glimpse of herself in a make-up counter mirror and felt like a stranger was staring back. She had cut her dark hair boyishly short in Europe and it was growing back into her usual straight bob. She'd lost weight, making her face look more angular and her mouth somehow wider. She sighed and pushed her buggy toward the registers.

Standing in line at the checkout, she saw Princess Diana's face on every tabloid cover. A woman in front of her was clutching a stack of magazines, staring at them forlornly, blinking away tears. Diane rolled her eyes. She had agreed to stand along the funeral route in London with Martin and Irène to watch Euan walk in the procession as a representative of one of Diana's charities. Diane hoped she would have time to discuss her plans with Martin and Irène, maybe even try to befriend the old woman. It was a small price to pay for a new life.

After standing in line for half an hour, she was loading the trunk with her purchases when she sensed someone watching her. Diane looked over her shoulder and noticed a car parked directly across from her, two people sitting inside. The sun cast a glare over the windshield, so she couldn't see their faces. Diane rolled her cart to the return corral, felt a bead of sweat roll down her back. The man and woman were now standing together behind their car staring at her. Diane shielded her eyes from the sunlight and felt her stomach drop. They were David McLaren's parents.

The last time she'd seen them was at the Memphis Airport when she had returned with the students, sans David, after the terrorist attack on the Saint-Michel station near Notre-Dame. Diane and Martin had taken the students to the cathedral that morning and they had all been caught up in the aftermath of the deadly bombing. There had been a crush of reporters and cameras, her principal, the school superintendent and David's father threatening a lawsuit and calling her a cunt. She'd slapped him across the face and hid in a bathroom waiting for her flight to be called so she could return to Paris. The last thing she needed was David's crazy parents meddling in her life. Diane fumbled with her car keys and started to unlock her door.

"Excuse me," the woman called out. "May we speak with you?"

Diane said nothing, her hand trembling so much that she dropped the keys on the pavement. By the time she retrieved them, David's parents were standing next to her. His mother was short and had cropped hair and wore very little make up. She looked exhausted and haggard. His father was tall and wore a polo shirt tucked into jeans. There was something both haunted and angry about the set of his mouth and the look in his eyes. Diane guessed he was probably replaying the slap and thinking how he'd like to return the gesture. She struggled to remember their first names from the one or two teacher conferences she'd had when David was her student.

"I'm Kathy McLaren and this is my husband Bill," the woman said.

"I know who you are," Diane said, trying to keep an even tone to her voice. "What do you want?"

"Can we go somewhere . . .a restaurant or bar?" Bill asked, an edge to his voice that made Diane wary. "We just want to ask you a few questions."

"A restaurant or bar?" Diane asked incredulously. "I don't think so. I seem to remember you calling me an irredeemable cunt the last time we met . . ."

Bill cut her off. "Can we not do this in the parking lot?"

Diane opened her car door and started to get inside. "It was two years ago. You got your precious son back. You won. Now leave me alone."

Diane started to shut the door, but Kathy put her hand on

the frame. "Please, Ms. Jacobs, we need your help."

"I gave at the office," Diane sneered and pulled the door closed, but Bill yanked it back hard. "Get your fucking hand off my car or I'm gonna start screaming rape."

"David is missing!" Kathy shouted, then dissolved into tears.

Bill slowly took his hand off the door and put it around Kathy's shoulders. He wouldn't look at Diane or his wife, his gaze set on some stoic middle distance.

Diane slowly got out of the car. "There's a coffee shop . . . let's go over there."

They walked in silence to the Starbucks, the McLarens trailing behind her, holding hands. Diane felt a cold panic growing inside her stomach. She had an almost pulsating image of David in her mind, the way he had looked that summer. The little bastard was coming back to fuck with her life again.

They awkwardly stood in line ordering iced lattes before finding a booth in the back of the coffee shop, the McLarens on one side and Diane on the other.

"Look, I realize you and this Martin are friends. Or whatever you are," Bill said.

Diane drew back. "You're already pissing me off, Mr. McLaren. If you want my help, keep your insinuations to yourself or I'm outta here."

"Martin Paige is the reason our son is missing in the first place," he said.

"Martin hasn't seen or heard from David in two years . . . count 'em . . . two, and neither have I. If you're trying to blame Martin . . ."

"David came back from that trip to Europe a different person. He was a totally different person than we put on the plane. He was out of control. We found all these . . . love poems that Martin had written to David. It was disgusting."

37

Kathy McLaren leaned in, her voice almost a whisper. "Our son is not a homosexual. He played sports, made good grades. He had a girlfriend." David's mother had convinced herself of these things, but she secretly knew the truth, Diane thought. She almost felt sorry for her.

Bill was talking again. "When he came back from that goddamn trip, he started drinking. Drinking a lot. He went to college and right after he got there, he was arrested for drinking and driving and assaulting . . ."

"That's not important, Bill," his wife interjected, touching his shoulder.

"The hell it's not. It has something to do with whatever happened while he was over there. He went to some bar and these faggots were hitting on him and he beat one of them up. The fag called the cops and David got locked up."

"He left school and we put him in rehab," Kathy said, trying to divert the conversation.

Diane was sitting with her arms crossed over her chest, looking back and forth at the couple. She shook her head. "You two are a piece of work. Let's clear up a couple of things right now. David was already drinking before he came on the trip. I know it's a hard pill to swallow that your golden boy has a few flaws, but get your heads out of your asses."

Kathy broke down and started to cry, she curled into her husband's chest. "I just want my son back. He's been missing since February. We're desperate."

Bill nodded vigorously. "He left the rehab center and said he was going to do some traveling and clear his head before going back to school. The last we heard of him, he was in Paris and said he was coming home. We wired him some money. That was months ago. We've spent thousands and thousands of dollars on a detective—nothing. The police have looked for him, but they say he's an adult and can do whatever he wants. They don't know our son like we do. He's in trouble."

Diane sat back in the booth. Yes, David was in trouble, but they didn't know him at all. That was how the trouble began. "I told you outside, I haven't heard from David. If he had contacted Martin in Paris, I would have heard. It sounds like David needs some space to figure out his life."

"David is not a faggot," Bill said, poking his finger in Diane's face.

"You're a delusional son of a bitch," Diane said, batting his hand away. "David chose to stay in Paris that summer, I didn't force him and neither did Martin. Your son disappeared then, too, and I went back to find him. You think Martin forced David to have sex with him? Please. David was a cocktease from the moment we landed in Europe."

"Please, let's not talk about this," Kathy pleaded.

"You two need to wake up," Diane said. "You pushed David out the door with your homophobia."

"Just a goddamn minute," Bill said, the same menacing tone in his voice when he was up in Diane's face at the airport. "Our son was an all-American kid. Then he meets this Martin and he starts sitting in his room and turning into a moody little girl. He had a future. He was going to Auburn University on an athletic scholarship, for god's sake. He fucking threw it all away because Martin Paige fucked with his head. He tried to turn him into a queer."

Everyone in the coffeehouse was looking at them now, as Bill's tirade had gotten louder. Diane picked up her purse and slid out of the booth. "You know what? I hope you never find him. I hope he keeps running away from your crazy ass. What kind of father are you?"

Bill jumped out of the booth and grabbed Diane by the arm.

People in the coffeehouse were leaving and the employees looked nervous. "Ma'am, do you want us to call the police?" a teenage barista asked from behind the counter.

"No, honey, I got this," Diane said and brought her knee up swift and hard into Bill McLaren's groin. He instantly let go of her arm and doubled over, falling back into the booth with a groan. His wife let out a little shriek. Diane leaned over him as he gasped for breath.

"Here's some free advice. You want your son to come back? Stop being a judgmental, angry, homophobic fucktard. Your son is gay and he's got a drinking problem. Deal with it."

"He'd be better off dead," Bill gasped.

Kathy pulled away from him, stunned. "Don't say that! How could you say that? If anyone drove him away, it was you. You're such a bastard." She tried to stand up in the booth, then crawled over the table and ran out of the coffee shop.

Diane shook her head. "God, you really are a douchebag."

"I'll have you locked up," Bill spat, still clutching at his crotch. "I'll fucking sue."

"Come and get me, motherfucker," Diane said, flipping him off behind her back as she walked out of the coffeehouse.

Diane walked quickly back to her car. David's father would probably call the police, or the employees would. Irrationally, she thought of going straight to Memphis Airport and getting the first flight out to Europe. She was getting into her car when she looked over and saw Kathy McLaren sitting on the pavement between the shopping cart corral and another car quietly sobbing. Diane sat for a moment, her hands gripping the wheel, the oppressive summer heat inside the car nearly suffocating her. "Fuck," she muttered under her breath and opened the door.

Diane knelt down in front of the woman, whose chest heaved. She looked up at Diane and wiped tears and sweat from her face.

40

"I'm sorry about my husband," she said between spasms.

"He's an asshole."

"He just doesn't understand."

"Mrs. McLaren, your son is gay. You have to accept it and so does your husband or you'll never see David again."

"I don't care if he's gay. I can't stand not knowing where he is and if he's okay," Kathy said, putting her face back into her hands.

"I wish I could help you, but I honestly don't know where he is."

"The detective we hired thinks David will try to contact Martin in Paris."

Diane swallowed hard. The last thing Martin needed was David—penniless, drunk and out of control—back in his life. "If David contacts Martin, I will let you know. You have my word."

Kathy grabbed Diane and hugged her hard. "Thank you, thank you."

Holding the woman while she sobbed, Diane reinvested in her hatred for David McLaren and his cowardice. All her hard work those weeks in the summer of 1995, practically holding David hostage and convincing him to come out of the closet and admit his feelings for Martin had been a waste. As soon as David had returned to America, he had been whisked away by his parents and denounced any feelings for Martin. He had gone off to college and then vanished all together, dropped off everyone's radar. Alice down the rabbit hole.

For months after she left Paris, Diane believed that Martin and David were living in bliss back in Memphis. Then a gnawing feeling came over her and she sent a postcard to Irène's apartment in Paris with an email address. In Dublin, she checked her inbox at a cyber café and found out what had happened. David's parents had been waiting at the airport to rescue their son from Martin's clutches, and David had willingly gone with them. Martin had quit his job as a law clerk and returned to Paris.

Diane could easily imagine David living a lie. He'd marry some hapless sorority girl, impregnate her and then she would discover in some horrible way that her husband was a closet case. Just as Diane had discovered her own husband's double life. A mind's eye snapshot she carried with her always: her husband fucking the teenage boy, her student, in their bed. The look of horror and shame on her husband's face, his long-held secret exposed in a careless moment of lust. Diane had let her husband off the hook without a fight. Let him have the house and most of the money, she only wanted to be away from the lie. She had gone to a grief-counseling workshop at the encouragement of her mother and fellow teachers. And that's where she had met Martin, still reeling from the death of his boyfriend, Peter. Martin called their meeting synchronicity, another link in a chain of pre-destined events that would eventually connect them to David and Irène. Diane thought it was all hooey, and she vowed once again to stop David from interfering in their lives.

# 4 Reset

In the taxi on the way from Orly Airport, sheets of rain lashed the windows. By the time Diane reached the city it was a cold drizzle, too cold for the first week of September, she thought. Martin and Irène had wanted to pick her up at the airport in Irène's old convertible, but Diane had told them she would just get a cab. She feared the old woman might have one of her panic attacks and freak out at the busy curbside or crash the car all together. Martin said Irène was cured, for the most part, of her agoraphobia, but Diane was not taking any chances. As she passed familiar monuments on the way to rue Rampon, she silently cursed David McLaren for ruining her return to Paris.

Diane sometimes cursed herself for bringing Martin to Paris in the first place, when he was still fragile over Peter's death. She often fantasized about turning back the clock and rearranging the scenarios that had put Martin and David on a collision course and left her without a job. If she had told the principal "no" when he asked her to fill in as chaperone for the students on their graduation trip, hadn't been thinking selfishly of a free vacation and a way to shake Martin from his torpor, where would she be now? Those thoughts ran parallel to the questions that also plagued her: What if they had never gone to Paris? Would Martin still be grieving over Peter, drifting through life in his dead end job as a law office clerk? Would she be going to teach every day, burned out and uninspired? Paris was a blessing and a curse. Like the bomb that ripped through the train station that day at Notre-Dame, the trip to Paris had exploded Diane and Martin out of their routines. Hit the reset button on their lives.

As the taxi swung onto rue Rampon, she saw Martin and Irène standing in the doorway to the apartment. Martin rushed out to embrace Diane as she got out of the taxi, while Irène hung back in the doorway.

"What shitty weather you're always having," Diane said as she wrapped her arms around Martin's neck. She knew from the happy look on his face that David had not made contact while she'd been en route from Memphis.

She accepted an embrace from Irène, whom she had never really warmed to. There was a mutual respect and not much else. Diane felt as if she had entrusted Martin into Irène's care, and she could see he was no worse for wear. He had a job, he was writing and he was seeing the man who lived across the hall. It was more than he would have done had he returned to Memphis and shut himself up in his overpriced apartment. Diane would give credit where credit was due.

"It's wonderful to have you with us again, Diane, despite the sad circumstances," Irène said.

"It just shows you that we're all mortal," Diane said. "No

matter how famous you are, you're still going to check out sooner or later."

They lugged her bags up to Euan's apartment and Martin used his key to let her in. "Is this up to your standards, milady?"

Euan's apartment was much like Irène's—lined with bookshelves and statues, photographs he had taken of his travels, expensive art prints. The giant bed was an heirloom from his mother's side of the family.

"My god, it's a ship. I'll need a rope to pull myself up into it. Did you change the sheets?" Diane teased.

"Why don't you get settled, have a bath, then come over and join us? Irène is cooking dinner."

"And first class tickets on the Eurostar," Diane said, hopping up onto the bed and sprawling out. "Now this is living."

"We're going to a funeral, you know. At least pretend to be moved."

"We're going to a spectacle, baby. The most famous woman on earth being towed down the street to a celebrity gathering that puts the Oscars in the shade."

"Try to fight your penchant for sarcasm around Euan. He's taking this very hard."

"One trip to an AIDS hospital and she was the thinking gay man's icon. Is that it?"

Martin sighed loudly. "You don't have to go to the funeral. You could stay here."

Diane rolled over on the bed and propped her face in her hands. "I do want to go. I admired Diana. She unloaded that ugly husband, although it took about five years longer than it should have. She had great taste in clothes and that older son of hers is going to be a piece of serious ass in a few years."

"Why wait? Go for him now."

"That's your department, Martin. I like men. Grown

45

men."

"So not a lesbian yet."

"Sorry, no."

"Couldn't even muster the courage to try it in Amsterdam?"

"My tongue went limp at the thought."

They both laughed. It broke some of the tension. Only emails and a few phone calls had passed between them since her last visit, before she went to Spain and then back to America.

After Martin had gone back across the hall, Diane luxuriated in Euan's bathtub. She had yet to tell Martin and Irène she wanted to stay permanently, but that had all gone out the window as every time she phoned Paris prior to her departure, it was all about Euan's grief over Princess Diana and the plans to attend the funeral in London.

She was back in Paris with a check from her father, no job, no place to live and David McLaren was probably lurking somewhere in the arrondissement ready to ring the doorbell and disrupt their lives. Diane slid down in the tub until her head slipped under the water, and she wondered if she would ever find peace of mind again.


Irène made soup as the first course of their meal. She spooned a taste into Martin's mouth. "More salt," he suggested. She tasted it. "More pepper," she decided. They cooked in silence, the television in the living room playing non-stop coverage of Princess Diana's death, the plans for the funeral at Westminster Abbey, the role of the paparazzi, the alcohol level of the chauffeur. The trip to London would be Irène's first out of Paris since she was a young woman, when Jean-Louis had been alive.

Martin silently fretted that Irène would faint in the masses that would throng London's streets, but Euan's participation in the funeral left them no choice. He also worried about Euan and Diane clashing during the visit. Euan had met Diane only once and felt put off by her abrasiveness, the way she calculated words to do the most damage. Martin had that quality as well, but it was tempered by his past and his deference to Irène's more even-handed approach to life and loss.

"Diane looks well," Irène said.

"She's as sharp as ever."

"She still doesn't like me very much."

"Unlike you, Diane takes her time warming up to people."

"Two years and counting."

"You two will get along fine. This little trip will give you a chance to bond."

Irène muttered in French.

"What was that?"

"Nothing at all," she said with a huge smile.

"Yeah, right."

"I was just curious . . ." she let her words trail away as she stirred the soup.

"About?"

"Don't you find it curious that Diane has come to Paris now when she should be teaching school? Doesn't school begin after your last summer holiday?"

"It did in Memphis, but she's teaching at a private school. Maybe they start later. What are you getting at?"

"This sudden appearance seems out of character. So does her wanting to go to Princess Diana's funeral and associate with me and Euan."

"She likes Euan."

Irène smacked her lips. "Hmmm . . ."

"Spit it out, Irène. What's her ulterior motive?"

She tasted the soup again, pronounced it perfect. "I'll let you know."

Dinner at Irène's was convivial and full of small talk. Gerard, the publisher who employed Martin and Irène as editors, arrived with flowers and blustery talk of the famous authors he had met. He was still sweet on Irène after all these years. Diane was chatty, almost too chatty, and was putting up a concerted effort not to offend. Martin sensed she was dancing around a subject she would rather not discuss. He could see that Irène was watching her carefully, looking for any crack that might reveal intent. Irène had made him paranoid that Diane was there for another reason as well. After all, Diane had secretly returned to Paris in the summer of 1995 to flush David out of hiding—and the closet. Although her scheme had been a colossal failure, it proved she was capable of anything. On the other hand, her desire to see the Princess of Wales' funeral could just be more erratic behavior.

Outside, the rain continued to fall and darkness began to overtake the City of Light. Even with her senses on full alert, Diane missed the glowing tip of the cigar that appeared in the hotel window across rue Rampon. Disembodied, watching, waiting.

The rain turned to drizzle again and Irène went out on the balcony to have a final smoke before going to bed. Her cat, Pierre, darted out the French doors and took cover under the table, flicking his tail in displeasure at the weather.

Irène let the mist wash over her, found her hand straying toward the binoculars sitting in their case on the tabletop. The Bel Air Hotel was only partially full since tourist season was over. All the school groups were gone, the college students, the honeymooners. Now it was just businessmen looking for a cheap room and a few tourists who found a bigger bargain by coming off-season. She could see all the rooms on the floor opposite and partially into the ones on the floor above and below. As always, Irène trained her binoculars on the room just across from her. A light was on in the main room and also in the bathroom.

Through the partially cracked curtain, she saw no one moving about. She had almost decided to look elsewhere, when something caught her eye. There was a hard shell case open on the bed and a camera with a long telephoto lens resting inside. Beside it, there was a small tape recorder with a huge microphone. Partially obscured behind the case was a stack of file folders, spilling pages and photographs she could not make out. Irène knew instantly that this was a detective's gear. When she had met with the detective helping her track Frederick Dubois, he had all these accoutrements in his office and showed her how he used them. She wondered who the man across rue Rampon was watching. A philandering husband or wife more than likely, possibly a businessman embezzling funds. This was the kind of thing she lived for, why she could never put away her binoculars. The intrigue of watching others' lives unfold had sustained her all of her adult life while she had been a prisoner of her agoraphobia and panic attacks. Now, she could walk to the market or take the car to the publishing house and even ride the metro when it wasn't horribly crowded. Martin had arrived and set her free. But her voyeurism would never go away.

The detective appeared between the crack in the curtains and picked up the camera. Irène retreated back inside her doorway, to lose herself in the shadows of the dark apartment. The man—a cigar clamped in his mouth, a little overweight, balding and wearing a suit with an open collared shirt—took the camera and pushed its long lens through the curtain. He was aiming down at the street, then at the apartment building. *He's watching someone here*, Irène thought. She made a mental list of the tenants in the building and who might have a detective on their trail. The most obvious choice was the businessman who said he ran an import-export firm and was rarely ever home. She always thought there was something sneaky going on with him, but she knew he was not in his apartment. There was poor Julie, who cared for her father deteriorating with Alzheimer's disease, and the retired flight attendant who could not possibly afford the apartment she lived in, not on her pension.

Irène heard the street door of her apartment building open and close with a loud click. The detective swung the camera to follow the person, snapping photos madly. Irène had to see who it was, had to give herself away. She rushed to the railing and just caught a glimpse of Diane as she turned onto Boulevard Voltaire toward République Square. Irène jerked her head back toward the window and found the detective staring at her, his camera half-raised, surprised to find he had been discovered. Irène took her binoculars and put them up to her eyes. He raised his camera and snapped a few photos of her. She stood there defiantly, meeting the dark eye of the camera with two of her own. Slowly, she extended her right arm in front of her and raised her middle finger. He dropped the camera and leered at her for a moment, a smirk on his paunchy face, then he snatched the curtains closed. She could see herself reflected back in the dark window glass, trembling.

# 5 Possibly Maybe

Irène woke up the next morning on the couch with Martin and Diane standing over her. She had fallen asleep waiting for Diane to return, to confront her. Irène sat up, her joints stiff from where she had slumped over. A glass of wine sat half empty on the coffee table next to a manuscript she had tried to edit to pass the hours.

"Were you boozing it up last night?" Diane asked. She was showered and made up, but Irène could see she'd had little sleep. Irène had last checked the clock at a quarter of six and Diane had not returned.

"I was working and fell asleep," Irène said, fixing an eye on Diane. She wanted to ask her right then and there, but did not want to alarm Martin.

"I'm going to take Diane to the Anglophile," Martin said. "Do you want us to bring anything back? Breakfast?"

Irène stretched and shook her head. "I'll get

something here or walk around the corner to the café."

"Suit yourself," Martin said. "We'll be back."

Irène could not stop staring at Diane, watched them leave and the door shut. She wanted Diane to look back, make eye contact, acknowledge that something was going on. Diane had brought trouble with her and Irène would be damned if it would interrupt their lives on rue Rampon.

Across the street, the curtains were still shut in the room occupied by the man with the camera. Breakfast would have to wait.

In the metro on the way to the bookshop, Martin told Diane he was thinking about going to see a psychiatrist again. Shortly after they had met, Martin's parents committed him to a psychiatric hospital. They had found Martin huddled in the kitchen, which he had destroyed in a grief-filled rage, with a gun in his lap. David's arrival might be just the tipping point to send Martin back to the loony bin, Diane thought.

"Really? What does Irène have to say about it?"

"I haven't mentioned it to her yet. She thinks I don't need a shrink if she's around."

"Of course. I told you she has delusions of grandeur about being Madame Freud."

"Yeah, yeah. Give that a rest."

"And why do you think you need to see a headshrinker again?"

"I feel stuck. Euan wants a relationship, and Irène thinks I'm leading him on."

"You need to pay some quack a hundred bucks an hour to help you work through that? Write me a check and I'll be your shrink. If you don't love Euan, you don't love him. See? It's all worked out."

"You're oversimplifying."

"Are you still waiting on David?" It was the first time she'd said his name since her return, and, as usual, it stung.

"I know he's never coming back to Paris. I've accepted that."

"Okay, so why not take a shot at Euan? He's not my type, but he's cute."

"He's older and he wants to settle. Hell, we already have sex like an old married couple. If I want it more than a couple times a week, then I'm a nympho. And any suggestion that we do it somewhere else besides his bed, you know, for a little variety, then I'm a whore."

"Yeah, but is he any good in bed?"

"Well, yeah. I mean, he gets me off, but it's not intense."

The train shuddered to a stop at St. Sulpice station and they went aboveground and walked toward the Anglophile.

"Want some more advice?" Diane asked.

"That's a rhetorical question, I take it?"

"If you're trying to find a David substitute, just stop. Most guys—Euan included—are never going to look like David, fuck like David, or drive you around the goddamn bend with their indecisiveness like David. Sorry to break it to you. Most people are not like David."

Martin thought of the boy from Saturday night who, if he squinted, reminded him of David. They both had the same type of lean body and aggressive sexuality. He fucked Martin hard, kissing him, bruising his mouth, making them come in a scream of release. Euan had never even come close to that kind of lovemaking, that intensity. Euan had passion, but it was restrained. He was fussy and particular, and made awkward attempts to sound like a free spirit to try and keep Martin interested.

"What would you do if David showed up here again?" Diane ventured.

"That would never happen. He's banging sorority girls and living the lie for his Nazi parents."

"But if he did?" Diane persisted.

"I don't know. If he came back and was cleaned up and serious . . . possibly. Maybe."

"Does Euan even know about David? Or did you give him the Cliffs Notes version?"

"I told him everything."

"And he's still around? That's impressive."

"Euan wants to pretend like David was all some big acid trip I once had. He keeps telling me I was just young and carried away by my first trip abroad, and he thinks if he says it often enough I'll believe it, too. Plus he thinks Irène and I are wasting our time looking for Frederick Dubois."

Martin and Irène had tried numerous times to explain their symbiosis to Euan, that they had dreamed about each other for months before they actually met in the summer of 1995. They both subscribed to Carl Jung's belief in synchronicity, that nothing was coincidence. If Martin had never come to Paris, Irène would have never discovered Jean-Louis' journal with its details about his affair with Frederick Dubois in the tumult of 1968. Whenever they were frustrated after hitting another dead end in the search for Frederick, Euan would try to convince them the search was fruitless. Frederick was either dead or living in another country and even if they did find him, there was no proof that he had anything to do with Jean-Louis' death.

"You know, Euan does have a point," Diane said.

"His lack of support is disappointing. He doesn't understand how important this is to Irène."

They were standing in front of the Anglophile, and even

Diane had to admit it was charming with its stalls of books on the street and the name of the shop in flourished script stenciled on the windows. The Anglophile had an impressive collection of English novels, poetry and nonfiction. Euan had renovated the space, leaving beams exposed, original gas sconces on the wall, but he had painted the walls white and installed a light hardwood floor. The tall shelves were also painted white, giving the space a gallery look and feel. It was an unexpected mixture of old and new Paris. The Anglophile spanned two floors—the storefront below and a former apartment on the second with more books, a small kitchen and office space. There was also a rooftop that Euan opened for special parties and events, such as watching the fireworks on Bastille Day.

The shop door opened and a young man came out. He was maybe nineteen or twenty, of mixed race, maybe half black, Diane thought, but what was unmistakable was his reaction to Martin.

"Hello," the man said, a smile breaking across his face.

"Hi," Martin said, his voice going up an octave. "How are you?"

"I'm well," he held the door for Martin and Diane. "Are you coming to the next open mic?" He had an indeterminate accent as well, French but something else, although he was obviously fluent in English.

"I'm always there," Martin said.

"I've heard you read. Your poetry is beautiful."

"Really?" Martin said, sounding bashful. Diane rolled her eyes.

"Yes. I always look forward to hearing you."

"You've never read before, have you?"

"Not yet. I usually sit in the back. I will next time."

"I look forward to it," Martin said eagerly.

"Well, goodbye then," the young man said and headed off down the street. As they went in the shop, Diane saw the boy look back over his shoulder and grin.

"Uh . . . who was that?" Diane said watching him go. He was tall, maybe a little too skinny, but he had an amazing ass in tight jeans.

"I don't know his name, but I've seen him at the open mic. He's hot."

"Watching gay boys flirt is weird," Diane said, scrunching her nose. "You were fucking each other with your eyes."

"And you were checking out his ass."

"It was hard to miss."

"I try not to hook up with guys I meet at the shop. It's weird with Euan always hovering around. You know that old saying, never shit where you eat."

"How thoughtful," Diane said. "Hallmark should make a card for that."


The detective opened his hotel room door, setting a suitcase and camera equipment in the hallway. He didn't notice Irène, back against the wall, smoking a cigarette, until he stepped out. His face registered surprise, and Irène relished that she'd been able to sneak up on him.

"Bonjour," she said. "I am Irène Laureux."

The man picked up his bags and walked down the hall toward the elevator. He was a large man, so he was easy to keep up with and the old hotel owner had locked the elevator on the first floor, so she was in no danger of losing him. He had checked into the hotel days ago, but there had been so much hubbub at the apartment with Diane's sudden arrival, that she had lost track of the comings and goings at the Bel Air.

"Why are you taking photographs of me and my friends?" Irène asked, walking behind him. "We've done nothing wrong."

The man did not look back. At the elevator, he poked at the down button with the corner of his suitcase, but it failed to light up. The old hotel owner had locked the elevator on the ground floor. Irène stood next to him. "The lifts are dreadfully slow here, Mr. Sullivan," she said.

At the mention of his name, he jerked his head toward her and his double chin swayed. "Pardon me," he muttered and turned and walked toward the door to the stairwell.

"Bernard Sullivan . . . a very Irish name," Irène said. "Employed by Smith Private Investigators in London."

Sullivan pulled on the stairwell door, only to find it locked. His shoulders slumped and he dropped his bags on the floor. He turned to face Irène, and pulled a handkerchief from his pocket to mop his brow.

"Why were you taking photos of Diane Jacobs last night?"

"You've got the wrong end of the stick, madame," he said in a lilting brogue.

"Do I?"

"Aye, absolutely."

"Then you're watching me?"

"I'm watching everyone. There's plenty to see."

Irène was unnerved by his answer, but she didn't show it. "Then why are you checking out so soon?"

"I have what I need," Sullivan said, fighting a grin.

The elevator suddenly dinged and the doors opened. The old owner was standing there, holding his walking cane like a bat. He let out a little gasp when he saw Irène and Sullivan standing there. The cane slipped from his fingers and clattered on the floor of the elevator. "Are you all right, Madame Laureux?"

Irène sighed. "Fine, thank you."

Sullivan's fat face broke into a wide grin and he stepped into the elevator. The old owner slipped around Sullivan and cowered behind Irène.

"Who are you working for?" Irène asked.

"That's confidential," Sullivan said as the doors closed.


After the encounter with Sullivan, Irène decided to walk and get fresh perspective on the matter. She found herself at Père Lachaise standing in front of Jean-Louis' grave. She brushed away leaves that had fallen there and, as always, traced the engraving of his name with her fingertips. The stone had weathered badly over the last thirty years while Irène was held prisoner by her agoraphobia at rue Rampon and unable to tend the plot. A crack was beginning to form in the center of the headstone and seemed to deepen with each visit. Eventually, it would cleave Jean-Louis' name, which seemed appropriate because Jean-Louis had lived two lives in his last days on earth.

Irène sat on the bench opposite Jean-Louis' grave and stared at the crack, learning its every twist and crevice. Any tourists who might have been there were somewhere else, smoking pot or spray-painting graffiti on the grave of the resident rock star. She felt nauseated, her mind trying to come to terms with the fact that life on rue Rampon was about to change again. It was in the air. As long as questions remained unanswered and people from the past were elusive as ghosts, there would never be peace.

A sharp crack from a snapping twig or branch reported from somewhere behind Irène. She turned, catching her breath. An image of the leering detective popped into her mind. Irène stood up and walked toward the sound. There was a mausoleum ahead, vine-covered and slowly disintegrating under a giant oak.

Irène started to call out, but was startled to see a tall, chiseled young man with slick-backed hair and wearing a tailored grey suit emerge from behind the mausoleum. The man saw Irène, nodded his head slightly and walked quickly down the path.

After he was out of sight, Irène walked around the mausoleum, which backed against the trunk of the ancient oak. There was a small alley in between, littered with used condoms, fast food wrappers and tinfoil stained with dark residue that once contained drugs. She smelled the familiar scent of Gauloises and near her foot was the remnant of one, a curl of smoke still rising from the tip. Irène crushed the cigarette out, pushing it into the soft ground with the tip of her shoe until it was buried under the mud. Irène had the feeling, once again, that she was being watched.

*In the dream, it is nearly December and the weather has taken a turn for winter. Irène is walking down a long path toward a giant glass house. It is a hothouse filled with soaring tropical plants. Even from a distance, she can see the condensation dripping down the panes of glass that reflect the overcast sky. The road seems to contract and she is suddenly at the doorway to the conservatory. The metal handle is warm and damp to the touch, but Irène pulls it open and steps inside. The air is wet and humid and the building seems even larger than it did from outside. There are high-pitched shrieks from some type of animal, a bird flutters over her head and perches in a tree. There is a gravel path before her and it leads deep into the center of the hothouse. She pushes away leaves and branches, marveling and a bit frightened by the flora and fauna that inhabit this little world. She sees a break in the path up ahead. The path is becoming a garden and a giant statue sits in the middle. The leaves and trees give way until Irène is at the center of the hothouse. The ceiling rises high above her and water drips from unseen places and fills her eyes. She brushes the drops away, focuses on the statue. It is smooth and armless; it stares at her with empty eyes and a downturned mouth. Condensation drips down the stone folds of the skirt that covers its thighs and legs. A spider crawls over the exposed foot. Irène looks up at the statue in awe. She hears footsteps behind her then a hand covers her mouth, drags her down. The last thing Irène sees before darkness overtakes her is the giant statue of Venus de Milo.*

Irène woke with a start. She was lying across her bed. It was late in the evening and Pierre was nuzzling her hand. As she became aware of her surroundings and the time, she could hear Martin in the kitchen talking on the phone. The smell of pasta and the garlic he chopped for the sauce drifted down the hall. He was talking to Euan, making final arrangements for their departure the next day. They were staying at a private house Euan had arranged through his charity contacts. There wasn't a hotel left in London for Princess Diana's funeral.

The clock said it was after nine. Irène went down the hall into the kitchen where Martin cradled the phone under his chin while he stirred. She took the wooden spoon from him and shooed him away.

"Hang on a second. Irène's up," Martin said into the receiver. "Euan says hello."

"Bonsoir, my dear," she called out, trying to sound happy and nonchalant when she felt neither. Irène's encounter with the detective and the mysterious man at Père Lachaise made her feel anxious. She desperately wanted to speak with Diane alone, but there hadn't been a single moment.

"Okay, we're having dinner. I'll call you in the morning. Love ya." Martin clicked the off button on the cordless phone.

"Do you?"

"Do I what?"

"Love him?"

"I didn't say I loved him. I said love ya—it's different connotation."

"Maybe not to Euan."

"Irène . . ."

"Nevermind. Where is Diane? Should I go and get her?"

"No. She's in one of her moods and not feeling well. I gave her one of your pills. I thought you wouldn't mind."

"Oh . . . that's fine."

"I may take one myself. I need a good night's sleep before we leave."

"I agree. I'll clean up and you can rest."

They sat on the sofa, eating from plates on their laps. Irène forced herself to eat, to keep up appearances, debating on whether to tell Martin about her discovery of the detective. She felt her suspicions were turning to paranoia, and bringing it up would cast a pall over what was already going to be a somber and awkward weekend in London. It couldn't be a coincidence that Diane and the detective had shown up at the same time. Irène had called her own detective, the one looking for Frederick Dubois, and asked him to make inquiries about Diane's movements in America and since her arrival in Paris. His efforts to find Frederick had come up empty, so maybe a new mystery might re-engage him.

# 6 Requiem

The Eurostar rolled silently toward Waterloo Station. Sun beamed, but all around Martin the faces of its riders were somber and voices never rose above a whisper. England was in mourning for its lost princess and the grief-stricken were converging on London for the funeral procession.

Irène sat transfixed by the sights outside the train window. Martin pointed out the giant Battersea Power Station, a hulking, disused relic made famous by rock band album covers. Its four giant white smokestacks rose from each corner and gleamed in the sky. Euan once told him Battersea was the most welcoming and most depressing sight in London. "You are happy to see it when you arrive, sad to see it pass by when you leave, but it's always quite sinister," Euan said when they had come to the capital earlier in the year.

Euan's father had grown up in Battersea—the wrong side of the river, as he always reminded his son—and made a fortune in the stock market. His parents now lived in tony Hampstead, and while they weren't happy with Euan's "lifestyle choice," they had grown to accept it. Euan had always been discreet about his relationships and his parents had never met Martin or any of his boyfriends.

Martin wrote in his notebook, glancing up every now and then to observe Irène's tempered excitement. Diane had her nose stuck in a magazine, but Martin noticed that she had not turned a page since they crossed through the Channel Tunnel. Diane and Irène had been acting strangely all morning, both subdued; even when there had been a delay at Gare du Nord, Diane had remained uncharacteristically quiet.

As the Eurostar pulled alongside the platform, Martin could see Euan just beyond the barrier mixing with those arriving and departing. The look of expectation on Euan's face as he scanned up and down the train cars was almost more than Martin could bear.

Martin had desperately tried to love Euan, to forget David and move forward into the stable relationship offered to him. Euan was kind, out of the closet and not addicted to drugs or alcohol. He simply wanted a quiet, unassuming life with only modest surprises, and a boyfriend who didn't smoke or want to have sex three times a day.

Martin moved away from the window and collected his bags, helping Irène do the same. As they prepared to exit the car, Diane came up behind him and bumped her bag into his butt.

"Are you okay?" she asked.

"Yeah, I guess. It's going to be weird."

"Better get your game face on. There's lover boy," Diane said, nodding toward Euan as they stepped onto the platform.

Euan was upon them, grabbing Martin in a tight embrace. He was taller than Martin, had strong arms that could envelop him completely. Martin loved this part of Euan, this first embrace, the comfort. Euan was wearing his funeral clothes, a long black coat over more black. Euan untangled himself long enough to embrace Irène and give Diane an awkward half hug, while Diane patted him on the back unenthusiastically with a limp hand.

"I'm so glad you're finally here," Euan said. "It's been absolutely awful. I've borrowed a car, so we won't have to queue for a taxi. The flat isn't far," he said squeezing Martin's shoulder as they walked.

"Did you say flat?" Diane asked walking behind them. "I thought we were staying in a house?"

"It's a huge flat, almost a house," Euan said. "It's better than a hotel, trust me."

The newspaper stands in the Waterloo terminal screamed Princess Diana's death from every magazine and tabloid cover. Euan went on and on breathlessly recounting the Royal Family's horrible response to Diana's death and the Queen's "too little, too late" address to the grieving nation planned for that evening. The mood at Waterloo was a precursor for the rest of the weekend. The entire station was more silent than usual. Passengers walked with their heads down or peering into a newspaper with more details of the tragedy, television sets in the waiting areas were wall-to-wall coverage of the funeral.

The flat was actually a loft overlooking the Thames. It was in a renovated building on the South Bank with a terrace and a view of Tower Bridge. The ultra-modern interior was all gleaming hardwoods, chrome fixtures and soaring ceilings. Diane was so thrilled that she grabbed Euan's face and kissed him on the mouth.

"It's beautiful," Irène said. "Who does this belong to?"

"A girlfriend of mine. Rebecca. Martin, you remember me talking about her. She's out of the country for a month.

64

International banking."

"She must be rich as hell," Diane said. "This place can't be cheap with that view. Is she married?"

"No. Why?" Euan asked, looking at Diane strangely.

"My lesbian tendencies creep out when money is involved," Diane said, luxuriating on the couch.

"Lesbian tendencies?" Euan asked, looking at Martin.

"She's kidding," Martin said.

"Oh, yes . . . well, right then. Why don't you ladies settle in? There are two bedrooms through there and Martin and I will share the upstairs." He pointed to a cylindrical staircase in the corner that led up to a second floor. "I managed reservations at a fairly decent restaurant just down the street. We have an about an hour."

"You're so kind to us, Euan," Irène said. "Thank you."

"Anything for Martin," Euan said absently as he took Martin's hand and led him upstairs.

After they had gone, Diane said, "Did you notice he said *anything for Martin*? Like he's doing us some big favor."

"He didn't mean it like that," Irène said.

"Hmmm . . . I bet."

"I'm going to nap for an hour," Irène said, taking her suitcases down the hall.

"I think I'll sit out on the terrace and start getting drunk now," Diane said. "I think I'm going to need it to get through this weekend."


Euan pulled Martin against him and hugged him tightly once they were in the dim bedroom, which was dominated by a king-sized platform bed. Martin kissed Euan hungrily, but as Martin backed him toward the bed, he felt the older man's body go rigid.

"Not right now," Euan said.

"I haven't seen you in a week. There's time."

"It's not that . . . it's just . . ."

"The funeral. Gotcha. When does the official mourning period end?"

"That sounds like something Diane would say," Euan said huffily.

"I learned from the best."

Euan sat on the edge of the bed, looking up pleadingly at Martin. "Let's not fight."

Martin sat down next to Euan and took his hand.

"It's been so incredibly sad here, Martin," he said. "I feel as if I've lost a member of my own family. Isn't that strange? I think if my mum were to die tomorrow, I wouldn't grieve nearly as much."

"Princess Diana was an icon. You grew up with her. She was like family, in a way."

"It's just . . . Diana's passing dredges up all these memories and she was just on the verge of being happy again. It's the worst thing that's ever happened."

Martin wanted to comfort him, but felt repulsed. If this was the worst thing that had ever happened to Euan, he must have lived a more sheltered life than he'd let on.

"No, my love, there are much worse things than this. I know for a fact."

Martin remembered holding Peter, covered in his blood, watching his life ebb away. He remembered the faces of all those killed and injured in the bombing of the Saint-Michel station. And he remembered David walking away down the airport terminal, dragged along willingly by his parents, only to disappear out of his life forever. Euan knew these things about Martin, but only secondhand. Martin had never broken down and wept over the retelling, so maybe Euan didn't understand how deeply the pain ran beneath his skin. Not so much Peter anymore, but he could not escape David. Was not ready to let him go completely.

"You're not really mourning for Diana, you're mourning for yourself and all the things you've lost and the time that has slipped away," Martin said. "You're right, though. Things will never quite be the same. You'll always look at things differently. She was part of your childhood and now she's gone."

Tears rolled down Euan's cheeks. "It's not like she was Santa Claus. She wasn't just some fantasy. I met her several times, we'd spoken on the phone about events for the charity."

Martin pulled Euan's head into his chest. "Yes, but you didn't *know* her. She didn't call you up to confide in you about her affairs. She was a business acquaintance. Think about how her children feel, her family."

Euan untangled himself from Martin and lay back on the bed. He pulled Martin down to him and put his arms around him. "I know, Martin, I do. But I am just devastated."


Martin, Irène and Diane stood on Whitehall Street waiting for Princess Diana's funeral cortege to pass by on its way to Westminster Abbey. Rising before them was the Cenotaph, the city's memorial to the war dead, surrounded by flowers from the grieving masses. Euan had left for Kensington Palace before dawn for a final briefing on the funeral and to meet the hundreds of other charity representatives walking behind Diana's coffin.

Martin kept an arm around Irène's shoulder and craned his neck to see over the heads of the mourners lining the street. Irène was holding up, but Martin had spotted the telltale beads of sweat along her hairline.

"I'm fine," Irène said. "The breeze helps."

The mourners—some had been camped on the sidewalk for days—were restless, but kept it in check. What Martin would remember most about that day was the sound of the great bell from Westminster Abbey tolling every minute as Princess Diana's casket approached. There was a ripple in the crowd, what seemed like a great sigh being expelled and the distant sound of voices. Everyone who had been sitting on the pavement stood up, surged forward a bit.

In a few moments, the first members of the cortege approached. Soldiers in full dress, followed by a team of horses pulling the gun carriage that bore Princess Diana's flower draped casket. There was an arrangement of flowers at the head of the casket with a white card that simply read *Mummy*. The crowd screamed and cried out Diana's name. Flowers were thrown at the casket and at the five somber figures who walked behind it—Prince Charles and his father, Diana's brother and her two sons, their heads bowed, fighting back tears. The sight of the two princes made the crowd surge again and Martin could feel the weight upon his back. He felt Irène shrink against him, begin to go limp. She seemed so small surrounded by the grieving, hand-wringing masses that enveloped her. She fainted.

Martin caught Irène before she fell, began pushing his way back through the crowd toward a block of buildings. Diane grabbed Irène's other arm, telling people to move out of the way, cutting a swath toward the open air. Together they were able to get Irène to a bench in the building's entryway. They lay Irène down and Martin slapped at her face gently, calling her name. She came to after a minute, waking with a start, unsure of her surroundings.

"Damn," she muttered and tried to sit up.

Martin pressed her back against the bench. "Don't move," he said. "Take deep breaths."

Irène rubbed at her eyes. "Did we miss Euan?"

Diane stood on the bench next to Irène and could see the backs of the charity workers moving down Whitehall and out of sight. "Afraid so," she said.

"I ruined it," Irène said. "I am so sorry."

"Well, we don't have to tell him," Diane said. "Euan's stiff upper lip has been put to the test, so we should just smile and nod and tell him he did a good job."

Euan and the other charity volunteers would watch the funeral on screens set up inside St. Margaret's Church next to the Abbey, so Martin, Irène and Diane walked past Parliament Square and found a taxi to take them back to the flat. When they arrived and turned on the television, the funeral was underway. They watched Elton John sing his rewritten tribute and Diana's brother give his angry and impassioned speech denouncing the media and the royal family.

When Euan didn't return after the funeral, the trio decided to walk down the street to a small Italian restaurant and left a message for Euan to join them, but he never did. When they returned to the flat, Euan was in the bedroom watching the BBC's coverage of Diana's casket being driven through the gates at the Spencer family estate where she would be buried.

"Come downstairs and have a drink with us," Martin encouraged him.

Euan shook his head. "You go ahead. It's almost over now."

"It's been over."

"No, I mean . . . I can't explain. I just need a little more time."

Martin sat on the terrace, his laptop open on the table. He had run the phone cord outside to connect to the Internet. He had found a boy within twenty minutes who was in walking distance of the flat. He signed off and quietly crept back inside, unplugged the phone, closed his laptop and headed for the door. He didn't want to wake Euan, who had finally turned off the television and gone to bed. Martin came into the dark entry hall and was about to open the door when he felt a hand reach out and grab his.

"It's a little late to be going out," Diane said.

Martin's eyes adjusted and he could see her sitting on a bench, chewing gum, waiting for him.

"I was just going . . ."

"For a walk? Yeah, right. You were going out to meet some little tricky you met on the computer."

Martin was silent for a moment. "So what?"

"Hey, it's no skin off my ass, baby. You go out and find you some sweet meat and fuck his brains out if that's what turns you on. Just promise me you're being safe."

"Of course I am."

"You should end it with Euan and stop leading him on. I think Irène might be right, and you know how I hate to admit that."

Martin sank onto the bench next to her. "I don't know what to do. I feel like I'm floundering again. I thought moving over here would be the cure all, but it isn't.

"Duh. Bullshit travels." Diane stood up and stretched. "Why don't you skip the trick and go to bed? We have to be up at the crack of dawn."

They stood staring at each other in the darkness. Diane turned to go back to the bedroom, expecting to hear Martin padding along behind her. Instead she heard the front door click open and close and Martin was gone.

Diane stopped at Irène's room and found her sitting up in bed reading a book.

"I told you he would go out," Irène said.

"I wouldn't get your French panties in a twist over it," Diane said. "He's a young gay man. It's pretty normal, if you ask me."

Irène made some little harrumph noise.

"Oh, please, madame. Don't tell me you're passing judgment on little Martin. We're no angels, are we?"

"I suppose not," Irène said.

"Good night."

"Diane . . . when do you have to go back to teach?"

"In a couple of days. Trying to get rid of me?"

"I was just curious," Irène smiled.

Diane cocked an eyebrow. "Uh-huh." She saluted Irène in an exaggerated gesture and walked down the hall. Irène set down her book and pulled the blanket under her chin. Tomorrow they would go home, and she was uncertain what would happen once they arrived. She had a sense of foreboding and was anxious to return to rue Rampon, but it would not be quite the same as when they left it.

# 7 a Door Half Open

A cab dropped Irène, Martin and Diane at rue Rampon, but Euan said he was going on to the Anglophile. He had left his manager in charge, and while he trusted her, he was still paranoid that something might have happened. He kissed Martin's cheek and said, "Thank you for being so patient with me. Your coming to London means everything."

As the cab pulled away from curb, Diane put her arm around Martin's shoulders. "Oh, be a sport, give him some sympathy nookie tonight. If you're not too worn out." Martin shrugged her off and Diane picked up her bag and headed across the street to the hotel.

Martin and Irène lugged their bags upstairs. As they came down the hall, they both stopped in their tracks. The apartment door was standing half open.

"Tell me you forgot to lock the door," Martin said.

Irène dropped her bag and rushed towards the

apartment, Martin on her heels. She pushed the door open and they both gasped. The living room was littered with their clothes, half eaten food and liquor bottles. Irène's laptop was missing from her desk.

"I have lived here for fifty years and this has never happened," Irène said in despair. "I go away one weekend in all that time and someone breaks in."

"Call the police," Martin said, putting his arm around her. "It's happened. Let's just take stock. Don't touch anything."

Dirty dishes filled the kitchen sink and the fridge had been cleaned of its contents. They walked slowly down the hall toward the bedrooms and heard a scratching noise coming from behind the closed bathroom door. Irène opened the door and found Pierre inside unharmed. He had shit and pissed all over the floor, but the robbers had filled the sink with water and left a can of food open. Irène cradled Pierre in her arms as he wiggled and squirmed, angry that he had been left behind and subjected to such bad treatment.

Martin's room had been ransacked. Most of the clothes were missing from his closet. His bed had been slept in. Irène called from her room that some of her jewelry was missing.

"The bastards. Some of those pieces belonged to my aunt. They are irreplaceable."

"They must have taken up residence all weekend long," Martin said as they met in the hallway.

Irène had the phone in hand and was dialing the police. "Bonjour, this is Madame Laureux at 233 rue Rampon. I would like to report a burglary."

Martin went back to his room and noticed that a sheaf of his poetry had been spread out on the desk. His journal was open and face down on the floor.

"The police are coming," Irène said, standing in the doorway.

"What else is missing from your room?"

"I'm still looking. They read my journal and my poetry is spread out on the desk, but it's all still here. I don't know whether to feel happy or sad about that."

The doorbell sounded and Irène went to the intercom. "I need my hairdryer . . ." Diane said and Irène buzzed her in.

A few moments later, Diane came into the apartment and stopped short. "Hey, what the fuck happened in here?"

"We've been robbed," Irène said.

In Martin's room, Diane saw Martin's poems fanned out on the desk and his journal on the floor. Diane's mouth went dry and her mind whirled. She already knew who had been in the room, had made himself at home and caught up on Martin's life. Diane reached down to pick up Martin's journal, but Irène caught her arm.

"Don't touch it," Irène said, her grip tighter than it should be. "Fingerprints."

"Right," Diane said, pulling away.

"What is it, Irène?" Martin said, looking at the two women curiously.

"I . . . I . . . just feel violated," Irène said.

"You should make a list of what's missing," Diane said. "Wanna start in the living room?"

Martin went to find a piece of paper and Diane followed him, but Irène made a hissing sound under her breath.

"Why are you here?" Irène demanded.

"I put my hairdryer in Martin's bag."

Irène shook her head. "You know what I mean. Why are you in Paris?"

"I don't like your tone, Madame Laureux," Diane said and went into the hall.

Irène was certain that Diane's arrival had something to do

with the detective at the Bel Air and the robbery. Pierre came back and sat in the doorway, cleaning his paws, watching Irène and her inability to decide on a course of action.

Two uniformed policemen arrived at rue Rampon to take Irène and Martin's statements and assess the crime scene, followed by an inspector with the Paris Police named Michel Arnaud. He was almost a cliché image of a Parisian policeman: mid-forties, rumpled raincoat, slicked back dark hair, medium height, weathered face.

"Oh, my god, it's Inspector Clouseau," Diane said.

Arnaud wandered about the apartment, inspecting things closely. He peered at the titles of all of Irène's books on the shelves that lined the living room, at the two desks pushed together, the sleeping arrangements in the apartment. He noted that the French doors to the balcony were locked and the curtain pulled over them. The policemen dusted for prints and bagged evidence while Martin and Irène stood near the front door watching the whirl of activity. Arnaud eventually approached them and spoke in English for Martin's benefit, a mix of classroom learning and working narcotic stings with Scotland Yard in London.

"This is not the first burglary of this kind we have seen," Arnaud said.

"Is it drug users?" Martin asked.

"We believe it is a gang of youths from the banlieue. They find empty homes, live there for as long as possible, steal items that can be sold for drugs. In this case, there seems to be a great deal of physical evidence left behind." Arnaud pulled a plastic evidence bag from his coat pocket and held it up. A blackened, rolled up piece of tinfoil was inside. "This was in the garbage pail in the toilet. There are fingerprints."

"What is that?" Irène asked.

"It's a crude pipe for smoking heroin," Arnaud said. "We are also taking your bed linen, Monsieur Paige, and I recommend you buy a new mattress. There were traces of semen found. You cannot be too careful. Many of the drug users have AIDS."

"What happens now?" Martin asked.

"I am going to speak with your neighbors. Since this is a locked building, we want to find out if someone let the criminals in or remembers seeing anyone suspicious. We are taking fingerprints in the lobby, but those will probably be inconclusive."

"Thank you for coming so quickly," Irène said and extended her hand. She fought the urge to tell him more, her suspicions.

Arnaud shook her hand. He started to turn away, but then turned back. "Forgive me, but I was curious about your living arrangement here."

Irène bristled. "Thank you for curiosity, Inspector Arnaud, but it has no relevance to the robbery of my apartment."

"Of course," Arnaud said, backing down with an almost patronizing smile. "I just wanted to rule out other suspects. Husbands, boyfriends, girlfriends."

"You can safely rule them out, Inspector," Diane piped up from the sofa, where she was pouring another glass of wine. "This is a love-free zone."

Arnaud regarded Diane curiously. "Yes, very good then."

He went back to the kitchen to confer with the officers, leaving Martin and Irène to exchange glances.

"I'm not sure I like his inferences," Martin said.

"Let him wonder," Irène said, shooting daggers into the inspector's back with her eyes.

Diane laughed. "What's he supposed to think? You're the Harold and Maude of the 11th arrondissement."

"Are you drunk?" Martin asked.

"I expect to be very soon. You should both join me."

After the police cleared out, Euan swept in with bags of food and took charge of the situation. Martin watched with vague amusement as Euan fussed around the apartment straightening things and commanding Martin's presence in the kitchen to cook dinner.

While they were in the kitchen, Irène called Diane onto the balcony and shut the door. "Why are you really here?" Irène demanded.

"I'm visiting my best friends in the whole wide world."

"Stop it," Irène snapped. "A detective was taking photos of you the night before we left for London. Why would a detective be following you?"

Diane wouldn't meet Irène's gaze and picked up the bottle of wine to refill her glass. Irène snatched the bottle out of her hand.

"Hey! Don't be so hostile, old woman."

"I refuse to believe that your arrival here, the detective taking photographs and my apartment being robbed are a series of unrelated coincidences."

"Then why didn't you turn me in to Columbo? Why didn't you mention your suspicions?"

"Why is a detective following you?"

"Irène, I have no idea what you're talking about. There's no detective following me. I went out the other night for a drink. I couldn't sleep. That's my story, and I'm sticking to it. Walk down to Café Richard and ask them. I have an alibi."

"I'm not sure I believe you."

Diane snatched the bottle back and drained the rest of the wine into her glass. "I don't care if you believe me or not. Maybe you've made some enemies."

"Maybe."

Diane leaned forward. "I was kidding. Who would be your enemy?"

"My late husband's lover. I have a detective looking for him. Maybe he's getting too close."

"Uh . . . you're scaring me a little bit."

"But why would the burglars spend so much time in Martin's room? They had spread all of his writing out on the desk and read his journal." Irène rubbed at her temples. "Oh, my god, what if it was one of the boys Martin met on the Internet?"

Diane swallowed hard. "That's a possibility, I guess."

"I'll have to speak with him about it."

"I think I'll sit that conversation out."

Irène went back inside and Diane gulped the rest of her wine. She went to the balcony railing, looking up and down rue Rampon. She could feel David's presence.

# 8 Changing Rooms

The next morning, Irène was sitting at her desk trying to arrange the manuscripts that had been scattered across the floor by the burglars. There was a loud knock at her door, and she was so startled that the manuscript she had just gotten back into order slipped from her hand, sending the pages sailing around the living room again.

"Who is it?" Irène called out.

"Oh, for god's sake open up," Diane said. "I haven't come to rob you."

Irène opened the door. "How did you get in?"

"Some old man was leaving and held the door for me."

"Martin has gone to the bookshop with Euan."

"I know. I wanted to talk to you alone."

Diane followed Irène into the kitchen and sat down at the table. Irène poured cups of coffee and mentally braced herself for Diane's revelation.

"I do have an ulterior motive for being here,"

Diane said. "You asked when school was starting and I thought you might have guessed something was up."

"I don't understand."

"Remember when I called and told Martin I was coming back to Paris? Well, what I was going to tell him before the whole Princess Diana circus came up was that I coming to stay permanently." Irène's countenance did not flicker or show any emotion at all, which Diane admired. "I should have never gone back to America. I've got some money to tide me over, but I'm going to need a place to live and a job."

Irène crushed out her cigarette and lit another. "That will make Martin very happy."

"But not you."

"No, I did not mean it to sound that way. It will just take some getting used to. We have a routine here at rue Rampon."

"Routines are dull. That's why I'm here. To shake you out of your doldrums."

"Hmm . . . I suppose Martin could move in with Euan across the hall and you could have his room."

Diane threw her head back like she'd been hit in the face. "Wha-what? Live here with you?"

"Martin said that he was going to try and make it work with Euan, so maybe this would jumpstart things."

"Wow," Diane said, pushing back from the table. "That is some cold-blooded matchmaking. Something tells me Martin is going to have a few words to say about that."

They both jumped at the sound of a key in the latch. "He's here," Irène murmured.

"Ah, the ladies who lunch," Martin said as he walked into the kitchen.

"You're back so soon," Irène said, overly cheerful.

"The shop is dead and I wanted Euan to take me to a movie,

but he wouldn't, so I came back here to drag you two along."

"Diane and I were just talking about her staying in Paris," Irène said, and Diane sighed loudly.

"For how long?"

"Permanently," Diane said. "Or until you bore me to death."

Martin squealed and grabbed Diane, dancing her around the kitchen.

"Don't get too excited," she said. "I'm a poor relation. I have hardly any money, no job and nowhere to live."

"We'll work that out," Martin said.

"We were discussing it," Irène interjected, "and the easiest solution might be for you to make the move across the hall and Diane could have your room."

"Oh," Martin said, trying to hide his displeasure.

Diane smirked. "Or not."

"No . . . it's just . . ."

"Don't worry, Martin," Diane said and patted his cheek. "I'll make do. I'm sure I can find a flophouse somewhere. I can stay at the hotel."

"That's ridiculous," Irène said. "Martin, you spend many nights at Euan's. What is the difference?"

"There is a difference," Martin said. "It may seem like a small gesture to you, but to Euan it will be huge. I said we were going to try and make it work. 'Try' being the optimum word. I don't want to give him false hope."

"Oh, Jesus," Diane muttered. "Well, I'll just trot back over to the hotel and give the old man my last shekels. Don't mind me."

"This is insane," Irène said. "You can't live at the hotel."

Euan knocked on the apartment door twice and then walked in. He came into the kitchen and stopped short to see the three of them standing there. "I changed my mind about the cinema,"

81

he said. "I thought you were flying back across the pond today, Diane."

"I think I might be staying on a little longer."

"How long?"

"Forever," Diane said in a looming voice.

"Oh . . . really . . ." Euan said, forcing a smile.

"Yes, indeedy. The Jewess is here to stay and needs a job and a place to live."

Euan, always taken aback by Diane's brassy ways, had no comment.

"You have an extra bedroom, Euan," Martin said. "Why don't you rent it out?"

Euan cut his eyes at Martin. "Well . . . I . . . I barely know Diane. Couldn't she stay here with Irène?"

"We've come full circle," Diane said. "This hot potato is going back to the hotel and cut a deal with the old man there. Maybe I can scare him into hiring me as a maid."

Diane left the kitchen and they all stood staring at each other until they heard the front door close.

Euan was outraged. "Staying at my flat for a few nights is one thing, but offering it to her permanently is outrageous. Just because she arrives with no resources doesn't mean we have to accommodate her." Martin and Irène stared at him like he was an alien. "Well, I'm right, aren't I?"

"I have nothing else to say about the matter," Irène said and went back to her desk.

Martin shook his head and walked out of the kitchen.

"I'll be at the shop. As if any of you give a damn," Euan yelled as he slammed out of Irène's apartment

Diane flung open the doors to the Bel Air, much to the horror of the old owner, who looked up from his newspaper with a look of dread on his face. Diane argued with him until he moved her to the large room across from Irène's balcony. She wanted the double room for the single price and refused to take no for an answer.

"I'm a good paying customer," Diane said. "I filled up this hole with kids a couple of summers ago. Cut me a deal, old man. The place is empty."

The old owner finally conceded after Diane threatened to camp out in the lobby. She had flopped down on one of the couches, put her feet up and pretended to go to sleep.

The hotel room had not changed in the slightest, which was somehow comforting. At least with winter coming, she wouldn't have to worry about dying of heat stroke. Diane lay across the bed in the dark hotel room feeling guilty. Her plan to move to Paris and live quietly and harmoniously with Martin and Irène had already gone sour, and David was out there skulking around, waiting for an inopportune moment to reappear.

Diane fell asleep on the bed, waking up hours later. It was almost six o'clock. She opened the curtains and saw Martin on the balcony setting the table. "Soup's on," he called to her.

Martin and Irène had come to a truce, but Euan was in his own apartment and refused to come to dinner. "If he's going to act like a child, then let him sit over there and pout like one," Martin said, stuffing bread into his mouth.

"He didn't think I'd seriously move in with him, did he?" Diane asked. "How uncomfortable would that be? And I'd have to listen to you two sodomizing each other every night. Thanks, but no."

"We're going to have to find a solution," Irène reminded them. "Diane can't live in the hotel forever."

"Actually, I could. The hotel is empty. I'm doing the old

man a big favor. We came to an agreement."

Irène pursed her lips. "Yes, he called me near tears. You must drive a hard bargain."

"Sometimes the Jew comes out in me," Diane said between bites of food.

Irène was rinsing dishes in the kitchen when she heard a soft knock at the door. Diane and Martin were still on the balcony drinking coffee and passing a cigarette. Irène opened the door and found a sheepish Euan standing in the hallway.

"I'm really sorry about all this," Euan said. "It's been a very confusing day."

"It is strange for all of us," Irène said. "Come in and have coffee with us."

"Wait," he said. "I want to ask you a question. I know you and Diane haven't always been on the best of terms, and I want your opinion."

"About?"

"I thought I could smooth things over a bit with Martin and try to make a truce with Diane. My manager informed me that she's become engaged and is leaving the shop. I thought about offering the position to Diane."

Irène's face lit up and she grabbed Euan by the shoulders and shook him gently. "You are remarkable." She pulled him out onto the balcony.

Euan made the offer, keeping an upbeat and positive tone in his voice. Diane eyed him suspiciously.

"What's the catch?"

"There's no catch," Euan said with exasperation. "You just have to be friendly to the clientele."

"Oh, well, there's the catch," Martin said.

"Fuck off," Diane said and punched Martin's arm. "I'm just desperate enough to take it, but you can't ride my ass over every little thing. I like to be independent."

"Your main duties will be running the store while I'm away or working on other business upstairs."

"How many staff members will I have under me?"

"You are the staff."

Diane rolled her eyes. "Can we negotiate salary?"

"No."

"Fine. I'll take it."

"Crisis averted," Martin said, and kissed Euan's cheek. "Now we just need to find an apartment for you."

"We'll worry about that later. I kinda like living across from you guys. Free meals, good company and cheap rent."

"You can't live in the hotel forever," Irène said again.

"We'll see," Diane said blowing a smoke ring into the air.

# 9 At the Anglophile

Diane had worked retail in college, so working the counter at Anglophile was, as she put it, "no big whoop." Anal-retentive Euan wanted the place kept like a library, so Diane's main duties were keeping the shelves in order, scanning new books into the computer and running the register. It was easy work and left her time to read, so she began to relax. David had not materialized, although she was positive he had broken into Irène's apartment while they were in London. The McLaren's slob of a detective, Bernard Sullivan, agreed.

Since there was no sign of David, Sullivan had taken to following her around, popping out of doorways with flowers and offering to buy her drinks. When he had information to pass along or wanted a report from her, Sullivan would stand outside the Anglophile browsing through the used books Euan put out to attract customers. Once Diane saw him, he'd walk down the avenue and around the corner to a tiny coffee shop. Weeks had gone by with no sign of David and Sullivan's source inside the police department said detectives were still convinced that Irène's robbers were teenagers from the banlieue.

There were three customers in the shop, none of them bothering her, and Diane had a book open on the counter and a hot cup of tea at her fingertips. She was almost forty-five years old, working retail and living in a hotel room. A sense of contentment, or something close to it, washed over her. The simple fact that she could sit somewhere quietly and read a book without her mind hop-scotching from worry to dread made her sigh with relief. Then she thought, *oh, fuck, I'm getting old. A good book and hot tea is the first step. All I need now is twenty cats to feed.*

The door to the shop opened and the annoying bell that supposedly sounded like Big Ben bonged loudly. She was going to rip it off the door the first moment she got when Euan was away. A boy entered wearing a tight sweater and jeans, a woolen hat pulled down over his ears. He looked familiar at first glance, but Diane dismissed him. She was at a good part of her book and if she made eye contact he might want her to help him find something. He wandered over to the rack full of English newspapers that Euan had shipped in daily, along with magazines from America and the U.K.

Diane returned to her book, but then felt someone standing in front of the counter. It was the young man she and Martin had met in front of the shop before they had gone to London, who had flirted and praised Martin's poetry. He was staring at her with his beautiful blue eyes and full lips slightly parted to reveal perfect teeth. She did love perfect teeth.

"Can you help me?" he asked in almost a whisper, as if he were in a library. "I'm looking for a book of Rilke's complete poems. Are you all right, madame?"

Diane snapped out of her reverie, blushed. "Sorry. I'm new. I couldn't remember for a second where the poetry was. It's upstairs. I'll show you."

The boy walked ahead of her and she followed him up the stairs. Although she knew he was gay, she couldn't help but marvel at his body. *I am sooooo pathetic,* she thought to herself. *Why am I always attracted to homos? Aren't there any cute straight boys left who want to be seduced by an older woman?* Maybe Bernard Sullivan was the best she could hope to do at this stage of her life. The idea made her shudder.

Diane showed the boy several editions of Rilke, and directed him to one she thought had the best translation. It was the same book she had given Martin so many years ago. She left him to browse and found Euan waiting on the stairs.

"That was very helpful of you, Diane," he said coming down behind her.

"What?"

"Helping the customer with your knowledge."

"Don't try to motivate me," Diane said returning to her perch behind the counter. "If I know something about a particular piece of literature, I'll recommend it. If I don't, I'll just point and grunt and they can figure it out for themselves."

Euan's shoulders slumped and he went outside to straighten the books in the bins by the front door. Diane went back to reading, but then she looked over the top of her book again and saw Bernard Sullivan walk up to the bins. He began pulling titles out and glanced up at Diane through the window. To her horror, Euan walked over and engaged him in conversation. "Oh, fuck-a-doodle-doo," she said aloud.

"Pardon?" The boy was standing in front of the counter holding the volume of Rilke and a slim edition of Anne Sexton's selected work. He put the books on the counter, waiting for Diane to ring up his purchases, but she was distracted by what was going on outside.

"I've seen you here before," the young man said. "You're Martin's friend, Diane."

"What? Oh, yes. What was your name?"

"I'm Christian," he grinned. "Martin writes such beautiful poetry."

"He does, indeed," Diane said absently, trying to keep an eye on Euan and Bernard. They seemed to be having a lively conversation.

"I hope to see you at the next reading," Christian said and walked out of the shop just as Euan was coming in. Sullivan sauntered off down the street, leering at Diane as he went. Euan was pulling the bins inside the shop, asking for Diane's help.

"Diane, I'm talking to you," Euan snapped. "Hello?"

Diane jerked her head toward him. "What?"

"We're closing. A little help from my manager would speed up the process. I'm taking Martin to dinner and I don't want to be late."

"Look, fussbudget, just go," Diane said. "I think I can handle locking the doors."

Despite his fear of being late, Euan still puttered around the shop, running back up and down the stairs to his office. Sullivan would be waiting for Diane at the coffee shop around the corner and she didn't want to risk him coming back to the shop hunting her down.

Diane made sure Euan was gone and not coming back before dashing to the coffee shop. Sullivan was sitting at a window table, stuffing his face with a mile-long baguette. Diane came in. She bumped the table with her hip, making his coffee splash onto the table and his jacket.

"Oy, you bastard . . ." he yelled, then saw it was Diane and broke into a wide grin.

"What the fuck? What were you saying to Euan?"

"Just exchanging pleasantries. He was thrilled to meet a fellow Brit."

"You're Irish."

"Northern."

"That explains a lot," Diane said, shrugging off her coat and trying to get the waitress' attention. "Do you have anything to share or is this just another courtesy call?"

"I was hoping we might get to know each other better," Sullivan said. "You're a spitfire."

"And you are a pig bastard. I'd rather sew my snatch shut than have you anywhere near it."

Sullivan laughed, choking on the baguette. "You're a dirty bird."

"Are we done now?"

"I thought I might drive by rue Rampon one more time and take some photos of Madame Laureux for old time sake. She does get flustered."

"You've got the old woman scared half to death. Let her alone."

"She should hire me," Sullivan said, slapping his sausage fingers on the café table. "I checked out that Hugo bastard she's hired to find her dead husband's boyfriend. What a useless cunt."

"It's her money," Diane said, looking out the window, afraid someone might see her with Sullivan. "Now run along, Bernard. Don't you have some McLaren checks to cash?"

Sullivan laughed heartily. "I do, I do."

"Be honest, how hard are you actually looking for David?"

"Oh, I was doing my dead best early on," Sullivan said,

finishing off his third beer. "Then that cunt father started rubbing me the wrong way, and after you told me what really happened with David here in Paris, I became . . . let's say . . . distracted."

"I'm glad you listened to reason," Diane said.

"I don't have anything against the poofs. As long as they aren't bothering me, live and let live, I say. But that father is pathological about the queers. You know what they say, methinks he doth protest too much." Sullivan laughed at his own joke.

"Close enough."

"David McLaren is twenty years old. I don't think he's missing—he just doesn't want to be found. The more we search, the more he disappears."

"But are you sure David has left Paris?"

"Almost one hundred percent certain. But I do know one thing. I know how David McLaren got into the apartment."

Diane looked up from her tea. "Wait . . . what? Why didn't you tell me that when I got here? How did you find out?"

"I was doing a little exploring on rue Rampon yesterday and decided to have a closer look around Madame Laureux's building. Did you know there's an attic?"

"What were you doing snooping around the apartment? Are you outta your fucking mind? What if Irène . . ."

"No one was home. What do you take me for? I'm a professional," Sullivan said huffily.

"A four hundred pound will-o'-the-wisp, you are," Diane deadpanned.

"As I was saying, there's an attic and there's a trapdoor that leads to the roof. It had been pried off its hinges. David could have easily leapt from the roof of the hotel onto the roof of the apartment."

"But the old man who runs the Bel Air didn't see David and neither did anyone else."

Sullivan snorted. "I don't see Christ and yet I still believe."

"Right. It doesn't prove anything."

Sullivan shook his head. "I saw the police report and the photos. Things were taken that were easy to sell—the old woman's jewelry, the computer. You think a typical burglar would have taken time to sit down and read Martin's poetry? He's a talented bugger, but let's be serious."

"And the dope in the bathroom?"

"Not surprising. You said he was an alcoholic. Someone probably turned him on to heroin while he's been seeing the world."

Diane swirled the dregs of her tea around the bottom of her cup, hoping it might give her a sign. She wanted Sullivan to reassure her that David would not show up on rue Rampon. "I still don't get why David would take such a risk."

"Love and drugs. Dangerous combination, if you ask me."

"But you're sure he's gone?"

"He's gone. Back to America is my guess. That's where I'm headed next."

"God help them. Well, Bernard, I'd like to say it's been a pleasure, but it's been absolute hell." Diane stood up and offered her hand to Sullivan.

With surprising speed, Sullivan hefted his large frame out of the chair and pulled Diane close to him, pressing his fleshy lips against hers. Diane tried to scream, but she didn't want to open her mouth for fear Sullivan's thick, probing tongue would make entry. Diane slapped at his arms until he let her go.

"I'd been wanting to do that since the first night we met at Café Richard," Sullivan said. "I'm Bogey and you're Bacall."

Diane was frantically wiping at her mouth. "I'm going to put my lips together and puke," she yelled. "And it wasn't Bacall, it was Bergman, you fat bastard."

The entire café was looking at them, and Sullivan, for once, actually looked embarrassed. Diane started to walk out, then stopped, came back and looked at Sullivan. She stood on tiptoes and kissed him on the cheek.

"We'll always have Paris, Bernard," she whispered.


At Euan's urging, Martin began hosting the poetry open mic at the Anglophile twice a month. The place was always jammed with every available chair filled and people sitting cross-legged on the floor.

The attendees were an eclectic mix of students from the nearby Sorbonne and École des Beaux-Arts and smartly dressed thirtysomethings, which pleased Euan. He wanted the store to be a hip meeting place for English-speaking students and expats. The poetry was a mix of the horrible and surprisingly good-for-amateurs.

Christian had become a regular fixture at the readings, and girls—and more than a few guys—were always flirting with him, but Christian only had eyes for Martin. The boy's caramel skin, wavy hair and pouty lips even had Irène entertaining thoughts of kissing him. He was tall and handsome, always immaculately dressed and unfailingly polite to everyone.

Euan blithely overlooked the flirtation between Martin and the stranger, darting around the shop engaging everyone in animated chatter. Irène wanted to slap him for blathering on, but he was trying hard to drum up business since tourist season had ended. Martin always began the reading with one of his own poems. Irène noticed his voice was evolving, becoming more mature. Christian sat at Martin's feet, staring up at him in near reverence.

We arrived in Paris on a rainy Sunday.
I remember this now,
as I lift the veil you shrouded me in,
made me complicit in your indecision.

While the others walked under umbrellas,
we lay on opposite beds in the Marais,
our hands reaching across the chasm,
my fingertips tracing your open palm,
every line a dead-end.

We made love through a litany
of favorite things: films as foreplay,
music for kisses, books our orgasm,
a rush of words safe between hard covers.
We should have been covered in sweat,
sticky with the unspoken,
a tangle of limbs and lips.
We are those people in an alternate world,
where hallway voices hold no sway.

I remember this now, your eyes
before the door opened, broke the spell.
Your hand moving away, all the lines
suddenly on fire, a map gone to cinder.
This ephemeral day, even the afterglow.

Euan clapped loudly, too enthusiastically as Martin finished the poem, Irène thought. She edged her way over to the checkout counter where Diane was leaning.

"That poem was about David," Irène said. "I wonder what Euan thinks it's about?"

"He probably thinks it was inspired by him."

"He couldn't possibly!"

Diane started singing. "You're so vain . . ."

They saw Euan coming toward them through the crowd, beaming. "Martin is amazing isn't he?"

"We're almost out of coffee. I'll just go put on a new pot," Diane said. As she walked away, she sang, "I bet you think this song is about you, don't you, don't you."

Euan stared after her, shaking his head. "Diane's in a jolly mood."

"She's settling in," Irène shrugged, trying to change the subject.

Christian got up and stood before the microphone when Martin started the open mic. He cleared his throat and began reciting Anne Sexton's "With Mercy For The Greedy" from memory.

My friend, my friend, I was born
doing reference work in sin, and born
confessing it.

Irène watched Martin as Christian continued. She could see his face was flushed and he was enrapt in the boy's melodic voice. Christian recited the entire poem looking directly at Martin. The whole shop was quiet, as if everyone was holding their breath. Irène searched Euan's face for a reaction, but he seemed to be in a daze.

Christian finished the poem and the room erupted into sustained applause. The young man moved toward Martin, who looked like he was about to swoon. Christian took Martin's hand and shook it, leaning in to whisper in Martin's ear over the applause. Whatever he said made Martin blush.

"Ooooh, boy," Diane said, sliding up next to Irène. "I've

seen that look on Martin's face before—when he first met David. Heavy petting and seat wetting, ahoy."

Martin made his way toward Irène, Diane and Euan at the register.

"That was amazing," Martin gushed.

"Anyone can memorize," Euan said dismissively.

"He writes, too," Martin said, ignoring Euan's tone. "He said he would bring some of his own work to the next open mic."

"Delightful," Euan scowled. He checked his watch and wandered off into the stacks.

"What's his problem?" Martin asked, but didn't wait for Diane or Irène to answer. He stalked back to the microphone to introduce the next poet.

"Meow," Diane clawed the air. "Looks like Euan has finally bought a vowel and solved the puzzle."

Irène looked at Diane quizzically. "Euan's reactions to Martin are very . . . selective. Is that what I mean?"

"Oh, honey, I don't know what you mean half the time," Diane said as customers approached with books to purchase. She went behind the counter, still singing, "I bet you think this song is about you, don't you, don't you . . ."

# 10 V. Hugo

The talk of strikes began in mid-November. It was typical, Irène thought. Every other winter, just before the holiday season, the transportation workers would become unhappy with their wages, or the sanitation department would decry their working conditions in Paris, or the truck drivers who brought goods in from around the country and Europe would bemoan their long hours. This would mean traffic snarls, no food on the shelves and garbage piling up in fetid stacks on the sidewalks.

Irène put these thoughts, and those of the last three months, out of her mind as things settled back into cautious routine. Martin and Euan were still together, and Martin seemed to have curtailed his night wanderings. Diane seemed happy at the Anglophile and had softened toward the owner of the Bel Air, who was letting her stay in the room across from Irène's apartment for next to nothing.

Irène was able to sleep at night, but she watched

the comings and goings at the Bel Air Hotel more closely and trained her binoculars up and down rue Rampon frequently just to reassure herself. The useless police department had no leads in the robbery, just as they had let Jean-Louis' death go unsolved. She wondered if she was on some kind of watch list because of Jean-Louis' connections during the riots in 1968. In the attic, she frequently checked the lock that had been installed on the trapdoor that led to the roof of the building.

Nearly a week after she and Martin had returned and found the apartment ransacked, Irène went up to the dark and dusty attic to go through Jean-Louis' trunk. She wanted to bring everything back downstairs, surround herself with all of his things as she prepared to press her detective to double his efforts to find Frederick Dubois. It was in Jean-Louis' trunk, in a secret compartment, that she and Martin had discovered Frederick's letters and her husband's journal that chronicled their affair in the spring of 1968.

Irène had climbed the stairs into the attic, feeling her way along the wall until she could reach the cord for the hanging light. As she neared the top of the stairs, however, she saw weak light beaming down from above. The trapdoor was only half covering the rectangular opening, a patch of dazzling blue sky visible through the crack. She remembered climbing through the trapdoor in the summer of 1995, startled by sounds and a distant voice coming from above, only to discover David on the roof of the Bel Air drunkenly singing and twirling around. Because of rue Rampon's odd acoustics, she realized that David had been eavesdropping on her conversations with Martin on the balcony.

Once again, Irène pushed together boxes and crates as a makeshift ladder and slowly climbed atop them, her fear of falling and breaking a hip racing through her mind. The trapdoor was completely off its hinges, the interior latch broken and splintered. Someone had driven something between the trapdoor and the frame to pry it loose from the outside. Irène pushed the door aside and poked her head through, shielding her eyes from the light and dust.

Rue Rampon was so narrow that anyone with any physical agility could have easily leapt from the hotel's roof onto the apartment building. But the trapdoor was hidden behind the chimneys, so someone would have to know it was there to access it. Irène ticked off who knew about the trapdoor other than her neighbors, but she couldn't shake the image of David atop the hotel.

Then Irène remembered Martin's journal and poems spread out on his desk after the robbery. David. She turned his name over in her mind, thought about Diane's sudden return to Paris. It raised the hairs on the back of her neck, but she dismissed it. Diane had been in Paris for three months and there had been nothing else suspicious about her movements. Irène had the old hotel owner keeping an eye on Diane and monitoring her telephone calls. But if it wasn't David, then who?

Irène had pulled the trapdoor back into place and sat on Jean-Louis' trunk deciding what to do next. She probably should have called the police, told Martin about her discovery in the attic, but David was not a topic she relished. Instead, she called Gerard while Martin was out for the afternoon and had him send the publishing house's handyman over to repair and install a sturdy lock on the trapdoor. For the rest of September and most of October, she regularly checked the lock. By November, she was allowing herself to relax a bit and to harass the detective looking for Frederick Dubois.

The detective was named Victor Hugo, a fact that Irène did not find out until after she had hired him. His card read V. Hugo, and upon their first meeting she had casually asked if he was related to the author. "Distantly," he said and quickly moved onto another topic. During their third meeting at his tiny office near Place Monge, he had gone out to photocopy portions of Jean-Louis's journal. Irène felt guilty about this, but it was all for the investigation. She wandered about V. Hugo's office looking at photos on the wall and then came to several framed documents. One was V. Hugo's detective license, which included his full name—Victor Jude Hugo. She had almost laughed out loud, but then decided the joke was probably on her. She cast Frederick in the role of Jean Valjean and V. Hugo as the always one step behind Inspector Javert. She tried not to let her hopes sink, because V. Hugo was actually a very nice man and intrigued by her case. He had also lived through the revolution of 1968 and understood her need for closure. V. Hugo was tall and patrician and wore little spectacles on the bridge of his nose. He had served on the city council at some point in his life, had come from a prominent family, but there was a hint of exhaustion about him. His search for Frederick Dubois would be his biggest case in years, since most of them involved spying on other people's spouses and waiting outside homes until the wee hours to glimpse some type of indiscretion.

Gerard had recommended V. Hugo to her, having published the detective's mystery novel in the early 1970s. "The book, as they say, flopped," V. Hugo said as he pulled a worn copy from the bookcase behind his desk. Irène held it in her hands and saw the publishing house's imprint on the dust jacket. For a moment, she wondered if she might have edited it, but Gerard rarely sent her genre books. The endless string of interns Gerard had hired for the office since it opened in the 1950s would have handled something like this.

"Gerard has always been a very supportive friend," V. Hugo

said as Irène handed the book back to him. He returned it reverently to its space on the shelf. "I am honored to be working for his best editor."

V. Hugo said he had sources inside the French police and Interpol and would tap into those to find Frederick's whereabouts. He would go to the suburbs and watch Frederick's mother's apartment. Irène and Martin had gone there once and the old woman, confined to a wheelchair, had a revolver concealed under her lap robe. The old woman claimed to not know her son's whereabouts, but Irène knew Frederick sent money to her through a courier.

By her calendar, Irène had hired V. Hugo in the spring of 1996. He had been on the case for nearly two years and all the leads had gone nowhere. Irène continued to write monthly checks to V. Hugo, because he swore the case was still his top priority, but there was a tone in his voice that indicated defeat was not far behind. Martin urged her to fire him, but she could not.

"Javert eventually caught up with Jean Valjean in *Les Misérables*," Irène reminded Martin.

"I don't do musicals," Martin said.

*Irène runs through the streets of Paris, carrying the statue of Venus de Milo that Jean-Louis had given her, cradled like a baby in her arms. There are mountains of trash, smoldering remains of barricades and teargas lingers in the air. Her eyes burn. It is 1968. She is at Pont d'Arcole, the bridge that leads to Île de la Cité and Notre-Dame, its spires shrouded in a ghostly mist. The day suddenly turns to night. The statue is heavy, and Irène's arms ache, but she tightens her grip and runs across the bridge. In the plaza outside the cathedral, Irène sees a man, his back to her. She knows instinctively that it is Jean-Louis and screams his name. He turns, recognizes her, and a smile breaks across his face. But it is a fleeting expression that quickly turns to one of horror. He raises his arm and points at her, shouting something, but he has no voice. Blood drips from his forehead into his mouth and, suddenly, Irène feels a hand grab her by the hair, yank her so violently backwards that her feet leave the ground and the Venus de Milo flies from her arms, seems to float between Irène and Jean-Louis, who runs toward the falling statue, his arms open to catch it.*

# 11 Breaking Glass

It was a meager Christmas for the residents of rue Rampon. The city drifted through the holiday in a fugue of Christmases past when the city was not paralyzed by strikes. Supermarket shelves were barely stocked because only a few trucks were running. Retailers started closing early because the metro was running a limited schedule and, in the spirit of the holidays, taxi drivers had jacked up their fares to double the usual cost.

Irène had a nasty incident at a Carrefour on the other side of the city where she had gone with Martin and Diane when rumor spread that a big delivery of food had been made to the supermarket. Half of Paris had heard the same rumor and the crush inside the overheated store was more than Irène could stand. She fainted in the checkout aisle and a woman snatched up the loaf of bread that had slipped from Irène's hand. Martin had helped her up while Diane screamed at the woman in a mixture of English and French as they struggled over the bread, eventually ripping the loaf in half.

"This is why I preferred having my food delivered," Irène said on the way home. "Agoraphobia has its practical side."

On Christmas night, Irène sat on the balcony smoking cigarettes and unwinding from the day. She had cooked a small meal for herself, Martin, Euan and Diane and they had exchanged gifts. A small tree twinkled with white lights near the French doors. Euan had driven out and hacked it down in the woods off a motorway because he was horrified that Irène and Martin had not put up a Christmas tree. Irène had held her breath as Martin unwrapped a small box that Euan had given him, and could see the tentative look on his face. She found herself gripping the arms of the chair, white knuckled. Martin opened the box, slowly pulled out a silver ring and held it between his fingers. He searched Euan's face.

"Don't panic, it's not an engagement ring," Euan said, but Irène could detect disappointment in his voice. Euan had obviously expected a different reaction from Martin, who tentatively kissed Euan as he slid the band on his finger. It would have been a disaster if Euan had forced some kind of commitment, Irène thought.

Diane, for once, kept her mouth closed. Euan had asked her to come up to his office at the Anglophile one day early in December. He was looking at rings online and asked Diane what type she thought Martin might like.

"A cock ring," Diane suggested. "Maybe one of those kind you hook to your nipples."

Euan looked up at her in disgust. "I want to buy him a promise ring."

"What's the promise? Not to fuck any of his little poetry groupies?"

Euan winced at the mention of the open mics Martin hosted at the store, which had now become weekly events by popular demand. Diane marveled at how Martin transformed at the microphone; he was funny, flirty and seemed to be enjoying himself immensely. Martin had also lost weight, grown out his hair, and his clothing, while always black, seemed to fit more snugly in the right places. Peter's death and David's betrayal were loosening their hold and the real Martin was emerging. Diane had often wondered what Martin would have been like if his life had taken a different turn, and she was finally getting a glimpse. An inordinate number of gay boys from the Sorbonne and Beaux Arts School had discovered the open mic and were there every week, and some dropped by the Anglophile during the week just to see if Martin was in the store.

Christian never missed the readings and his flirtation with Martin had only intensified. They would stand too close to each other, whispering conspiratorially and sharing private jokes. When he was leaving the Anglophile, Christian would put an arm around Martin's waist and kiss him on each cheek, wavering as if he might kiss him on the mouth. Diane and Irène watched every week as Euan struggled to maintain his composure and hold his tongue. Euan's nostrils would flare and a trickle of sweat would invariably appear on his forehead. There was a break in the readings because of the holiday, and Euan was glad.

"I can't believe Martin hasn't been knocking boots with that Christian kid yet," Diane whispered to Irène at the last reading before the holiday. "He's seriously hot."

"Martin has been sleeping at Euan's apartment almost every night. I think he has grown fonder of Euan in the last few months."

"You're usually a better liar than that," Diane said, nudging Irène. "Our boy is growing up and moving on. Euan is about to get the full-tilt boogie whiplash of what it means to be the rebound boyfriend."


After everyone said their goodnights, Irène sat at her desk and picked up a manuscript she had been struggling to edit for Gerard. The twinkling lights of the Christmas tree mesmerized her. Pierre was asleep under her feet, but he was soon awakened as Irène moved restlessly about the apartment. She finally went out on the balcony, pulling her robe around her to fight off the chill. Irène lay with her head back, blowing smoke toward the stars and fast moving lights of airplanes jetting high above.

The phone rang inside the apartment, breaking her reverie. She guessed it was Martin calling from across the hall, picked up the receiver and said, "How may I help you?" in a teasing voice. There was silence from the other end, then the sound of a throat being cleared.

"Madame Laureux?"

Irène was flustered, surprised to hear another voice on the line. "Yes. Who is this?"

"It's Monsieur Hugo."

"Ah, V. Hugo. Joyeux Noël."

"I am sorry to disturb you on Christmas Day, but I wanted to ask if you had read yesterday's *Le Monde*?"

"No."

"I thought not, or I would have heard from you."

Irène tightened her grip on the phone. "What was in the paper?"

"An obituary for Frederick Dubois' mother. She passed away on December 23 at her apartment in Argenteuil."

Irène held the phone to her ear, but could not speak. Her mind whirled. Sympathy for the old woman who had died alone, confined to a wheelchair and pining for her son who was in hiding. A twinge of grief for Frederick Dubois, wherever he was.

"Are you there, madame?"

"Yes, I apologize. It is a shocking thing to hear."

"But a tremendous break in this case. This will draw Frederick Dubois out of hiding."

"He won't come to the funeral. It would be too easy."

"This is true, but there will be arrangements to be made. Money to be paid for the funeral service and burial. I can track him this way." There was a note of excitement in V. Hugo's voice that Irène found offensive.

"Let me know what you find out," she said and rang off quickly.

For years, Irène had thought about what she would say to Frederick Dubois when they finally met face to face. She envisioned screaming at him, calling him a coward and maybe slapping him. But as time wore on, she decided the unfettered truth would do; no glossing over or sugar coating of facts to spare her feelings. If Frederick Dubois knew whether her husband was murdered or committed suicide, she was prepared to accept either answer.

After she finally went to bed, the dream came again. The giant hothouse and Venus looming over her, a hand covering her mouth and water filling her eyes.


On New Year's Eve, Euan held a party on the roof of the Anglophile, and they watched the fireworks blaze over the Eiffel Tower to usher in 1998. The party was a good diversion from waiting to hear from V. Hugo about Frederick Dubois. His mother's body was being kept in cold storage awaiting instructions from the family. V. Hugo said he was watching the funeral home and had tapped an inside source in case contact was made by phone, letter or email.

Earlier in the day, V. Hugo had come to rue Rampon and presented Irène with a stack of letters about an inch thick. He had gone to Madame Dubois' apartment in Argenteuil, forced the door and performed a late night search. The detective breaking into the dead woman's home and rifling through her things was distasteful to Irène, but she said nothing.

"Have you read them?" Irène asked, starring at the tiny bundle held together with a thick rubber band.

"Yes. I checked them for postmarks or any mention of his whereabouts in the lines. I found nothing. The letters were all hand delivered."

"Another dead end."

"Not at all," V. Hugo said animatedly. "Look at the one on top. It's the most recent." It was a small Christmas card and it had been dated December 5 on the inside.

*Dear Mama,*

*I hope this card finds you in better health. I apologize for the early date of this Christmas message, but I wanted to be sure it reached you in time. I have been keeping myself busy with many activities and have been re-reading Proust's grand work again. I know how much you adored his writing, Mama, and I think of you every time I open a page. I wish I could be with you this season, but as you know, that is not practical or safe. I am sending a gift under separate cover that should carry you through the next few months.*

*All my love,*

*F.*

Irène ran her fingers over the card. It was on a thick, creamy paper with a small drawing of a tree on the front and blank on the inside. The mark on the reverse indicated it was made in France. V. Hugo said he had called about the cards, which were sold in upscale boutiques and gift shops around the country. He was already getting a list of the stores.

"You're very thorough," Irène murmured, but could not take her eyes off the writing in the card. Frederick's handwriting had changed very little from the letters he had sent to Jean-Louis in 1968.

"I have even taken the liberty of phoning libraries and book shops to find out if copies of Proust have been checked out or purchased in the last six months."

Irène handed the letters back to V. Hugo and thanked him for his hard work.

"Please read the letters," he said. "You may notice something I have missed."

She wanted to tell V. Hugo to return the letters, but on New Year's Day, they still sat on her desk unread.

After the party at the Anglophile, Irène came home feeling unexpectedly exhausted and fell asleep quickly. It was nearly four o'clock in the morning when she was awakened by the sound of breaking glass. She thought it was a dream, but then heard an alarm going off. Irène scrambled out of bed, pulled on her robe and went out onto the balcony. Diane was awake as well, leaning out of her hotel room window and looking down at the street.

Irène saw broken glass glittering on the street outside the tobacco shop next door to the Bel Air. The owner, Anton, used to live in the tiny apartment over the shop, but had moved the year before to a larger space on the other side of République Square. Irène yelled to Diane over the wailing alarm to phone the police.

A figure emerged from the shop, almost tumbling through the window, carrying two bulging plastic bags. Irène heard the distinct sound of a police car siren approaching, and the robber heard it, too.

"Hey, asshole," Diane shouted and the robber looked up at her. He seemed stunned for a moment, uncertain what to do.

He was dressed in a dark sweater and pants, wore trainers and a baseball cap with the brim curved and pulled low over his eyes. Although Irène couldn't see his face, something about his demeanor was familiar, and she felt panic well up inside her. There was a reason he wasn't running.

"David," Irène called down and the robber's head jerked her way, almost looked up.

Two police cars turned onto rue Rampon and the robber ran in the opposite direction. One car stopped in front of the tobacco shop, while the other pursued the fleeing figure. Diane stared at Irène across the narrow street, her mouth open in surprise.


Diane and Irène huddled in the doorway of the Bel Air as a policeman took their statements. Martin and Euan had come out to check on the sirens, but Irène convinced them to go back to bed since they had seen and heard nothing. The policeman went to confer with the officer who was inspecting the broken window. Anton, the owner, arrived and bellowed his indignation at being robbed. He thanked Diane and Irène for trying to stop the thief. The robber had busted open the cash register and taken expensive cigars and hundreds of packs of cigarettes. After Anton and the policemen went inside the shop, Irène glared at Diane.

"Why are you looking at me like that? You don't actually think that was David," Diane said.

"Yes, I do. You saw him. You saw how he responded when I called his name."

"How much champagne did you drink at the party?"

"Stop it. I wondered why you showed up here, and now David's here, too. Is that a coincidence?

"Whoa, Nancy Drew, cool your heels."

"The robber who got into my flat came in through the trapdoor in the attic. Only a handful of people know about that, and David was one of them. And Martin's journal and poetry... I thought I was being paranoid, but I know I am right, and I know you are involved."

Diane started to protest, but a dark sedan pulled up in front of the hotel and Inspector Arnaud stepped out.

"Oh, Christ," Diane whispered.

Arnaud walked over to the women, pulling off his hat. "Your little corner of Paris has become quite the crime capital," he said, pulling a small notebook out of his coat pocket. "I understand you both witnessed this robbery."

"We've given our statements to the officers," Irène said.

"Of course," Arnaud said, "but I have a few other questions."

"Of course you do," Diane muttered.

Arnaud jotted something down on his pad and Diane craned her neck to look, but he pulled the pad away.

"I came by looking for you and Monsieur Paige earlier in the week, but no one was home," Arnaud said. "I wanted to give you a report on our findings."

"Are there findings?" Irène asked. "I haven't heard from you in months."

"We have been unable to match the fingerprints found in our known offender files," Arnaud said. "But I believe we have determined how the thieves entered your apartment."

Irène felt her insides knot. "And how was that?"

"Through the trapdoor in the attic," Arnaud said. "The one that was padlocked *after* the robbery had taken place."

Irène was poker-faced. "Really?"

"The other tenants in your building said they had not installed the padlock, and rarely visited the attic," Arnaud said, writing in his notebook. "I haven't asked Monsieur McEvoy, but I would surmise he knows nothing of the attic as well. That would leave you and Monsieur Paige. Shall I ask him?"

"No," Irène said, too quickly. "He knows nothing about the lock."

"So you admit that you had the lock installed."

"She doesn't admit anything," Diane chimed in. "What is this? An interrogation? We called to report a break-in at the tobacco shop."

"Be patient, Madame Jacobs," Arnaud said. "I will be with you shortly." He looked again at Irène. "What do you have to say, Madame Laureux?"

Irène shrugged with a smile on her face. Arnaud pursed his lips and put the notebook back into his pocket.

"You're a very intriguing woman, Irène," Arnaud said, taking on a more casual air. "Everyone speaks so highly of you. Those at the publishing house, your neighbors, the private detective you employ."

Irène was unshaken by Arnaud's revelation. "Perhaps if you spent more time investigating the robbery and less time inquiring into my personal life, you might catch the thieves. You act as if I robbed my own apartment."

"Oh, no, madame," Arnaud said. "We believe there was a robbery. What we don't understand is why you are trying to protect the robbers."

"That is ridiculous," Irène said.

Arnaud stuck his hands in his coat pocket. "I would like to

help you, Madame Laureux, but you do not seem to want it. We will catch those who broke into your apartment and the tobacconist with or without your assistance. If you have any idea who committed these crimes, we would be more lenient in our charges. I am sure you are aware we have taken a strong position on drugs in the city. Drug users, dealers and those who commit crimes to supply their habit are dealt with harshly, no matter the circumstances."

Arnaud walked back to confer with his men. Every few moments, Arnaud would look over at Irène and Diane. Finally, he bowed his head in their direction, got in his car and drove away.

"Your attic is quite the tourist attraction," Diane said. "You should start charging like the Anne Frank house."

"Be quiet. I am sick of your nonsense. I want to know what you know."

"I don't know anything. I haven't seen or spoken to David in over two years, same as you and Martin." Irène sensed she was telling the truth, just not the whole truth.

Back in her room at the Bel Air, Diane rummaged through her wallet until she found Bernard Sullivan's grease-stained card. She counted back the hours to American time, then picked up the phone on her nightstand. For a moment, she held the receiver in her hand then hung up. She went to her purse and dug through it until she found the mobile phone Sullivan had suggested she buy in case the old hotel owner was monitoring her calls. Diane punched in Sullivan's number with her hand shaking.

# 12 Saint-Étienne

Three weeks after the death of Madame Dubois, V. Hugo arrived in a taxi at rue Rampon to take Irène and Martin to Gare de Lyon. The trio was heading to Saint-Étienne in southeast central France where Frederick's mother was to be buried. Irène fussed about the distance, the cost and showing up so abruptly at a private function. Martin and V. Hugo had stared her down until she relented.

All three were dressed in funeral black as they set off from the apartment. Irène wore a hat with a veil that partially covered her face. Martin wore an ankle length black coat over more black, while V. Hugo was elaborately dressed in a waistcoat and bowler hat.

"Is it a funeral or a costume party?" Diane asked Martin as the taxi driver loaded their bags. V. Hugo overheard her comment, sniffed loudly and slammed the taxi door hard as he got in the front seat. Diane wanted to go with them, but Euan said he needed her at the Anglophile.

"Run along on your little adventure," Euan said with barely contained condescension. That morning, he and Martin had argued after Euan called the trip "another wild goose chase."

As the taxi pulled away from the curb, Martin felt a sense of relief. He desperately needed a break from Euan and what felt more and more each day like a charade. Since Princess Diana's funeral, Martin had been trying to make things work with Euan, but he felt increasingly bored and unfulfilled. Martin looked forward to the poetry readings each week at the bookstore and to seeing Christian.

Martin held Irène's hand as the TGV sped toward Saint-Étienne. V. Hugo sat across from them, uncomfortable with their silence. He attempted to make small talk, told them in hushed tones how he had found out about the burial site of Madame Dubois and the possibility of personal harm to them all.

"What are you talking about?" Irène asked, her eyes turning from the rushing landscape to V. Hugo. "It's a funeral, not a war zone."

"Frederick Dubois, or André Sarde as he is now known, is not just a radical youth from the 1960s, madame," V. Hugo said in a huff. "He is well connected with a number of underground political movements, extremists. If my sources are correct, and I believe they are, he has a large source of income that he uses to finance candidates for political office. His parents were very wealthy."

"Then why did his mother live in such a tiny apartment?" Martin asked.

"She preferred it," V. Hugo said. "She did not want to call attention to herself."

"Who is going to be at this service?" Irène asked.

"That is the unknown factor. Of course, we hope Frederick Dubois is there."

"But there is no guarantee," Martin said, slumping back in his seat. "We may be traveling hundreds of miles to see a woman buried who would have just as soon shot us."

"It is a risk that Madame Laureux agreed to take," V. Hugo said. "It may be our last chance to meet Dubois face to face. Now he has no connections to the past. He can go more deeply underground. He can vanish without any trace at all."

"If he was any deeper underground, he'd be in China," Martin said wearily.

Irène smiled at the joke, but V. Hugo obviously did not get it. He cleared his throat and excused himself to the bathroom.

"I can't believe you're paying him," Martin said to Irène as they watched V. Hugo careen up the aisle.

"He's better than he seems. No one has ever gotten this close to Frederick." She tightened her grip on Martin's hand, her thumb rubbed over the surface of his tattoo. "I must say I am very anxious."

"Try and relax."

"I have this very clear picture in my head of how the meeting should be. I dreamed about it. I am outside of my body and I can see myself coming up behind him. Frederick is standing alone at the grave and I come behind him and call his name. He turns, I lift my veil and for a moment he does not know who I am, but then it slowly sinks in. He is too stunned to say anything."

"Very cinematic."

"He answers all my questions and we go our separate ways again."

"What if the answers aren't what you expected?"

"I have accepted that Jean-Louis might have killed himself over this. In a way, I almost prefer it."

"Don't say that."

"It is a harsh thing to say, but at least there is a reason. If it is murder, then that leaves more questions that may never be answered. The police and the government will never tell the real story. It is thirty years ago this year that Jean-Louis died. I just want closure."

Irène stared out the window as the train sped south. Snow stood in patches and the sky was grey and heavy. She could see her own and Martin's reflections in the glass. She wished she could take back her words about Jean-Louis committing suicide. Martin rarely mentioned Peter anymore, but when he did, there was always a tone of sadness in his voice. In a moment of insanity, Peter had planned to kill Martin and himself, but Martin's sense of self-preservation had kicked in. The act had nearly consumed Martin, and Irène often wondered if a similar scenario had played out between Jean-Louis and Frederick. What could have possibly happened that day in May 1968 that could have sent Frederick Dubois running for three decades?

An ancient, hearse-sized black sedan picked up Irène, Martin and V. Hugo at Châteaucreux station in Saint-Étienne. The driver was an elderly, stooped man wearing a driving cap and suit that seemed several sizes too large for him.

"This is the employee of the funeral home that arranged Madame Dubois' service," V. Hugo said. "He will take us directly to the cemetery."

"May I open the window?" Irène asked once they were inside. The car reeked of stale cigarette smoke and the heater was blowing at full blast.

The driver spoke quickly in French to V. Hugo. "He asks that you not. He says it will slow down the car and the cold wind makes his joints seize."

"Fabulous," Martin said under his breath.

"We wouldn't want that, would we?" Irène said, trying to be cheerful. "Let's go quickly then. Very quickly."

The cemetery was more than an hour outside Saint-Étienne, and Martin and Irène dozed against each other's shoulders as the driver kept the heat cranked up to an oppressively high level.

"This could be a trap, you know," Martin whispered to Irène.

"How so?"

"The heat and the smell in here, it's combining to create carbon monoxide poisoning. The old fart is trying to kill us off."

This tickled Irène unexpectedly. "Don't make me laugh, Martin."

"I'm sorry," he said and covered his mouth to stifle a snicker.

"No, you're not."

"No, I'm not."

They both burst out laughing, snorting in near hysterics. The old driver veered all over the road at the commotion, while V. Hugo looked back at them with a mixture of horror and disgust.

"We're delirious from the heat," Martin said to V. Hugo, which made Irène double over with laughter. "Tell the old man we're going to crack the window whether he likes it or not."

The driver mumbled and muttered as Martin and Irène leaned toward the glass to let the cold wind buffet their faces. The mood became somber again as they saw a sign pointing toward the church and cemetery.

"A few more kilometers and we will be there," V. Hugo said, checking his watch. "And on time as promised."

Irène clutched Martin's hand. "I feel sick suddenly," she said.

The car turned off the main road onto an unpaved path

leading to a small stone church. It was a barren landscape that greeted them; the trees gnarled and twisted by the winds in the dead of winter. The graveyard lay in the shadow of the church surrounded by a crude stone fence that had been built in some other century. A small white tent was set up at the far corner of the cemetery. Madame Dubois' casket was already resting over the open grave and four or five people were gathering under the tent, including a priest in full robes.

The driver pulled up behind the hearse, a silver Mercedes and a white van with dark, tinted windows. V. Hugo leaned closer toward the glass to get a look at the people under the tent.

"Is he there?" Irène asked.

"I cannot tell," he said as he got out of the car. He opened Martin and Irène's door and they slowly climbed out into the bitterly cold air. "We should hurry," V. Hugo said. "They are about to begin."

V. Hugo led them through the rusted iron gate of the cemetery. Martin and Irène walked slowly, his arm around her shoulders.

"I think I may faint," Irène said.

"Don't you dare," Martin said, tightening his grip, just in case.

There were three women, all of them ancient looking in their funeral garb, sitting in a row of uncomfortable wooden chairs at the grave's edge. Behind the women, a tall young man with slicked-back hair and a dark suit stood with his hands clasped behind his back.

A priest stood at the head of the casket with a prayer book already open. All of them turned their eyes to V. Hugo, Irène and Martin as they hovered at the edge of the tent. The priest looked worriedly at the three old women for some type of sign. The one closest to him nodded, but never took her eyes off the strange trio that had suddenly appeared.

The priest stammered and stuttered through a short ceremony, while the three old women crossed themselves over and over, but remained stone-faced throughout. When it was done, two old sextons in gray jumpsuits moved quickly to lower the casket into the ground and began covering it with dirt. No one moved as the clumps of frozen earth hit the casket lid like rocks. The church's side door opened and the driver of the hearse came out and stood speaking with another priest. The two men shook hands and the driver walked quickly to the hearse, got in and drove away. Martin craned his neck and saw the driver of their car was fast asleep, his head tilted back, mouth open. He'd be useless in a pursuit.

The younger man touched each of the women lightly on the shoulder, then turned and walked toward the van. The priest moved to help one of the old women to her feet, and V. Hugo decided it was time to make his move. With his hat pressed against his chest, the detective approached the mourners.

"He's not here," Martin whispered to Irène.

"I didn't think he would be," she said, both disappointed and relieved that a nasty confrontation had been avoided. "It would have been too easy."

The howling wind cut off much of what V. Hugo said, but Martin and Irène caught the name Frederick numerous times. The old women—Bibles and rosaries clutched to their chests— glared scornfully at V. Hugo, then turned in unison and moved toward the Mercedes parked outside the gate.

Irène watched as the young man walked toward the van, which she noticed had a wheelchair lift fitted onto its sliding side door. The young man spoke into a small walkie-talkie, which he must have been carrying in his pocket. He sensed Irène's gaze upon him and turned to look back at her. She realized she had seen him before, but where? Then she remembered: Père Lachaise—the young man who had startled her when she was visiting Jean-Louis' grave.

The young man opened the sliding door and appeared to be speaking to someone. Irène crossed the distance between the gravesite and the van quickly, taking notice of the darkened windows. Someone was inside observing the funeral.

The man shut the sliding door with a slam and was startled to see Irène standing behind him at the passenger door.

"We've met before," Irène said.

"I don't think so."

"Not formally. You were at Père Lachaise in September."

"You are mistaken."

"I'm sorry for your loss," Irène said. "How did you know Madame Dubois?"

The young man said nothing and walked around Irène to the driver's door. Irène followed him, trying to get another glimpse inside the van, but the windows were opaque.

"I knew Madame Dubois' son."

The young man fumbled with they keys. "You should not have come here."

"Do you know who I am?" Irène asked, startled.

A tight smile played across the man's face. "I cannot help you."

"Who is in the back of the van?" Irène demanded, trying to keep her voice calm.

"Not who you are looking for," the young man said, getting inside and slamming the door.

Irène knocked on the window. "Oh, please, you must help me. Let me speak to him. Is it Frederick Dubois?"

The engine started up and Irène ran alongside the van pounding on the darkened windows, calling Frederick's name.

The van accelerated, spraying her with dust and dirt as it sped down the road. She turned to call to Martin, but saw that V. Hugo was in a heated exchange with the driver of the old women's Mercedes. The driver was all muscles and Nordic looking, wearing a severe black suit and cap. He held the back door open as the women slowly crowded in.

Irène moved toward them, but had only taken a few steps when the driver, in one swift move, shoved V. Hugo away from the car. The detective stumbled and fell back onto the ground. Martin moved to intervene, but the driver slammed the sedan's back door closed, brushed Martin aside and got into the car. Martin slammed his fist on the hood of the car and the driver gunned the engine. V. Hugo grabbed Martin and pulled him out of the way as the car made a wild u-turn and drove fast down the dirt road.

"Motherfucker!" Martin screamed at the retreating car. He bent down, picked up a rock and threw it at the back window, but it fell far shot of its target.

Irène rushed up to them. "Are you all right?"

"He almost ran me over! What the hell is wrong with these people?"

"We got too close," V. Hugo said, dusting himself off.

"Yes, we did," Irène said. "I believe Frederick was watching the funeral from the van. That young man had a radio."

"Did you get the license plate number?" V. Hugo asked.

"No," Irène said, "I didn't even think about it."

"I got the sedan's number. I'll have it traced," V. Hugo said, pulling a notebook from his jacket and jotting down the numbers. "The only piece of information I obtained was that those women were Madame Dubois' sisters."

Irène told Martin and Hugo about seeing the young man at Père Lachaise. "He said the person in the van was not who I was looking for, but it was Frederick. I feel it."

They looked around the churchyard for the priest, but he had gone. V. Hugo went to speak with the sextons, while Martin and Irène went to the church. It was locked. They walked around, knocking on other doors and trying to peer inside windows.

"There are two priests," Martin said. "One of them has to be in there."

"But they won't come to the door," Irène said. "Frederick paid them off."

V. Hugo joined them and said the sextons had no information. "I think we have done everything we can do here," he said, and they all walked back toward the car under a darkening sky.

Once they were back on the train to Paris, V. Hugo tried to engage Irène and Martin. "We can have someone watch the cemetery," he offered.

"He won't come back," Irène said. "He paid his last respects and made a clean getaway. Frederick was there and we let him escape."

"What else could we have done?" V. Hugo asked, irritation in his voice. "I was assaulted."

He wanted to protest further, but Irène's and Martin's stares silenced him. He eventually went to sleep, troubled that he had lost the last thread of the case that could have been his entrée back into the respectable rank of detectives. V. Hugo dreamed of cracking the case wide open, while Irène and Martin stared out the window all the way back to Paris.

# 13 Disquiet

Inspector Arnaud was waiting for Diane in the lobby of the hotel when she arrived from work. She didn't notice him sitting in the corner and went to the desk to retrieve her room key. When she turned around, he was standing behind her. She jumped back a bit and scowled at him.

"I'm sorry to frighten you, Madame Jacobs," Arnaud said, but she could tell he was not sorry at all.

"What do you want?"

"I was looking for Madame Laureux, but she does not seem to be at home, nor her little friend."

"They've gone to a funeral," Diane said and walked toward the elevator.

"Just a moment."

Diane turned back with a frown. "They aren't home, so you've come to harass me?"

"I was planning to see you also, so I can make my inquiry now. I have just a few more questions," the inspector said, pulling a notebook from his coat and flipping through it. "Are you living here at the hotel, Madame Jacobs?"

"I'm a paying guest."

"How long do you plan to stay?"

"I haven't decided."

"Are you working for Monsieur McEvoy?"

"I'm helping at his shop."

"He is paying you a wage."

"No."

Arnaud did a double take. "You are working for free? I find that hard to believe."

"You can ask him yourself. Check his records. I receive no checks."

Arnaud tapped his pen on the notebook. "Paying you . . . how do they say . . . under the table. We strictly enforce immigration and labor laws. I am sure you are aware your passport only allows you leave to stay for three months and it is illegal to work for money. You would need a visa and a work permit."

"Thanks for the newsflash," Diane said. "Are we finished?"

"I am quite serious, Madame Jacobs."

"So what are you gonna do, Inspector, kick me out of the country?"

"I will follow the law."

"So you'd persecute me, yet let every other Algerian, Iraqi and African stay forever and take other people's jobs and live off the taxpayers."

"It is a problem, but we will end this problem and everyone will be handled the same way. Just because you are American, it will not give you any special privileges."

"I'm sure you would make Jean-Marie Le Pen proud," Diane said. "Are you an anti-Semite and homophobe as well?"

"My political affiliations are none of your business."

"I'll take that as a yes," Diane said. "Your National Front scare tactics might work here, but I come from the land of radical Christian loonies. I don't scare easily. Now, if you'll excuse me, I have things to do."

"I will be back," Arnaud said.

Diane got on the elevator. "Police are the same everywhere, aren't they? Always looking for things that aren't there, while the real criminals run the streets."

Arnaud started to answer her, but the elevator door closed.

In her room, Diane flopped across the double bed she had made by pushing the two singles together. It was warm in the room and she crawled over the bed to open the window.

If someone had asked her three years ago where she would be in her life, she would have said teaching in Memphis, dating some guy who probably bored the shit out of her and hanging out with Martin. Nothing exciting. She still couldn't believe she was living in a Paris hotel, that her life had taken such an unexpected turn. All because she'd agreed to fill in as chaperone on a trip to Europe. Maybe there was something to Martin's and the old woman's babbling about synchronicity. Diane looked around the room that she was slowly making a home. She'd taken the ugly artwork off the wall and put up her own, bought a cheap microwave and was thinking of buying a mini-fridge. The hordes of tourists would start arriving in the spring and she'd have to leave and find a real apartment.

Diane was lost in her thoughts of the future when she heard voices on the street below. Arnaud's voice, she was certain, and another man. She crept off the side of the bed and opened the window further so she could peek down to rue Rampon. It was Euan coming home late from the Anglophile. The cold air made her shiver with dread at what that bastard Arnaud might be saying to Euan. Then she heard her own name float up. She wanted to leap out the window onto Arnaud's back and claw his eyes out. She heard Euan raise his voice, trying to assert his authority.

"She's simply doing me a favor," Euan said heatedly. "How dare you question me like this."

Arnaud was completely unruffled by Euan's outburst. "I am simply reminding you of the labor laws in France," he said officiously. "They are very specific."

"I am aware of the law, sir," Euan said pulling his coat tighter. "If that is all, it's freezing and I have other work to attend to."

"When do you expect Madame Laureux and Monsieur Paige?"

"I don't know."

"Bonsoir, monsieur," Arnaud said.

Euan went inside the apartment building and Arnaud looked up and tipped his hat at Diane. She almost ducked her head back inside, but instead she hocked up a wad of spit and surprised herself by landing it at Arnaud's feet. The smile faded from his lips and was replaced by a scowl. Arnaud stared at the spit that gleamed on the sidewalk and then slowly walked away down the street. Diane wondered if her comment about Le Pen had been correct. What if this fucker was a member of the National Front that wanted all foreigners, especially Jews, out of France? And he was a member of the police. For a brief moment, she felt what her father must have felt in Poland all those years ago when dread turned to panic.


Martin and Irène were in a funk after returning from Madame Dubois's funeral in Saint-Étienne. They moved around the apartment quietly as snow closed down the streets and brought the city to a peaceful standstill. Euan had asked persistent questions about the trip, but neither Martin nor Irène felt like answering them. He bristled about Inspector Arnaud's questioning him in the street, and Irène had held her breath waiting for Euan to drop some unexpected bombshell.

"If he begins investigating me, I may have to lay off Diane," Euan said.

"You can't," Martin and Irène chorused.

"She's working illegally."

"I'm working illegally," Martin said. "You do what you have to do."

"I can't let the shop go under."

"Why was he here asking about Diane?" Martin wanted to know.

"He was looking for you and Irène, and when I told him you were away he started in on the shop."

"He's an idiot," Irène chimed in. "I don't think he gives a damn about our robbery or the tobacco shop."

But Arnaud did not return and their days slipped back into routine. Martin tried to find comfort in Euan's arms, but it was elusive. Where he used to fantasize about David, lately Martin's thoughts turned more and more to the beautiful boy from the Anglophile who had read Anne Sexton to him at the open mic. Whether he was masturbating or having perfunctory sex with Euan twice a week, Martin would close his eyes and conjure up Christian's face and body, could almost feel the boy's mouth and hands upon him, followed by an orgasm so intense that it would leave him gasping for breath.

# 14 Falling Further In

Martin sat in front of a computer at Café Orbital across from Jardin du Luxembourg. He should have been back at rue Rampon editing manuscripts with Irène, but he was restless. It was mid-afternoon and there were few people in the downstairs part of the café—some students and locals, but no tourists jockeying for position on the café's computers. It was a cold, dreary February day and Martin did not want to be alone.

He found himself back in the chat rooms, a curiosity too strong to be denied. He had offers from around the city, most were from older men looking for something quick before they went home to their wives. There were students from the Latin Quarter, some were within walking distance, others just a metro stop away, but they couldn't have company. Martin's hour on the computer was almost over when a private message popped up on Martin's screen: *Hello, Martin*

Martin paused, felt a wave of panic wash over him. *Who is this?*

*A fellow poet*

*Did we meet somewhere before?*

*At the Anglophile*

Martin almost signed off. He felt the urge to flee the café. What if Euan had discovered he was meeting strangers on the Internet? He didn't want to hurt Euan, but maybe the revelation would end the stalemate of their relationship. But it wouldn't be Euan, Martin thought, because he hated computers.

*Is this Christian?*

*You will have to come and find out. 24 Avenue Junot in Montmartre*

Although he had hooked up dozens of times, Martin was always nervous, always felt a wave of nausea, guilt, excitement, eroticism. There was something dangerous about the invitation, but Martin was already hard in his jeans at the idea that it might be the beautiful boy from the open mic.

*I'm on my way*

There was poetry in sex with strangers, Martin thought as the taxi wound its way up the hill to Montmartre. The first glance, first touch, first kiss, the embarrassment of nudity, the exhilaration of being gently or roughly pushed back onto a bed or floor or sofa, the fumbling to find the right position, the electric shock of penetration. And just before orgasm, it seemed perfectly reasonable that a total stranger could be the long desired soulmate.

The address was an elegant townhouse on Avenue Junot, a brick-paved, tree-lined street not far from the domed Sacré-Cœur Basilica that dominated the district. Martin paid the taxi driver, went up the steps and rang the bell. After a moment, the door opened with a rush of air and Christian was standing before him with a grin on his face.

The object of Martin's desire was standing in the doorway wearing nothing but loose fitting, drawstring pants low on his hips. Christian's body was lean and muscled, his abs well-defined; a thin trail of hair led from his belly button to a curl of pubic hair peeking over the waistband. He was obviously not wearing any underwear.

"Oh, my god, it is you," Martin said, feeling color rise to his face.

"Are you surprised?"

"Surprised is one way to put it."

"I must confess that I have seen you in the chatrooms before."

"Why didn't you message me?"

"I was afraid," Christian said. "Maybe a little embarrassed. I've wanted to talk to you at the Anglophile, ask you to dinner or for a coffee, but there are always so many people around you."

"I've thought about you so often," Martin said, resisting the urge to rush into the boy's arms.

"What have you thought about me?" Christian asked, leaning against the doorframe.

Martin smiled. "I thought you were beautiful."

"Come in out of the cold," Christian said and held out his hand to Martin.

Christian pulled Martin inside and shut the door. The house was cool in a damp sort of way, and Martin shivered. In the late afternoon gloom, Martin could see the house was ornate and expensive. Artwork lined the entrance hall, wool rugs spread across the floor and a chandelier twinkled overhead from the high ceiling.

"My parents are in Berlin at a conference, so I closed this part of the house," Christian said. "It's nice and warm upstairs."

Christian stripped Martin of his coat and scarf, discarding them on the stairs, then pulled Martin into his arms and kissed him gently on the lips. "I've wanted to do that since the first time I saw you in the Anglophile."

Martin wrapped his arms around Christian and kissed him hard, feeling light-headed and weak-kneed at the same time. Martin shivered violently, and the strange sensation that he had suddenly snapped back into his own body, into focus, came over him. He pressed himself even more tightly against Christian.

"Are you all right?" Christian asked, cupping Martin's face in his hands.

"I'm more than all right."

Christian ran a thumb slowly, sensuously over Martin's lips. "I have fantasized about kissing you for months. That sounds crazy, doesn't it?"

"No," Martin laughed. "That's the most sane thing anyone has said to me in ages."

"Let's go up."

It was warmer upstairs, and Martin felt as if he were gliding down the long hallway to Christian's room at the end. Christian pushed open the door and let Martin go in before shutting it behind them. The room was big and well furnished, but slightly messy with clothes draped over chairs and discarded on the floor. Chinese take out cartons sat next to a laptop computer on a desk in the corner. The giant bed was unmade, the sheets rumpled and pillows tossed all about.

They stood next to the bed and kissed before tumbling back into the tangle of bedclothes. "How long can you stay?" Christian whispered.

"I have the rest of the day."

"Good," Christian breathed into his ear, raining kisses all over him, slowly peeling off Martin's clothes.

They each came four times in the space of five hours, the last two hard won and exhausting in the most liberating way.

Never once did Martin's mind stray away from the boy, never once did thoughts of Euan or Peter or David intrude. Even as he lay panting for breath in Christian's arms he felt lighter, as if the act of making love to Christian had unburdened him. In a city full of millions, they had found each other, their need and desire so strong that it reached through wires and circuits to bring them together.

Martin fell asleep in Christian's arms and it was dark and snowing outside when he woke. Somewhere deep inside the house, a clock chimed eight. Irène would be wondering where he was. Martin moved ever so slightly and felt Christian's arms tighten around him.

"Don't go yet," he said.

"I'm not," Martin said.

"Are you hungry? I'm starving."

"Very."

"I will see what's downstairs." Christian kissed him and crawled out of bed. Walking toward the door, he turned to look back at Martin. "Are you staring at my ass?"

"Yes, I am," Martin said, aroused again.

Christian stood at the door, stroking his dick with a grin on his face. "I'll be right back."

Martin went to get his mobile out of his bag, but remembered it was downstairs in the foyer. The phone had probably rung a dozen times. Martin looked around and saw a phone on the bedside table. He picked it up hesitantly, then dialed Irène's number. It rang twice before Diane answered.

"Where the fuck are you?" Diane asked.

"I'm at a lecture at the Louvre, we're in the middle of a break," Martin said convincingly, or so he thought.

"A lecture at the Louvre," Diane repeated, rolling the words around on her tongue to test them. "That would loosely translate to: I've been out fucking some punk all afternoon and just realized what time it was."

"Where are Irène and Euan?"

"Kind of you to ask about Sir Euan."

"Diane . . ."

"He's still at the shop, but Irène is hovering right here beside me and trying to rip the phone out of my hand."

"Put her on."

"Lovely speaking to you as well."

There was a rustling of the phone, Diane complaining of the cord being caught in her hair and several muffled expletives before Irène came on the line. "I called you twice on the mobile phone."

"I had it turned off."

"I'm preparing dinner. Should we wait or do you want us to save something for you?"

"Save something for me. I'll be home in a couple of hours."

"Give me the phone," Diane said in the background.

"He has to go. Be careful. Call if you need anything."

"Wear a rubber," Diane yelled.

Martin hung up and sank back into the bed, luxuriating in the warmth and happiness he felt. Christian returned balancing a tray with a bottle of wine, a carton of noodles and half a loaf of bread. "I haven't gone to the market," he said, embarrassed. "I hope this is okay. We can share it."

They lay on their stomachs, side by side, feeding each other the warm noodles and tearing off pieces of bread. Martin realized he had never eaten in bed with anyone. He never had the chance with Peter or David, and Euan thought it was impractical and would lead to a mess to "contend with" later.

"Tell me everything about you," Martin said when they were done, and were again nestled under the sheets.

"That would take some time," Christian laughed. "Why don't you stay tonight and I'll tell you all of it."

"I can't."

"But do you want to?"

Martin was silent, looking into Christian's eyes, tracing his mouth with his fingertip. "I don't think I can put it into words how much I want to."

Christian would be twenty before Martin was twenty-five. They were Cancer and Virgo, signs that don't usually attract or last. Christian's story was not fantastical or unbelievable; just one of growing up in a different culture to parents who had struggled to become well off. His father was Rwandan, his mother was from Belgium, and Christian had been educated in England. His mother and father had met in Paris when they were students and vowed to live in the City of Light one day. Christian was finished with school and was in the middle of his gap year before deciding which university to attend. He had been out to his parents since he was fifteen and they were initially stunned, but accepted him nevertheless. He made decent grades, stayed out of trouble, was a voracious reader and had aspirations of being a writer. He had only had one serious boyfriend, a relationship that lasted three years and ended only after the boy moved away to Hong Kong with his family.

Martin poked Christian in the shoulder. "What was that for?" Christian asked.

"Just making sure you're real."

"Of course I am. Now tell me about you."

Martin told him everything: Peter's death, his friendship with Diane and Irène and how he had met a boy named David who had broken his heart. Christian brushed Martin's hair back and traced the scar on his forehead.

"Where did this come from?"

"Were you in Paris in the summer of 1995?"

"No, I was in England for the summer."

"I was here. This is a souvenir from the bombing of the metro that summer."

"Did someone you know die?"

Martin ran that horrible Sunday through his head like a movie in fast forward. Diane's long-held secret about her husband's affair with one of her students had been revealed, Irène had been liberated from her apartment after thirty years, the reality of Peter's and Jean-Louis' deaths had been brought to the surface. "No one died, but things changed. It changed me."

"For the better?"

"I'm still trying to figure that out."

They kissed again, lazy and slow. Christian propped himself up on one arm and looked down at Martin. "You're leaving out one thing."

"What's that?"

"Your boyfriend."

Martin felt himself go red even in the dimness of the room. "Oh, yeah . . . that."

"It's ending then?" Christian asked.

"It never really began."

Christian frowned. "I don't understand."

"Euan is a nice guy, but he got me on the rebound from David. Irène sort of pushed me into dating him. And with no other offers, I just fell into a routine. I'm not in love with him. We have hardly anything in common except we both love art and books."

"How long have you dating?"

"Almost two years."

"That is a long time to have a relationship with someone you're not in love with."

"Now I sound like a flake," Martin said. "It was a mistake and I let myself make it. Euan never took my breath away."

"Did I?" Christian asked in a teasing tone.

"Did you ever."

"I want to be with you. I've fantasized about being your boyfriend for months and months, since I first heard you read your poetry at the Anglophile."

"Even now that you know I'm a chatroom whore?"

"I have had sex with men I met online. There is no shame. It was casual. I want something more, but not with someone who already has a boyfriend."

Martin closed his eyes. There was the gauntlet thrown down, an ultimatum he would either have to run with or away from. He thought of the manuscript of poems he had left for David at his apartment in Memphis nearly three years ago. *This is no time for indecision,* he had written in one of the poems, and David had made a decision. He never returned to Paris. Staring into Christian's eyes, Martin realized that David's hold on him had loosened, could be escaped. Christian was a doorway and he had to be brave enough to walk through it.

"I want to be with you, too," Martin said.

"Prove it."

"How?"

"Stay here with me tonight. I can't imagine letting you go right now. The house would be so empty. I want to wake up with you in the morning, have breakfast with you. I haven't had that in a long, long time."

Martin could feel his heart beating, thudding in his ears along with the sound of his breath. The entire room seemed to be alive, holding its own breath, waiting for Martin's decision.

"Can I use your phone? I just need to let my friends know where I'll be."

137

The next morning, Martin met Irène at the Louvre. She was sitting in the circular room that housed the Venus de Milo, the first place that they had gone together after her liberation. She had smuggled in coffee from the museum's café. Her face was a mixture of worry and relief.

Martin was giddy with exhaustion. He looked and felt, as Christian had put it, "well fucked." His body felt loose and light, his hair was messy and fell in his eyes. Martin flopped down on the bench next to Irène with a sigh of relief, but he couldn't look at her. She handed him the cup and he sipped from it.

"How long do you think it would take security to get here if I lit a cigarette?" Martin wondered aloud.

"I was thinking the same thing," Irène said. "I always want to smoke in the most inappropriate places and times."

They sat quietly, drinking the coffee, waiting for each other to begin. Irène finally did.

"Euan is devastated."

"What did you tell him? "

"I didn't have to say anything. It was obvious. Things are too familiar on rue Rampon, my dear. You don't come home and what other explanation is there?"

"Shit."

"Are you going to tell me who kept you out all night?"

"Christian."

"The young man from the Anglophile?"

Martin nodded.

"I've seen the way he looks at you. The sex must have been wonderful."

"It was more than just sex. He turned me on emotionally and physically like no one has since Peter or David."

"How old is Christian?"

"Nineteen."

Irène sighed and leaned back against the wall. A couple of tourists wandered into the rotunda and talked too loudly about the Venus de Milo. Martin and Irène stared at them until they became uncomfortable and left.

"Do you believe that a nineteen year old boy is going to make you happy? That he is mature enough to give you what you need?"

"He's smart, he's out to his parents, he's going to university, he writes, we love the same music and films."

"I am not going to try and talk you out of this," Irène said.

"Why would you want to?"

"Because it feels like a mistake."

"But this is different," Martin said. "It's not like Peter or David. There are no secrets or lies."

"But he is still a stranger."

"You are the last one to lecture me on meeting strangers and falling into bed with them after all your stories about meeting men at the Bel Air. And I seem to remember that Jean-Louis was a one-night stand . . ."

"I am not lecturing you," Irène said huffily. "This is different and you know it, Martin. Things are different now; times have changed. And you have a boyfriend. I never cheated."

"Well I did. I cheated. Is that what you want to hear?" Martin said, his voice rising.

"You should have broken up with Euan."

"You're the one who pushed me into dating him in the first place. From the minute you saw him in the hallway, you had your matchmaker hat on."

"You liked Euan, you told me you did," Irène scoffed. "You were trying to seduce him at the bookstore."

"I just wanted to sleep with him, not marry him!" Martin's voice echoed through the rotunda. He turned away from Irène, who shook her head.

"Things are too entangled," Irène said. "Euan lives across the hall, he gave Diane a job to make you happy. It is all going to unravel."

"Is he at the shop this morning?"

"Yes."

"I'll go there now. I'll end it."

Irène was silent, so Martin gathered up his things and walked down the hall. Irène stood up and called his name.

"I beg you not to do this, Martin. End it with Euan if you must, but do not become involved with Christian. Take time to realize what you really want."

"You said you weren't going to try and talk me out of it."

"I know, but . . ."

"Be happy for me, Irène. Don't ruin the moment. I wish I could tell you how happy I feel. This morning on the way here, I finally realized that I could put David behind me. I feel released."

Irène took a deep breath. "All right," she said quietly. "I love you."

"I love you, too. I don't want to fight. I hate when we have these little quarrels."

Irène watched Martin make his way down the long gallery. She had planned to tell him about her suspicions that David was in Paris; that David had robbed the apartment and the tobacco shop, and that a detective was following Diane. But when she saw how happy Martin was, she couldn't go through with it. Things had been quiet on rue Rampon, but Irène could not shake the sense of foreboding that had been invading her sleep and was now seeping into her waking life. She looked up at the Venus de Milo, who always played some part in her horrible dreams of Jean-Louis and Frederick, and fought the urge to jump the barrier and push the statue over.

# 15 the Space Between Us

Neither Diane nor Euan were at the counter when he came into the shop, but Martin knew things were going to be bad when he heard the music playing. Euan had put on Fairport Convention, which would surely be followed by Kate Bush and Dusty Springfield. This trifecta of music was a signal that things were not right in Euan's world. Martin stood on the threshold, the cold wind still blowing around him as Sandy Denny's voice keened over "Who Knows Where The Time Goes." He almost went back out, but he heard footsteps on the stairs and then saw Diane rushing toward him. She grabbed him by the arm and pulled him into the stacks at the back of the shop.

"Do not go up there," Diane said.

"I have to."

"Do it tonight when I'm not around."

"I don't want him to sit here and stew all day."

"Like he hasn't been stewing? Get your head

out of whoever's ass you've had it in all night."

Martin started to push past Diane.

"Wait a second," she said, putting her hands on his shoulders. "You know this will put me out of a job, too. I may have to leave again. I'm a little worried."

"Gerard will give you a job at the publishing house. I've already called and asked him. Are you trying to talk me out of this?"

"I don't know."

"You and Irène have dithered back and forth on me breaking up with Euan more than I have. And you don't even like him."

The floor above them creaked and they both froze looking up until the sound subsided. Diane spoke in a loud whisper. "I don't dislike him. I just feel . . . I don't know . . . sorry for him, I guess. He's a real sad sack, but not a bad guy."

"Get out of the way," Martin said.

"Jesus, you sound mean about it. Don't go up there and be mean. Try to do it gently."

"I'm trying to hold it together, Diane. I'm just on the verge of chickening out, so if you don't get out of the way, I'm afraid my resolve is going to fail."

"Are you going to tell him the truth?"

"Yes."

"Which is what?"

"That I slept with someone else."

"Just the one?"

"Diane . . ."

"I know, I know. Move out of your way." Diane stepped aside ceremoniously. Martin was halfway down the aisle, when she spoke again. "Was it worth it?"

Martin turned back. "Yes. This wasn't a one-night stand. This was something else entirely."

"Who is he?"

"It's Christian."

"I knew it! I told Irène it was only a matter of time. What is he . . . nineteen?"

"We'll talk later."

Martin was already going up the stairs, taking them slowly and gripping the railing. The door to Euan's office was half open and Martin approached it tentatively. Euan had his back to the door and was staring out the window, his arms folded across his chest. Martin stood in the doorway, about to speak, but Euan already knew he was there.

"I wondered if you would come," Euan said.

"I almost didn't."

Euan turned to face him. He looked tired and older. "It was a mistake from the beginning, wasn't it? Getting involved with the neighbor across the hall. I knew if it ever went pearshaped, it would be uncomfortable for everyone involved. Namely me, at this point."

Martin came into the office and shut the door behind him. He sat down in front of Euan's desk. "I'm not happy, Euan. You're not happy either."

Euan laughed lightly. "I was coping with the situation. A rough patch. All relationships have them."

"I couldn't cope," Martin said. "The difference, the space between us is just too wide."

"Perhaps, but did that mean going out and sleeping with someone else to prove the point? Couldn't you have just come to me and said, this isn't working out or I need a break or just told me to piss off?"

"I was trying to make it work. I've been trying since September."

"That's a bloody lie. God knows what else you've lied about."

Martin sat back in the chair. "You're just trying to provoke me into a fight. I don't want that." Martin pulled off the silver ring Euan had given him at Christmas and placed it gently on the desk.

Euan seemed to sag in his chair. He stared at the ring, but would not touch it.

"Who is he?" Euan asked. "I think I have a right to know."

"I met him here. At the open mic."

Euan nodded over and over. "I suspected it. I see how they all flock around you and how you flirted outrageously with all of them. Which one?"

"Christian."

"Of course, the one you were mooning over. He was in the shop the other day talking to Diane. You've probably been sleeping with him for months."

"That's not true."

"So, you met him yesterday and tumbled into bed with him. Is that it?"

Martin stood up. "I know what I did was wrong. I cheated, I'm a whore, I'm unfaithful. Whatever you want to call it. I'm sorry."

"Sit down," Euan said harshly.

Martin sank back down into the chair. He should have to listen; it was his repentance.

"I have wasted so much of my life chasing after boys and men who could not or would not love me, but I persisted anyway, hoping each time it would be different. When I met you, I thought the chase was over. I had finally found my soulmate. I knew you still had feelings for David, but when he never returned to Paris, I thought you would forget him and we would be happy. Instead, you've decided to replace the fantasy you had with David with someone just like him."

"Christian is nothing like David . . ."

"Please let me finish. I know I'm not young and on heat twenty-four hours a day, but I love you. I have tried to be good to you and give you what you need, but I see that's not enough. You're headed down a very dark road, Martin. I don't know what you think that boys like David and Christian can give you. If you're trying to replace Peter, then you are going to be very lonely. Perhaps you will always be chasing after ghosts."

Martin felt tears slide down his face, but Euan was dry-eyed and unwavering. Martin wanted to say something to Euan, but he was afraid he would sob.

"Now you can go," Euan said and swiveled his chair toward the window.

Martin stood up and went out the door, slamming it behind him, harder then he had planned to. He took the stairs two at a time, and went past Diane at the counter without saying a word. The Big Ben chime sounded as the door closed behind Martin.

Diane got up from her perch behind the counter, walked over to the door, reached up and snatched the bell mechanism from the frame with a vicious yank. She dropped it on the floor and kicked it across the room. Standing in the middle of the empty shop and breathing hard, she tried to maintain her composure. From upstairs, she heard one great sob and then it was quiet for the rest of the day.


Gerard danced around Irène like a dervish as she settled into a chair in his office at the publishing house. He had called her the day before and asked her to come by, but she felt listless and ill at ease after her meeting with Martin at the Louvre. Gerard was pouring glasses of champagne for them and yammering on and on about a new day, a new beginning, but she was only half listening.

"Irène," he said her name sharply. "Are you all right? You seem a thousand miles away."

"I'm sorry. I've just had many things on my mind. I'm listening. Go on."

Gerard handed her a glass of champagne and raised his own. It was too early in the morning for a drink, she thought, and different scenarios flashed through her mind about why he wanted to toast before noon. *Please god, don't let him ask me to marry him,* she thought. He had threatened proposals before, but had never followed through. She had an image of the old gentleman struggling to his knee and producing a tiny velvet box.

"I have very good news," he said, the smile on his face threatening to wrap behind his ears. Irène gripped the stem of the glass until she thought it would snap in her hand. "I have sold the publishing house."

Irène released her breath in a very audible gasp of surprise as Gerard drained the contents of his glass. He waited for her to drink hers as well, but she was frozen with her mouth open.

"Do not worry, Madame Irène. I know it sounds shocking, but it is a wonderful thing. You will retain your job and no doubt get an increase in salary, as will Martin. I will stay on as publisher. Nothing will change except we will be a more formidable house. We will have, as they say, deep pockets."

Irène drained her glass and sat it back on his desk. "But why Gerard? You built this house. You created its reputation, and now you so easily give it away?"

Gerard looked deflated as he sat down. He leaned across the desk and looked at Irène with tired eyes. It was the first time in their decades as friends and business associates that she had ever seen him look anything but dapper. "I am getting old, Irène.

We both are. If I were to die tomorrow, this house would close or it would be gobbled up by one of the conglomerates. All that I had built would disappear overnight. Now, it will last forever. I have it in writing and locked in my safe."

"It's just so very shocking," Irène said, leaning back in her chair, feeling her age as if Gerard's words had suddenly made her realize a truth she regularly hid from. She was getting older. Her time on earth was drawing to a close. She wasn't afraid to die. That fear had passed thirty years ago, but she was afraid to leave those she loved behind.

"I have also taken the liberty," Gerard said, "of putting aside a sum of money in an account in your name. It is a gift, a nest egg if you will, for future days." He opened a file on his desk and slid a piece of paper across to her. It showed the balance was over one hundred thousand francs.

"I can't accept this," Irène said. "This is too generous."

"My dear, I am rich. I have been rich for many years, but now that I have sold the house, I have money to spare. You can do with that money whatever you like. It is in an interest bearing account."

She held the paper in her hand and brushed away tears that had sprung to her eyes. "I don't know what to say."

Gerard gallantly pulled the handkerchief from his pocket and handed it to Irène. "You do not have to say anything. All I want is a promise that you will remain here as my top editor. That we will grow old together as friends." He came around the desk and opened his arms, and Irène hugged him affectionately.

"I thought you were going to ask me to marry you," she laughed through her tears.

"I had thought of it," he said. "But I know you are not the marrying kind anymore. You are a free spirit, as I am. I have dreamed of marriage, but I think I am too set in my ways. You and I would eventually murder each other if we married."

"So who is the man with all the money that is our salvation?" Irène asked.

"His name is Simon Temple; he's Irish or Scottish, I believe, peculiar accent," Gerard said. "He contacted me a month ago and expressed interest. I said no at first. But then he sent me a letter a few weeks ago and it gave me pause to consider."

"What did the letter say?"

"It said that he had lived in France as a child and his parents were great fans of the books that came from the house. He listed many of them and said they were still in his collection although his parents had passed away. He said he was a lover of literature and wanted to make sure that the house never closed, as a legacy for his family. Diversifying his portfolio or something like that. He said he would leave day-to-day operations to me and nothing would change. How could I let that offer slip away?"

"You couldn't," Irène said. "It is wonderful, Gerard. Maybe there is hope in the world after all."

"We don't have to worry about the lean seasons anymore," Gerard said with delight. "There will be no more lean seasons. While other houses cut back, we will move ahead. I have big plans."

There was a knock on the door and Gerard's secretary came in and handed him an envelope. "An Inspector Arnaud was just here and said I should give it to you," the girl said.

Irène felt her body stiffen. Gerard opened the envelope and pulled out the folded piece of paper.

"What is it?" Irène asked, a catch in her throat. She had a very bad feeling.

"It's a missing person," Gerard said. "This face is familiar to me."

Irène dug her nails into the chair's leather arms.

"Is this the young man we followed once? When Martin was first here? What was his name?" He pushed the paper across the desk to her.

There was a photo of David McLaren on the piece of paper. All his vital statistics were included, as well as a note that both the FBI and Interpol were conducting a joint search. David's last known whereabouts: Paris.

She had been right all along.

"Madame Irène, you look pale. Are you all right?" Gerard asked anxiously.

"Can you drive me somewhere? I'll tell you on the way."


Diane did not know how long Inspector Arnaud had been observing her through the window of the Anglophile before she noticed him. After Martin had left, she tried to lose herself in a magazine, but the words would not focus and she found her mind racing. The shop was empty and she was able to stare into space undisturbed. All was silent upstairs in Euan's office.

She was staring at the row of photography books on the opposite wall, but not really seeing them. It felt like the summer of 1995, before the bombing of the metro. There had been signs everywhere, little hints and warnings that something bad was going to happen: the evacuation of the Underground in London, the warnings on television, the newspaper she read while sailing along the Seine when the long shadow of Notre-Dame had fallen across the boat. Diane had the creeping sense that another explosion was imminent and it would totally disrupt all their lives.

Diane felt someone was watching her and she looked up and saw Arnaud standing outside the shop. He pulled a piece of paper from an envelope he was carrying under his arm.

Diane suddenly felt her mouth go dry. He was coming to deport her. The racist son-of-a-bitch. He looked at the piece of paper and then looked back at her. He did this several times until Diane was enraged. She got up and strode to the door; Arnaud appeared there behind the glass and startled her.

"What the fuck do you want?" she said loud enough so he could hear.

Arnaud took the tip of his finger, put it into his mouth and then touched it to the window leaving a large wet spot. Diane was repulsed and fascinated by this and watched as he did it again, leaving another spot next to it. Then he took the piece of paper and slapped it hard against the window. Diane shrieked and stepped back. She heard Euan call her name from the top of the stairs, then his footsteps. Arnaud peered around the piece of paper, wagged his finger at her and walked away.

"What the hell is that?" Euan asked, coming up behind her.

The weak winter light was filtering through the glass and it looked as if David was almost beatific. She put a hand to her throat, feeling as if she might be sick.

Euan stared at the paper stuck to his shop window and did not comprehend at first. "What's this in aid of then? Is this someone's idea of a joke?"

Diane could only shake her head.

"This says David McLaren is a missing person. Is this Martin's David?"

"Who else would it be?" Diane managed.

Euan drew back from the glass as if stricken. "Is that who Martin is really seeing? He's harboring David McLaren somewhere? The thing about meeting that kid here was all just a cover up."

"No," Diane said. "You have no idea."

"Well, perhaps you'd like to explain. There must be some

explanation for all this insanity and why that cop is always around. You and Irène are involved in all this somehow."

And just as those words left his lips, Irène was at the door. She opened it and came face to face with Euan and Diane. Gerard, right at her heels, touched her shoulder and said, "Look, Madame Irène." She turned to see the missing person's report stuck to the glass, David's face juxtaposed with her own reflection.

"Has Martin seen this?" Irène demanded.

"Not yet," Diane said.

"You've known all along, haven't you? That's why you came back to Paris."

Irène pulled the piece of paper off the glass, wadded it into a ball and threw it in Diane's face.

# 16 Mistaken Identity

Gerard drove Irène back to rue Rampon, threading through traffic as a light snow began to fall again over the city. Irène had refused Diane and Euan's request to come with them, and they were following in a taxi. She hoped Martin had gone to Christian's rather than coming back to the apartment, where surely Arnaud would turn up next.

Gerard pulled up in front of the apartment and Irène told him to go home, but he was concerned about her state of mind.

"Gerard, please, just go. This is a personal matter. You have been so wonderful, but you cannot help now." Irène leaned over and kissed him on the cheek, as the taxi carrying Diane and Euan screeched up behind them.

Both Irène and Euan rushed toward the building, their keys ready to open the door, jabbing at the lock, until Irène slapped his hand away. As they scuffled, the door opened and Arnaud was standing there, an almost amused look on his face.

"Are you a fucking twin?" Diane asked.

"If only that were the case, Madame Jacobs," Arnaud said. "I am glad to see you have come so quickly, but Martin is not here."

"Let's go inside," Irène said.

Arnaud held the door open for them as if he owned the place. "How did you get in here exactly?" Euan asked. "This is bordering on harassment."

"Madame Jacobs and Madame Laureux have information about David McLaren and about what has happened here on rue Rampon, but are colluding to pervert justice," Arnaud said.

Euan looked incredulously at the women. "Is that true?"

"No," they chorused.

"They are trying to spare Martin's feelings, which is noble but also illegal."

Irène would not be moved. "I have no information about David McLaren. I haven't seen him in more than two years."

"Neither have I," Diane spat.

"But you knew he was missing," Arnaud said. "You met with David McLaren's parents before you came to Paris, no?"

Both Irène and Euan looked at Diane, but she stood with her arms folded over her chest. "I'm not saying another goddamn word until I talk to a lawyer."

"Would someone please explain to me what is going on here?" Euan shouted. "This is nonsense."

"Shut up, Euan," Diane said. "Just stand there and be British."

Euan stepped up to Diane and put his finger in her face. "Don't tell me to shut up."

Diane grabbed his finger and bent it back until Euan yelped in pain. "Don't put your finger in my face or I will break it off and stuff it up your royal ass."

"Stop it," Irène snapped. "Martin will be here any moment. I'd like to settle this and send the inspector on his way."

"I must speak to Monsieur Paige," Arnaud said.

"He knows nothing," Irène said, a pleading tone creeping into her voice. "Getting him involved will not help your investigation. He has no idea where David is, has no idea he is missing or has been in Paris. What could you possibly hope to gain?"

"That may be the case," Arnaud said, "but from what I have learned, Martin is the reason David is here. For that reason alone, I must speak to him."

The door to the downstairs apartment opened and Julie, the young woman who took care of her elderly father, came into the lobby. "What is going on? Why all the shouting? You are disturbing my father."

"My apologies," Arnaud said graciously. "You remember me? I am investigating the break in at Madame Laureux's apartment and the tobacconist."

"Oh, yes," Julie said. "Has something else happened?"

"We believe we have a suspect," Arnaud said, producing the image of David and handing it to her. "Have you seen this young man on rue Rampon?"

Julie looked at it closely for a moment. Her father shuffled into the lobby leaning heavily on a cane and looked over her shoulder

"Who is that?" the old man asked.

"The inspector believes this is who robbed Madame Laureux's apartment," Julie said gently. "Do you remember that?"

The old man took the paper out of Julie's hand and held it up closely to his face. "That's not him. Looks nothing like him."

"Father," Julie said with an almost embarrassed tone. "How could you know that?"

"Because I saw the little bastard," the old man said. "It was the day of Princess Diana's funeral. I was sitting here in the lobby in that chair waiting for you to come out so we could go to the market. He came down the stairs carrying a computer under his arm and a bag full of clothes. When he saw me, he was startled and ran out the front door."

"Dad! Why didn't you tell me?"

"I'm telling you now," her father said dismissively. "The one I saw was black. One of those thieving drug addicts from Montfermeil would be my guess. Tall, wearing a hat, baggy clothes. They all look the same." He folded up the paper and handed it back to Arnaud. "You're looking for the wrong man. Why am I not surprised? Now stop bothering us. My wife is napping and all this noise will wake her. I pay taxes . . ." he muttered, walking back into the apartment and slamming the door. His wife had been dead for years.

All eyes turned to Arnaud, who looked stunned. "Well, this is an interesting turn."

"I am so sorry about this," Julie said. "Sometimes my father is still very lucid. He forgets things and then something will trigger them and it will be like he's remembering something that just happened."

"Will you please go now, Inspector?" Irène implored.

Arnaud slowly folded the photo of David in half and stuck it back into his jacket. "For now."

There was the sound of a key in the lock and the front door opened. Martin came in and his face registered shock to see the group gathered in the lobby. "What's happened?" he asked. "Has there been another robbery?"

Martin's face was red from the cold, his eyes puffed from crying. He looked expectantly at Arnaud. Irène could see all this unfolding in the mirror that hung over the credenza in the lobby, the mirror she broke on the way out the door that day to rescue Martin after the metro bombing. She watched Julie slowly edging back into her apartment, Diane fighting to maintain composure and Euan standing on the stairs with his arms crossed tightly over his chest. Arnaud reached into his overcoat and Irène held her breath. Something flickered across Arnaud's face, pity perhaps, and when he withdrew his hand from his pocket he held a pen and small notebook instead of the photograph of David.

"Just following up," Arnaud said, jotting something down in the notebook and returning it to his coat. "No leads on the break in here, I'm afraid. We couldn't match any of the fingerprints we lifted from the apartment. Bonsoir."

Arnaud paused and looked at everyone standing in the lobby and shook his head before exiting.

"He gives me the creeps," Martin said, looking at Irène, who was leaning on the credenza for support and Diane, who looked wild-eyed and out of sorts. "What's going on?"

"Arnaud was waiting when we arrived," Irène said as nonchalantly as possible. "He gave us a fright."

"He's a shitty cop," Diane chimed in. "He's probably on the make."

Martin nodded, but Irène could tell he didn't quite believe them. "I'm not staying," he said, glancing at Euan. "I just want to grab a few things. I'll be back in the morning."

Martin kissed Irène's forehead and went up the stairs past Euan, who stepped aside and pressed himself against the wall.

"We must agree to say nothing to Martin," Irène said, "not until we're certain it really is David."

"I don't want any part of this," Euan said, and started up the stairs.

"Euan, please," Irène pleaded. "I know Martin's hurt you,

but you cannot possibly understand what he, what we all, went through with David McLaren. It will only divide you further."

Euan did not turn around, but his shoulders slumped. "Fine."

"I have your word."

"Yes," he said, as he trudged up the stairs.

Irène turned to Diane, who was sitting in a chair with her head in her hands. "I knew it. I knew your coming here had an ulterior motive."

"Oh, you don't know anything. You just think you know."

Diane pulled a mobile phone from her pocket. It was making an almost inaudible buzzing sound. She flipped it open and said hello. After a moment, Diane said "okay" and put the phone back in her pocket.

"Who was that?"

"There's someone who wants to speak to you," Diane said. "Wait until Martin leaves and come to the hotel."

Martin had wandered about in the snow after he slammed out of the bookstore. He had fought back tears standing next to a reeking, overflowing garbage can at the Palace overlook. The Eiffel Tower glowed an almost ghostly red in the winter light. The snow whipped around the spire; the numbers on the giant clock counting down to the millennium seemed to quiver in the wind. Millennium approaches, he thought, and I am unprepared.

Martin walked back to rue Rampon. It was a long walk and his legs ached from the combined exertion of last night with Christian and trekking over Paris' uneven boulevards. He vowed not to let guilt overtake him about Euan. He would convince Irène and Diane that he was making the right decision. All his thoughts kept turning back to Christian waiting for him upstairs in the big house on Avenue Junot. He wanted to be there snuggled against him under the covers.

When he arrived back at rue Rampon and found everyone in the lobby with Arnaud, Martin sensed something else was going on; it was in the air. Euan wouldn't look at him, his contempt palpable. Things were going to be very uncomfortable in the building. He felt certain Euan would move out and sell the apartment rather than stay there across the hall, constantly reminded of Martin's unfaithfulness. He'd probably fucked Diane out of her job, too. Maybe Arnaud really was sniffing around trying to find illegal workers to deport. Euan had railed about Arnaud showing up at the apartment one night and quizzing him about Diane's work visa. If Arnaud went to the publishing house, that would put Martin's own job and status in question.

He heard Diane and Irène talking in the kitchen as he stuffed clothes into an overnight bag. He desperately wanted Christian, but he also felt adrift as well. Like those days when he first came home from Paris to his apartment in Memphis without David and no one to talk to. Irène and Diane had been out of reach then, but now they were just in the next room and he didn't know what to say to either of them.

When Martin left the apartment to go back to Christian, the overnight bag slung over his shoulder, it was like he was leaving all over again, Irène thought. She knew that things could have turned out differently. If David and Martin had stayed together in America, he wouldn't be in Paris. And for the first few months after Martin came back to Paris in the fall of 1995, she braced herself for the day David would turn up, but as the months went by and then the years, she and Martin had settled into their lives.

The search for Frederick Dubois helped ease Martin's restlessness, the leisure of their lives gave him time to write, and she had wrongly thought Euan would be the antidote to his melancholy. Once again, she had miscalculated, overplayed her hand. If she had carefully examined her own heart, she would have realized that Martin would have no peace until things were settled with David. In just a few months, it would be the thirtieth anniversary of Jean-Louis' death and she was still unsettled and haunted by his memory, the lack of closure, the fear that even getting answers might not be enough. All these things were on Irène's mind as she crossed rue Rampon to the Bel Air Hotel. She looked up and saw that the curtains were drawn in Diane's room.

Irène stopped at the front desk to talk to the old owner, but he peeped his head out of the back office and said he was busy. He looked very flustered, waved her off and shut the door. She took the elevator to the third floor and walked slowly down the hall toward Diane's door, her hand trailing along the wall to steady herself. She felt dizzy, wanted to turn around and go back to the apartment. Lying to Martin was a repulsive idea to her, but she knew whatever Diane and the stranger in her room were about to tell her would make her even more of an accessory.

Diane opened the door at her first knock, and Irène could see a man sitting in the shadows of the hotel room, which was filled with cigar smoke. Diane stood aside and Irène hesitantly entered, her eyes adjusting to the gloom. The man stood up and Irène saw that it was the detective, Bernard Sullivan.

"We meet again," Sullivan said.

"What game is this?" Irène asked, looking at Sullivan and then back to Diane.

"He's going to tell you everything, and so am I," Diane said.

"Remember when I said you had the wrong end of the stick, Mrs. Laureux? Well, here's the right end."

159

# 17 Avenue Junot

Martin sat on the steps of Christian's house on Avenue Junot. The snow had stopped, but it was bitterly cold and he sat shivering and smoking cigarettes, trying to clear his mind. Christian was not at home and he realized they had never exchanged numbers. He didn't even know if Christian had a mobile phone. Then he realized he didn't know Christian's last name. This somehow struck him as funny and he laughed out loud. Maybe this was madness. Maybe he needed to see a shrink again before he cracked up.

Avenue Junot was mercifully quiet. Lights glowed from the windows of other townhomes, and there was the distant sound of classical music wafting through the bare trees that lined the street. He saw Christian walking fast up the other side of the avenue out of the corner of his eye. Martin stood up to greet him, and Christian seemed startled to find him there. He stood in the middle of the road, as if he might turn and flee.

"What's wrong?" Martin asked, coming down the steps.

"Oh, you scared me," Christian said. "I didn't realize it was you at first." He took Martin into his arms and kissed him. His body felt warm and he smelled of sweat, in the musky, male way that always made Martin hard.

"Where have you been?"

"I've had quite an adventure. I walked to the library and planned to take a taxi back, but realized that I had left my wallet and keys in my other jeans. I'm going to have to break into the house."

"Oh, I've done that before. That sucks. Is there a spare key hidden somewhere?"

"No, but there's an unlocked window in the kitchen. Wait right here and I'll come and let you in."

"I can come with you. I'm not scared of climbing."

"It's a little precarious. I'd feel better if you wait here." He pulled Martin closely to him. "I think I might want to carry you over the threshold."

"Careful. That's why I left my last boyfriend."

"Your last . . ." Christian said, suddenly comprehending. "Was it bad?"

"The worst."

Christian kissed him again. "Wait here. We will talk it through. I don't want you to be sad."

He sprinted down the steps and scaled the fence that led into a narrow side yard. Martin sat on the steps, pulling his coat closer around him. Snow flurries were falling again, glistening in the streetlights. The music grew louder, and Martin recognized it as Barber's *Adagio for Strings*. The music that had been playing when he met Irène, that she still put on from time to time to remind herself of Jean-Louis. It was nearing the crescendo, the

161

strings moving up the scale to their highest registers, then that moment of sustained silence. It never failed to move him.

"Who are you?"

Martin snapped out of his reverie and saw a smartly dressed woman standing on the street in front of him. She was clutching her purse tightly against her chest. "The Rivas are out of the country. There is no one home," she said.

"Oh, yes, I know. I'm a friend of their son. I'm waiting for him."

"Son? I don't remember a son. They have two daughters," the woman said, squinting her eyes at Martin.

"I can assure you they have a son. He's just locked himself out."

"I'm almost positive the Rivas don't have a son."

The townhouse door opened and Christian stood there in silhouette. "Sorry that took so long."

The woman craned her neck to see, shielding her eyes from the glare of the streetlight to get a glimpse of him.

"It's all right. I was just talking with this lady," Martin said standing up.

"Come out into the street and let me see you," the woman demanded. "I don't remember you at all."

"Oh, go away, busybody," Christian hissed. "My mother said you can never mind your own business." He took Martin by the hand and pulled him inside, closing the door on the woman's protests.

"What a bitch," Martin said, laughing. "She must have thought I was casing the place for a robbery. She had her purse in a death grip."

"Ignore her. She's a pain in the ass," Christian said, kissing him.

"I didn't even know your last name was Riva until she said

it," Martin laughed. "That's terrible."

"A minor oversight."

"Do you have sisters?"

"Two."

"You didn't mention them when I was grilling you."

"I'm sure I did. You just weren't paying attention . . . you were still in the afterglow."

"Oh, is that it?" Martin asked playfully, kissing him harder. "I wouldn't mind that again, actually."

"It would be my pleasure."

"I'm not feeling sad anymore."

Martin shucked his coat as Christian pushed him against the front door, curving into him. Soon they were naked in the cold vestibule, but Martin's body was on fire as Christian's hands and lips moved up and down his body. When Christian turned him around and entered him roughly, Martin rested his face against the cold wood, could feel a tiny draft coming from where the door met the frame. It was an overload of the senses as Christian wrapped one arm around Martin's chest and the other hand found his cock. Christian pulled Martin's head back and kissed his neck and ears, whispered pornography in his ears, the kind of thing Euan would never do. They came together, loudly, Christian's body heavy on Martin's back, pressing him against the door. Even in the cold, they were both drenched in sweat. It steamed off their bodies as they kissed, then slid down to the floor onto the pile of coats and clothes and began again.


Martin sat at the kitchen table wearing nothing but Christian's long coat, watching him scramble eggs and sear thin strips of steak in a pan. Christian was naked and kept jumping back as grease popped out of the pan onto his torso. Martin laughed, felt aroused again, watching this beautiful boy move around the kitchen like a master chef.

"Are you amazed I have real food in the house?" Christian asked.

"I don't care. Bread and water would have been fine as long as you served it."

"Flattery will get you everywhere."

"It already has."

Christian dumped the fluffy eggs onto the plate in front of Martin and used a fork to lay the perfectly cooked piece of steak next to them. "Voila! Steak and eggs. My secret recipe."

"There's a secret recipe to scrambling eggs and frying meat?" Martin teased.

"Yes," Christian said, taking the fork and feeding Martin some of the eggs. "It instantly tastes better when I cook it naked." He gyrated a bit like a stripper, and Martin flashed on David. He knew he would forever be attracted to edgy, beautiful boys like this. It would be his curse. "Do you like it?"

Martin realized he was still chewing the eggs, and swallowed. "They're perfect." He cut into the steak; it was still rare inside and Martin took a piece and fed it to Christian. A little trail of juice and blood ran down his chin.

"It's hot," Christian said, fanning his mouth. "But good."

Christian sat across the table and they stuffed the food into their mouths. They were both ravenous after their lovemaking.

"Are you going to tell me now?" Christian ventured.

Martin sighed. "Do I have to?"

"Please."

Martin put down his knife and fork on his almost empty plate. "The short version. I told Euan we had slept together and he said I was throwing my life away because you would never love me like he could."

164

Christian reached across the table and took Martin's hand. "I will prove him wrong." Martin took Christian's hand and kissed it. "This is crazy, isn't it? We don't even know each other. Not really."

"Don't you believe in love at first sight?"

"I used to, but I think maybe I'm a little blind," Martin said, pushing his glasses onto his forehead. "It's all a bit blurry."

"I won't rush you. I promise. We'll take it slow and just let it unfold day by day. That's how I live anyway," Christian said, adjusting Martin's glasses.

"What if you had missed me in the chatroom? We wouldn't be together right now."

"I believe we were fated to meet."

Martin felt a chill pass through him, a shiver of recognition. "I feel like we're in a dream together. Like time is contracting and expanding and any second I'm going to wake up and you won't be there."

"Then we won't wake up."


It was after three in the morning. They had made love again, this time slowly, exploring every inch of each other's bodies, mapping all the places a touch, kiss or breath brought pleasure. There was nothing furtive or hurried. There was no guilt. When they were done, Martin felt like he was melting into the bed. He was exquisitely sore and raw, well past exhaustion.

He watched Christian crawl out of bed and walk over to the desk where the laptop softly hummed, a swirling kaleidoscope screensaver casting light on his body. He picked up what appeared to be a small tin box, slid open the cover and pulled something out. When he crawled back into bed, Martin saw a joint dangling between his lips.

"I thought you didn't smoke," Martin said.

"I don't," Christian mock protested. "This isn't smoking. It's toking."

Christian lit the joint with a tiny lighter and took a long drag. Martin hadn't smoked a joint in ages, remembered passing one back and forth with Diane some nights in the apartment in Memphis. Diane would invariably get the munchies and microwave an entire box of popcorn.

Martin took a long drag, pulling the smoke deep into his lungs. "Any other drug habits I should know about?" he teased.

"I'm pretty sure I've tried just about everything. Coke, ecstasy, acid, mushrooms, heroin."

"You've done heroin?"

"Once. I didn't like the way it made me feel."

"Which was?"

"A little too good," Christian said, taking the joint from Martin. "The rush was indescribable, but I also felt out of control. I don't like that feeling."

"I tried coke once. It made me feel jittery and horrible. I don't know how people can snort that shit all the time."

"And ecstasy?"

"Never tried it."

"I have to admit, I like it. It makes you very sensitive, tactile. You want to be touched and kissed and held. It's sensual. I'll do it with you if you want."

"Uh-oh," Martin said. "Drug pusher."

"Do I look like a drug dealer to you?" Christian narrowed his eyes to slits and sneered. "Come here, little boy, I have some candy for you."

Martin smiled drowsily. "Mmmm . . . I think I'd buy anything you were selling."

Christian smiled and put the joint in an ashtray next to the

166

bed. He pulled Martin to him, their legs intertwining under the sheets. "I'm only selling love today."

Martin giggled. "That is really, really, *really* corny."

"Love and rainbows and unicorns and roses," Christian said in a singsong way. They giggled into each other's necks for a long time, until sleep overtook them as dawn was breaking over Montmartre.

# 18 Love and Anger

Irène's head swam with all the information Diane and Sullivan imparted in the hotel room. Diane told her about meeting David's parents and her contact with Sullivan, who had been looking for David since his disappearance. Both were convinced he had gone back to America, but the break in at the tobacconist and Inspector Arnaud's involvement changed everything.

"But it wasn't David who robbed the apartment," Irène said. "Julie's father saw the robber and said he was black."

"Doesn't mean anything," Sullivan said, chewing on a cigar. "David could have gone over the roof while the black fellow came downstairs."

"It doesn't make any sense," Irène protested. "Why would David do this?"

"He's snapped, obviously," Diane said. "I mean, Christ, that father of his is a monster."

Sullivan said that when he went to America to

meet with the McLarens, the father refused to believe that David wasn't hiding in Paris with Martin and Irène. He accused Sullivan of taking a bribe and colluding with those "faggots and brainwashers." McLaren fired Sullivan and said he was going to call Interpol, the FBI and the Paris Police to get someone to help him find his son.

"He made good on his word," Sullivan said. "Arnaud was instantly tipped off. He won't let this go. My guess is that he thinks David is an addict and thieving to support his habit. Maybe working with a group of lads who regularly rob homes and cars so they can sell the items for quick cash."

"There's no way to keep Martin out of it," Irène said. "We're going to have to tell him before Arnaud does. He should hear it from us. We can't lie."

Diane picked up a pillow off the bed and punched it. "Two years later and David McLaren is still fucking with our lives. I'd love to beat him to death."

"When Martin comes home, we'll sit him down and tell him," Irène continued.

"He's going to freak out big time," Diane said.

Irène nodded absently, then looked up at Sullivan. "If the McLarens fired you, why are you back in Paris?"

"I'm working for her now," Sullivan said pointing his cigar at Diane. "Besides, I'm between assignments and that McLaren cunt really got on my tits."

"And you're not getting on mine," Diane said, grabbing Irène's hand. "I've got a witness. You're coming nowhere near my tits."

Sullivan chuckled under his breath and stood up. "I'll leave you ladies. I'm going to check on a lead."

"What lead?" Diane asked. "You just got here."

"I've always got my fingers in many pies, my nose to the

ground, ear to the wall, so to speak," Sullivan said. "I got a tip about a hotel where the addicts go to shoot up and sleep it off. Stolen goods are sold and bartered there, too."

"Yeah, you won't be conspicuous at all," Diane said.

"Sometimes the lads are looking for a daddy figure," Sullivan said.

"I don't want to know what that means," Irène said.

Diane followed Sullivan to the door. "You are one sick bastard."

"Aye, but I'm your sick bastard." Sullivan picked up Diane and planted a wet kiss on her forehead. Diane flailed against him until he dropped her on the bed. He was laughing as he went out the door. Irène looked at Diane, horrified.

"Not a word," Diane said, wiping at her forehead.

"I wouldn't even know where to begin."


Martin woke before Christian and lay watching him sleep. He lightly stroked the boy's face and kissed him before nestling down again into the crook of his arm. As he was drifting off again, Martin heard his mobile ringing and decided not to answer it. The phone was in the pocket of his jeans, which were strewn somewhere on the bedroom floor.

"Are you going to answer it?" Christian asked, nuzzling against Martin.

"Oh, I'm sorry, it woke you."

"I was already sort of awake," he said, pulling Martin even tighter against him. "It is almost noon."

"Is it?" Martin said, rolling over to look at the clock. "I'm sure Irène is wondering where the hell I am. I've got so much editing to do, and I've totally blown it off."

Christian rolled on top of him, and Martin could feel how

170

hard he was. Martin wrapped his legs around Christian, kissing him deeply.

"What will you do with yourself while I'm working?"

"I might go to Jardin des Plantes."

"I've never been there."

"I love to walk there, even when it's cold. They have these old hothouses where all the tropical plants grow and the sculptures are amazing. I love to take a book and read in the Natural History Museum. It's so quiet and peaceful. I think it's my favorite place in all of Paris. I'll take you there."

"I'd like that."

Martin could feel Christian rubbing against him, his kisses a bit more insistent. "Is there time?"

Martin looked at the clock. "Yes. One for the road."

After they made love, Martin went back to sleep, and when he woke, it was nearly three o'clock. Christian was also asleep, and Martin watched his chest rise and fall in even breaths, resisting the urge to touch him. Martin quietly and carefully slid out of bed and found his jeans. He dug out his mobile and there were several messages. Martin went out into the hallway and softly closed the bedroom door. He dialed Irène and she answered on the first ring.

"I was worried," Irène said.

"I'm fine. I'm at Christian's. I'm coming home shortly and we can get back to work."

"Yes, I'll make something for dinner."

"Irène, I need to tell you something," Martin whispered. "I think I'm falling in love. I know it's crazy, but David has finally moved out of my heart. I didn't think it was possible to feel this way again."

Irène was quiet on the other end of the line. "Why don't you . . . why don't you stay at Christian's tonight and come home in the morning. We can get started then. I'll look over what you've edited so far and we'll pick back up early tomorrow."

"Are you sure?"

"Yes, I'm sure. It will be fine," Irène said. "Martin, I'm so happy that you are happy again. I love you very much."

"I love you. I can't wait to tell you everything."


Irène put the phone down and looked at Diane, who was sitting opposite her across the desk she usually shared with Martin.

"Why didn't you tell him to get his ass back here?" Diane demanded.

"Because he's falling in love."

Diane nearly tipped backwards in her chair. "Jesus fucking Christ. Here's another one he barely knows. Why does he do this?"

"He should have one more night of happiness before we tell him. He said David was moving out of his heart. It's going to crush him."

"Maybe not," Diane said. "Maybe he'll be angry. Maybe this will be the final nail in the coffin, so when David does show up, Martin will tell him to fuck off good and proper."

"Do you know that for sure?"

Diane hesitated. "No. This is uncharted water, madame, and it's full of sharks."

"Martin has been . . . lighter. Happy. How can we ruin this?"

"You said it yourself. We have to tell him before someone else does. And they will."

Irène felt rage building up inside her, directed at David. She picked up the manuscript on her desk and threw it across the room. It clipped the Winged Victory statue and the binder loosened, sending pages sailing around the living room. Pierre

172

jumped at them, excited by something new to do while the humans sulked around the apartment and showed him no affection.

"Atta, girl," Diane said, pouring herself another glass of wine.

# 19 the World Spins

The next morning, Martin could still feel Christian's lips on his as he sat in the taxi on the way back to rue Rampon. The clouds had parted and the sky was shockingly blue. It was still cold, but the snow was almost melted away and everything along the avenues seemed to jump out in bright relief. The streets were packed with people on their way to work and school and everyone seemed to have an extra spring in their step.

Martin was definitely falling in love and he couldn't stop grinning and giggling like an idiot. It wasn't just happiness, which was a foreign emotion to him, but also joy. He laughed out loud and fell back against the seat in the cab, the driver watching him in the rearview mirror with a nervous eye.

At rue Rampon, Martin gave the driver an extra big tip and bounded up the stairs to the apartment. He put the key in the lock, but realized it was already unlocked. He swung the door open and the tableau stopped him in his tracks. Seated around the coffee table were Irène, Diane and Euan, and standing near the French doors onto the balcony was a large, florid looking man with an unlit cigar clenched between his teeth. It looked like mourning. Or an intervention. Or . . .

Martin's mind flashed on a million things: one of his parents was dead, and he hadn't talked to either of them in months; there was news about Frederick Dubois; he or Diane were in trouble for working illegally in France, and they were going to be deported back to America. He felt his bowels liquefy in fear.

"What's going on?" he asked, refusing to step over the threshold.

"Come in." Irène held out a hand. "We have some news to tell you and we thought we should all . . ."

"David is in Paris," Diane interjected. Everyone in the room winced.

Martin dropped his bag on the floor with a thud. "He's here?"

"No . . . he's . . . it's a long story," Irène said.

"Oh, what the fuck is wrong with you people? It's like a band-aid; let's rip it off." Diane stood up and walked up to Martin and grabbed him by both shoulders. "David has been missing for a year. His parents contacted me because they thought he was here with you and Irène. The lummox over there by the window is the detective they hired to find him. David broke into the apartment while we were in London and also robbed the smoke shop across the street. There, see, that wasn't so bad."

Diane felt nauseous; she let go of Martin and went down the hall into the bathroom, slamming the door. Euan stood up and went to Martin, touched him briefly on the shoulder and then went back across the hall to his own apartment. Irène and the detective were looking at Martin, who had slumped against the doorframe.

"Why?" Martin asked in a strangled voice. "Why would he?"

Irène went to Martin and put her arms around him in a fierce embrace. "Come in and sit down," she said, guiding Martin toward the sofa. "This is Mr. Sullivan. He will tell you everything."

Sullivan moved from the window and sat down in the chair opposite the sofa. He spoke in a warm, Irish brogue, leaning forward and filling in the details that Diane had left out. Martin listened impassively as Sullivan explained the situation. He pulled a thick folder out of a battered briefcase and opened it on the coffee table. There were grainy security camera images of David taken in stores both in America and Europe. There were notes from David's father filled with angry diatribes, bank statements, other scraps of paper that all became a blur as Sullivan's voice faded in and out of Martin's head.

Martin remembered the dream he'd had about David just before he left America to return to Paris. He and David on the top deck of the Eiffel Tower and David slipping over the edge, chasing the mechanical bird Martin had bought him. In the dream, Martin grabbed David as he went over, pulled him back over the edge and into his arms. The look of joy on his face had made Martin weep, and he was crying when he woke from the dream. There was hope then. Hope that David would read the poems Martin had left under the statue of the Venus de Milo and he would decide to come to Paris so they could begin their life together. Martin often wondered what David had done after he read the poems, but none of the scenarios he ever envisioned led to this moment.

"Are you all right?" he heard Irène ask him, but it sounded like someone speaking underwater. Martin looked up and saw Diane standing in the hallway. The door to the apartment was still open and he saw Euan leaving with two large suitcases, not even a passing glance at Irène's door. It was all coming apart. He was coming apart. Martin closed his eyes tightly and he saw Christian on the stairs of the house on Avenue Junot, his hand outstretched.

"Mr. Sullivan, is it?" Martin asked, looking up at him.

"Yes, sir."

"Mr. Sullivan, make him go away."

"I'll do my best."

"If you find him, tell him . . . tell him, maybe one day we'll speak again. But not now. I just can't."

"There's one thing," Sullivan said. "That policeman is looking for him, too. And my guess is that if he catches up to David first, he'll lock him up."

Diane had come into the living room, her face scarlet. "Oh, fuck, don't tell him that."

"He should know," Sullivan said.

Martin closed the file on the coffee table and handed it back to Sullivan. "Then you have to find him first. You have to get David out of Paris. I don't want him in jail. I couldn't live with that."

"Maybe if you spoke to him," Sullivan suggested. "Told him to go."

Martin sat back on the couch. "No . . . no, no, no. I can't help him. I can only fuck him up more. Fuck me up more. Just get him back to America safe and sound. Here, I'll give you some money . . ." Martin pulled his wallet out and started rifling through it for francs. "I only have about 100 on me, but I'll get more."

Sullivan reached out and touched Martin's arm. It was almost fatherly, reassuring. "Money's not a problem. It's taken care of. You just rest your mind now, lad." He patted Martin's shoulder and stood up, gathering his things. He tipped his hat to Irène, and Diane followed him into the hall.

Sullivan was halfway down the stairs when Diane poked him in the back. He half turned and suddenly Diane was hugging him.

"Oh, you pig bastard. You're one of the most decent men I've ever met."


Irène stood at Martin's bedroom door, watching him pack. "You're going back to Christian's?"

"I think it's a good idea temporarily. Don't you?"

"I don't know."

"Why is he playing this game? Why now?"

"Because he's confused and lost."

Martin sighed and sat down on the bed, where Pierre was rolling about on the bedspread. Pierre batted Martin playfully with a paw, but realized the mood in the room had darkened. He slinked off the bed, rubbing against Irène's legs as he made his way to the kitchen and food.

"I'm not in love with David anymore," Martin said softly. "It really hit home when Sullivan opened that folder and I saw the pictures of David. I've fantasized about him and the sex and the dream of making a life with him, but I know now it's because there was no one else in my life. I know you wanted me to be with Euan, but it would have never worked."

"I know," she said.

"And now I've met Christian and he does have feelings for me. He turns me on, he's smart, he's gentle. He gets me in a way David and Euan never have. In just the little time we've been together, it's like he knows instinctively what I need. And I don't feel like he's a placeholder until someone better comes along."

"I'm glad, Martin. I truly am. I just don't want you to get hurt."

"We are going to take it slowly. I promise. I'm not going anywhere," Martin said, standing and coming to put his arms around Irène. "You're stuck with me."

"This is your home for as long as you want it to be," Irène said, hugging him. "I just want you to be completely happy without complications. If Christian can offer that, you have my blessing."

"Is this a group hug situation?" Diane asked from the hallway.

Martin moved back to the bed and continued packing. Irène went out, whispering to Diane, "Tread gently."

Diane came in and sat down on the bed watching Martin pack. "Am I in the shithouse again?"

"Were you ever out of it?" Martin said, turning his attention to the stacks of papers on his desk.

"Okay, okay . . . I should have told you about David when I first got here. But seeing how I fucked it all up last time, I was trying to avoid a similar situation."

"What were you gonna do if David showed up? Take him hostage and force him out of the closet again for old times sake?"

"Actually, I was going to threaten to kill him if he didn't go back to America and deal with his parents. Nice and simple this time."

Martin was incredulous. "And I would have never known?"

"That was the plan. Because I didn't think you could handle it."

Martin slammed his desk drawer shut. "Thanks for the vote of confidence. How am I doing now?"

"Better than I expected."

"What paper did I sign that gave you the right to try and control my life like this? To decide what information I was allowed and what would be kept from me?"

"Because you've always been fragile. You tried to kill yourself right after we met, remember? Who sat with you? Who got you through it? It wasn't your parents or any of those fair-weather friends you made working at the law office. It was me. You put your life in my hands, and I accepted it. I love you, Martin. I will always love you. I told you before . . . I know you better than anybody. I know what you can handle and what you can't handle, or at least I thought I did."

"Fuck you. I am not that person anymore. If you'd been around the last couple of years, you'd know that."

"Oh, sorry, I missed the Internet whoring and rebound gone wrong part of your life," Diane said.

Martin pointed at the door. "Get out."

"Don't be a drama queen." Diane got up and went to the door. Instead of going out, she closed it and stood there barring Martin's exit.

"All those months I spent traveling around Europe, I thought you and David were back in America buying tasteful furniture and fucking on it every night. I'm sorry he left you. I've never been sorrier about anything in my life. I thought my plan had worked, but he fooled me. He said what I wanted to hear and I blithely sent you to him and went off gallivanting on my victory tour. I wish I could take all that back, but I don't know what I would have done differently. The outcome was always going to be the same whether I had a hand in it or not. David is a fucked up little boy made that way by his equally fucked up parents. He's going to have to decide for himself if he's going to cut that cord and live his own life or keep using it as an excuse to act out and play games."

Martin pushed his bag onto the floor and sprawled face down across the bed. "I can't believe we're even having this conversation.

That it's two years later and we're still talking about David in Paris on rue Rampon. It's like nothing has changed at all."

"No, Martin," Diane said, coming to stand over the bed. "You have changed. Remember I said I *thought* you couldn't handle it? You're stronger now. You've moved on. It's David that hasn't changed. You know that, don't you?"

"Yeah," Martin mumbled, his face in a pillow. He rolled over and stared up at the ceiling. Diane crawled onto the bed and lay down next to him, watching the afternoon sun move across the wall. "I just feel like an idiot. All this time I've wasted waiting for David to come back, dreaming of him and crying about it. And now he's here and I just want him gone. I never thought those words would come out of my mouth."

Diane rolled on her side and put her arm across Martin's chest. "I know it's wrong to say, but that's music to my ears."

"You'll always be inappropriate, Diane."

"You still love me, right? Even if I am a meddling, lying, crazy old Jew bitch?"

"I guess."

"That almost sounds like yes, so I'll take it," she said, rolling off the bed. "Oh, and just so you know, if Sullivan finds David and I get the chance, I'm gonna punch his fucking lights out."

# 20 Soixante-huit

*Irène drives her red Mercedes convertible down a road surrounded by snow peaked mountains, Martin in the passenger seat. The top is up and wind buffets the small car, leaves dance across the windshield. It is late afternoon and the sky is a layer cake of clouds shot through with bands of orange light, casting a warm glow over the long, flat valley. There is an old stone bridge ahead, arching over a river. The bridge is covered in leaves, brown and crackling in the wind, yet they do not blow away. Irène drives onto the bridge and stops at its center. Martin opens the door and gets out, his feet crunching across the brittle leaves, to look over the edge. He says the river is made of glass. Irène opens the door and steps outside. The color of the sky has deepened and the setting sun sends arcs of light dancing across the valley. Irène can see herself reflected back in the motionless stream below; it's almost like a mirror. Martin says, Let's have our photo taken. There is a man in a rumpled trench coat with an ancient looking camera. Irène and Martin pose, holding each other, their cheeks touching.*

*The photographer pulls a white square out of the side of the camera, fans it in the air, then peels the paper back and hands the photo to Irène. In the photo, Irène's image is sharp and clear, but Martin has faded into a ghostly halftone, as if she's holding onto thin air. Over her shoulder, in the photo, is a giant glass house. She looks up and realizes that Martin, the photographer and her car have disappeared. Irène turns to look back at the house, and it shimmers like a mirage, ripples in the wind.*

Gerard arrived late in the afternoon to drop off manuscripts for Irène and Martin to edit. She was still trying to piece together the dream she'd had, the second appearance of the glass house and the anxiety she felt at Martin's ghostly image in the photo. Gerard was chattering about the new owner advancing a large sum of money to purchase new manuscripts and how the publishing house was going to be busier than ever. He was considering hiring new staff and applying for a work permit for Martin to make him a full-time and legal employee.

"That's wonderful, Gerard," she said absently, bundling up the manuscripts she'd finished.

"You should be excited, Madame Irène," Gerard said, a hint of disappointment in his voice that his jubilance was not being acknowledged or returned by his best editor.

"I'm sorry," she said. "There has been so much happening here . . . I am distracted."

Gerard pressed her, and Irène gave him an abbreviated update of the robberies, David's return and her search for Frederick Dubois. She assured him that things would settle down and they would be back to a normal schedule soon.

"That's good," Gerard said, relieved. "We're going to be very busy. Monsieur Temple will be pleased."

"When do we get to meet the new owner?"

"He's made no requests to meet the staff. As I said, he's not interested in the day-to-day operations; he just wants to make sure the house is solvent. Look at this letter." Gerard opened his briefcase, pulled out an envelope and handed it to Irène.

The envelope was heavy and made of a rich, creamy paper. Irène turned the letter over and saw the embossed company name in the top left corner: Soixante-huit.

"That's the name of the company?" Irène asked. "Sixty-eight? How odd."

"I suppose it has some meaning for Monsieur Temple," Gerard said. "It's a branch of a larger company. He said he was expanding his holdings and created this one for publishing and media."

"He must be quite rich," Irène said, removing the letter from the envelope.

*Dear Gerard,*

*Thank you for signing the papers so quickly and making this transaction such a pleasure. I look forward to many fine new books, and as a token of my regard, I am advancing you the sum of one hundred thousand francs to purchase new manuscripts and redesign the fall catalogue as you requested. With your excellent eye and the good work of your editors, I know the house will produce a fine selection of literature that will bring new attention and acclaim. I have been making time to read quality literature every night before bed rather than business reports, and am currently re-reading the works of Monsieur Proust. He had such insight into how the minute and mundane of our everyday existence can trigger memories we had thought lost forever. If you have not read Proust, or have not read his works in many years, I highly recommend it.*

*Good wishes for the new year,*

*ST*

The letter triggered a memory for Irène, a recent one. She touched the stationery again, felt the grain of it underneath her fingers. Marcel Proust's name seemed to glow from the page. Soixante-huit—sixty-eight. 1968.

"Did you . . ." Irène choked on her words. "Did you meet Monsieur Temple?"

"Of course," Gerard said. "I went to his office in Calais."

"What did he look like?"

Gerard tried to recall any specifics. "Slender, grey at the temples. Handsome, I suppose, but not extraordinarily so."

"How tall was he?"

Gerard shrugged. "I have no idea. He never stood up. He was behind a desk. I did think it was odd, maybe even rude, that he did not stand when I entered his office. Then I noticed his movements were sometimes a bit stiff—when he was reaching down to open a drawer. I guessed he had an injury."

"He wasn't in a wheelchair?" Irène asked, urgently leaning forward, the letter nearly crumpled in her hand.

"No, he was in a large leather chair. Irène, what are all these questions?" Gerard asked, trying to pull the letter from her hand. "Do you know this man?"

Irène seemed to snap out of a trance; she leaned back and smiled at Gerard. "I'm sorry. "I'm having a bit of involuntary memory. Perhaps it's the mention of Proust."

Gerard wiped at his brow. "I'm worried about you, madame."

Irène took his face in her hands and kissed him on the nose. "I am fine, but I do have a strange request, a bit of an indulgence."

"Anything for you."

"May I keep Monsieur Temple's letter?"

"Yes," Gerard said uncertainly. "But why?"

"I may write and introduce myself to him . . . if you have no objections?"

"No, not at all. You are my best and most senior editor. Monsieur Temple will be delighted to hear from you."

"Good," Irène said, smoothing out the letter on the desk before folding it and putting it back in the envelope. She stood up, signaling the end of their meeting, and Gerard hurried to stand up as well. "Martin and I will get to work on these new manuscripts immediately."

She ushered Gerard out with a promise to have him over for dinner soon. As soon as he'd gone, Irène rushed back to her desk and picked up the phone, dialing with shaking fingers. "V. Hugo. I need you."

V. Hugo arrived half an hour later, huffing and puffing as if he'd run all the way to rue Rampon. He opened his briefcase and pulled the letter Frederick had written to his mother before she died. It was in a plastic evidence bag, and V. Hugo removed it carefully as if it were an artifact. An impatient Irène snatched it from his hands and put it on the desk next to the letter from Simon Temple written to Gerard.

"It's the same stationery," V. Hugo said, picking up both letters. He ran his fingers over the surface and weighed them both in his hands. Then he took the letters and held them up to the lamp on Irène's desk. There was the same unmistakable watermark.

Irène braced herself on the desk. "It's him."

"I'll need to do more analysis," V. Hugo said.

"They are both reading Proust," Irène nearly shouted. "The company is called Soixante-huit. How many coincidences do you need?"

"It doesn't make any sense," V. Hugo said, reading the letter. "Why would he reveal himself this way? Make these errors?"

"Obviously, he wasn't expecting his letters to be read. You stole the one from his mother and I'm sure he never expected Gerard to show me this."

"But why now? And why does he want the publishing house?"

"That's what I'm paying you for, monsieur. To find out."

"Of course."

"When do we leave for Calais? I think we should go tomorrow and visit the offices of Soixante-huit."

"Perhaps I should go alone," V. Hugo suggested. "It would be more subtle. After what happened at the funeral . . ."

Irène rushed to her bedroom with V. Hugo following her. He stopped up short at the threshold. She pulled an overnight bag out of the closet and tossed it on the bed, making Pierre leap out of the way. "I will book tickets and let you know when to meet us at Gare de l'Est," she said.

"But madame . . ."

"Go home and pack, V. Hugo."

# 21 Calais

The late morning train to Calais was only half full. V. Hugo sat across a small table from Irène, nervously looking through a notebook and occasionally making notes. A cup of coffee sloshed on the table in front of Irène, while Martin sat across the aisle and nibbled at a sandwich he had bought at Gare de l'Est. It tasted like plastic, but he ate it anyway.

Martin was relieved to have the distraction of being back on the search for Frederick; it would give him time to process the last forty-eight hours, which seemed like weeks. He instinctively knew things were moving too fast with Christian, but he couldn't help himself. It was so easy to be around Christian, reminding him of the early days with Peter. There was no second-guessing or doubt. With David, it had been all about pursuit and the sexual tension between them. None of these things were a factor with Christian. It was as if the best parts of Peter and David had been synthesized into the perfect lover. That morning, before Martin had left for the train station, Christian had kissed him tenderly on the steps as the taxi driver waited impatiently.

V. Hugo eventually dozed off while Martin and Irène talked about the manuscript she was reading and the one Martin was late returning to Gerard. They were still talking shop when the train pulled into Gare de Calais-Ville.

The old part of Calais sat on an island surrounded by canals and the English Channel. The address for Soixante-huit was near the ports where all the ferries and cargo ships departed for the U.K. and beyond. There was no snow in Calais, but it was bitterly cold and the sky was a steel grey.

A taxi took them to an address at the end of rue Margollé, which sat opposite the ferry and shipping docks for the Port of Calais. The imposing ships and cranes made for an industrial, disconcerting backdrop. V. Hugo suggested he go in alone, but Martin and Irène gave him a withering look that meant his idea was defeated.

"But what if he is inside, madame? There will certainly be security cameras. I am sure he can escape easily if he knows you are here."

"Something tells me he already knows," Irène said. "I have the feeling he is always one step ahead. It would be too easy to walk in the door and find him."

The door was locked, so V. Hugo rang the buzzer, but no one answered. They searched the roofline for cameras, but saw nothing. Drapes were pulled across the windows.

"Now what?" Martin asked.

"Let's go around and see if there is a back entrance," V. Hugo said.

The trio huddled close as a piercing wind whipped off the channel, but the back of the office building yielded no clues.

There was a walking path that separated the building from an expanse of greenspace where there was a statue of a fisherman about to cast a rope and looking intently across the water. On the opposite side of the park was a row of pubs and restaurants.

"Why don't we get lunch and watch the building from that restaurant?" Irène suggested.

V. Hugo went to pay the taxi, while Martin and Irène walked over to look at the statue, the Monument des Sauveteurs, commemorating those lost at sea and their rescuers. "Everything seems like a hidden message now," Irène said. "I imagine Frederick picking this spot out of spite."

Irène, Martin and V. Hugo took a table by the window of the small café at the corner of rue Margollé and rue Jean-Pierre Avron where they could watch the Soixante-huit building. They asked the waitress about the building and its comings and goings, but she knew nothing and called the owner from the kitchen. An older woman appeared, wiping her hands on a crisp apron.

"I have seen a few people come in and out of the building, but it seems empty most of the time," the café owner said.

"Have you met Simon Temple?" Irène asked. "Has he ever come in to dine? He might be in a wheelchair."

"If he has, he's never introduced himself," the woman said, "and I don't recall a gentleman in a wheelchair recently. Are you the police?"

V. Hugo produced identification and said he was a private detective. "We're trying to locate a missing man."

"I haven't heard about any missing persons cases in Calais," the woman said. "How long has he been missing?"

"Thirty years," Irène said.

They had lunch and drank endless cups of coffee, but no one ever came to the Soixante-huit building. As the light began to fade, V. Hugo said they should either take a train home or find a hotel.

"Have either of you ever been arrested?" Irène asked.

Both V. Hugo and Martin shook their heads, glancing at each other and then at Irène.

"Neither have I. What do you think the punishment is for first offense breaking and entering?"

"Madame . . . I don't know what you're thinking, but I will have no part of it," V. Hugo said. "I could lose my license."

"Then why don't you go find a hotel for us," Irène said. "We'll keep you out of it."

"We?" Martin chimed in.

"I cannot leave Calais without seeing what's inside that building."

"Let's think about this for a moment," Martin said.

"I'll break the window and crawl inside if I have to," Irène said.

V. Hugo stood up, buttoning his coat. "You are on your own. Monsieur Paige, I urge you to make her understand reason. This is not how these matters are handled. If you will not take my counsel, Madame Laureux, then I will remove myself from this case. I wish you luck."

V. Hugo left the café and walked back toward rue Margollé. Irène stood up and went out after him, but instead of following, she pulled a packet of Gauloises from her pocket and lit up a cigarette. Martin paid the bill and joined her.

"I knew V. Hugo would crack under the pressure," Irène said. "Perhaps I should hire Mr. Sullivan. He wouldn't be afraid."

"You seriously want to break into that building?"

"I do."

"If we're caught, I could be deported."

"Then we should do it quickly and carefully."

191

It was getting dark and the temperature was plunging. They walked back to the rue Margollé side of the building. There was no traffic and the port building across the way appeared empty.

Martin knelt down and looked at the door. "I think this is the only lock. I bet I could pick it if I had a bobby pin."

A voice from behind them made them both jump. "Move out of the way," V. Hugo said. He produced a small leather case from his jacket pocket and unzipped it. Inside was a series of hooked tools—a lockpicking set. V. Hugo inserted two of the picks into the lock and fiddled with them until there was an audible click. He pushed on the door and it swung inward.

"Inside, quickly," V. Hugo said, returning the case to his jacket.

"You are full of surprises," Irène said.

Martin felt for a light switch, but V. Hugo told him to stop. He produced a small flashlight from another pocket. The reception area of the building was empty. Not a desk, chair or any type of furniture to indicate it was an operational office. Along the back wall were a series of offices, but they also turned out to be empty. Martin pointed toward a staircase and V. Hugo led the way, his flashlight beaming up into darkness. Like downstairs, the upstairs room was empty. It was as if the building had never been inhabited.

"Martin, lend me your mobile," Irène said.

He handed her the phone and she dialed a number. "Hello, Gerard. I am sorry to bother you at home, but I have a strange question. When you went to Calais, you said you met Monsieur Temple at his office. Was the office on rue Margollé across from the port?" She listened for a moment. "Was it a typical office? I mean to say, was it full of furniture and people? Yes, I know it's odd, Gerard. I was just curious. I must go, but I will call you soon. Bonsoir."

She pressed the disconnect button and handed the phone back to Martin. "Gerard said this building was full of people and desks. He said Simon Temple's office was upstairs and was full of expensive furniture and artwork." They surveyed the large room, each trying to imagine Frederick Dubois here.

"How long ago did Gerard meet Temple here?" V. Hugo asked.

"In the autumn."

"More than enough time to clear out," V. Hugo said. "The building has been stripped." He walked around pointing the flashlight at the walls. There were no traces of holes where pictures might have been hung, the wooden floor gleamed under the beam of light. "Professionals," V. Hugo concluded. "They left no trace."

"But why? Why would he set up a fake office just to meet with Gerard? He could have met him anywhere. It doesn't make sense," Irène said, frustration in her voice.

"I will make some inquiries about the building," V. Hugo said. "Find out when the electricity and telephones were in use. Perhaps that will give us some clue."

"Let's get out of here," Martin said. "It's freezing."

They slipped out of the building unnoticed, and Irène suggested they go back to the café and call a taxi, but V. Hugo said it would raise more suspicion. They walked further up rue Jean-Pierre Avron to a bar and Martin called for a taxi from his mobile. Irène ordered them each a drink as they waited.

Irène swirled the Scotch in her glass. "I have to warn Gerard. The publishing house is in jeopardy."

"I advise you to say nothing," V. Hugo said. "We will let Dubois or André Sarde or Simon Temple or whatever he calls himself now make the next move."

"Yes, but we aren't even in the game," Martin said.

"Monsieur Paige, *we* are the game."


The trio checked into a small hotel near the Calais train station.
V. Hugo had encouraged Martin and Irène to take the last train
back to Paris, but Irène said she was tired and wanted to be
around if he found anything out about the building or its owner.
V. Hugo forced a smile and went into his room and shut the
door without saying goodnight.

"I think you're trying his patience," Martin said.

Irène unlocked their hotel room door. "It's good for him.
Character building, as they say."

Martin called Diane to update her and she said there had
been no word from Sullivan, but Euan had ignored her all day
while he set up an apartment in his office at the Anglophile.
"You're never going to believe this, but he gave me the keys to
his apartment," Diane said. "Okay, he kind of threw them at
me as he was going out, but, hey, that means I'm out of the
hotel. Now we're just two single gals living in the same building.
I'm the Mary and you're the Rhoda. And I guess Irène is like
Phyllis."

"I'm hanging up now."

"You know, your sense of humor has turned to shit since
you . . ."

Martin ended the call and dialed the number Christian had
given him for the townhouse on Avenue Junot. The phone rang
and rang, but there was no answer. Irène sat in a chair by the
window smoking a cigarette.

"Maybe he wanted us to find out that he had bought the
publishing house," Irène mused. "Something to dangle over our
heads as a subtle threat. Keep quiet or else. Gerard and the
publishing house are all that's left of those days. Maybe he wants

to take them away. Is that crazy?"

"Nothing seems crazy these days," Martin said.

Irène nodded. "Then maybe this won't sound crazy. Before you arrived in Paris, there was a sense of something about to happen. There was an anticipation that I could almost taste. Those strange, waking dreams I had about you and that you were having about me."

"I remember."

"Are you having any dreams like that now?"

Martin shook his head. "No."

"I am. They started months ago." She told Martin about the dreams of the giant greenhouse and the Venus de Milo statue, of Jean-Louis bleeding outside Notre-Dame, of the presence always behind her, but never seen.

"You think it's Frederick?"

"I know it is. He's out there lurking in the dark. Following me even in my dreams."

# 22 Closer

Diane left the Anglophile, pulling her hat over her ears. She was tired of cold weather and ready for spring. She felt oddly at peace, although the lives of everyone around her were in upheaval. She was growing fonder of Paris and she felt a giddy sense of anonymity. Diane passed the metro and walked toward the Seine. The night sky was clear and full of stars and a huge, bright moon hung over the city. She might walk all the way to rue Rampon, burn off the calories from the heavy dinners Irène always prepared.

She was lost in thought, unaware of the car that had been trailing her until it pulled up alongside her on Boulevard Saint-Germain. Diane glanced out of the corner of her eye at the BMW, noted the tinted windows and how the car kept pace with her. She walked faster and the car accelerated to keep up. Diane stopped in her tracks and turned toward the car, which also stopped.

"What?" Diane shouted at the car, but it just sat there idling, exhaust creating a cloud over the avenue. Diane stepped off the curb, went up to the driver's side window and rapped loudly on the dark glass. "Hey, motherfucker. You wanna talk to me? Here I am."

The window slid down and Diane stepped back. Bernard Sullivan stuck his head out the window, a cigar clenched between his teeth.

"You are going to get yourself killed one day," Sullivan said. "Do you always walk up to strange cars following you on the street? I could have been a sexual pervert."

"Could have been?"

Sullivan touched a button and the passenger door unlocked with a click. "Get in."

"I was going to walk by the Seine. I was having a pleasant evening. Are you stalking me?"

"I want to take you to a hotel," Sullivan said.

"I'm gonna scream rape," Diane said, stepping back onto the sidewalk.

"I thought I was the most decent man you'd ever met."

"I'm reconsidering."

"This is official business. There's someone at the hotel you'll be wanting to speak to."

"Oh, really? And who might that be?"

"David McLaren."


Sullivan turned down a narrow street in the 18th arrondissement on the city's north side. It wasn't far from Montmartre, but seemed a world away from the Paris tourists flocked to every year. The street was full of shops that appeared to be selling everything from tacky souvenirs to exotic meats. Furtive eyes glanced at the BMW as it passed, and Diane was sure she saw more than one hooker.

Sullivan pulled the BMW up to the curb in front of the Americana Hotel. It looked dark and empty.

"Well, ain't this the Ritz," Diane said.

Sullivan switched off the engine. "From what I've heard it's one of Paris' finer drug dens."

Sullivan led Diane through a set of greasy, double glass doors. The lobby was a narrow corridor finished in fake marble, adorned with cheap cardboard pictures of Paris in tacky wooden frames. An opening on the left near the end of the hall revealed what used to be a bar and small café, but was now serving as a storage area. A cluttered alcove revealed the check-in desk and the garrulous desk clerk who worked the overnight shift sitting in a chair listening to a crackling radio station.

Sullivan flashed his credentials at the man, who stood up so quickly he knocked the chair over.

"Take it easy," Sullivan said. "We're not the gendarmes. We're looking for an American."

"All Americans are alike to me," the clerk said, righting his chair and sitting down again. "I cannot keep up."

Sullivan leaned over the counter so that he was eye-level with the clerk. "Keep up with this. I'm looking for someone who is a fugitive. Do you understand that word? F-U-G-I-T-I-V-E. A criminal. If you don't want the police here, you'll answer my questions."

The man perked up at the mention of the police. "What do you want from me?"

"I understand there's a young American staying here," Sullivan said, handing the clerk a photo of David.

The clerk studied the photo and handed it back. "Non."

"Has anyone checked in at all?" Diane asked, looking around

in disgust.

"No Americans," the man said, sneering back at Diane. "We are not for tourists. We have people who scrape enough money for one night out of the weather. It is a serious problem here, you know. Runaways, drug users, child prostitutes. I give them a room if they can pay."

"He's a regular Mother Teresa," Diane said under her breath.

Sullivan pushed the photo back across the counter. "Think hard. David McLaren is his name."

The man sighed and drummed his fingers on the counter. "There was a guy here a few nights ago, but not the person in this photo. He had an American name, but he didn't sound American."

"Has he checked out?" Sullivan asked. "Can you check your guest book?"

"We have no guest book."

"Even the Bates Motel had a guest book," Diane said.

Sullivan reached into his pocket and pushed francs across the counter. "Anything you can remember would be helpful."

The clerk looked at the money for a moment and then put a hand over the top of it and slid it over the edge. "He checked out yesterday."

"We'd like to see the room," Sullivan said.

The clerk produced a key with a cardboard tag. "Fourth floor. Elevator is in the corner or take the stairs."

"There's an elevator?" Diane asked. "My god, the 19th century is a marvel."

The elevator was tucked into a corner next to a growling ice machine. The door opened revealing room for two passengers at the most, one if there was luggage. Sullivan and Diane jostled and repositioned so they could both get inside, smashed against one another. The door slammed shut so hard the carriage swayed back and forth. There was an unmistakable smell of urine and it was at least ninety degrees in the tiny box. Diane gagged once, loudly, and the car rocked.

"Press the fucking button," Diane said.

"It's behind you," Sullivan said, snaking his hand around Diane's thigh.

"Hey . . . hey," Diane said, slapping his hand away. "Time and a place, Sullivan, and this ain't either."

Diane started pressing every button on the panel located somewhere behind her back. The elevator lurched upwards and she shrieked. The lift stopped on the third floor with a violent screech and the door opened half way. Diane thrust her head out of the elevator and gasped for air and Sullivan snatched her back just as the door slammed closed again.

"This thing is a fucking guillotine," Diane said. "No wonder it smells like piss in here. People were wetting themselves in fear."

The elevator lurched again and then stopped with a thud at the fourth floor. For a moment, the door threatened not to open and Diane started pressing buttons behind her until it slowly slid back with a whisper.

"This is officially the worst hotel ever," Diane said. "And I stayed in some real shitholes in Poland."

They stumbled out of the elevator, Sullivan leaning against the wall to catch his breath, dabbing at his forehead with a handkerchief.

"You'd better not have a coronary," Diane said, taking big lungfuls of air. "Because I'd hate to explain to paramedics what we're doing here."

"I'll be fine," Sullivan said, looking at the tag on the key. "The room is right here."

Sullivan put the key in the lock and pushed the door open.

The smell of feces wafted out of the room and made Diane gag. Sullivan turned away and leaned back against the wall. "Mother of God," he said, cupping his hand over his mouth and nose.

Diane took a big gulp of air and stuck her head into the pitch-black room. "Where's the fucking light switch?"

She advanced slowly into the room, her face tucked into the crook of her arm to mask the stench, while running her hand up and down the wall. She had only gone a few steps when she screamed and the room swallowed her.

"Diane!" Sullivan shouted. "What's happened?"

Sullivan held his hand over his mouth and slipped into the room, groping for a light. A cord brushed his face and he grabbed it. A weak overhead light illuminated the room. Diane was face down on the bed, which took up the majority of the space. Rusted, misshapen wire hangers lined a rack over the head of the bed, while a TV was mounted near the ceiling. Sheer fabric that was once white, but was now yellowed by nicotine and age covered a sliver of window. A sink was in the other corner, dripping and stained green. Another door that must have led into the bathroom was cracked open.

Diane rolled over and knelt on the bed. "Fuck. I'm most definitely going to need a Silkwood shower after this."

Sullivan pulled a handkerchief from his pocket, covered his nose and started edging around the bed. He went to the sink and knelt down. There was a rusting trashcan underneath and Sullivan used the sleeve of his coat to pull it out. There were greasy cartons and fast food wrappers at the bottom, but a square of white paper stuck to the side caught his eye. Sullivan pulled the paper out of the trashcan, studied it closely, then leaned across the bed and handed it to Diane.

"What's that?" she asked. "I don't want to touch it."

"Look at it."

Diane pinched the paper between her fingertips and held it up to the weak light. It was a cash register receipt from the Anglophile dated a week ago.

Diane tried her key on the Anglophile door, but Euan had bolted it from the inside. Sullivan pounded on the door until they saw a light come on at the top of the stairs. Euan appeared at the door wearing a bathrobe and a sour expression.

"What is this about?" he shouted through the door.

"Let us in," Diane said. "We need to look at the security camera footage."

"It's almost midnight," Euan said. "Why do you need to see the camera?"

"Just open the door," Diane said, exasperated.

Euan unlocked the doors, and Diane and Sullivan pushed inside.

"What's this all about?" Euan demanded.

Sullivan produced the receipt they had found at the hotel. "We need to watch the video footage from this day and time."

"I wasn't working that afternoon," Diane said. "You were."

"Who are we looking for?"

"David," Diane said, and Euan's face froze.

"He was here? In the shop?"

"That's what we need to find out."

Euan led them upstairs to the office where he kept a VCR and monitor in a cabinet. He showed Diane how to fast forward and pause the tape, then said goodnight.

"What do you mean goodnight?" Diane asked. "You're going back to bed?"

"I wasn't asleep," Euan said, "but I don't want any more of the drama. It's why I moved out of the apartment."

"We can manage, Mr. McEvoy," Sullivan said, nudging Diane with his elbow. After Euan had walked out: "I wouldn't take it any further with him. He is your boss."

"Worried you're not going to get paid?"

"I'm worried your mouth is going to get you in trouble one day."

"You are far too late for that."

Diane popped in the tape for the day listed on the receipt and began to fast forward. The camera was mounted behind the checkout area, giving a wide view of the front area of the shop. Diane watched the back of her head fly by on the tape. She had her head down reading a book most of the time, unless a customer came in or the phone rang. Occasionally, Diane would spin around in her chair and throw her head back in a silent scream.

"Boredom," Diane said under her breath.

Just after lunch, Euan came downstairs and Diane left for the day. He fussed over some paperwork, but for the most part, sat staring out the window. Customers came and went, and only one or two bought anything. Then, at around three o'clock, according to the tape, the door opened and a man came in, wearing a baseball cap pulled low over his forehead.

"Stop right there," Sullivan said, and Diane hit pause. "Go frame by frame."

Diane fiddled with the buttons, accidentally rewinding and fast forwarding while muttering obscenities. When she finally got the tape to advance by frame, both she and Sullivan practically put their noses on the television screen. Euan was using the slowest recording speed to get the most footage on the tape, which made the image grainy.

The man in the baseball cap was wearing a non-descript black peacoat jacket and jeans, but Diane couldn't tell if it was David. With the brim of the cap pulled so low, it created a shadow over the face that hid all his features. He could have been anybody. The man moved toward the stairs and out of frame.

"Is there a camera up here?" Sullivan asked.

"No," Diane said, jerking her head back toward the door. "He hasn't gotten around to it yet."

"Shame."

After fast-forwarding a bit more, the man came back into frame again and approached the register. "Here we go," Diane said.

"I still can't get a good look at his face," Sullivan said. "Let it play at normal speed."

Diane clicked the button and they watched as the man reached into his pocket, and pulled out francs and put them on the counter. He dropped some coins on the floor in front of the register and bent down to retrieve them. When he stood up, the light played directly across his face for a moment.

Sullivan snatched the remote out of Diane's hand and rewound. "Who is that?"

Sullivan's meaty fingers stabbed at the remote, once again advancing until the frame where the man stood up was frozen on the screen.

Diane felt lightheaded. "It's Christian."

"We need a photo," Sullivan said. "Is there a way to print an image from the screen?"

"Are you kidding? We're still using dot matrix because Euan likes the 'satisfying clack of the machine.'"

"Do you think Martin has any photos of Christian?"

"I doubt it . . . wait . . ." Diane snapped her fingers. "We took photos at some of the poetry readings." Diane went to Euan's desk and pulled open all the drawers, rifling through the contents. "Euan, goddamn it!" she shouted. "Where are those photos?"

Euan appeared in the doorway with packets of photos that had been developed at the camera store around the corner. He threw the packets toward the desk, but they landed on the floor, photos and negatives scattering across the rug.

"Prick," Diane muttered.

Diane knelt down on the floor and saw most of the pictures were of Martin, which gave her a little twinge when she realized Euan had kept them in his room. She tossed most of the photos aside, sending them sailing around the office, until she came to one of Christian standing at the microphone. He looked angelic.

"It doesn't make any sense," she said, handing the photo to Sullivan. "I've met this kid and he doesn't seem like a junkie. I mean, look at him. He's hot."

Sullivan cut his eyes at her. "You and Martin have the same taste in men, I see. Young and damaged."

Diane started to protest, rising up on her knees, opening her mouth. But Sullivan was right.

Sullivan stuffed the photo into his jacket pocket. "Strike a nerve?"

"A little."

Sullivan drove through the streets of the 1st arrondissement, not far from Forum des Halles, the underground shopping arcade in the center of Paris. He turned down the narrow, restaurant-lined rue de la Reynie. At the intersection of rue Saint-Denis, Sullivan turned onto a pedestrian mall that led toward the Fontaine des Innocents.

"What the fuck," Diane said. "This is a sidewalk."

"It's after midnight. We're fine. There's a big drug trade around Les Halles and the fountain plaza is where the punks like to skateboard."

Sullivan pulled up alongside the Fontaine des Innocents, which was surrounded by spindly trees and old lampposts. The four-sided Renaissance-era fountain rose out of the center, its bas-relief nymphs and tritons cavorting on carved columns as water gurgled down steps into a round pool, which had a skim of ice. Shops and apartments surrounded the square, but it was deserted save for the clacking sound of more than a dozen boys' skateboards hitting the paving stones.

"Well, this isn't obvious at all," Diane said. "Why don't you just drive right into the plaza?"

"Some of these skaters are dealers and prostitutes, or both. This is a favored hangout."

"You take me to all the best places, Sullivan."

Sullivan turned off the engine. He got out of the car, and leaned against the door and lit a cigar. Diane scooted over into the driver's seat and rolled down the window. "Uh, is this a smoke break?"

"Wait for it."

It was if a ripple had gone through the skaters in the plaza. Before Sullivan pulled up, they had been jumping off the edge of the fountain and the low concrete benches that surrounded the square, noisily chiding each other for a missed trick, a tinny-sounding boom box was turned up as a French rapper's lyrics echoed off the concrete. As the detective stood there, relaxed and casual, the skaters were still in motion, but they were now moving slowly, checking in with each other to see who the stranger was and what he might want.

One of the skaters who had been hanging back on the far side of the plaza finally moved toward them. He was maybe sixteen, lanky with a buzz cut, wearing a silver puff jacket and baggy jeans. As he rolled toward the car, he stepped off the skateboard, popped it with his heel and into his hands.

"What do you want?" the boy asked, anger in his voice. "I told you everything."

"You told me David McLaren was staying at the hotel. I was just there and he most definitely was not. And never was."

"Not my problem."

"Oh, it's your problem," Diane said, leaning out the window.

The boy looked at her and grinned. "You're pretty. Are you the fat man's wife?"

"Hell, no," Diane snapped, but was oddly pleased the teenager had called her pretty.

Sullivan pulled the photo of Christian from his breast pocket and held it front of the boy's face. "Who is this?"

"That's him," the kid said.

"This is David McLaren?" Sullivan asked, waving the photo in front of the boy's face.

"Yes."

Sullivan snatched the cigar out of his mouth and threw it at the boy, who jumped back as the lit end hit his jacket. He brushed frantically at his coat as if he might be on fire.

"You're lying!" Sullivan said.

"Fuck you, fat man," the boy yelled. "Leave me alone."

With a speed that defied his size, Sullivan snatched the boy's skateboard and held it high over his head. The other skateboarders had stopped and were watching silently. Diane poked Sullivan in the back. "What the fuck are you doing?" Diane whispered. "We're outnumbered here."

"Tell me more, lad, or your board is kindling," Sullivan said. As the boy was trying to decide whether he should fight for the board or run, he looked back at the other guys watching. "They aren't going to help you. Every man for himself." Sullivan waved the board back and forth as if it might fly from his fingers.

"He was dealing. He said he grew up in the United States.

He said his father was black and he grew up where Elvis lived."

"Memphis," Diane said, her head swimming.

"Yeah, that's it. Memphis and Graceland. Now give me my board."

Sullivan tossed the skateboard from hand to hand. "I showed you a photograph of the real David McLaren and you identified him as the one staying at the hotel."

"My mistake. Americans all look alike to me," the boy said and leaped to try and grab the skateboard. In one swift motion, Sullivan grabbed the boy by the jacket and dropped the skateboard to the pavement. He raised one of his meaty legs and brought it down hard in the center of the board. It cracked loudly.

"You fat fuck!" the boy screamed, squirming in Sullivan's grasp.

Sullivan pulled the boy's face close to his. "You've disappointed me. I could bring a river of shit so deep over your head, you'd be drowning in turds. The police would love to get their hands on you and your punk friends," Sullivan said, punctuating the words so that they carried to the other skaters who were watching. "I told you from the beginning I was trying to find one kid, just one. I gave you money, bought you food and this is how you repay me?"

"I need more."

"I'm going to give you a choice now, lad, and you'd better think carefully. You're going to tell me everything, *everything*, or I'm dumping you in the Seine."

The boy squirmed again and looked back over his shoulder. The other skateboarders were disappearing into the night, leaving him to hang.

The boy's shoulders slumped in defeat. "They were together at Eureka. The guy in the picture and the American."

Sullivan opened the back door and pushed the kid inside.

"You think I'm a fright, just wait until my lady here gets done with you."

# 23 As If to Nothing

Martin and Irène took a mid-morning train back to Paris, while V. Hugo remained in Calais to follow up on loose ends that they all knew would lead nowhere. They had gone to the town hall to inquire about the owner of the building, but the file on the building had mysteriously disappeared.

"No one loses a file like that," Irène said. "It was stolen."

Martin had called Christian a number of times from pay phones, but there was still no answer at the house in Montmartre. He had forgotten to charge his mobile and it died the night before. Martin felt a vague sense of anxiety that only grew as they neared Paris. At Gare de l'Est, Irène took a cab back to rue Rampon, while Martin took another to Avenue Junot.

As the driver wound up the streets into Montmartre, the sunlight gleamed off the Sacré-Cœur and Martin found himself leaning forward in the seat as if it might streamline or hasten the taxi through morning traffic. When the taxi arrived at Avenue Junot, a dozen police cars lined the street. Martin felt nauseous and sweat sprang to his brow.

"I'll get out here," Martin said, tossing francs over the seat and jumping out of the cab.

As he'd feared, officers were coming in and out of Christian's house. Residents watched from across the street or hung out their windows to see what was going on. As Martin neared the house, he saw the old woman who had harassed him on the steps a few nights ago. She was talking to an officer, who was making notes on a small pad. She saw Martin approach and pointed an accusatory finger.

"There! There's another one. I told you I saw him on the steps. That's him!" she screeched. The officer turned and looked at Martin, as did several others.

"What's happening?" Martin demanded.

The officers quickly took Martin by the arms, pulled his overnight bag from his shoulder and walked him toward the steps.

"Sit down," one of the officers commanded, reaching for handcuffs on his belt.

"Those won't be necessary," a voice said from the top of the stairs. Martin turned and saw Arnaud standing there. "I know this man."

"He's a thief," the old woman barked. "I saw him break into this house."

"Go home, madame," Arnaud said, coming down the steps. The officer who had been taking her statement hustled the old woman away from the house. She looked over her shoulder at Martin and continued to declare him guilty.

Martin stood up and faced Arnaud. "Why are you here?

Where is Christian?"

"You should come inside."

"Is he here?"

"No," Arnaud said. "I see Madame Jacobs and her detective did not reach you."

"No. The battery on my mobile is dead."

"That is unfortunate."

They were standing in the entry hall where Christian and Martin had made love, the coolness familiar and, unlike before, chilling. Martin felt his whole body shake. He moved toward the staircase, but Arnaud caught his arm.

"Not yet. The detectives are still gathering evidence."

"Evidence for what?"

"Burglary," Arnaud said.

"Was Christian here when it happened?" Martin flashed on Christian being confronted by robbers, trying to defend himself.

"Christian is the accused," Arnaud said.

Martin laughed. "Accused of breaking into his own house?"

"Monsieur Paige, the house does not belong to Christian. He has deceived you. This house belongs to a pair of doctors. They've been out of the country for weeks, and Christian has been squatting here."

"That can't be true," Martin cried. "I've been here. All of his things were here. He made dinner . . ."

"I can assure you, it is true," Arnaud said. "The owners are in the kitchen making a list of stolen items."

Martin looked down the hall toward the back of the house and the owners were standing in the doorway, staring at him. It was a man and woman, tastefully dressed in business suits, wide-eyed looks on their faces. "I want to speak to them," he said and started down the hall.

"That wouldn't be a good idea," Arnaud said. "They may

want to file charges against you as well."

Martin stopped and turned back to Arnaud. "Against me? For what?"

Arnaud motioned down the hall and an officer ushered the owners back into the kitchen and shut the door. "You were squatting here as well, were you not? Did you not drink their wine, eat their food, use their home as if it were your own?"

"That's crazy," Martin said. "I had no idea. Where is Christian? Have you arrested him?"

"He got away," Arnaud said. "Through the back door and over the garden wall. We're looking for him now. He left some interesting things behind in his haste to get away." Arnaud started up the stairs. "Come along."

As Martin followed Arnaud up the stairs, memories of Peter's suicide came flooding back. He had climbed the stairs in Peter's house, filled with dread, until he had come face to face with his lover sitting with a rifle between his knees. What would he find at the top of these stairs?

At the door to Christian's bedroom—or the bedroom Martin had believed was his—Arnaud stopped. "Let us have the room," Arnaud said to the detectives who were collecting fingerprints; one was peering over the bed with a blue light searching for DNA evidence. They all quickly filed out of the room. Martin noticed that Christian's laptop was still on the desk, its whirling screensaver engaged.

"Do you recognize the computer?" Arnaud asked Martin.

"Yes, Christian has had it ever since I met him."

"Look more closely."

Martin walked over to the laptop. He pushed the screen down and realized it was the same brand as Irène's computer that was stolen from the apartment. "Irène had one just like this."

"No, Monsieur Paige, that *is* Madame Laureux's computer.

The serial numbers match."

Martin closed his eyes, wanted to sit down, felt as if he might faint.

"Do you need assistance?" Arnaud asked. He pulled the desk chair out and guided Martin toward it, a firm hand on his shoulder.

"Are you saying that Christian broke into Irène's apartment?" Martin asked incredulously.

"It appears so," Arnaud said. "There's something else I need for you to identify. This might come as a bit of a shock to you."

Arnaud picked up a notebook from the desk. Martin had seen Christian carrying it at the Anglophile. It was more of a portfolio, really, with a clasp closure. Arnaud opened the flap and offered the notebook to Martin like a menu. There were loose pieces of paper with typewritten words on them. Poems.

"It's Christian's notebook. I've seen him with it."

Martin took the notebook into his hands. It was a rich brown suede; it felt silky under Martin's fingers. He put the notebook on his lap and picked up the first poem delicately, as if it were an artifact. Martin read the first lines and it took him a moment to realize he was reading his own poem. "What is this . . . ?" Martin choked.

Martin pulled the stack of paper from the notebook and flipped through it, feeling lightheaded. The papers slipped from his fingers and scattered on the hardwood floor. His poems for David. The ones written and left behind in the empty apartment with the statue of Venus. Martin's head felt like it was being gripped by a vise, as if his brain was trying to escape the maddening truth.

"There's more," Arnaud said, taking the notebook from Martin's lap. The detective pulled a rumpled piece of paper from a pocket inside the notebook and it handed it to Martin.

With trembling fingers, Martin took the piece paper and unfolded it. It was the letter he had written to David the year before, telling him that he was moving on with his life.

"You wrote that letter to David McLaren?" Arnaud asked.

Martin could only nod. Arnaud called for one of the officers in the hallway, handed him the notebook and instructed him to pick up the papers on the floor. Martin watched the detective gathering up the poems with gloved fingers.

"No, stop," Martin said, slipping out of the chair onto the floor. "This is mine. This is my poetry." He snatched the notebook from the detective.

"Leave it," Arnaud said to the detective, who got up and left the room. "Do you want to know what we believe has happened?"

Martin nodded, but he was outside his body again, watching himself crawl around the floor collecting the poems.

"Christian and David met early last year. We believe it was Christian who broke into the apartment and the tobacconist. Whether David was involved is less certain. We do know that Christian assumed David's identity. Detective Sullivan was able to verify that last night through one of his sources and he wisely contacted the police out of fear for your safety. Against Madame Jacobs wishes, I might add. We had no idea this burglary was connected until one of the officers found the stolen property and the notebook with your writings. Are you having difficulty breathing? I will call the medic."

"No," Martin said, although his heart felt as if it would burst through his chest. Blood was pumping in his ears.

"I need you to come to my office and make a full statement about your relationship with Christian. You may have information that can help us find him and David McLaren."

"It doesn't make any sense. Christian wouldn't do this. It must be some kind of trick or set up. Something David is doing."

"I understand you have feelings for Christian, but he deceived you, monsieur. It's what his type does. They adapt to any situation that will give them an advantage. They are always looking for another opportunity and they are always looking for the vulnerable to recruit, which may be the case with David McLaren. Christian is not unknown to the police. He has been picked up before for petty theft and drug possession under different names." Arnaud consulted a notebook from his coat pocket. "His real name is Baptiste Kigali."

"But there was no opportunity, as you call it, with me," Martin said. "What could he possibly gain from me?"

"Don't be naïve, Martin," Arnaud said. "He has given you a false name, broken into your home, the tobacconist and is possibly involved in David McLaren's disappearance. If I am brutally honest, he was probably using you as an alibi. Did you give him money?"

Martin was on his feet. "He never asked for a cent from me. It wasn't like that between us. He wasn't using me. What if it's the other way around? What if David put Christian up to it?"

"Martin, really, let's be serious."

"I am serious. David has been missing for a year. He's obviously unstable and I can tell you that he is one of the best liars I've ever met."

"I don't doubt that, but there is no evidence at all that David McLaren has been in this house or that he is still in Paris, for that matter. We have stepped up our search for David. He might be in danger, and there is now pressure from your state department, thanks to David's parents."

"You'll never find David if his parents are allowed to direct the search," Martin said.

Arnaud's eyes narrowed. "No one directs the investigation but me, I can assure you."

Martin had touched a nerve. "You haven't met David's parents yet."

Arnaud smiled thinly. "We're finished here. Let's go to my office."

They went downstairs and the owners of the townhouse were in the entry hall, talking to another officer. Martin saw that the man was white, but the woman was black, just like Christian. Was that why he had chosen this house? So that he wouldn't seem out of place? What nerve to not only break into someone's home, but to take up residence so nonchalantly and without fear. He realized he didn't know Christian at all. Diane and Irène were right again, and he was the fool.

The man and woman stared at him, the husband's face red with rage, but the wife looked at him with what seemed like pity.

"I'm so sorry," Martin said to her as he passed, and Arnaud quickly hustled him out of the townhouse and shut the door behind them.

An unmarked police car was waiting at the bottom of the steps. Over the roof of the car, Martin saw Irène, Diane and Sullivan standing behind a police barricade.

"Where the fuck are you taking him?" Diane called out.

"Monsieur Paige has to make a statement of the facts," Arnaud said. "We will have a car bring him home."

"Don't say anything without a lawyer," Diane yelled.

"Madame Jacobs, you are public nuisance. I will have you cited for disorderly conduct," Arnaud said as he opened the car door for Martin. "I should have you arrested for obstruction of justice."

"Yeah, come and get me," Diane sneered, but Sullivan slapped his hand over her mouth and physically picked her up and carried her off down the sidewalk as she flailed in his arms.

Irène leaned over the barricade. *I love you*, she mouthed. *I love you*, Martin mouthed back. *I'll be fine.*


Martin stared out the window of the car. Two officers were in the front seat and Arnaud sat beside him in the back. No one spoke and the silence was only occasionally broken by the radio dispatcher. Martin didn't know how long they had been driving before he realized they were not headed for the police station.

"Where are we going?" he asked. "Why are we headed out of the city?"

"I want you to see something," Arnaud said. "Something most tourists or Parisians never see."

Martin realized that the unmarked car they were in was sandwiched between two other unmarked cars. They came to an intersection and Martin saw a directional sign that read Montfermeil, one of the northeast suburbs. The deeper the cars traveled into Montfermeil, the more grim the surroundings became. Graffiti was the only color in the bleak landscape of gray concrete apartment buildings. Vandalized cars lined the streets and grimy children of all nationalities paused to stare as their cars moved slowly toward the area's notorious Les Bosquets apartments. "Fuck The Police" was spray painted in giant red letters on the side of a building.

"This is where most of the immigrants live," Arnaud said, his eyes cutting back and forth across the street. "There's no direct link to Paris by transport and no jobs or industry. It is like a war zone. A war to survive."

"Careful, Arnaud, you sound almost sympathetic," Martin said.

Les Bosquets was a hulking complex of buildings. Balconies

were littered with junk and drying clothes. Youths, mostly male, lounged against walls and railings and came to attention as the police cars crawled along the street. Some disappeared into the warren of buildings, while others stood defiantly. Three women dressed in colorful African regalia carrying shopping bags saw the police cars and began to walk faster down the street, fearing a clash.

"Why are we here, Arnaud?" Martin asked.

"Because when we arrested Christian the first time, he listed his address as Les Bosquets."

Martin looked at the boys standing along the street, some with fists clenched at their sides ready for a fight, and he could suddenly picture Christian there. Some of the boys had Christian's coloring, his features, the café au lait skin.

"You'll come to understand our situation and position, Martin," Arnaud said. "The immigrants know they will end up here or somewhere just like it, and still they come. Why come to live in this decay when you could stay in your own country?"

"Maybe this is better than where they came from," Martin said. "These guys all look African. You do know what's going on in Africa, don't you? Genocide and civil war. Maybe they thought they would be protected here."

Arnaud shook his head. "We are not the enemy."

"It's hard to tell."

Arnaud started to protest, but Martin cut him off. "Look, I got in the car to go and make a statement. We're wasting time. Even if Christian came from here, he won't come back."

"Don't be so sure, monsieur. This is the easiest place to hide."

The radio crackled and Arnaud spoke to the officers in the other cars. "Go door to door. Show the picture, if anyone acts suspicious, pull them out for further questioning."

"What are you doing?" Martin asked, fear rising. He saw

three armored police vans appear out of nowhere.

"You may not like our tactics, but they will get results," Arnaud said, and then into the radio, "Allez, allez, allez!"

The doors to the vans slammed open and heavily armored officers emerged with shields, batons and assault rifles. Almost immediately, objects began flying from the balconies: overripe fruit, a bike tire, plates and cups. The men held up their shields and created a plexiglass umbrella as the officers made their way to the stairwells.

Something hit the roof of the car Martin was in and everyone instinctively flinched. A youth with a bandana covering his face appeared at the driver's door and heaved a brick. The window cracked like a starburst. "Go now," Arnaud said, slapping the back of the seat and the driver hit the gas, barely avoiding a mob of youths running up the sidewalk. A bottle bounced off the trunk and shattered, but they were pulling away from the flashpoint. Martin was shaking. Arnaud was completely unruffled.

"Welcome to the other Paris, Monsieur Paige."

# 24 Fate

Martin sat at a table in a sterile interview room at the police station on rue des Saussaies, not far from the Champs-Élysées. A tape recorder was fixed to the wall next to the table, an old television and VCR on a cart were pushed into a corner and there was a one-way mirror at one end of the room. Martin wondered if someone was sitting on the other side, observing him and making notes about his demeanor. He decided to sit quietly, hands folded on the table and eyes fixed on the empty wall.

Martin had run every possible scenario of how Christian and David met until they were a jumble of images and ideas, none of which made any sense. The weight of Christian's betrayal was slowly settling in and it didn't feel much different than when he was waiting downstairs at Peter's house, covered in his lover's blood from trying to revive him. Martin wondered if his mind would fracture again and force him back into a mental hospital.

The idea sent fresh waves of panic through his muddled brain.

The door to the interview room opened and Arnaud entered with a uniformed female police officer. They sat across the table from Martin, while Arnaud opened a manila folder and flipped through a stack of papers inside. He turned the folder around and pushed it toward Martin. On top was a mug shot of Christian from a year ago.

"That is the top of the stack," Arnaud said. "Multiple arrests, multiple names. We believe he's the errand boy for one of the city's most sought after drug suppliers."

Martin shuffled the papers, watching Christian age backwards until he was fourteen, his first arrest, head shaved and face defiant. "What can I do?"

"He will contact you," Arnaud said.

"And then he goes to jail."

"He is a criminal, Monsieur Paige."

"Look, I'm not an idiot, Inspector. I know where I am. This is the organized crime division of the French National Police. What I want to know is what that has to do with David McLaren? Something doesn't add up here."

"There is evidence that David might have sold drugs," Arnaud said. "Recruited by Christian for his boss. David might have valuable information."

Martin closed the folder and pushed it back across the table. "Are you serious? What's your evidence?"

"Monsieur Sullivan's contact gave a statement that he had seen Christian and David together in a nightclub known to be a distribution point for drugs," Arnaud said. The female police officer handed Arnaud an accordion file.

"So it's one drug dealer's word against another? Is that all you have?"

Arnaud reached into the file and pulled out a videocassette.

"We have it on tape, too. Let's watch." He handed the tape to the officer who turned on the television and pushed the tape into the VCR.

After a moment of static, an image with a greenish hue appeared. The camera was mounted above the bar and Martin instantly spotted Christian sitting there shirtless and talking to the bartender. David entered the frame and sat down next to Christian and soon after, they were conversing. Arnaud hit the fast-forward until the two got up and left the club together.

"These images were captured last March. Monsieur McLaren, we have learned, had been in France for three weeks. We have obtained the immigration records showing David entered the country on February 25, 1997. He had been to the United Kingdom and Holland before entering France."

Martin closed his eyes and put his head back. "Is he still in France?"

"We don't know. There is no record of his departure, but that means nothing. He could have forged documents."

"I don't know how can I help you," Martin said. "You seem to know more than I do. I'd like to go home."

Arnaud sat back in his chair. "Which home is that, Martin? Your illegal home with Madame Laureux or in America?"

"I'd like to make a phone call. I want to speak to a lawyer."

"Of course, monsieur. However, I'm not sure you will be able to find a lawyer who can defend your illegal residency in France, not to mention the publishing house paying you under the table. That won't look good for Gerard or you."

"What do you want, Arnaud?"

"Christian will contact you. He will want to meet, and then we will capture him. He has answers we both want. It's a . . . how do you say it . . . a win-win situation. And for your cooperation, we will make sure your residency issue is handled with haste."

Martin shifted in his chair, looking from Arnaud to the female officer. "Let me get this perfectly clear. If I don't help you arrest Christian, you're going to have me deported?"

Arnaud stared at him, stone-faced. Martin stood up, knocking his chair backwards. It slammed loudly against the linoleum floor. Arnaud and the officer didn't flinch.

"Since I'm not charged with anything, I'm free to go," Martin said. "Right?"

"You're obstructing my investigation," Arnaud said. "If you walk out, you take your fate into your own hands."

Martin considered Arnaud's words. "I'll show myself out."

# 25 Contact

Martin, Irène, Diane and Sullivan sat in the living room at rue Rampon. The detective had spotted two unmarked police cars at either end of the street, which meant Arnaud had placed them all under surveillance. Christian would never risk coming to rue Rampon and Martin's every move would be followed.

"We need to switch focus," Martin said. "Instead of finding David, we need to find Christian before Arnaud."

"Aye," Sullivan said, shifting the cigar he was smoking to a corner of his mouth. "I'm sure they'll try to follow me as well, but I can give them the slip."

Diane rolled her eyes. "Yeah, you're a regular Houdini. You can disappear like a puff of smoke."

"You'd be surprised," he said.

"Christian took David to a club called Eureka in the Marais," Martin said. "Arnaud suggested it was prime turf for drug dealing, so maybe there's a way to get a message to Christian there. A bartender or bouncer."

"I've been there before," Sullivan said. "I might have a contact."

Irène lit another cigarette. "How long before Martin is deported? That's my only fear."

"Arnaud would have to make a report to immigration," Sullivan said. "He's not going to do that while there's still a chance Martin will lead him to Christian."

Diane started to speak, then stopped herself. She had been short with Martin and obviously had something on her mind.

"Go on, Diane," Martin said. "You've been wanting to say something all evening."

"I can't believe you'd risk being deported over this kid who has lied and stolen from you. It's crazy even for you. He makes David look like a pillar of truth and justice."

"Fuck off," Martin said. "You don't get it."

"Oh, right. Right. I never get it. We both know that's bullshit. You're trading one asshole for another."

"Please," Irène pleaded. "Let's not do this."

"I agree," Sullivan interjected. "It's counterproductive."

Diane turned to Sullivan. "Nobody asked you. Shouldn't you be out on the streets, Poirot?"

Sullivan snatched the cigar out of his mouth and shoved it toward Diane's face as if he meant to extinguish it in her eye. "I swear to Christ, woman, I'm this close to choking you to death."

Irène stood up, put her hand on Sullivan's shoulder and guided him toward the door. They went out into the hallway and Irène pulled the door closed. Martin and Diane stared at each other across the coffee table.

"I'm just gonna say one more thing," Diane said.

"Yeah, right."

"When I extricate you from this mess, I'm done. I'm officially handing off all responsibility to Irène. I can't keep doing this."

"No one is asking you to do anything. It's not like your success rate in solving my problems is anything to brag about."

"I'm here, aren't I? Still here and still helping you clean up your shit."

"Why don't you just leave then? I don't want your help."

Diane stretched and yawned, an exaggerated move that infuriated Martin even more.

"I'm serious. Get the fuck out."

"Christian must have whipped the dick on you good if you're willing to lose Irène and your home for him," Diane said. "You're not thinking smart."

"I just want the truth."

Diane snorted. "Okay, Tommy Cruise, I'll give you some truth. You've been fucked over by two guys who don't give a shit about you, but you're such a self-absorbed drama queen that you think there's some big mystery to be solved here. They're a couple of fucked up kids. One's a closet case and the other is a thief. End of story. They are never, I repeat *never*, going to make your happily ever after fantasy come true. They can't fill up the hole you have inside. Only you can do that. So stop fucking digging it deeper."

"Christian loves me. I know he does."

"Yeah, so did David until he got home. God, you're not this stupid."

"You weren't there," Martin said. "Christian is nothing like David."

"The fact that you're making up excuses for the little goon boggles my mind. Christian was probably giving David the hot beef injection and then getting his jollies slipping it to you. A little double dipping."

Martin raised his hand to slap Diane, but she caught his arm. "Let's not do something you'll regret."

Martin snatched his arm away, then stalked away to his bedroom. Diane looked up and saw Irène and Sullivan standing in the doorway watching her.

"What?" Diane spat at them.

Irène shook her head. "Nothing."

"Someone had to say it."

Sullivan shifted his cigar. "Aye, but you'll never be a diplomat."

As Sullivan expected, he was also being followed by the police, which restricted his movements and made it more difficult to touch base with his contacts. Sullivan discovered that not only was rue Rampon being watched, but the Anglophile and the publishing house were as well. Irène believed their mail was being opened before it even arrived at the apartment and the phones were tapped. But Martin was still certain a message would come.

Two weeks later, it did.

Diane was at the counter of the Anglophile trying to pretend like everything was normal. Euan had called and said he needed her to watch the store while he went to a meeting, which sounded like a lie even as he said it. Maybe Arnaud had recruited Euan to spy on them and he agreed to do it out of spite. She picked up the phone to dial Irène's apartment, then remembered that Sullivan said the phones were most likely bugged.

She tried to read a book, but found herself staring at the lines of text until they blurred, so she straightened books that didn't need to be straightened and even dusted. There were two other people in the shop; one was a woman who had been perusing nearly every shelf, and Diane was certain she was a cop. There was also a man in an ill-fitting suit who was sitting at the back of the store in one of the large leather chairs. He had a stack of books on his lap and one open on top of them.

An hour before closing time, a young woman Diane recognized from the poetry readings came into the store. Her dark hair was pulled back into a ponytail and she wore an oversized jacket over a short skirt with leggings. The boys who weren't flirting with Martin or each other were usually flirting with her. Diane was relieved to have a familiar face in the shop, and she went back to the counter and tried to relax.

The girl wandered around for nearly thirty minutes, then approached the counter with a slim volume of poetry in her hand. Diane rang up the purchase and the girl reached into her coat and pulled out a stack of green handbills and put them on the counter.

"May I leave these here?" she asked sweetly. "There is a poetry reading at the Jardin des Plantes on Thursday night," the girl said. "It's in the evening after the garden is closed at the Natural History Museum."

Diane didn't even look at the advertisements, pushing them next to the postcards and bookmarks. "No problem."

"Merci. Perhaps, you'll give one to Martin," the girl said expectantly.

Diane reached over and picked up one of the handbills, folded it in half and stuck it in her pocket. "Sure thing."

"Bonsoir," the girl winked at Diane and left the shop.

A moment later, the woman who had been loitering in the shop for hours crossed by the checkout desk and also left the shop. Diane reached into her pocket and pulled out the handbill for the poetry reading. There didn't appear to be any hidden message, but the girl had specifically told Diane to give one to Martin. Diane picked up the stack of handbills and flipped through them. They were all the same.

The man who had been sitting in the back of the shop approached with a stack of books to purchase. While Diane rang up his purchase, the man picked up one of the flyers for the poetry reading left by the girl.

"Give Inspector Arnaud my best," Diane said as she handed the man his bag of books. The man didn't respond, but stuffed the handbill into the bag and left the shop.

When Diane returned to rue Rampon, Irène, Martin and Sullivan were huddled around the coffee table. The television was on with the volume turned up too loud.

"What the fuck?" Diane asked.

Sullivan stood up, putting a finger over his lips to shush her. Since the cops couldn't get in Irène's apartment to bug it, Sullivan was taking precautions in case the cops were using listening devices from outside.

Diane sat on the floor and the others huddled close to her as she recounted the scenario with the girl and the undercover cops at the Anglophile. She pulled the handbill from her pocket and handed it to Martin.

Martin's eyes lit up. "This is a message. Christian told me Jardin des Plantes was his favorite place in Paris."

"Would he chance showing up at this poetry reading?" Sullivan asked, scanning over the handbill. "Seems very risky. Especially since the undercover cop at the Anglophile took one of these notices."

"I've never heard of a poetry reading at Jardin des Plantes," Martin said.

"It could be some kind of decoy," Sullivan suggested. "Something to throw the cops off the scent."

Diane was skeptical. "This doesn't compute."

"I'm going," Martin said. "Maybe there will be another message at the reading."

"You won't be able to move freely," Sullivan said. "Arnaud's minions will be all over you."

"I'm going with you," Irène said.

"We're all going," Diane said. "I wouldn't miss this for anything."

The next morning, Martin and Irène sat at their desks trying to edit manuscripts, but their minds wandered. Martin turned on the television and they sat on the sofa drinking wine at ten o'clock in the morning watching Hitchcock's *Vertigo* with Jimmy Stewart and Kim Novak dubbed in French. Novak's double identity and Stewart's obsession with her were not lost on Martin. Just as Novak took her swan dive off the tower at Mission San Juan Bautista, the phone rang on Irène's desk.

Gerard was on the line, telling her the courier was on his way to bring a new manuscript that needed immediate attention. Irène sighed and told him she would work as quickly as possible.

"Tell the courier he'll probably be stopped," she said. "We have police watching us like hawks. And listening in."

Less than half an hour later, the buzzer rang. The courier was a pimple-faced teenager Gerard had employed for years, who was notorious for ringing the buzzer and leaving the envelope on the street for Irène to retrieve.

"I'll go get it," Martin said, but then the buzzer rang again.

Irène went to the intercom and clicked the talk button. "Hello?"

"I have the manuscript from Monsieur Gerard," the courier's voice crackled over the tinny speaker.

"Just leave it outside the door as usual."

"Wait," Martin said. "When has that little shit ever rung the buzzer and brought up a manuscript? Buzz him in."

Irène looked at Martin and then pressed the button. "Bring it up."

Martin opened the door and heard the courier's feet slapping on the marble steps. The teen was wearing a starter jacket and a baseball cap turned backwards with a lollipop stuck in his mouth. He was balancing a fat yellow manuscript on his palm like he was a waiter carrying a serving tray.

Rather than handing the manuscript to Irène, the courier gave it to Martin. "Monsieur Gerard needs this back by eight o'clock tonight."

Martin and Irène exchanged a brief glance. "Eight o'clock doesn't give us much time," Martin said, looking for any flicker of acknowledgement from the courier.

The courier pulled the lollipop from his mouth. "He apologizes for the short notice, but he said time was of the essence."

The courier put the lollipop back in his mouth, turned on his heel and went back down the stairs two at a time, singing some rap song. They went back into the apartment and Martin ripped open the envelope. It was a manuscript, but it was one both Irène and Martin had edited months ago.

"Let me see that," Irène said.

She took the manuscript, went to her desk and put on her reading glasses. After a moment, she motioned for Martin to turn up the volume on the television. Bernard Herrmann's music blared from the set.

"Same book, different name," Irène whispered in Martin's ear and handed him the first page of the manuscript. Typed there was a single word: *Venus*.

"What does it mean?" Martin said. "This is maddening."

Irène walked over to the bookcase behind her desk. She ran her fingers along the row of oversized art books Jean-Louis had brought to the marriage, found the one she was looking for and pulled it off the shelf. A trail of dust followed and she blew on the edges of the book before opening it. Jean-Louis had taken her to Jardin des Plantes when she was still able to go out. Venus had triggered a memory, something she had seen and forgotten. She flipped through the pages until she found it.

Irène brought the book to her desk and opened it to the page she had marked with her finger. There was a color photograph of a statue surrounded by flowers in front of an ornate building. Underneath was the inscription *Venus Genetrix (1810) Charles Dupaty, Jardin des Plantes, Paris.*

Martin put his arms around Irène. "We just can't seem to get away from her."

"She is persistent," Irène agreed.

Martin looked at the mantle clock. He had exactly eight hours to figure out how to get out of the apartment unnoticed.

# 26 Escape

That afternoon, Martin and Irène went to the Anglophile, where a large crowd was gathered inside and spilling onto the street to have Margaret Atwood sign her new book of collected poems. Euan had worked all his connections to get Atwood there at Martin's suggestion, but her appearance was a perfect excuse for them to be at the bookstore and Arnaud's detectives would be hard-pressed to get close.

Diane was already at the store, looking harried behind the counter ringing up purchases of the book. Euan stood near the stairs with his hands clasped behind his back, a satisfied look on his face until he saw Martin and Irène out of the corner of his eye. His shoulders slumped and he crossed his arms over his chest. He was textbook defensive.

"Bonjour, Euan," Irène said gaily, kissing him on both cheeks.

"Good afternoon," Euan said curtly. "You missed the reading."

"We were unavoidably delayed," Martin said, trying to keep his voice neutral. "This is an amazing crowd."

"As you predicted," Euan said. "Diane's already had a book signed for you, so you don't have to wait in line."

"Actually, I need to speak with you," Martin said.

"This isn't the time."

"It might be the only time," Martin said out of the corner of his mouth. "I could be deported any day now. Diane, too."

Euan chewed on his thumbnail, his face turning red. "Come up." He marched up the stairs with Martin close on his heels.

"Don't go up," Martin said. "Let's just talk here on the stairs. They probably have it bugged up there."

"This is ridiculous," Euan said, turning to look down at him. "Is this what's getting you off now? Playing Bonnie and Clyde?"

"There's no time for this, Euan. I need your help."

"How could I possibly help you? I don't want anything to do with this. I told Arnaud everything I know in hopes he would keep his people from loitering around my store all day, but he seems to think my shop is the conduit for intrigue and secret messages."

"Well, remind me not to tell you any more secrets. You'll be up in front of a Senate committee naming names."

Euan pushed past Martin. "I'm going back downstairs."

Martin put his arm out and blocked Euan's passage. "I'm in trouble. Serious trouble," he said softly. "I didn't want to come here asking for favors, but there's no one else."

"What do you want?"

"I got a message from Christian. I have to meet him tonight, but we need a diversion."

Euan's eyes widened. "Are you seriously asking me to help you go and meet your lover?"

From the bottom of the stairs, Irène made a shhhh-ing noise

and glared at them.

"He's not my lover. Not anymore. He's a liar and he screwed me over, but he knows what happened to David."

"Who bloody cares what happened to David? You haven't spoken to him in three years. Surely, if he wanted to talk to you he would have made contact, and yet you're running after him. David and Christian are probably in this together and they are playing you for a fool."

"David came to Paris to see me."

"Why didn't he, then? Why was he with Christian?"

"That's what I have to find out."

"What could it possibly matter? You say you're not in love with Christian or David, so why not tell them both to fuck off home and get on with your life?"

Martin slammed his fist against the wall. "I just want to make sure David is alive and extricate myself from this mess so I can stay in France," he yelled. "I want a little fucking closure for once!"

Irène came up the stairs. "We need to leave."

"Let's go," Martin said. "He's not going to help."

"Wait . . . goddamn it," Euan said. "What do you want me to do?"

Martin turned back. "Are you sure?"

Euan sighed. "I guess."

"No," Martin said. "You're either all in or you're out."

"And this will be the end of it?"

"Yes," Irène interjected, before Martin could speak.

"I love you, Martin," Euan said, a catch in his voice. "God help me."

"I know," Martin said.

That night, Sullivan watched Irène's apartment from his room at the Bel Air. Martin and Irène were preparing dinner, and he watched as they set a table near the wide-open French doors. It had been a surprisingly warm day and it lingered into the early evening. Darkness was falling, but rather than turn on lights in the apartment, Irène lit candles, which turned her and Martin into silhouettes.

Sullivan glanced at his watch. It was almost half past seven and dusk was fading into night. Occasionally, the click of silverware on the plates and little snatches of conversation would drift across to him. He saw Irène stand up and disappear for a moment, then heard music. She returned and sat back down at the table. Martin picked up the bread basket from the table and stood up. He was gone for less than a minute then returned with the basket and sat back down at the table, ripping a piece of bread from the new loaf and handing a piece to Irène. The candlelight danced around them as they continued to eat.

Sullivan peered down into the street. A plainclothes policeman was staring up at Irène's apartment. The policeman saw nothing suspicious and walked back toward the unmarked car parked near the corner of Boulevard Voltaire. Sullivan looked down at his watch and then knelt down on the floor in front of the window so he could see the roofline of Irène's building. In the half light, a large shadow suddenly passed over rue Rampon, as if a bird had flown across the beam of a streetlamp. All was silent; the policeman had noticed nothing.

A few minutes later, there was a knock on Sullivan's door and Diane and Martin entered.

"He's hurt," Diane said.

Martin sat on the edge of the bed and looked down at the rip in his jeans. He pulled the torn cloth back to reveal a cut on his knee. There were also abrasions on his hands from where he had landed on the roof of the hotel.

"That might need a stitch," Sullivan said, and went into the bathroom.

"I'm okay," Martin said, breathing hard. "I thought I'd twisted my ankle, but it's okay."

Sullivan returned with a bottle of rubbing alcohol and a piece of toilet paper. Martin winced as the alcohol met his torn skin and Sullivan blotted at it roughly. Sullivan reached into his pocket and pulled out a super-sized bandage and started peeling off the wrapper.

"That's the biggest band-aid I've ever seen, " Diane said

Sullivan slapped the bandage on Martin's knee. "I get blisters."

"I bet you do."

"Stand up and walk," Sullivan ordered Martin.

Martin did so and felt just a twinge in his ankle, but adrenaline was coursing through him and he felt superhuman. "It's fine," Martin said. "It'll hurt like hell tomorrow."

Taking a running jump and leaping from the roof of the apartment to the roof of the Bel Air Hotel looked easy; Christian had done it to get inside their building. If Martin had miscalculated, he would have wound up dead in the street or clinging to the side of the building. It was a huge risk, and even during dinner, Irène had tried to talk him out of it. Martin knew he could make it and would not be moved by Irène's pleas. As he sailed across rue Rampon, Martin had kept his eye on Diane, but his foot snagged the ledge and his plan to roll into the landing had failed. He'd gone down on one knee and used his hands to stop himself pitching face forward into the roof. The fact that nothing was broken was a small miracle.

Martin went toward the window, but Sullivan grabbed his shoulder.

"Not too close," Sullivan said.

"I just want to see."

Across rue Rampon, he could see himself and Irène sitting in silhouette having dinner. He could hear snatches of Miles Davis' soundtrack for *Elevator to the Gallows*, which Irène said seemed appropriate for the occasion.

"You need to go," Sullivan said. "Are you sure you won't take a taxi?"

"I don't want to stand on République Square flailing for a taxi," Martin said. "And I don't want some cab driver trying to be a hero and turning me in for a reward later. It's safer on the metro."

Martin pulled a black Kangol hat out of his coat pocket and put it on, pulling the brim low over his eyes so his face was in shadow.

"Are we coordinated now?" Sullivan asked. "Diane's going out through the front door and walking to the liquor store, while Martin and I go out the back."

"Right," Diane said, hugging Martin before he went into the hall. "Don't wind up dead."

Sullivan raised an eyebrow. "What about me?"

Diane rolled her eyes, stood on tiptoe and kissed Sullivan's cheek. "Happy?"

Sullivan winked at her. "Nearly ecstatic."

The trio took the elevator to the lobby where the old owner of the hotel was standing behind the registration desk. Diane gave the old man a little salute as she went out onto rue Rampon and turned toward Boulevard Voltaire. The old owner looked white as a ghost and was visibly shaking, but he led Sullivan and Martin through the small breakfast room and into the kitchen. The hotel owner unbolted the door to the service entrance of the hotel and quickly closed it as Sullivan and Martin went out. The old man slumped against the door. Although he didn't know what intrigue Madame Laureux and her strange friends were up to, it was certainly illegal. He felt an odd mix of fear and excitement that he hadn't felt since his days in the Resistance.

Martin followed Sullivan down a series of passageways that connected the hotel with other buildings in the triangle of rue Rampon, Boulevard Voltaire and Avenue de la République. Sullivan had a flashlight the size of a baseball bat and Martin was worried it would arouse suspicion, but as they crossed courtyards, nothing stirred. They finally came to the end of a passageway and a large wooden door.

"When you go out this door, turn left and you'll see the square. Cross over as quickly as you can and stay along the periphery under the trees until you get to the metro entrance. Do you have your ticket?"

Martin pulled the blue stub from his pocket. "I've got it. I'm ready."

Sullivan pulled the bolt back on the door. "One day, you're going to have to tell me how you persuaded Euan to be your double tonight. I thought he wasn't speaking to you ever again."

Martin frowned. "He's in love with me."

He thought of Euan's face in the kitchen as they made the switch. Euan was as skeptical as Irène about the plan for Martin's escape, and urged him not to follow through. Euan was also afraid. One of the policemen had stopped him as he was coming into the building, questioning his return to rue Rampon.

"If they catch us, we're all going to be deported," Euan had whispered to him in the kitchen. "I cannot believe I'm doing this."

Sullivan opened the door enough for Martin to slip through onto Avenue de la République, locked it behind him and walked slowly back along the passageway. He stopped for a moment to rest, leaning up against the wall. He pulled a cigar from his pocket and stuck it in his mouth. Sullivan thought about Diane hugging him, telling him he was one of the most decent men she'd ever met. He rubbed at his cheek where she had kissed him. Somewhere along the line, Sullivan's idea of needling Diane for sport had shifted to affection.

"Shit," he muttered, finally admitting to himself that while Diane was a shrew and borderline crazy, he might be in love with her.

# 27 Venus in the Underworld

The metro was packed with people, so Martin had no trouble blending into the crowd. He stood in the corner of the car, away from the windows, but with access to exit doors on both sides and the connecting door to the next car.

At Châtelet, Martin got off the metro and switched to the RER headed south toward Mairie d'Ivry. Martin took an aisle seat, keeping his head down and avoiding eye contact with those around him. He could feel sweat rolling down his back and his cut knee throbbed underneath the tight bandage. The Jardin des Plantes had been closed for hours and Martin was still unsure how he was going to get inside once he got there.

Sullivan had ruled out simply going to Gare d'Austerlitz and walking across to the botanical garden. It was a huge station, sure to be filled with police and guards, and he would have to cross the busy traffic circle to get to the entrance to Jardin des Plantes. They finally decided he should take the RER to Place Monge and make his way through the residential area to the entrance on rue Geoffroy Saint-Hilaire. There was tall gate with spikes on top that he would surely never be able to scale, yet Martin wasn't worried. In the back of his mind, he pictured the gate open or someone there to let him—some kind of guidance. He knew he was going in unprepared, and there was no escape route should something go wrong, other than Sullivan's advice to "run like hell."

Martin got off the train at Place Monge and took the steps two at a time up to the square. The dismantled stalls for the outdoor market were skeletal in the lamplight, and Martin made sure to stay close to the buildings as he walked the few short blocks to the entrance of Jardin des Plantes.

As he crossed over rue Geoffroy Saint-Hilaire, Martin saw the botanical garden's gate was indeed closed. Martin pulled on the gate, but it wouldn't budge. He slipped his hand through the bars to see if there was a release mechanism and his fingers brushed past a heavy chain and padlock.

The intersection was too busy to try and scale the fence without someone noticing or calling the police. "Is anyone there?" Martin called through the bars, but there was no response.

Martin checked his watch and saw that he only had minutes before he was supposed to meet Christian. He walked back along rue Geoffroy Saint-Hilaire and noticed an ornate drinking fountain jutting from the stone wall. The fountain had a deep bowl and a curved cornice that went halfway up the wall. Martin leaned on the fountain hard; it was made of some heavy metal that would surely hold his weight.

Martin waited for the light to turn and the intersection to clear, then with a deft move that surprised him, he put his foot in the basin, another on top of the cornice, and vaulted himself to the top of the wall. He tried to slide under the low tree branches, but they whipped at his face and knocked his hat and glasses askew. Martin hung from his fingertips on the other side of the wall. It wasn't a far drop, but Martin winced as his hurt leg hit the ground. He crouched down to catch his breath and listen for voices or movement in the darkness that surrounded him.

The moon drifted in and out from behind clouds and Martin could see a pathway through the trees. He followed the path up a hill, remaining in the shadow of the tree line until he was standing at the entrance to the labyrinth, a yew-hedged circular pathway that led up to a wrought iron gazebo with a weather vane on top. Martin followed the pathway, the hedge making for excellent cover until he was at the top of the hill. From there, Martin could look across the entire garden and over his shoulder to see the glittering lights of the city. He had to make his way down the other side of the hill alongside the enormous old greenhouses and somehow dash across the plaza in front of the Natural History Museum. The Venus Genetrix stood on a trellised pathway that ran along the front of the Galerie de Minéralogie on the other size of the plaza.

As Martin crept alongside the massive tropical hothouse, its windows streaked with condensation, he felt dizzy with fear. The full weight of what he was doing and the possibility of deportation suddenly hit him like a ton of bricks. He trembled violently, the undulation seeming to come from the core of his body as if he were expelling a demon. He took a deep breath and stuck his head around the corner of the hothouse so he could see the plaza. Standing at the corner was a security guard. Martin froze, unable to even gasp, but the guard simply stared at him, his hand resting on his gun holster. The guard appeared to be in his late twenties, of some Middle Eastern descent with swarthy skin and a thin mustache.

"I . . . I . . . was just cutting through . . ." Martin stammered, inching backwards, prepared to run.

The guard said nothing, his face blank. He jerked his head back toward the Galerie de Minéralogie and whispered, "Dépêche-toi." Hurry up. The guard walked past Martin toward the zoo without looking back. Martin exhaled loudly then took off running across the plaza, his feet crunching in the packed gravel. The moon slipped from behind a cloud and it was almost like daybreak.

The main entrance to the mineralogy building was bisected by a long rose garden that ran the length of Jardin des Plantes. Martin turned left down the path and could see the Venus Genetrix statue, the white marble almost glowing in the dark. She looked skyward, cupping a breast in one hand while holding a horn in the other. At her feet was a globe of the world with an eagle sitting at the North Pole, poised to fly. Martin stepped off the path onto the grass and put his hand on the cold stone. "Hello," he called out softly.

"I'm here."

Martin was startled by the voice. He turned to see Christian standing underneath a wrought iron trellis just down the pathway from the statue.

"I'm sorry for all the subterfuge. Sending Madeleine to the bookshop with the handbills for the poetry reading was very risky," Christian said. His voice sounded different, harder somehow, Martin thought. "I know you must hate me now."

"I don't know who you are. Baptiste, Christian or another fake name."

"I love you," Christian said, moving from under the trellis. He was dressed in black and had let his beard and mustache grow in. "You don't believe me, I don't expect you to after . . ."

245

"No, I don't believe you. I want you to tell me where David is and then I'm gone."

"That part is easy," Christian said. "It's what comes afterward that is more complicated. I'm not the person the police make me out to be."

"All I want is information," Martin said, looking around, feeling exposed.

Christian moved to touch him, but Martin stepped back and shook his head.

"It was last winter—March. I was at the Eureka. The dealer I work for sent a message that some American kid was trying to sell on his territory and I was supposed to scare him off. That's how it began."


Christian leaned against the bar at the Eureka club. He was shirtless and his chest glistened in the strobe lights; it was a good sales tool, especially for the gay guys looking to party with what he had to sell. If the guy was hot, he might sell something else: a few minutes in a toilet cubicle or in the alley behind the club. If the guy had a lot of money, he might go home with him. His boss had issued a clear directive: sell the drugs first and your ass second. Christian rarely prostituted any more; he made enough selling cocaine, heroin and ecstasy to live without being a whore. The last couple of times he had been paid for sex, Christian felt unsettled by it. Empty. Although he'd been on the street since he was fourteen, he had never admitted that he was lonely, that maybe he wanted more.

Christian lived in a foul-smelling room at the Americana Hotel paid for by his supplier, but one of his favorite hobbies was squatting in other people's houses while they were away on vacation. He had become an expert at casing homes, getting inside and making it seem like he belonged there even if approached by suspicious neighbors. He'd squatted for nearly two months in an apartment in the Marais, reveling in the luxury, impressing people he met at the clubs with his wealth. Christian thought of calling his father in Montfermeil and asking him come to the apartment so he could slam the door in his face. Christian's father had physically thrown him out of their squalid apartment at Les Bosquets and called him a dirty little queer. Christian had sat inside a burned out car and cried, looking at the graffiti and patchwork of broken windows, and vowed he would never live there again. He would change his name, live in Paris, be free of the oppressive banlieue.

He drummed his birth name, Baptiste, out of his head while smoking heroin in alleys, while giving old, fat men oral sex in their parked cars, while teaching himself not to cry as some brutal man came inside him. A year after living on the street, he met the drug supplier who became his patron. Christian was at a club, dancing in his underwear, when the supplier came up behind him and started grinding against his ass. "We could make a lot of money together," the supplier had whispered in Christian's ear.

The supplier told Christian he was pretty and pretty boys were better salesmen, that club kids—boys and girls—would rather buy their narcotics from someone hot. He advised Christian to work on his body and not be a common whore. "No one respects a whore," the dealer said after he had sucked Christian off in the Eureka toilets. Now, the Eureka was Christian's main distribution point and, like his supplier, he didn't want anyone cutting in on sales.

Christian was leaning back against the bar, surveying the club, showing himself off, when a young guy sat down next to him. Even over the loud music and voices, Christian heard the guy order Jack Daniels and Coca-Cola with a distinct accent. Christian watched the guy belt back the drink and order another.

"Can I buy you a drink? I like your accent. Where are you from in America?"

The guy paused, looked Christian up and down uncertainly. "I'm . . . uhhh . . . Tennessee. Memphis."

"Are you visiting Paris or are you a student?" Christian asked, leaning in closer. He wanted to see if the guy would pull away. He did not.

"Visiting," the guy said. "Unfinished business."

"I'm Christian."

"I'm David."

Christian kept the drinks coming, kept getting closer to David, who became drunk very quickly. "What's your unfinished business?"

"It's a long story," David slurred in his ear. "You don't want to hear it."

"Of course I do," Christian said, resting his hand on David's thigh.

David leaned in and said loudly. "I'm not gay."

Christian grinned. "Then why are you in a gay club?"

"I was . . . uhhh . . ."

"Selling drugs?"

David pulled away. "Who told you that?"

"Word gets around. A friend said a really cute American guy was selling at Eureka. I was hoping I might run into you."

"I'm not a drug dealer, dude," David said. "I just need to make a little money to get back home."

"Come with me." Christian stood up and took David by the hand. David pulled his hand away and stared at Christian, but then slid off the barstool and followed him into the dark recesses of the club.

The toilet was fetid and filled with men jockeying for position around the sink, waiting for a stall to open up, and some were engaging in various sex acts in the open while others watched. Christian pushed his way through the sweaty bodies, pulling David along behind him. At the last stall, Christian knocked loudly and a voice from behind the door yelled, "Fuck off." Christian reached up and grabbed the top of the stall and pulled himself up, his biceps and abs flexing so that many of the men in the toilet stopped to watch.

Inside the stall were two teenagers awkwardly trying to fuck over the dirty commode. "Get out," Christian said. The boys looked up, saw Christian and hurriedly started pulling up their jeans. They fled the toilet still trying to get dressed; the other men in the bathroom laughed as they made a hasty exit. "Step into my office," Christian smirked and grabbed David by the shirt and pulled him into the stall.

"Hey, I said I'm not into this," David stammered. "I mean it's cool, but I . . ."

"I didn't bring you here to fuck. Show me what you have to sell."

"Oh," David said. "Oh, right." He fished into his pocket and produced a couple of small baggies filled with cocaine. "This is all I've got left."

Christian took the baggies and weighed them in his hands; he'd become an expert at that, too. "Look, I'm going to do you a favor and take this off your hands for a fair price, and then I'm going to give you some friendly advice." Christian slipped the baggies into his shorts and pulled out a roll of bills in a rubberband. His shorts were low on his hips and he wasn't wearing any underwear, and he noticed David's eyes were having trouble focusing above his waistline.

Christian counted out the bills and handed them to David.

"That should be almost enough to buy a one-way ticket. And I suggest you buy it and get out of here. You've been selling on someone else's territory and they aren't happy about it."

Fear flashed across David's face. "Man, I didn't know. I just . . . I was just trying to get some money so I could go home."

"It's okay," Christian said, putting his hand on David's chest. "I believe you."

David was hot and Christian didn't believe he was straight, so he moved closer, backing David against the stall. The din of the music and voices swirled over their heads. Christian pushed his body against David, moved in to kiss him. David's eyes were wide, but he didn't move and he let Christian kiss him gently on each cheek and his neck. Christian was hard in his shorts; he groped David and found him erect, too. Christian started to kiss David's mouth, but David turned his head away.

"I don't wanna do this," David said.

"You're very hard," Christian said.

"My dick always gets me trouble," David said as he retreated to a corner of the stall.

"Why do you say you're not gay?"

"I've fucked around with guys . . . well, with one guy. I mean, when I drink I get horny and I wind up doing stuff I wouldn't normally do. That's why I'm in Paris. I met this guy a few years ago and things got out of hand."

"How do you mean?"

"Meaning I thought I was in love with this guy. I was in a weird place mentally and I led him on. I was a total asshole and he didn't deserve it. I came here to apologize. To explain. That's my unfinished business."

"You came all the way from America to tell this guy you aren't in love with him?" Christian asked skeptically. "Why didn't you just write him a letter?"

"It's complicated. Like I said, a long story."

"So how did he take it? The guy you came to see?"

"I never saw him . . ." David's voice trailed off.

"You couldn't find him?"

"No, I know where he is, but there never seemed to be a right time and I started feeling stupid." David looked at Christian. "Why the hell am I telling you this? Thanks for your help, but I need to get out of here."

Christian reached down and flipped back the bolt mechanism and the stall door sprang open. "Thanks," David mumbled and he slipped out.

There were catcalls from some of the men as David pushed through the men crowded into the toilet. "There's another one Christian has made walk funny with his giant cock," one of the men said, grabbing at David's ass.

"Get your fucking hands off me, faggot," David yelled.

There was an outcry from the men, who yelled obscenities at David and started to surround him. Christian moved quickly through the crowd to diffuse the situation. He grabbed David around the waist and started pulling him toward the door. "Leave him alone, boys, he's drunk and new at the game," Christian yelled.

Christian grabbed David by the back of the neck and threw him toward the door. "Keep quiet or I won't be able to get you out of here in one piece," Christian hissed in David's ear.

Once they were on the sidewalk, Christian pulled a hoodie over his head he had picked up at coat check, while David tucked his shirt back in his jeans, still muttering obscenities under his breath. David was indeed very drunk and he staggered on the street.

"Where are you going?" Christian asked.

"I gotta get my stuff," David said, "then I'm getting the fuck

251

out of here."

"What about your friend? You're going to leave without seeing him?"

"Yeah. He'll be okay. He's got someone else now. I'd just screw things up."

"Why don't you get your things and stay at my place tonight?" Christian asked.

David shook his head. "I don't take it up the ass."

Christian laughed. "I can be a gentleman. You can sleep in the guest room." Christian was squatting at a luxurious townhouse near Luxembourg Gardens and there were rooms to spare. The owners were due home in a few days, so Christian knew he would be moving back to the hotel until he could find another empty house. "Where are your bags?"

"In a locker at Gare du Nord."

"Let's go get them."

"Do you have anything to drink at your house?"

"Everything."

They took a cab to the train station and Christian waited while David went inside. He was gone for nearly twenty minutes, then came out carrying a duffle bag in one hand and a backpack haphazardly slung over his shoulder. "I couldn't find the right locker," David said as he fell into the cab.

Christian had decided in the cab that he was going to fuck the American. It would be a personal challenge to get this uptight boy to give in and surrender himself. A few more drinks and David would be begging for it.

At the townhouse, David sat on the sofa in the living room and stared at the plush surroundings. "Are you rich?" he asked as Christian handed him another Jack and Coke, heavy on the whiskey. "How old are you?"

"I'm almost nineteen," Christian said, sitting on the sofa

next to David. Close but not too close.

"So this is your parents' house?"

"No one's here," Christian said.

"I saw all that money you had in your pocket."

"I usually have a lot of money on me. People buy their drugs with cash."

A lightbulb suddenly went off in David's head. "Oh, man, I had no idea I was selling on your turf."

"That is behind us now."

"Cool," David said and took a big swig from his glass.

Christian moved a little closer to David. "Tell me more about this guy you came to see. It sounds fascinating."

David was silent for a moment. He stared into space, the drink resting on his lap. "I fucked up. I told him I was in love with him because I thought I was. I had convinced myself I was. We had sex. A lot of sex."

"But you're not gay."

"Yeah . . . I mean . . . sex with Martin was better than any bitch I'd ever fucked. We did stuff a girl wouldn't even think about doing. It was hot. He was kinda like a girl, I guess."

"Why didn't you stay with him?"

"I couldn't do that. My parents went ape shit. They're really religious and conservative and when they found out I'd been fucking Martin, it was . . . bad. A nightmare. I told them it was just because I was drinking, so they sent me to rehab. My dad said if I didn't go, he was throwing me out and would never speak to me again. He sent me to this place where the shrinks said they could cure me of wanting to fuck dudes. Man, that was fucked up."

"I don't understand," Christian said, recoiling a bit. "They said they could cure you of being a homosexual?"

"Yeah . . . can I have another drink?" Christian brought the bottle back to the couch and handed it to David, who swigged the whiskey directly from the bottle. The more he drank, the more he talked. "I was at this rehab place for months and then they said I was cured, so I went home and got a job working at a car wash. I had gone to college for a while and my grades were total shit, but I was going back. Then I got a letter from Martin a couple of months ago saying he still loved me, but was moving on with his life."

Christian's seduction plan fell by the wayside as he listened to David's story. He felt an unexpected empathy with David as he realized their lives had been similar in a way.

"If you're in love with this Martin, you should go and tell him," Christian said.

"I can't . . ." David was starting to slip into unconsciousness, the almost empty bottle of Jack Daniels resting between his legs.

"Why not?"

"I can't be gay."

David's eyes finally closed and he slumped into the corner of the sofa. Christian took the bottle and put it on the coffee table and then moved David so he was lying on his side on the sofa. The last thing Christian needed was for this sad, closeted boy to choke on his vomit and die in the townhouse.

Christian was going upstairs to bed, then noticed David's bags sitting by the front door. He quietly picked up the bags and took them across the hallway into the library. He went through the backpack first, but found nothing of interest or value except reeking clothes. The duffel bag was filled with clean but rumpled clothing, and he found a plastic wallet with one travelers' check and David's passport inside. He opened up the blue booklet: David McLaren, Memphis, Tennessee, United States of America. The passport had been issued in 1995 and the photo showed a grinning, cocky boy without a care in the world.

In any other circumstance, Christian would have pocketed the passport instantly; they were worth a fortune on the black market. He rarely had a conscience when it came to lifting people's belongings, but he felt a wave of pity for David, and stuffed the wallet back into the bag. He dug to the bottom of the duffel bag and his fingertips brushed what felt like a book. Christian pulled out a leather notebook and flipped it open. There were pockets on either side and both were filled with sheets of paper that appeared to have poetry written on them. Christian sat down at the ornate, mahogany desk in the library and started to read.

What would you do for this moment
I place in your hand?
A penny or a pound,
you must set its worth.

There was no signature and Christian flipped through the poems until he found what appeared to be a cover page: *What Remains* by Martin Paige. Christian sat at the desk reading Martin's poems until he realized that the room was full of light; morning had come. He also realized that his cheeks were wet, that he had been crying over the outpouring of love and heartbreak that David had visited on Martin. The words stirred up emotions he had suppressed since his father had thrown him out. There was a wave of longing to connect with someone who was full of passion, who would love him unconditionally, who wasn't afraid of being out and open. Christian wanted someone to guide him in a different direction because he was beginning to wonder if the rest of his life was going to be spent squatting in other people's houses, selling drugs and thoughtlessly fucking strangers.

Christian thought of his mother who had died of cancer when they were still living in Belgium. She was a teacher and had passed on her love of literature and art, encouraged her son's curious nature. Christian's father managed a market and was a quiet presence in their house, but after his mother died, his father changed. He drank too much and stupidly agreed to invest in a business scheme with Rwandan cousins in France. The business went belly up in a matter of months and they wound up living in Les Bosquets. His father did odd jobs but the alcohol, the lingering grief over his wife's death and their descent into poverty had turned him into an angry religious zealot. Christian was caught having sex with a boy in an empty flat and when word got back to his father, there was a terrible fight and his father beat him. Christian, bleeding from the nose and his face bruised, had gone to the boy's apartment down the road. They had talked about running away together to Paris or the south of France. "We have to go," Christian said. "There's nothing to keep us here." But the boy said he could not leave his family. Christian was on his own.

Christian stifled the sob that rose in his throat. He closed the pocket doors to the library, leaned heavily against them until he gained control again. Then he took the duffel bag and backpack and put them next to the door, but the notebook full of poems he stashed in the desk. David did not deserve those beautiful words.

David woke up, still intoxicated. He sat up on the couch, clutching his head. "Oh, fuck," he said. "Where's the bathroom?"

Christian pointed him down the hall and then went into the kitchen where he grabbed several bottles of beer from the refrigerator and brought them back to the living room. When David returned, he shoved one in his hand. "What do they say about the morning after drinking . . . hair of the dog?"

"Exactly," David said, opening the bottle and taking a long swig.

"What are you going to do now?"

"Go home, I guess," David said, flopping back on the couch. "I just want to disappear for awhile. But you need money for that."

Christian chewed on his thumbnail for a bit. He had several schemes at once going through his head. If he wanted to drop out of the game, he needed a new identity. If David wanted to return to America anonymously, so did he. "Would you be willing to trade passports?" Christian asked.

David laughed. "Funny. Even a blind man could tell we look nothing alike. What are you, anyway? Part black and what else?"

"Rwandan and Belgian. I have a friend who could get you a new passport. You give me yours and I'll pay to have the new one made."

"Why would you do that?" David asked suspiciously.

"Because in my line of work, you always need an escape route."

"Okay, but I'm still not going to have any money."

"Call your parents and tell them you're coming home, but you need some money and have them wire it to you in Paris."

"They won't do it. They are probably so pissed. My mom is probably going crazy."

"Trust me," Christian said, leaning forward. "If you cry a little and tell them you love them and that you will change and be a better person, they will trip over themselves to get to the bank."

David was quiet. "Dude, no offense, but you kinda scare me."

"None taken. I'm a businessman offering a business transaction.

You need a solution and I have it."

They went to a phone box in the middle of Paris, across the street from a Western Union office, and David called home. "Sorry, Mom, I know it's early. I know. I know. I'm okay, really. I'm ready to come home, but I need money. I'm at a Western Union office in Paris." He gave her the address three times to make sure she had it down. "Yeah, maybe a couple thousand. I gotta pay off the hotel and then the flight will be expensive. I love you, too, Mom. No, don't put Dad on. I don't wanna get in a fight with him. I'll try to get a flight out today. If not, then tomorrow for sure. Yeah, I know I was stupid. I know. Okay, this phone card is about to run out. I'll see you soon. Okay, bye."

David pulled the card out of the slot and disconnected the call.

"I told you they would send the money," Christian said.

They sat in a small café near the Western Union office for more than two hours, nursing cups of coffee. When the money came through, Christian said it was time for the next stop.

"You used your passport to collect the money, now you don't need it anymore. We'll go to my friend's apartment. We'll need new photos and he'll need time to work on the passports. We can take the metro. It's just a short walk from Place de la République."

David stopped short. "République Square?"

"Yes, it's not far."

"I know where it is. Martin lives near there on rue Rampon."

Christian had been on rue Rampon. There was a hotel, but he couldn't remember the name. He'd had sex with a man old enough to be his grandfather there. "What's the hotel on rue Rampon . . . I can't remember?"

"The Bel Air." David had gone pale. "Martin lives across the street."

"It's a small world. My friend lives over a shop on Boulevard Voltaire just past rue Rampon."

"Can't your guy use my old passport photo? I could just hang out here."

"You'll need a new one and you'll need to sign it before it's laminated. Come on."

David hesitated. "I'm not so sure about this now."

Christian put his arm around David's shoulder and steered him toward the metro station. "You're about to start a whole new life. Be happy."

As they walked down Boulevard Voltaire from the Place de la République metro station, David wanted to cross to the other side of the street before they got to the intersection of rue Rampon.

"No one will see us because no one is looking for us," Christian said.

They came to the intersection and David quickly looked to his left and dashed across to the other side. Christian, on the other hand, stopped in the middle of the street.

"Dude, come on," David said. "What are you doing?"

"Which apartment is it?"

"It doesn't matter. Come on."

"Is it the one with the balcony full of plants?" Christian asked, but he already knew that was it. Martin had mentioned it in one of the poems.

There was a car parked in front of the building with its emergency lights blinking. The door to the building opened and a man in his thirties with curly hair and carrying a stack of books under his arms stepped into the street.

"Oh, fuck," David said. "That's Martin's boyfriend. We gotta move."

David took off running down the street, but Christian was rooted to the spot. The man was already in his car when the apartment door opened again and a young man stepped out. He was blonde, wore glasses and a black coat that was fitted at the waist and came down nearly to his knees. The young man handed a book through the window and leaned down. They pecked lips and then the car accelerated toward Boulevard Voltaire. Christian stepped out of the street, but the man behind the wheel braked hard and mouthed obscenities at Christian as he turned toward Place de la République.

Christian stood under the awning of the brasserie on the corner and peered around the building. Martin was still standing on the sidewalk, talking to what appeared to be the owner of the tobacco shop across the street from the apartment building. He handed Martin several packets of cigarettes and a silver bucket appeared from above their heads. Martin and the tobacconist looked up. There was a grand looking woman standing on the balcony; she had lowered down money in the bucket. Their conversation was indistinct over the traffic, but Christian was only looking at Martin.

Christian jumped when he felt a hand on his shoulder. David was standing behind him.

"What the fuck are you doing?" David demanded.

"Martin is standing right there," Christian said.

"This is fucked up, man. Let's go."

"How can you . . ." Christian's voice faltered. "How can you not want to see him?"

"I do want to see him, but if he sees me it will fuck everything up."

Christian watched Martin go back inside the apartment. "I am sorry for you. Martin is beautiful."

"I can't be what he wants me to be," David said, his voice

260

flat. "Can we go?"

At Christian's friend's apartment—which was dark and cluttered with boxes and stacks of paper—the process of making the passport was extremely fast. The man was tall and black, wore loose fitting clothes and said very little, but when he did, it was with a heavy accent from some African nation. The Belgian passport David was receiving was a real one, a blank stolen from some government office. The man took David's picture with an Instamatic camera, typed information onto the blank page and, in less than an hour, David was officially Thomas Jannsens. David looked at the passport in awe.

"Now yours," Christian said, holding out his hand.

David scrounged in his duffel bag, pulled out his passport and tentatively handed it over to Christian. The forger held the passport up to a lighted magnifying glass. "I don't need it right away. I'll check back in a few days," Christian said to the man, then leaned over and kissed him on the cheek. The forger smiled.

"How do you know him?" David asked once they were back on the street.

"He's Rwandan, like me. He's in exile."

"What did he do?"

"He is Tutsi. He escaped the genocide. Do you not watch the news?"

"I guess not."

"You're an American. Things that happen in distant places don't matter very much. It is the same in France."

They took the metro back to Gare du Nord and David looked up at the departure board. "I could go anywhere, I guess. Maybe I won't go back to America."

"The passport is good," Christian reassured him. "You won't get caught. But I wouldn't come back to France. Ever."

David stared at him but said nothing. After a moment, he

stuck out his hand. "Thanks for your help."

"You helped me as well. More than you know. I hope you find happiness, Thomas."

"Why did you call me Thomas?"

"Because it's your new name. You need to memorize the information on that passport in case you're ever quizzed. And you need to learn to respond to Thomas Jannsens."

"Does that mean you're David McLaren now?"

"Not yet. But maybe one day when I need to find happiness."

David turned and walked into the throng of people in the terminal at Gare du Nord. Christian never saw him again.

Martin had stood listening impassively to Christian, his arms folded across his chest. He realized he was incredibly cold, actually shivering. The story Christian told was not what he had expected, and while parts of it rang true, he couldn't be sure. Some of it sounded too pat, too rehearsed. Martin realized he would probably never know the complete truth; this story would have to suffice.

"So David is alive and well and hiding somewhere—that's what you're telling me?" Martin asked.

"I don't know. I can only tell you what he told me, that he wanted to disappear, start again."

"I have to go," Martin said.

"Wait! I want to tell you the rest. What happened afterwards. One day, I followed you from rue Rampon to the Anglophile. I heard you read your poetry, started talking to you after the open mic. I couldn't understand how David could so easily walk away from you if he really was in love with you. I knew you weren't in love with Euan. I started watching the apartment and I would see you go out at night. I followed you a few times, and

262

I knew you were going to fuck other guys. I knew you were waiting for David to come back, and I thought I could replace him. I had his passport and your poems. I know it sounds crazy."

"Sounds crazy is the understatement of the century," Martin said. "How about total fucking insanity? And then you robbed our apartment."

"I didn't plan to steal anything, I just wanted to see where you lived. I got a little drunk, and then I thought your neighbors had called the police. I was out of my head for a bit. I sold off the last of what I had while I stayed in your apartment and then I dropped out of the game. I started looking for an empty house and, just by luck, I saw the people packing up to leave the house in Montmarte. They had trunks and bags and I knew they were going to be gone for a long time. It felt like divine intervention, like it was supposed to happen. I had Irène's computer and I found you online and you came to my door. And after that first night I knew for sure what I still know: I'm in love with you."

"Do you realize how many people are after you? Arnaud, Interpol, probably the FBI."

"They don't want me. They want the boss."

"Turn yourself in, then. If you give up this boss, Arnaud will wipe the slate of the burglaries and everything else. You can ask for immunity."

"I wouldn't be able to stay in France."

"Arnaud is threatening to have me and Diane deported, and I won't let that happen."

"So you would turn me in?"

"I've told Arnaud nothing. I wanted to hear your side of the story first, but I can't leave Irène. I didn't want to be in the middle of this, but you put me there."

"I know. I just want to be with you."

Christian was standing very close to Martin, looking down

at him. Martin refused to meet his eyes, knew that if he did, he would be taken in again.

"Christian, we're not going to be together. You can't expect me to just pretend none of this ever happened and we can just go back to the way things were. You can't expect me to trust you."

"I wanted to be better, you made me better. I never wanted anything so badly. After everything I'd seen and done, I didn't think it was possible to fall in love with someone. Please believe me. I do love you."

"If you really love me, then tell Arnaud what he wants to know. You can't keep running like this because they'll catch you eventually. Arnaud won't let this go, neither will David's parents."

Christian pulled Martin into his arms, but Martin pushed him away. "No, stop it. Goddamn it! I love you, but I can't forget that you lied. That everything has been a story you've immersed me in. The way you used David to get close to me is . . . it's sick."

"David is a coward," Christian said. "You know that. When my father threw me out, I could have begged to come home and changed to please him, but I never did that. I could not. I would have rather died. If David loved you, he would have done the same."

Martin walked away, back to the Venus Genetrix glowing in the moonlight. He walked around the statue, following her gaze up to the night sky full of dimly twinkling stars. Christian stood on the path watching him.

"Why did you want to meet here?" Martin asked.

"I know Venus means something to you. I read the poem you wrote to Irène about seeing the Venus de Milo in the Louvre. Since we couldn't meet there, I thought . . ." Christian's voice trailed off.

"The Venus Genetrix is the goddess of peace and domesticity. Did you know that?"

Christian shook his head. "But it's what I wanted with you. Don't you see? It's synchronicity. You said that nothing happens by chance, that if we listen closely, a pattern emerges in the chaos. I started listening and the message led me to you."

Martin walked back to Christian and held out his hand. "Let's go to Arnaud."

# 28 Exile

Martin sat in Arnaud's office sipping coffee. He was beyond exhausted. He had spent eight hours in an interrogation room with Christian as the inspector, other officers, Interpol agents and a stream of men in suits came to listen to Christian tell the same story over and over again. Arnaud asked him the same questions five different ways, but Christian never wavered from his answer. He admitted breaking into the apartment and robbing the tobacconist, and repeated the story about David almost word for word, but Arnaud quickly moved on to the real reason he wanted Christian—the drug syndicate.

Christian gave the name of his supplier, other dealers, where he picked up the drugs, where he sold them, how much money he made, how much he was allowed to keep. Christian refused to look at Arnaud, but instead told it all to Martin, as if he was confessing his sins once and for all. The only time he met Arnaud's gaze was when he asked for immunity from prosecution.

Martin heard the door to Arnaud's office open and the inspector came around and sat down at his desk with a stack of folders in his hand. He shuffled through them and pushed one across the desk to Martin.

"What is that?"

"See for yourself," Arnaud said, busying himself with the other paperwork.

Martin picked up the folder and opened it. Inside was a security camera photo of David at customs. It was marked Miami. The photo was stapled to a sheet of paper that appeared to be a photo of the interior of a Belgian passport issued to Thomas Jannsens.

"Belgian passports are easy to fake. Blank ones are stolen from embassies around the country and sold on the black market. Jannsens is the most common name in Belgium," Arnaud said. "Like Smith or Jones in America."

"So Christian is telling the truth."

"About this, yes. We are making inquiries now about the other information he has provided."

"But you're giving him immunity."

"You watched as I signed the paper."

"Yes," Martin nodded, but there was a tone of uncertainty. "What about David?"

"That matter has been turned over to the FBI. If they pursue, it's felony forgery, fraud and counterfeiting, all highly illegal."

"And you don't give a shit, do you?"

"It's out of my hands."

"And what about immunity for me and Diane?"

"Immunity from what? You've broken no laws, at least that is what you both say," Arnaud said.

"I trust immigration won't be knocking on our doors then."

Arnaud shrugged. "Who can say? No reports have been made to my office about residency status, so I have no reason to pursue it."

"Can I go now?"

"Of course. Your friends are taking up space in our waiting room and poor Madame Laureux has smoked two packs of cigarettes until the entire lower floor smells like a cafe."

"Good," Martin said sarcastically, standing up.

"One more thing." Arnaud leaned back in his chair and put his feet up on the desk. "I admire you, Monsieur Paige."

"Oh, really?"

"Oui, yes. You may not believe it, but when we discovered that you had slipped away from the apartment, I laughed out loud. It was a bold move. I am also glad you were smart and convinced Christian to turn himself in. I know it seems unfair, but the information he has provided will save lives and take drugs off the streets not only in Paris but all of France."

"And you'll get a promotion. Everybody wins, except Christian."

"Be reasonable, Martin. The boy grew up in one of the worst situations imaginable and this will give him the opportunity to start a new life without having to worry about a home, food or money. For someone like him, it is like winning the lotto."

"I hope we never meet again, Inspector," Martin said, walking out of the office and slamming the door behind him.


Martin stood in the departure hall at Gare de l'Est, an overnight bag slung over his shoulder and hands shoved deep in his pockets. It was just past evening rush hour and passengers hurried around him making their connections.

Through the crowd, Martin saw Christian coming toward

him flanked by two other men, who were obviously plainclothes policemen. They stuck out like sore thumbs, Martin thought, stiff and shifty-eyed. Christian was clean-shaven, wore baggy jeans and a hoodie to help obscure his face.

Christian leaned down and kissed Martin awkwardly on the cheek. "Thank you for this," he said and Martin could barely muster a smile.

"I'm Coutard," one of the officers said. "I'll be accompanying you to Berlin."

They were taking an overnight train from Paris to Berlin, where Christian would begin his new life under an assumed name. Arnaud didn't think Berlin was far enough away, had suggested South Africa or even America, but Christian refused to leave Europe. For turning over evidence, France had essentially set up Christian for life. He would have a free place to live and money would be deposited into an account in perpetuity. To blend in, Christian would be required to enroll in school or take a low-key job. Any evidence of criminal activity would mean immediate extradition back to France. And while it sounded like the opportunity of a lifetime, Christian would forever be looking over his shoulder, even when the drug syndicate was busted.

Martin and Christian settled into their seats. Coutard and the other policeman were standing at one end of the car talking quietly. After a moment, they shook hands and the other one left. Coutard came down the aisle and took a seat behind Martin and Christian.

"If you need the toilet, food or even to stretch, I have to go with you," Coutard said. "Lucas is in my care until I hand him over in Berlin."

Martin looked at Christian. "Is that the name you chose? Lucas?"

"Yes. It's an easy, ordinary name to remember," he said with sadness in his voice.

The train shuddered and began to move out of the station. The other officer was still standing on the platform and waved as the car moved past.

"We're clear now," Coutard said. "Let's go."

"Go where?" Martin asked.

"We have a compartment. It's been thoroughly checked."

There were bunk beds on each side of the tiny compartment and metal ladders to access the top berths. Coutard flipped a switch and weak light filled the compartment. He pulled the curtain over the window and climbed to one of the top bunks, stretched out and pulled a paperback book from his coat pocket.

Martin and Christian sat down uncertainly on the lower bunk underneath Coutard. Christian unzipped his hoodie to reveal a fresh crew cut, which made his startling features and eyes even more noticeable. Without thinking, Martin reached out and ran his hand over the soft bristle of Christian's remaining hair. Martin caught himself and pulled his hand away.

"It's okay," Christian said softly. "I don't mind."

"It's not okay," Martin said, sliding off the bunk. "I'll sleep over there."

"Can't we talk a bit?"

"What else is there to say? We're never going to see each other again after tonight." It suddenly struck home how true that was, and Martin felt his throat tighten.

"I did what you asked. I'm going into exile for you. Not for any other reason. I could have run away without telling the police anything, but then I knew for sure I'd never see you again. This way, there's a chance."

They sat quietly, feeling the sway of the train, the clacking sound of the wheels on the tracks. Eventually, they heard Coutard softly snoring above them.

Martin broke the silence. "I'd give anything to be with you back at Avenue Junot. I felt so happy and safe there." Christian leaned in to kiss Martin, who pulled away. "Let's just talk. Like we used to afterwards."

Martin stretched out on the bunk on his back and Christian lay on his side looking down at him and tentatively rested a hand on Martin's chest.

"What do you want to talk about?" Christian asked.

Martin was distracted by Christian's hand on him, the rise and fall of his own breathing. He thought about Irène and rue Rampon. "Did David tell you how to get into the apartment?"

"No, you did."

"I did? When?"

"In one of the poems you wrote to David. There was a line about how the attic ceiling looked like an eclipse and you rose through it like a ghost until you were floating over the chimneys. Besides, most buildings like yours have access to the roof."

"I guess you would know that."

Christian ignored the implication in Martin's comment. "I've read your poems almost every day, so I could recite them backwards and forwards."

"Why didn't you just talk to me and tell me how you felt?"

"Because you were with Euan. When I saw you at the Anglophile, you were always distant because Euan was watching you. When I figured out you didn't love him and you were meeting guys for sex in the chat rooms, I knew I had a chance. I should have said something, but I liked the idea of meeting you online. It was hot. I had it all planned out in my head. You showing up at Avenue Junot, making love to you, making you fall in love with me. It was a silly game; I realize that now."

Martin sighed deeply. "And I fell for it."

"I was going to get an apartment and a job . . . a real job. Maybe go to school. The life I've been living was not supposed to happen. When my mother died, it was like time splintered. I promised myself that I would stop dealing and get off the streets. I robbed the tobacconist on rue Rampon to pay back the rest of the money I owed to my supplier. When I came out of the shop and Irène yelled David's name, it stopped me cold in the street. It was like she'd called my name. I had David's passport in my pocket."

Martin shook his head in disbelief. "Did it work? Did you pay off your supplier?"

"Yes, and then I disappeared. I became David. I found the house on Avenue Junot and stopped going to Eureka and the other places I used to sell. I disappeared just like I had planned. And then the people who owned the house came home early."

It seemed inconceivable to Martin that he would never see Christian again. Would never get to find out if he was serious about changing his life so they could be together. Christian would get off the train in Berlin, disappear into the crowd, become someone else and Martin would take the next train back to Paris. How long would it take for things to return to "normal" with Irène at rue Rampon? What would Euan do? And Diane?

Christian fell asleep; the exhaustion finally caught up with him. Martin was beyond exhausted. He hadn't slept in at least thirty-six hours and his body ached. Tears leaked from the corners of his eyes and he didn't bother to wipe them away. He listened to the steady rise and fall of Christian's breathing. Martin slid out of the berth and moved toward the door, quietly opening it.

"To the bathroom and back, quickly," Coutard whispered from the darkness.

"Right," Martin mumbled.

Martin walked along the corridor toward the end of the car where the toilets were located. Ahead of him, a compartment door opened and Diane poked her head into the corridor. Martin was startled by her sudden appearance on the train.

"What the fuck are you doing?" Martin asked.

"Shhhh," Diane said, coming out of the compartment and closing the door.

"Who's in there with you?"

"Sullivan."

Martin held up his hands in mock surrender. "I don't even want to know."

"I'm not fucking him. We're just keeping an eye on you at Irène's request. And mine."

"We have a police escort and I'm coming back to Paris tomorrow."

"But I'm not."

Martin was dumbfounded. "Where are you going?"

"I made a promise to my dad that I'd go to his village. Sullivan's going with me as my bodyguard. Want me to hum a few bars of 'I Will Always Love You'?"

"When are you coming back?"

"Not sure. But you know me. I always turn up like a bad penny. Now go piss before that cop comes looking for you."

Diane kissed Martin on the lips, pinched his cheek and opened the compartment door. Martin caught a glimpse of Sullivan stretched out asleep on the bed. It wasn't until he was back in his own compartment, his head resting on Christian's shoulder, that he realized Diane and Sullivan were sharing a single berth.

# 29 White Queen

Irène sat on the sofa staring into the darkness, a glass of red wine in her hand and a nearly empty bottle on the coffee table. It was past two in the morning and her sadness had turned to numbness. The idea of things ever being peaceful and settled on rue Rampon seemed impossible. She worried about Martin's state of mind and how the upheaval of the last few weeks would affect him emotionally. Christian was banished, David disappeared and any chance of a relationship with Euan was gone. Irène did not want Martin to return to trolling for strangers on the Internet, filling the empty space in his heart with empty sex. But he was right; she had done the same all those years she was trapped in the apartment. There was a string of one-night stands, and less, from men staying at the Bel Air who had caught her spying from the balcony. Anything to fill the loneliness left after Jean-Louis' death.

The apartment was silent; the noise from the

street seemed muted and far away. Pierre was asleep next to her on the sofa, his tail occasionally slashing the air as he dreamed. Irène desperately wanted to sleep, but knew another nightmare would come: Jean-Louis bleeding in her arms, the strange house near the mountains and the giant Venus looming over her as some unknown assailant grabbed her from behind. It was like puzzle pieces spread across a table and she couldn't make the notches fit correctly. She felt wrung out by both her waking and sleeping life, so maybe floating in a drunken daze was the best she could do.

Sometime after three, Irène began to doze, her chin resting on her chest. Distantly, she heard tires screech on the pavement as a car made a sharp turn onto rue Rampon. The car raced down the narrow street and then came to a stop with another screech, but by then Irène was breathing heavily, her sleeping mind transitioning into another dream.

*Irène is standing on the balcony when her red convertible comes racing down rue Rampon and pulls up in front of the hotel. The top is down and Jean-Louis looks young and handsome behind the wheel. Without opening the door, he vaults over the side of the car and stands on the street grinning up at Irène, his arms spread wide like a game show host presenting her with a prize. Irène runs back into the apartment. She flings open the door and takes the steps two at a time until she's in the lobby. When she opens the door to the street, rue Rampon has disappeared and she is standing in a room at Salpêtrière Hospital. A man is standing at the window in silhouette, but it is not Jean-Louis.*

*Do you remember 1968? the man asks.*

*Who are you? Irène asks.*

*The all-seeing I.*

*The man turns and she sees that it is Frederick. He advances toward her and Irène screams, but no sound comes out of her mouth. She tries to push the door closed, but Frederick holds it fast. Irène realizes she is once again in the lobby of her building on rue Rampon. She turns and looks back into the mirror over the credenza and sees Martin's reflection there. She puts her hand against the mirror and Martin does the same.*

*It's for you, Frederick says still standing at the door, and she hears a telephone ring. Irène looks down and there is an old-fashioned telephone sitting on the table. It rings loudly, urgently, the volume increasing until Irène clamps her hands over her ears. She looks into the mirror and sees Martin there, holding a cell phone to his ear. Irène snatches up the receiver, but the phone continues to ring.*

*Hello? Martin? Is it you?*

*A voice crackles down the line, as if it's coming from somewhere far away. She feels a tap on her shoulder, and Frederick is standing there with a telephone receiver in his hand, the cord coiled and dangling by his side, connected to nothing.*

*Frederick hands her the receiver and says, It's a poor sort of memory that only works backwards. Now wake up and answer the phone.*


Irène bolted awake and nearly tripped over the coffee table to answer the telephone ringing on her desk.

"Martin? Is it you? I've just had the strangest dream."

"No, madame, it is V. Hugo."

Irène was so sure that it was Martin calling that she was momentarily speechless as V. Hugo called her name.

"I am sorry," Irène said. "I . . . I was sure it was Martin. I was dreaming about him."

"There isn't much time and I have a very important message to give you. Do you have pen and paper?"

Irène moved around the desk to sit down. "What message? Where are you?"

"I am still in Calais."

"Why? It was a dead-end there."

"Madame, please . . . as I said, time is of the essence. Are you ready?"

"Yes, I have pen and paper. What is this about?"

"I received a message from Frederick Dubois. There are instructions."

The pen slipped from Irène's fingers. "What?" she whispered.

"I was given these instructions only once, so I hope I have written them down correctly. I will give them to you as they were given to me."

"They were given to you by Frederick?"

"Yes."

"I don't understand . . . instructions?"

"Directions, actually."

Irène's mouth went dry. "Directions to where?"

"First, will you go to your window and confirm that your Mercedes is parked in front of the hotel?"

"My car?" She flashed on Jean-Louis in the dream, pulling up in front of the hotel. "That's impossible. I have the only set of keys to the garage and the car itself." She dropped the receiver on the desk and went out onto the balcony. Light spilling from the Bel Air revealed that her convertible was indeed sitting in front of the hotel. She grabbed the railing to steady herself and went back inside and picked up the phone. "Yes, it's there."

"He said it would be. Now, write this down."

The instructions directed Irène to drive from Paris to Chambéry in the Rhône-Alpes. It would take five hours to drive there. In the center of the town, she would find the Fontaine des Éléphants and would receive more instructions to her final destination. A map was in her glove compartment with the route she should take to Chambéry and find the fountain. She was to leave precisely at 6 a.m. Her car had been filled with petrol and there was another can in the trunk, so she would not need to stop at any stations that might lead her to the temptation to use a public phone. She was encouraged to eat breakfast before she departed and to bring water and a snack for the road. And lastly, V. Hugo was to be the only person who knew her destination.

"He was very exact about the last item," V. Hugo stressed. "He specifically said you should not contact Monsieur Paige. Any deviation from the route or the instructions would mean immediate termination of the meeting. He also said to tell you . . . I hesitate to pass this on because you may find it upsetting."

"Out with it," Irène said, gripping the pen so tightly she could hear the plastic cracking.

"He said he could still see you standing on the sidewalk at République Square as he drove away with your husband. He was driving a Fiat. It was May 28, 1968. He said you were wearing a sleeveless dress with black and white geometric patterns and you were about to cross the street, but something held you back."

Irène felt tears in her eyes. "Yes, fear." She cleared her throat. "Perhaps if I hadn't been afraid, Jean-Louis would still be alive."

"Madame, it is my opinion that you should not go. It is too dangerous. There are too many unknowns."

"I have lived with unknowns for thirty years. It's almost five o'clock. I need to get ready."

"I beg you to reconsider. You are not yourself."

Irène laughed. "Oh, Victor, I am more myself than I have ever been. I will get the answers I'm searching for and if I die in the process, then so be it. I am ready. Today, I am going to cross the street."

Irène drove slowly at first, fighting back a panic she hadn't felt since before Martin arrived. She gripped the wheel of the Mercedes and took deep breaths. She wasn't going to dawdle like some old woman driving; she put her foot down on the gas pedal and the Mercedes, despite being thirty-five years old, responded with hardly a shudder.

As promised in the instructions, there was a map in her glove compartment with a route marked precisely in red pen, but she wouldn't need it until she had driven deep into the southeast corner of the country to Lyon, then she would head east toward Chambéry. It didn't seem so far away until she looked at the map and saw Chambéry was less than one hundred miles from both the Swiss and Italian borders.

Martin would just be arriving in Berlin with Christian, unaware that she was gone. Only V. Hugo knew her approximate destination, but if something happened to her beyond Chambéry, there would be no one to come to her rescue. Irène didn't turn on the radio, but drove in complete silence, the last thirty years on a constant loop in her head.

After stopping along the side of the road to refuel the car from the can in the trunk and navigating the ring road around Lyon, Irène arrived in Chambéry. She exited the motorway and drove into the warren of narrow streets, missing a turn before winding up on rue Victor Hugo. "How appropriate," she said out loud, and realized those were the first words she'd spoken since leaving Paris. Irène looped around a long narrow park lined with trees and benches. She found a parking space across from a cinema. Just ahead of her, the Fontaine des Éléphants was in a wide pedestrian plaza circled by shops and benches.

Irène got out of the car and walked toward the plaza. People were going about their daily lives, but the plaza was quiet. No one appeared to be waiting for her; the weather was still chilly, so no one was sitting on the benches having lunch. She walked up to the fountain, the life-sized heads of four elephants sculpted into its base and water pouring from their trunks into a pool below. On top of the base, a tall column rose into the sky capped by a statue of General Count Benoît de Boigne, one of France's most famous adventurers and military heroes, who settled in Chambéry after his illustrious career in India and devoted his life to charity.

The instructions given by Frederick said she would receive further directions here, but no one approached her as she slowly walked around the fountain, pretending to admire its beauty. After twenty minutes, she sat down on a bench, pulling her coat closed around her, and lit up a cigarette. Irène suddenly realized how exhausted she was and closed her eyes. When she reopened them, she saw a tall man wearing an overcoat coming toward her across the plaza. Irène instantly recognized him as the same man from Père Lachaise and Madame Dubois' funeral.

The man walked up to the bench and seemed to tower over her. He reached into the breast pocket of his coat, and Irène felt herself tense, wondering if he might pull a gun and shoot her. Instead, he pulled out an envelope and handed it to her.

"As before, follow the instructions without deviation," he said. "Do you have a light?"

She realized he had a cigarette dangling from his lip. Irène reached into her pocket and handed him her lighter.

"Merci," he said after he lit the cigarette, and handed the lighter back to her. The man walked into the park and disappeared.

Irène opened the envelope and pulled out a single piece of stationery, the same kind that Frederick had used to write his mother and, under his alias, to Gerard. She unfolded the letter.

*So close now. I can sense you. Drive toward Saint-Alban-Leysse. Before you reach Saint-Jean-d'Arvey, turn left onto a road called Chemin*

*des Pailles. You will see a small sign that says Château Vignes. Turn*
*right and follow the winding road. Put the top down on your Mercedes;*
*the view is quite impressive. Follow your dreams.*


The road called Chemin des Pailles twisted and turned around
the foothills of the Alps, which rose majestic and snow-capped
ahead of her. Irène drove carefully, hands locked in the three
and nine position on the Mercedes' steering wheel, the panic of
meeting Frederick compounded by oncoming traffic that
threatened to send her car careening off the road into the valley
below.

Eventually, Irène had the road to herself as it wound around
one of the smaller mountains. The road flattened and she saw
the tiny sign that pointed to Château Vignes. Irène stopped the
car and tried to calm her breathing. She had run hundreds of
scenarios in her mind over the years about what she would say
to Frederick, but now that their meeting was imminent, her
head was a jumble of thoughts and images.

Irène turned down a narrow, unpaved road that made a gentle
descent into the valley below. She could see the roofline of a
house rising above a stand of trees. The mountain range made
a cul-de-sac, so that the only way down to the château was along
this one road. It was almost like a fortress. She continued to
drive through the valley until she saw a bridge ahead. Her mind
flashed back to the dream of driving with Martin and reaching
a bridge covered in leaves, the stream below a ribbon of glass.
In the dream, Martin had disappeared—a harbinger of her solo
journey. The Mercedes rolled up to the bridge and Irène reached
up and released the latches of the convertible top.

Just like in the dream, the sky was cloudy and shot through
with dim sunlight. She slowly drove onto the bridge, the tires

crunching on the remains of leaves and pebbles. Irène stopped the car and got out, filling her lungs deeply with the cold mountain air. She leaned on the bridge railing and looked down into the placid stream, could see herself reflected back. The château's black windows and stone façade was visible through the trees on the other side of the bridge. More indistinct was a second roofline that seemed to be made of metal and glass that rose behind the château. The greenhouse from her dream. She desperately wished Martin was with her because, for all her bravado, she was frightened. Fear coursed through Irène, jolts of adrenaline making her forehead and underarms break out in sweat. The only time she could remember being this frightened was when she was hiding from the Nazis after her parents had been captured and taken to a concentration camp.

Tall trees on both sides of the road created a grand avenue up to the château. As the road emerged from the trees, there was a closed, ornate gate. Security cameras mounted on poles on both sides of the gate swiveled toward the Mercedes. Irène sat behind the wheel, waiting for the gate to open. A robotic voice from a call box nestled inside a bush startled Irène so badly that she felt her bladder release slightly in her pants.

"Leave the car and walk through the gate. The front door is unlocked. You'll know the way," the voice said, and then there was a loud clicking sound as the gate swung open.

As Irène got out of the car, she could hear a mechanical whirring as the cameras turned to watch her. Frederick watching her, waiting inside the house with answers. She walked through the gate, her legs feeling wobbly.

The yard in front of the château had been cut into a chessboard pattern, which was dotted with topiary shrubs shaped like rooks, pawns, bishops, knights and kings, but no queens. Behind her, the gate closed with a click.

Irène reached the tall double doors and put her hands on the handles. She gripped them tightly until her fingers ached, and then, taking a deep breath, pushed the doors open and walked inside.

Irène felt like she was floating down the wide central hallway of the château. All the doors on either side were closed, but ahead of her at the end of the hall were two glass doors beaded with condensation. Irène flashed on an old movie she'd watched one night when she couldn't sleep—Katherine Hepburn leading Montgomery Clift into a giant hothouse filled with Venus flytraps. What was it called? *Suddenly, Last Summer?*

She stood before the glass doors, streaked and clouded with water droplets, but there were no handles. Irène reached out to touch the doors, and they slid open silently as if it were an entrance to a supermarket. A wave of warm, moist air enveloped Irène and she stepped back. The hothouse was filled with tropical plants that rose almost to the glass roof. She heard water running and some kind of birdcall from the depths of the massive structure.

A pebbled path led toward the center of the greenhouse, and through the palm fronds, Irène could see a statue of the Venus de Milo. The statue, twice the size of the original in the Louvre, was oxidized green and stood on a pedestal over a fountain. This, too, was just like the scenes from Irène's dreams.

"Hello?" she called out.

There was a rustling in the trees and a multi-colored bird flew over her head and lighted somewhere else. Irène walked around the fountain and saw that the path continued into darkness that seemed to shimmer in the heat. She tried to see through the screen of plants, hoping to catch a glimpse of someone watching her, but the depths of the hothouse seemed endless. Irène stood gazing up at the face of Venus, then reached down and ran her fingers through the water. Tiny fish swam there and darted away as the water rippled.

"Do you like my Venus de Milo? It's a tribute to you and Jean-Louis."

Irène froze. The voice came from behind the fountain. It was a plaintive voice, not full of anger or menace as she had expected from the notes and dreams. Irène peered around the statue. On the other side of the fountain was a man sitting in a wheelchair, dressed in a black suit, hair thinning and slicked back. His face looked weathered and sunken. A grey blanket was draped over his lap where a pair of bruised hands rested. Frederick was only fifty years old, but the man sitting in the wheelchair looked ancient. The Frederick emblazoned on her mind was a beautiful, young teenager standing on the sidewalk at République Square.

"If you could see the look on your face," Frederick said, smiling. "Not what you expected?"

Irène stood before him and shook her head.

"Has my appearance shocked you into silence? Speak."

"No, not what I was expecting," she said. "You're Frederick Dubois?"

"In the flesh, Madame Laureux. I must say you are more beautiful than ever. The photos and video don't do you justice." A deep, phlegm-rattled laugh emitted from the man's throat.

"Are you ill?"

"I am beyond ill. I am dying. That is why we are meeting. Cancer has nearly eaten me alive. You didn't answer me. Do you like my Venus? And did you see the lawn? I finally have my White Queen."

"I didn't come to discuss your statuary or your lawn," Irène said crossly.

"Oh, but you did," Frederick said, a hint of glee in his voice.

"I have seen you through my looking glass and you have seen me. Just like you saw Martin. You were fated to meet him, just as our meeting was inevitable. I think Monsieur Jung would call it synchronicity. But I think that's just a fanciful name for magic. And your magic has only grown over the last two years. Once Martin arrived and you assembled all your players, I became powerless to stop this moment, although I tried very hard. The checkmate is yours."

"I am sorry you are ill, but I no longer wish to play this game."

"You're disappointed," Frederick said, wheeling closer to her. "You were expecting some robust man you could spar with, maybe even strike with your fists. If it will make you feel better, hit me. Slap me across the face. Tip over my chair."

"Why waste your energy on this subterfuge?" Irène asked.

"A wonderful word—subterfuge. My whole life has been subterfuge." Frederick twisted in his chair and called over his shoulder. "Bring the chair, please, Geoff."

The man from Père Lachaise, Madame Dubois' funeral and who had brought the envelope in Chambéry appeared from the shadows carrying a heavy wooden chair. How had he reached the château before her, Irène wondered.

"You have met my aide Geoff on several occasions," Frederick said. "He is my morning, noon and night."

Geoff sat the chair on the path in front of Frederick's wheelchair, then squeezed the man's shoulder and walked back into the darkness.

"Geoff has been with me for many, many years. He has made my existence almost bearable. Almost." Frederick gestured weakly toward the chair. "Please, sit. I want to tell you a story. No, not a story . . . a confession. That is what you have wanted. When you leave here today, you will have all the answers."

Irène slowly sat down. She was face to face with Frederick. Thirty years.

"Let's begin," she said.

Frederick sighed deeply, his chest rattling. "I killed Jean-Louis."

# 30 Frederick

Frederick had only intended to seduce Jean-Louis, not fall in love with him. The assignment had been very clear-cut: infiltrate the resistance, get close to its leaders and report any and all information. De Gaulle's agent had convinced him, his own father had convinced him. He was young and performing a service to the country that was moving toward a state of chaos. It would mean an important role in the government, money and perks only allowed the elite.

Frederick had been born in Paris, but his mother and father fled to Geneva just before Hitler invaded. His father was a doctor, but as Frederick grew older, he realized that his father was practicing more than medicine. There were phone calls and strange men in suits in and out of their apartment overlooking Lake Geneva. His father was gone for two years during the Korean War, leaving Frederick to be raised by his bored mother who drank too much, shopped daily and spoiled her only son. When he would totter into the living room in her high heels, an expensive dress dragging the floor and face smeared with make-up, she would laugh and twirl him around, telling him their special playtime should never be revealed to his father.

When his father returned, he often fought with Frederick's mother. Then one night, when he was sixteen, Frederick heard his father say that his absence and her influence had turned their son into a homosexual. He'd heard boys at school use the word— and much more derogatory terms—to harass other students, including himself, on occasion. It was true he had no interest in girls and often found his penis growing hard watching older classmates during physical education classes, and he'd had a crush on his English teacher for a year.

Frederick's mother encouraged him to be an artist, to find a boyfriend and defy his father's wishes to take up medicine, play football and visit whores in the local brothels. But Frederick believed his bohemian ways were the reason his father was always absent, had taken an apartment in Geneva to be, ostensibly, closer to his medical office.

To his mother's dismay, Frederick began spending time with his father, often staying for weekends at his father's apartment. It was during one of those visits that Frederick met the man who would recruit him as an informant. His father had met Yves Denis in Korea and they had become friends. Yves had since become a handsome intelligence officer in de Gaulle's government, who bedded Frederick in his hotel room and returned often to Geneva for "meetings" he would never elaborate on when they met for sex.

"Your father says you have a talent for art," Yves said. "Perhaps you would like to study in Paris."

"Will you be there?" Frederick asked, feeling himself falling in love with the man, images of living a blissful life full of sex and shopping on rue Saint-Germain dancing in his head.

"Of course. I'll help you find an apartment."

"Why can't I stay with you?" Frederick asked, disappointment creeping into his voice.

"I'm married."

"But I love you."

"Do you? Well, I have a way you can prove it," Yves said, and explained the communist, fascist and radical threat to France. It was 1967 and the country was a powder keg, Yves said, full of leftist provocateurs whose goals were to depose Charles de Gaulle's government. Even the United States and Britain were not to be trusted and were thought to be secretly agitating revolutionaries in France.

Frederick was on the verge of turning eighteen, and he'd ignored the early stirrings of the student and worker unhappiness, but as he lay spooned against Yves Denis, the intelligence officer weaved a tale so insidious that by the end, Frederick was propped on his elbow, an untapped fear beginning to bloom in his brain, and it mixed with adventure and romance. He would be doing a service for his country. He would make his father and Yves proud.

Whether Frederick's father knew his friend from Korea had been bedding his son as a tool of recruitment, Frederick would never know. There was some sort of grim pride on his father's face the last time they met. He said communism and fascism were threats to the planet, more dangerous than the Nazis, and what Frederick was doing was commendable.

"You must not tell your mother," his father advised. "She won't understand and she will cause a problem."

And while Frederick usually told his mother everything, he listened to his father's advice. She had already tried to talk him out of going to Paris, weeping over her abandonment in Geneva. She drank herself into a stupor while using a white chamois to clean the revolver she had bought to "protect herself." The room smelled of cleaning oil, a smell that would haunt him for the rest of his life.

That same day, a package arrived from Yves. It was a large box filled with clothing, a stack of record albums and a note that said, "Wear these and listen to this music." Frederick put on the tight jeans, black turtleneck sweater, black Italian loafers and stood in front of his mirror. His hair had already grown past his neck and had a bit of curl. As he listened to the Rolling Stones, he didn't recognize himself. He never would again.

By the time Frederick arrived for his first year at the École des Beaux-Arts, he had transformed himself almost completely. At Yves' insistence, he had read every article he could find about the current political climate in France and even read books about the country's evolution after World War II. He had been bored with school, but he absorbed the vagaries of French politics like a sponge. When Yves quizzed him the weekend before he left for Paris, Frederick answered every question correctly.

Frederick had lost weight, grown his hair even longer, loved British and American rock music. He had started smoking, too, and there was a strut to his walk once he was at school. He caught the eye of both men and women, could sense them watching him walk away. He instantly fell in with a group of radical students, young men and women who talked about revolution, smoked marijuana and had casual sex. All the years he spent dressing up and play-acting for his mother came in handy; he was just in a different kind of drag.

The apartment Yves found for him was nothing more than a dusty garret on rue Civigni on the Left Bank. Yves would appear like clockwork on Saturday afternoons to gather information and instruct Frederick on whom he should seek out and befriend.

"Can you get your cock hard for a woman?" Yves asked as they made love on the narrow garret bed.

"I don't know, I've never tried."

There was a girl in his printmaking class who was one of the most radical students. She often aimed angry diatribes at classmates in the student center or courtyard. France was being bought and sold by the bourgeoisie, she said, while the working class and students suffered and were robbed by the government of what little money they had. Frederick flirted with her, despite the fact that she had a shaggy-haired, lanky boyfriend who always seemed indifferent about his girlfriend's politics or the fact that she hung on Frederick, would kiss him and grab his ass in public.

One night, she came to his garret with the boyfriend in tow to smoke marijuana and listen to records. Before long, Frederick was sitting on the edge of his bed and she was on her knees with his cock in her mouth. The boyfriend sat on a chair across the room watching, and then casually pulled his own erect dick from his jeans and began to stroke it. He locked eyes with Frederick, who put his hand on the back of the girl's head and pumped his hips into her mouth. He shot his wad down her throat, and her boyfriend came all over the floor. Afterwards, they all smoked some more while she babbled about the demonstrations that were sure to come in the new year.

"I can get my cock hard for a girl," Frederick reported the following Saturday when Yves came to the garret for his regular round of information gathering and increasingly rough sex.

"That will be useful," Yves said, "but I believe you'll be able to use your true talents soon. Do you know one of the professors, Jean-Louis Laureux?"

"I've seen him. He teaches design and art history, I think."

"He has sympathetic leanings toward the students," Yves said. "We may need you to get close."

He remembered Jean-Louis quite clearly. Tall, wavy hair, impeccably dressed and he had an odd little tattoo on his left hand, where he also wore a wedding band.

Late one afternoon in January, he saw Jean-Louis go into the library. Frederick waited a few moments and then went inside, pretended to have lost his library card. The library was closing. He was pleading his case to the librarian when Jean-Louis appeared at the desk and offered to check the book—Hitler's *Mein Kampf*—out for him.

"You're Monsieur Laureux," Frederick said, flashing the grin he'd perfected in the mirror. "I plan to take your class in the spring."

As Frederick left the library, he knew Jean-Louis was watching, already fantasizing about him. It was almost too easy.


A week later, Frederick came to Jean-Louis' classroom. The teacher was putting papers in an attaché case and preparing to leave for the day.

"Did Herr Hitler suitably inspire your political ambitions?" Jean-Louis teased him.

Frederick perched on the edge of the teacher's desk. "Powerful men fascinate me," Frederick said. "I found parallels in Hitler and de Gaulle."

"Many do," Jean-Louis said, pulling a packet of Gauloises and a lighter from his jacket pocket. "Care for one?"

"Merci."

Jean-Louis handed the boy a cigarette and flicked the lighter. Frederick put his hand over Jean-Louis' to shield the flame, let his fingertips linger before pulling away.

"I saw that you registered for my design class," Jean-Louis said.

"Yes, I look forward to it." Frederick was wearing his tightest pants and he casually picked tobacco from his tongue, grinning at Jean-Louis the whole time.

"Who . . . what are your inspirations?" Jean-Louis stammered, sitting back down in his chair. Frederick was sure the teacher had an erection.

"Cinema. Godard, Truffaut, Chabrol, Rohmer."

"Ah, yes. La Nouvelle Vague. I'll be very interested to see your portfolio."

"I could bring it by one afternoon. I would love to hear your thoughts. Perhaps some critique before class begins in March."

"Yes, I'd be happy to. It would be my pleasure."

They talked art and design for several hours, smoking cigarettes, subtly flirting until the cleaning women showed up with their buckets.

Jean-Louis looked at his watch. "I didn't realize it was so late."

"I was going to ask if you wanted to go to a café? I was enjoying our conversation," Frederick said.

"Well . . ." Jean-Louis hesitated. "Just for a coffee. Have you been to that little place around the corner? Noisette, I think it's called."

"I go there often. I met a friend there last night who was telling me about what's happening in Nanterre. Things are heating up."

"I've heard that, too. I'd like to hear your opinion." Jean-Louis touched the small of Frederick's back as they went out of the classroom. It was a brief and subtle gesture, but Frederick felt an almost electric shock. He realized that seducing Jean-

293

Louis might be a pleasurable assignment.

As Yves had guessed, Jean-Louis was sympathetic to the plight of the students. He had already given over entire class periods so that the students could air their grievances. Jean-Louis had tried to moderate the conversations, play devil's advocate, but he agreed that de Gaulle had worn out his welcome in France and the bourgeois university system had to be changed. Jean-Louis had grown up poor in Nice, had struggled to put himself through university, had taken part in demonstrations and sit-ins to demand changes when necessary, but be believed that what was brewing in France was something bigger.

"There's an electricity in the air, a recklessness that anything could happen at any moment," Jean-Louis said.

"Are you frightened?" Frederick asked.

"I'm excited. It makes me feel, well, younger."

Frederick laughed. "You're not old. What are you . . . thirty-five?"

"Thirty-six."

"You look much younger. You're good looking."

Jean-Louis blushed. "Irène says that, too."

"Is Irène your girlfriend?"

Jean-Louis hesitated, started to speak then stopped. "No," he said finally. "I have a very liberal circle of friends, but they are more literary. Not particularly interested in politics or world affairs."

Frederick lit another cigarette and handed it to Jean-Louis. "That must be very unsatisfying for you. It's lucky I came along."

Frederick smiled. He knew that Irène was Jean-Louis' wife, that they had been married for nearly a decade, that she had bouts of agoraphobia and worked from home as a book editor. With very little hesitation, Jean-Louis had made Irène disappear and would never mention her again.

As January turned to February, Frederick and Jean-Louis were regularly meeting after class to discuss politics, books and whatever else came to mind. They usually wound up at Noisette, but then one evening, Frederick decided to escalate things by asking Jean-Louis back to his apartment.

"We can smoke some grass," Frederick said conspiratorially.

"Grass? What's that?"

"Grass, cannabis, marijuana."

"Grass, yes, that's what the Americans call it."

"Have you been to America?"

"Yes."

"Let's go back to my place. You can tell me about it while we get high."

They sat on the floor at rue Civigni, passing a joint back and forth while Frederick showed Jean-Louis his portfolio of sketches. The work was good, but Jean-Louis was over-effusive in his praise; he was high and happy.

Jean-Louis started coming to the garret three or four times a week, usually bringing a bottle of wine, and Frederick supplied the marijuana. Frederick wanted Jean-Louis to make the first move, and there were many evenings that they sat huddled on the floor facing each other in front of the tiny heater when Frederick was sure the teacher was going to lean in and kiss him. March was approaching and Frederick would soon be in Jean-Louis' design class, which might change the dynamic of their budding relationship.

"I think it would be unfair to the other students if they knew we were confidantes outside of the classroom," Jean-Louis said.

"Confidantes," Frederick said. "I like that. It sounds intimate."

Jean-Louis laughed nervously. "Yes, friends and confidantes." Then he leaned in and kissed Frederick on the mouth. Frederick returned the kiss, pulling the professor into his arms and easing them back onto the floor.

"Stay the night," Frederick said between kisses. "Let's be together."

Jean-Louis seemed to snap out of a trance. He looked down at Frederick and then rolled off him, lying on the floor panting. "No, we shouldn't do this. It's the wine making us take leave of our senses."

After Jean-Louis left, Frederick masturbated, imagining Jean-Louis inside of him. Yves' visits were few and far between as the political situation continued to simmer, but had yet to boil over, and Frederick had made it a point to be friendly, but make no friends with his fellow students. Jean-Louis was his only outlet. The professor treated him as an equal, never spoke down to him.

When the spring quarter began, despite their best efforts, it was obvious to the students that Professor Laureux favored Frederick, singling him out for example in the design studio. There were better artists in the class, but no student could disagree that Frederick's drawings and ideas had more of a contemporary edge. Frederick's grades in his other classes were dismal, but Jean-Louis began to tutor him—another reason to have the professor at rue Civigni. They had several more drunken fumblings, but Jean-Louis would never go all the way. He always checked himself emotionally. Frederick guessed that it was Irène who was keeping Jean-Louis from allowing himself to surrender completely.

On March 22, students occupied an administration building at the university in Nanterre and held a meeting in the council room to discuss societal discrimination and the political bureaucracy that controlled the school's funding. The administration overreacted and called the police, but the meeting ended with no arrests. However, students were outraged at the university's attempt to crack down on freedom of speech and assembly, and the month of April was dotted with showdowns between students and authorities. Nanterre turned into a flashpoint and all of France was watching as rumors spread that student demonstrations were imminent at universities and schools across the country.

Frederick created a poster in class that would eventually be seen on street corners around Paris as the revolution intensified. It was a clenched fist traced in white on black paper and spilling like blood from under the fist were the colors of the French flag—blue, white and red. It was a startling image and it was the first seed planted in what would blossom into the Atelier Populaire.

After the events at Nanterre, Yves resumed more regular visits, pumping Frederick for information about what the students, Jean-Louis and the other professors were saying, and warning Frederick that the situation was about to become more dangerous.

"The president is ready to send troops in to quell the unrest at Nanterre," Yves said as he unbuttoned his shirt. "There's already been talk of marches and protests at the Sorbonne. The Beaux-Arts school will be next. Let's fuck."

"We don't have to fuck," Frederick said. He could only imagine himself with Jean-Louis and sleeping with Yves almost seemed like betrayal.

"Of course we don't have to," Yves said and pushed Frederick onto the bed, rolled him over and took him roughly from behind. When Yves was finished, he continued to lecture Frederick about his duty.

"Don't let your feelings for Laureux get in the way of your assignment," Yves said. "Remember you are working for the government. The agitators and leftists want to destroy this country. The revolution they talk about is treason. Laureux and his Rive Gauche ilk will soon be in jail or exiled from the country, so keep your head."

"I have no feelings for Laureux."

"Don't lie, Frederick. The professor is here almost every night of the week and you're joined at the hip at school. He sees you more than his wife."

"You told me to get close, so that's what . . ."

Yves kissed Frederick hard. "Just do your job." He turned Frederick back over, ready to take him again. "My wife is out of town, so I can stay the night."

After Yves fell asleep, Frederick wrote his first letter to Jean-Louis, a long, gushing proclamation of his feelings and admiration that he eventually ripped up and threw in the trash bin. Yves was right; he couldn't let his loneliness and burgeoning feelings for Jean-Louis get in the way.

As he listened to Yves' heavy breaths, Frederick noticed the agent's attaché case sitting next to the sofa. Frederick pulled the case onto his lap and opened it. There were file folders inside and Frederick slid one out and flipped it open. There were lists of operatives working for the French government and their assignments. Other folders contained communiqués from agents about the movements of suspected agitators. Frederick put the folders back inside and closed the attaché case, but then looked at Yves still asleep on the narrow bed.

Frederick pulled the folders back out and took them to his desk. It would take him two hours to meticulously copy the information, which the next day he would mail to his mother's apartment in Geneva for safekeeping. Maybe the information could be used later in case he needed a bargaining chip.

On May 2, the university at Nanterre was shut down and the ripple effect across the country was instantaneous. Within days, hundreds of thousands of students and teachers were marching in the streets of Paris. De Gaulle ordered the police to raid the Sorbonne, where student unions were planning demonstrations and marches. The night the Sorbonne was closed, students rioted in the streets until dawn, throwing up barricades made from road barriers, trash cans and whatever else they could find, and ripped up paving stones to hurl at the baton-wielding riot police. It would be the first of many sieges.

By mid-May, workers had joined the students and more than ten million were on strike across the country. Students had occupied and closed the universities, including the École des Beaux-Arts. Students and teachers flocked to Jean-Louis' class in the lithograph department to talk about what was going on in the streets, when one student suggested creating posters that could be carried by demonstrators and put up all over the city. Jean-Louis held up Frederick's poster as an example and in a matter of hours, the Atelier Populaire was born. The first official poster was simple, the main tenets of the movement in bold words: *Usines, Universités, Union!*

Soon, the posters were everywhere. During the marches, hundreds carried posters created by the Atelier Populaire over their heads and they were posted in metro stations and on abandoned buildings. The posters carried provocative, colorful images: Arms raised over silhouetted heads and the message *La lutte continue*—The struggle continues. One of the most controversial featured a silhouette of de Gaulle in his famous military grab with his hand over a student's mouth and the inscription *Sois jeune et tais toi*—Be young and shut up. When word came that de Gaulle himself had ordered the posters removed and those making them arrested, the printing of the posters moved to secret printing presses across the city.

The Atelier Populaire gave the posters away for free and demanded that they not be hung up in rooms as artwork. They released a statement saying the posters belonged in the streets. They got their wish. That spring, as television cameras panned the streets full of rioters, the work of the Atelier could be seen. They were taped to the barricades as strikers clashed with police. Posters would be torn down and more would reappear hours later, which enraged the government and made the Atelier members euphoric.

Jean-Louis and Frederick volunteered to carry the poster designs to the printing presses, rolling them up in guitar cases for transport. They knew it was dangerous work, but it was also high adventure. They were drinking heavily; Jean-Louis rarely went home, preferring to stay at the Beaux-Arts building.

One night after they had returned to the Beaux-Arts school from one of the secret printing presses, Frederick pulled Jean-Louis into a secluded hallway and pushed him against a wall. Frederick had been drinking red wine all evening, so he was both buzzed and incredibly horny. They kissed roughly and then Frederick put his hand down Jean-Louis' trousers and began to masturbate him.

"I love you," Jean-Louis whispered, unbuttoning Frederick's jeans and grabbing his cock.

"Shhhh," Frederick said. "Don't ruin it."

They both came quickly, falling against each other, shuddering from the pent-up climax. They went into the toilet and cleaned up, then went back to the classroom where the students were at work making more posters. The orgasm had sobered up Frederick instantly and he realized his feelings for Jean-Louis were spiraling out of control. He remembered what Yves said. He ignored Jean-Louis for the rest of the night and was aloof for the next few days, keeping conversation strictly on Atelier business. Frederick would catch Jean-Louis looking at him, but forced himself to keep his distance. Secretly, he wanted to run into Jean-Louis' arms.

Working in such close proximity, it was hard for Frederick to ignore Jean-Louis. He knew the professor had gone home to his wife a few nights. He felt irrationally jealous. One night, he followed Jean-Louis to rue Rampon and stood in the doorway of the closed tobacconist watching Jean-Louis' and Irène's shadows moving behind the closed French doors. Frederick smoked cigarette after cigarette, hoping Jean-Louis might come outside, but he never did and Frederick walked back through the streets of Paris, piled high with garbage now that the workers were on strike. There was a stench in the air, a mixture of rotting meat and the lingering smell of teargas and Molotov cocktails in the flat, windless air.

It was nearly dawn when Frederick crossed to Île de la Cité and saw people going into Notre-Dame for early morning mass. He joined the line of worshippers, but once inside the cathedral, Frederick slipped away and climbed the long flight of stairs to the Galerie des Chimères. The panoramic view of Paris from the gallery underneath Notre-Dame's towers was breathtaking; he could see all the way to the Eiffel Tower, Montmartre and beyond. He inched along the narrow walkway looking at the gargoyles and chimeras that had kept watch over the city for more than one hundred years. One of the stone chimeras had its elbows propped on the gallery railing, head resting in its hands. From a distance, the statue looked menacing with its horns and wings, but upon closer inspection, Frederick saw that the beast was sticking out its tongue, wore an almost bored expression as it contemplated the city below. Leaning against the chimera, Frederick realized that he was in way over his head.

A week later, Frederick sat naked in the garret, his hand on the back of Jean-Louis' head as the older man sucked him off. They were both incredibly drunk, or maybe just Frederick was intoxicated. He could hear Yves' voice in his head telling him to do his job and not let his emotions complicate the issue, but Frederick was in love with Jean Louis. He had to convince Yves that the professor wasn't a revolutionary, but simply a confused man caught up in the fervor of the moment.

Frederick came in Jean-Louis' mouth, violently undulating his hips, and then passed out. When he came to the next morning, Jean-Louis was asleep on the floor, snoring softly. Frederick sat at his rickety desk staring at the man, wanting to wake him and make love to him.

Instead, Frederick quietly dressed and went outside to smoke a cigarette. When he opened the door to the street, he was met by a column of students and workers walking toward the Sorbonne. They carried posters from the Atelier, some had bricks and bottles in their hands. It was going to be another confrontation with the police. Frederick smoked a cigarette and watched hundreds pass by, some calling for him to join them. The door opened behind him and Jean-Louis appeared, a look of panic on his face.

"I woke up and you were gone," Jean-Louis said. "I thought something had happened."

"I just came out for a smoke."

Jean-Louis watched the marchers file past. "Let's go with them."

"What?"

"We sit in the Atelier day and night making the posters, but we have never joined the protests. I think it's time."

Yes, it was time, Frederick thought. Along with his feelings for Jean-Louis, he realized he was on the wrong side of the revolution. He should have never agreed to be a spy for de Gaulle; his sympathies had slowly turned to the students and workers. The government was corrupt and oppressive and Frederick suddenly knew he wanted no part of it. Yves would have him arrested, deported or worse. But he didn't care. He wanted to be in the streets.

"Let's go."

Frederick and Jean-Louis joined the tail end of the marchers, who were now singing *L'Internationale:*

> *This is the final struggle*
> *Let us group together and tomorrow*
> *The Internationale*
> *Will be the human race*

They hadn't walked far when they could hear shouting from somewhere ahead of them. Plumes of smoke rose, then there was screaming. The tide of marchers was turning, running back toward them. Jean-Louis grabbed Frederick's hand and pulled him along, trying to stay close to the buildings so they could get back to the garret. The students and workers had stopped just before the steps to Frederick's building and were piling trash onto the street; a café window shattered across the street and tables and chairs were being thrown atop the heaps of trash. A barricade was going up. The demonstrators were going to make a stand.

A phalanx of police with shields and batons approached, followed by more on horseback with rifles slung over their shoulders. The officers on foot carried teargas canisters, poised to throw them at the demonstrators, who were shouting obscenities at the police. Jean-Louis shucked his jacket and ripped off his shirt. He tore it in half and handed the other piece to

Frederick. "Tie it around your face," the professor instructed.

Standing in the street in his undershirt, Frederick could see the muscles on Jean-Louis' arms, his slim physique and the way his hair fell boyishly across his eyes. He was beautiful. Frederick could smell Jean-Louis' scent in the half-shirt as he tied it around his face, felt himself grow hard in his trousers.

Someone in the crowd threw a brick and it hit one of the policemen in the head, a sharp crack against the plastic helmet— and then everything exploded. The street disappeared in a haze of teargas, which penetrated the shirt around Frederick's face and made his eyes burn. Through his tears, he saw Jean-Louis swing a milk bottle at a policeman who was lifting his baton. Jean-Louis caught the officer in the face with the bottle, which shattered on contact with the visor of the policemen's helmet. The policeman stumbled backwards and fell. A cheer went up from those around Jean-Louis.

As the teargas dispersed, the air was alive with flying objects. Bricks, pieces of concrete, chairs, table legs, wood pallets, cans. Anything that could be a projectile was lobbed at the policemen, who were trying to break down the barricade. But it soon became apparent that the students outnumbered the police. When they began to withdraw back down rue Civigni, a cheer went up that was deafening.

Frederick grabbed Jean-Louis and they kissed deeply, arms wrapped around each other tightly.

"Victory," Frederick whispered in Jean-Louis ear.

Jean-Louis looked momentarily stunned, then Frederick took the professor's face in his hands and kissed him again. In the garret, they humped on the couch, kissing until their lips were bruised, rubbing their cocks together until they came.

While Jean-Louis dozed, Frederick went back out to try and find food. He thought there might be something left in the café, which had been trashed by the demonstrators. Rue Civigni was quiet and empty as dusk fell. Frederick walked through the shattered window and found bread and cheese. All the wine and beer had been looted. Walking back across the street, Frederick saw a dirty box tied with a piece of frayed cord sitting next to the steps of his building. Frederick bent down to pick it up, surprised by the weight. He looked up and down rue Civigni to see if anyone was there, then took the box inside.

Jean-Louis was sitting on the sofa naked, smoking a cigarette, when Frederick came back in. "What did you get for us?"

"Only bread and cheese."

"What's in the box?

"It was sitting on the street. No one was around, so I took it. It's heavy."

Jean-Louis got up from the couch, took the box and sat it on floor. "What if it's a bomb?"

Frederick laughed. "I don't think it's a bomb. I dropped it once on the way upstairs and it didn't explode."

Jean-Louis got a knife from the sink, knelt down and cut the cord on the box. He lifted the top flap and stared into the box.

"What is it?" Frederick asked.

Jean-Louis reached into the box and carefully pulled out a statue of Venus de Milo and set it gently on the floor.

"Oh," Frederick said, disappointed. "It's just someone's lost souvenir."

Jean-Louis was sitting cross-legged on the floor of the garret, his fingers templed under his chin, staring at the statue. His mood had darkened, changed the energy in the tiny room.

"What's the matter?" Frederick asked.

"This reminds me of . . ." Jean-Louis' voice trailed off.

"Of what?"

Jean-Louis stood up. "No one. I mean . . . nothing. I have

to pick up posters tonight at the printing press. Can you pick me up in your car this evening at République Square? I need to get a few things at my apartment. Let's say six o'clock."

"Yes," Frederick said. "Are you all right?"

"I'm fine."

Jean-Louis pulled Frederick against him and kissed him softly on the mouth. Frederick knew Jean-Louis was going home to see his wife.

That evening, Frederick parked the old Fiat on the curb at République Square just before six o'clock and lounged against it, smoking a cigarette. A minute after the hour, he heard Jean-Louis call his name across the busy street. Jean-Louis weaved through the cars until he was standing at Frederick's side. The professor embraced him, discreetly kissed him on the cheek. Across the street, a woman was standing on the curb watching them. Jean-Louis got inside the Fiat, not noticing his wife standing there. As he ducked inside, Frederick took one last look at Irène Laureux. The look on her face was a mixture of fear and uncertainty, maybe shock. Did she know? Had she guessed what her husband was up to all those nights away from home?

As Frederick began to merge into the heavy traffic around the square, he looked over at Jean-Louis, who sat stone-faced and still in the passenger seat.

"Who was that woman?" Frederick asked, trying to sound casual.

Jean-Louis jerked his head toward Frederick. "What woman?"

"There was a woman who followed you, she was standing across the street and looked like she was about to cross."

Jean-Louis was silent for a moment, too silent. "There was no one following me," he said at last.

Frederick started to ask another question, but Jean-Louis

changed the subject and was talking about Atelier business. Frederick looked in the rear-view mirror and could see Irène still standing on the corner.

# 31 the Parting of the Ways

After picking up the posters, Frederick dropped Jean-Louis off at the Beaux-Arts school and returned to rue Civigni. Seeing Jean-Louis' wife had shaken Frederick; the look on her face—the first flicker of recognition that something was going on besides the riots—haunted him. Maybe it was time to go back to Geneva.

When Frederick unlocked the door to the garret, he was startled to find Yves sitting on the sofa smoking a cigarette.

"I was beginning to think you would not return tonight," Yves said. "You've been a very busy boy."

Frederick stood in the doorway. "I've done what you've asked."

Yves blew smoke at the ceiling. "Yes, too well. You've become more involved than necessary. I think you're a liability."

"How?"

"You're emotionally involved with the professor,

we know that. You took part in the demonstration yesterday. We have photographs of the professor assaulting the officer and you kissing him in the street. Your lack of discretion is troublesome. You were too young and immature for this assignment; I realize that now. Too easily influenced."

"I had no choice."

Yves held up his hand. "Say no more. Your work is complete here. We have photographs from the demonstration, we have photos of Jean-Louis at the illegal printing press and statements from others of his acts of dissidence."

"You're going to arrest him?"

"Of course. Laureux is ultimately small potatoes, but we have enough evidence to end his career as an educator. We don't need his kind of rogue element filling our youth with the wrong kind of messages. Once his wife finds out about his indiscretions, she will leave him and he will leave France."

"And what about me?"

Yves stood up and walked toward Frederick. The agent looked much taller, menacing. Frederick took a step back.

"You can finish your education in Geneva. You'll be better off there. Staying in Paris might be dangerous for you."

"What if I decide to stay?"

Yves loomed over Frederick and backed him against the door of the garret. "Your departure from Paris is not up for negotiation, you little pédé." Yves grabbed Frederick by the throat and slammed his head against the door. "I recruited you for this job because you suck cock and take it in the ass. You're an embarrassment to your father, and because he is my friend, I offered to try and reform you."

"Is that what you call it when you're putting your cock in me—reform?"

Yves slammed his head against the door again. Frederick felt dizzy, as if he might pass out.

"Understand this—I have a wife and family. I do what I have to do for my country. Your type is not to be trusted. You're as dangerous as the radicals out there in the street, perhaps worse. At least they aren't trying to rape our children."

Frederick spit in Yves' face, a big gob that hit him in the mouth. Yves pulled back his fist and Frederick closed his eyes, awaiting the crushing blow from the agent's knuckles. Instead, Yves laughed as he wiped the spit from his face and smeared it into Frederick's hair.

"What a pathetic boy you are. Begin packing your things. You'll be leaving Paris in the next few days. Say nothing to Laureux. If you try to warn him, you will be arrested and thrown in jail. A pretty boy like you wouldn't last long there. That tight little ass of yours would be turned inside out."

Yves tried to kiss him, but Frederick turned his head away. "I was going to let you suck it again, but now that you've been soiled by the professor, I think not. He probably has gonorrhea."

Yves pushed Frederick aside roughly and went out, slamming the door behind him. Frederick could still feel the man's fingers around his throat and he could feel a lump on the back of his skull. Despite Yves' threat, he would have to warn Jean-Louis. There was still time for him to take his wife and get out of the country.


Frederick left by the back entrance of the apartment building and walked through the debris-filled streets to the Beaux-Arts school. The printmaking room was abuzz as more of the students were planning to go to another large demonstration, but Jean-Louis was not there. One of the students said he had come and gone quickly, but wasn't sure when he was coming back. Frederick went to Jean-Louis' classroom and sat down at his desk, prepared to write him a letter and then disappear.

He opened the drawers of the desk looking for a piece of stationery and came across a small, leather-bound book. The book bulged at the middle with envelopes. Frederick opened the book and saw it was all the letters he'd written to Jean-Louis over the last few months. There was writing in the book, too. It was Jean-Louis' journal. Frederick flipped to the end where Jean-Louis had written about the demonstration they'd been caught up in.

*I feel like I'm being torn in so many directions. My loyalties are being tested from every side.*

"What are you doing?"

Jean-Louis was standing at the door with a rolled poster in his hand. Frederick looked at Jean-Louis and down at the journal, his face flushed scarlet.

"I was going to leave you a note," Frederick stammered. "I thought this was just a notebook."

Jean-Louis walked silently to his desk, closed the journal and put it in his jacket pocket. "I shouldn't have left it here," he said, and smiled.

Frederick visibly relaxed. "I was looking for you."

"Daniel has been expelled back to Germany," Jean-Louis said.

Daniel was Daniel Cohn-Bendit, a student at Nanterre who had become the face of the student movement after the government and conservative press had labeled him a "Jew, a German and an undesirable." A photograph of his grinning face confronting a helmeted police officer in Nanterre had been transformed by the Atelier Populaire into one of the most recognizable posters in the movement with the words, *Nous*

*Sommes Tous Indésirables*—We are all undesirables. That was the poster Jean-Louis was carrying under his arm. He unfurled it and spread it across the desk face down. On the plain white reverse, Frederick saw words had been scribbled in the top corner.

*My Dear Frederick, Even as the revolution promises to change our world, we too shall be forever changed. Our hopes and dreams will be remembered for the ages. One day, we shall all be desirable, even as you are to me now. With love, Jean-Louis.*

Frederick felt his insides clench. Jean-Louis looked down at him expectantly, but Frederick could not face him.

"I appreciate the sentiment, Jean-Louis," Frederick said softly. "You are very important to me . . . your friendship has sustained me."

"Friendship," Jean-Louis said, dejection in his voice. "Is that all?"

"My parents want me to return to Geneva."

"At least look at me when we are talking," Jean-Louis said. He picked up the poster and rolled it tightly, his hands shaking.

"There's talk the workers are going to sign an agreement with the government," Frederick said. "If the workers capitulate, the revolution ends. The Gaullists will win."

There were frantic footsteps in the hallway and one of the students of the Atelier flung herself into the doorway. "Come quickly," she said breathlessly. "The police are on rue Bonaparte." She ran back down the hallway, leaving Frederick and Jean-Louis to stare at the doorway.

"Let's go," Frederick said.

Jean-Louis touched his shoulder. "I want to speak with you tonight. Please just hear me out. I have so many things I want to say to you."

The pleading look in Jean-Louis' eyes made Frederick pause. He had to tell the professor to take his wife and leave Paris, that his arrest was imminent. But instead he said, "I'm not in love with you, Jean-Louis."

Jean-Louis' hand slowly fell away from the boy's shoulder. "I don't believe you."

"We should go," Frederick said, starting toward the door.

Jean-Louis grabbed him by the arm and pulled him close, raining kisses on Frederick's face and softly on his mouth. Frederick melted into him, hungrily kissing him back.

"I'll come to the garret tonight and we'll talk this through," Jean-Louis whispered into his ear. "If you're going back to Geneva, I'll go with you. We can go anywhere you like."

"How can you, how could you just leave . . ." Frederick stopped himself before he said Irène's name.

Jean-Louis hugged him tightly. "My future is with you."


Frederick and Jean-Louis became separated in the melee on rue Bonaparte outside the École des Beaux-Arts. Students were trying to repulse the police with projectiles. Chairs from the school had been broken down into clubs and the students were fighting back against the baton-wielding police. Inevitably, teargas canisters clattered on the ground with the familiar sound of metal on concrete.

Frederick was sweaty, his eyes were burning and he could feel the sting of little cuts on his face and hands. He had taken out his anger on several policemen. When he smashed a policeman's visor with a piece of pavement, saw blood gushing from the officer's nose, he pretended it was Yves. He felt a murderous rage towards the intelligence officer, pictured Yves lying in a pool of blood with his skull cracked open.

A policeman was beating a girl about the head with his baton, and Frederick and several other students set upon him with their fists. As they wrestled the policeman to the ground, a concealed pistol fell from the officer's pocket. Frederick instinctively reached for it, thought about pressing it to the officer's chest and pulling the trigger, but instead he shoved it into his trousers. As he staggered to his feet, Frederick could feel the weight of the gun in his pocket. The students continued to kick the officer and other policemen rushed in waving batons to help their fallen comrade; Frederick pushed his way out of the crowd.

The sounds of the brawl receded as Frederick walked in a daze down an alley toward rue Civigni. By the time he reached the garret, he was out of breath. Climbing the steep stairs seemed impossible, but he trudged up to find the door to the garret ajar. Frederick froze on the landing and pulled the gun from his pocket. He pulled the hammer back and advanced slowly toward the door.

Frederick saw the lock was broken, the wood splintered; someone had forced the door open. He took a deep breath, raised the gun and kicked the door inward. The room was so small that even from the doorway, Frederick could see there was no one in the apartment. He went inside and closed the door, wedging the back of a chair under the doorknob to secure it. Frederick sat on the ratty sofa, the gun still cocked, staring at the door.

After midnight, when Jean-Louis had not shown up, Frederick started packing his clothes into a bag. He would go to rue Rampon, warn Jean-Louis and then disappear. He couldn't go back to Geneva; returning to that life seemed impossible. London, maybe, or even America. While he was packing, Frederick noticed that the statue of Venus de Milo he had found on the street and put on the windowsill was gone.

Frederick woke with a start before dawn. Someone was pounding on the garret door, the chair wedged there threatening to topple over. The gun had slipped between the cushions and he struggled to pull it free.

"Frederick, it's me. Are you there?" Jean-Louis' voice had an urgency that Frederick had never heard before.

Frederick tucked the gun into the back of his trousers, kicked the chair out of the way and the door swung open. Jean-Louis stood there, disheveled and sweaty. His eyes were puffy and there were little cuts on his face that had scabbed over.

"What happened to you?" Frederick asked as Jean-Louis stumbled clumsily into his arms. "Where have you been?"

"I think I was followed. We need to get out of here." Jean-Louis seemed to focus for a moment and saw Frederick's duffel bag and suitcase sitting in the middle of the floor. "Why are you packed?"

"I'm leaving. I'm going back to Geneva."

"Were you going without me?" Jean-Louis asked, his eyes full of panic.

"Jean-Louis, you have to listen to me now. You are going to be arrested. You need to go home, pack your things, take your wife and get out of France." The words tumbled out of Frederick's mouth before he could stop himself.

Jean-Louis' mouth popped open in shock. "My wife . . ." he said in a strangled voice.

"I've known about Irène all along. There's no time to talk now. We'll take my car and I'll drive you back to rue Rampon."

Jean-Louis looked dazed, older. "How do you know that I'm going to be arrested? Did someone come here? Did they threaten you?"

"I made a mistake, Jean-Louis. A huge mistake, and I'm trying to fix it now. Let's go." Frederick picked up his bags, but Jean-

315

Louis grabbed him by the arm, his fingers digging into the boy's flesh.

"What mistake? What are you talking about?"

"I'll tell you in the car."

Jean-Louis let Frederick go and walked over to the sofa and sat down hard. "I've left my wife, but I won't leave France unless it's with you."

"They will arrest you and put you on trial for sedition."

"Perhaps we should let them arrest us. Put us on trial so we can reveal what we know to the entire country," Jean-Louis said, his eyes flashing.

Frederick realized gentle imploring would not move the professor. "They won't arrest me, only you."

"Of course they would arrest us both . . ." Jean-Louis' voice trailed off. It was as if a light switch was flipped on in his head, the truth about Frederick suddenly illuminated. "Oh, Frederick . . . no."

"I'm an operative for the French government," Frederick said, the words sounding strange coming out his mouth. He had been so stupid and naïve, caught up in the idea of playing spy in Paris and being Yves' lover.

Jean-Louis dropped his head into his hands, his shoulders shaking. "What have you done? Oh, my god, Frederick."

Frederick stood before Jean-Louis and dropped to his knees. "I made a mistake. I realize that now. I had no idea what they were asking me to do, that I would be sympathetic to the revolution . . . to you."

Jean-Louis looked up. "Sympathetic to me?"

Frederick took Jean-Louis' face in his hands. "Yes, sympathetic. And that I would fall in love with you. It was forbidden . . ."

Jean-Louis grabbed Frederick by the wrists. "What are you saying?"

"You're hurting me," Frederick said, trying to pull away.

Jean-Louis stood up quickly, hauling Frederick up with him. "What was your assignment? Tell me."

"I'll tell you everything if you come with me now."

Jean-Louis tightened his grip on Frederick's wrists as if he might break them. "I'm not going anywhere until you tell me who you are and what you have to do with me."

Tears sprang to Frederick's eyes, a combination of pain and sorrow. He wanted Jean-Louis to punish him. He deserved it. "I was recruited to get close to you. To gather information and report on your activities and what was happening at the École des Beaux-Arts."

A guttural cry rose in Jean-Louis' throat, a cross between a roar and a scream, and he flung Frederick across the garret with what seemed like superhuman strength. Frederick struck the wall hard, his breath gone and sat down hard on the floor. He could feel the edges of the gun cutting into his lower back.

"You've ruined my life," Jean-Louis bellowed, tears streaming down his face. "Do you realize what you've done? I would have never left my wife if it hadn't been for you. Now she will be alone. I promised I would never leave her and you come along and seduce me away."

Jean-Louis crossed the distance between them, diving toward Frederick. The professor grabbed Frederick by the throat and held up his hand in front of his face. The tiny tattoo—the two interlocking crosses that he shared with Irène—seemed to pulse on the back of Jean-Louis' hand.

"Do you see this? You once asked me what this meant, and I lied and said it was nothing," Jean-Louis said. "It means something. It was a promise I made to my wife and you made me forget."

"I love you, Jean-Louis."

317

The punch Jean-Louis delivered made Frederick see stars. He tasted blood in his mouth and felt it trickling from his nose.

"I'm going to kill you," Jean-Louis said, his voice detached as he raised his fist to deliver another blow.

"Don't make me, Jean-Louis."

Frederick reached behind him and grasped for the gun as Jean-Louis punched him again. There was the sound of bones crunching and Frederick was unsure if it was his nose or Jean-Louis' knuckles. As the professor raised his fist again, Frederick brought up the gun and fired once. The bullet sliced along Jean-Louis' temple and sent him reeling back into the room. He lay on his back motionless, blood seeping onto the hardwood floor from the wound.

The gunshot rang in Frederick's ears like a bell and his entire head throbbed. The pistol suddenly seemed to weigh a ton and he let it drop from his hand and clatter against the floor. Frederick crawled toward Jean-Louis, calling his name, but was unsure if he was speaking out loud or in his own head. Frederick leaned over Jean-Louis, blood dripping from his nose and spattering on the professor's shirt.

Frederick laid his head on Jean-Louis' chest, could hear his heart still beating and feel his chest rising and falling in shallow breaths. Frederick slowly stood up, his knees threatening to buckle. He expected to see people from the building standing outside the door, but there was no one. Outside, it was still dark. There wasn't even a hint of morning light coming through the garret's window.

There was a telephone in the lobby, and Frederick knew he had to call an ambulance to get help for Jean-Louis before he bled to death. Frederick swayed in the doorway and lurched himself toward the stairs, grabbing onto the banister for support. He started slowly down the stairs, each step making his face pulse with pain. He lifted his t-shirt to his face to staunch the blood.

Halfway down, Frederick heard the street door open and the sound of footsteps coming quickly up the stairs. He started to turn and go back, but then Yves was there before him.

"Christ," Yves muttered and caught Frederick, who fell against him.

"I shot him," Frederick whispered. "He's dying."

Yves slung Frederick's arm around his neck and carried the boy back up the stairs. "We've got to get you and the body out of here," Yves said, his tone almost businesslike. "We'll tie up the loose ends."

On the top floor landing, Frederick could see through the doorway that Jean-Louis was no longer lying on the floor. He started to tell Yves, but Jean-Louis was suddenly in front of them, his face covered in blood, the gun Frederick had dropped clutched in his hand. He fired once.

Frederick's legs went out from under him and he was sitting on the landing, his legs splayed out in front of him like a dropped marionette. Before Yves could react, draw his own weapon, Jean-Louis took the gun and aimed it as his own chest. He smiled almost beatifically down at Frederick.

"Tell Irène I'm sorry and that I love her," Jean-Louis said, then pulled the trigger. The professor staggered backwards into the garret and crumpled to the floor.

Frederick tried to stand, but felt a searing pain shoot up his spine and spike in his brain, as if his head was going to explode. Before he blacked out, he saw Yves step over Jean-Louis' body, move quickly around the apartment, perhaps looking for any incriminating evidence. Yves picked up Frederick's bags and brought them onto the landing, pulling the door closed behind him. He pulled a walkie-talkie from his jacket and held it close to his lips while looking down at Frederick.

"I need a clean-up team at rue Civigni. One dead, possibly two."

Frederick separated from his body. He hovered near the ceiling looking down at his battered body on the landing. Frederick turned and was able to look through the wall into the apartment. Jean-Louis' eyes were still open, staring blankly into space. Frederick wanted to touch him again, to apologize and tell the professor he loved him, but he was like a balloon skittering against the ceiling unable to descend.

# 32 Aftermath

Irène could hear her own heart beating, blood pounding in her ears. She sat motionless in her chair, tears streaming down her face. As Frederick told the story of Jean-Louis' final days, she felt a panic attack flaring in her brain.

"Geoff, bring Madame Laureux a glass of water, or perhaps something stronger," Frederick said to his assistant, who hovered on the periphery of the greenhouse. "Yes, bring the brandy. I could use a drink myself."

Frederick rolled his chair closer to Irène, but she would not look at him.

"I was in the hospital for months," Frederick said. "There were several operations, but the bullet had severed my spine. I found out later that Yves and his cleaners had taken Jean-Louis' body to Île de la Cité and dumped it near Notre-Dame to make it seem like he was killed in the riots.

"When I was well enough to travel, the

government put me in a form of witness protection. They gave me a lot of money to be quiet, to live in the countryside as an invalid. I had information that could damage the government—names of operatives and their missions I had copied from Yves' files. They even provided me with a new name, André Sarde. It never suited me, so I took others."

Irène looked at Frederick, her head swimming in information overload. "Why didn't you come forward? Why didn't you go to the newspapers or television?"

"De Gaulle left power, and it seemed my secrets were no longer a bargaining chip. Yves stopped coming to visit me, the checks stopped arriving. They thought they were done with me, but when my father died, he left a great deal of money to me and my mother. With that money, I continued to buy and sell state secrets, to infiltrate, to make myself a boil that could not be lanced on the back of the government. It's amazing how much other countries will pay for the smallest piece of information."

Geoff appeared with two glasses of brandy and handed one to Irène and the other to Frederick, who downed it in two gulps with a shaking hand. Irène sniffed at her glass.

"Drink it, my dear," Frederick said. "I'm not trying to poison you. I could have had you killed years ago if that's what I wanted."

Irène slowly turned the glass upside down and let the brandy splash to the ground, then let the glass slip from her fingers to shatter on the flagstones that surrounded the fountain.

Frederick clucked his tongue in disapproval. Geoff moved to pick up the shards, but Frederick waved him away. "I've been watching you for thirty years, Irène. While you were afflicted with your agoraphobia and couldn't leave your apartment, I felt a very strong sympathy with you. France is not very kind to those with disabilities, so I've felt very trapped in my wheelchair."

Irène's tears had stopped; the panic attack seemed to retreat and was replaced by a dull ache in her head, as if a migraine were setting in. What had she expected Frederick to tell her? She had run so many scenarios in her head, always imagining Jean-Louis murdered, but to hear, finally, that Jean-Louis had taken his own life in such a violent and senseless way was incomprehensible. For a moment, she questioned whether Frederick was telling her the truth, but she intuitively knew that he was.

"Why did you wait thirty years to tell me? Why not a year later? Or five? Or ten? Why not just send a letter anonymously and explain?"

"I had planned to," Frederick said. "Every May, I thought I would contact you and confess, but then I would talk myself out of it. You believed the police or de Gaulle's agents murdered Jean-Louis, and as the years passed, I thought it was kinder to let you go on believing that. Then your little friend Martin arrived and changed everything. You must tell me . . . what did you find that sent you looking for me?"

"The journal."

Frederick leaned forward, his eyes glistening. "Where was it?"

"Hidden in a trunk in the attic, along with all the letters you wrote to Jean-Louis."

Frederick leaned back again. "I wondered what happened to it. I remember so clearly that afternoon he caught me reading it, and then slipped it into his pocket. I thought perhaps he'd burned it."

"I wish he had. I thought I wanted to know the truth, but now I realize the old cliché is true: ignorance is bliss." Irène stood up. "I must go now."

Frederick was flustered. "There's more to tell. Don't go just yet."

"What else could you possibly tell me? I've heard enough."

"You'll want to hear this. It has to do with your friends, with Martin."

"What do you know of Martin and my friends?"

"Not to sound Henry Jamesian, but I've had everything to do with you since you were released from your apartment prison. And Martin, too. I know where David McLaren is right now. I could pick up a phone and dial a number and he'd answer."

Irène held onto the back of the chair, her fingernails digging into the wood. "How could you possibly know that?"

"Pay attention, Madame Laureux. I told you, I buy and sell secrets, but I diversified my business. I needed something recession-proof, so I moved into the drug trade. Not to brag, but I control most of the cannabis, cocaine and heroin that comes in and out of the country. And I do it with the government's knowledge. The trade flourishes because money appears in certain politicians' bank accounts on a regular basis. Other criminal elements are kept at bay. Things could be much worse in France and the government knows it. I help keep things in balance. I never let them forget that they put me in this chair, the price I paid for being their informant. The price Jean-Louis paid."

Irène sat back down, her arms folded tightly over her chest. "What does this have to do with Martin?"

"Last summer, one of my men told me that a young American was selling drugs at the Eureka club, which I own by the way. I told him to take care of it, and rather than handling it himself, he stupidly assigned the task to one of his pretty errand boys."

"Christian," Irène said.

Frederick smiled. "Unfortunately, Christian let his heart get in the way of common sense. But Martin is very charming—

strong and fragile at the same time. So much passion. How could Christian not fall in love with him? Just like I fell in love with Jean-Louis. Surely you see it, Irène . . . the synchronicity. Our lives intertwine even without our machinations."

Irène covered her face with her hands. The dull ache was now throbbing, piercing. "You've ruined our lives."

"That was not my intention," Frederick said quietly. "After my mother died, I planned to commit suicide, but then I was diagnosed with cancer. As if being confined to this wheelchair wasn't penitence enough, God decided to punish me further."

"Where is David?"

"Tending bar at a tourist trap in the Vieux Carré in New Orleans. Geoff, bring me a piece of paper. I'll write the name and number down for you. Have one of your detectives check it out."

Frederick scribbled on a piece of paper, folded it and handed it to Irène. She snatched it from his fingers and stuffed it in her pocket. Irène stood up and walked toward the doors of the greenhouse. She could hear Frederick's wheelchair crunching over the gravel, following her.

"In my will, Gerard will find that I have left the publishing house solely to him with enough money to keep it running in perpetuity. You and Martin will always have jobs there. I wish there were something more to give you for all these years of suffering. You may not believe this now, but I am sorry. I loved Jean-Louis. You must believe that. I would have traded my own life that morning on rue Civigni. Please . . . forgive me."

Irène turned and leaned down so that she was eye to eye with Frederick, her hands resting on the arms of the wheelchair, holding him in check as if he might roll away. "God may forgive you, but I won't."

Frederick seemed to shrink in the wheelchair. He closed his

eyes, but tears escaped from the corners and ran down his cheeks. Irène felt her throat constrict, as if she also might cry again. She turned and ran out of the greenhouse, back down the long hallway and out onto the grounds. It was almost dark; the chess piece topiaries were silhouetted against the château in the fading light. Frederick had called her the White Queen, and yet there was no victory.

Irène thought she would feel relief knowing the truth about Jean-Louis, as if the weight of his loss would instantly lift from her shoulders. Instead, thirty years folded together like a paper accordion, and she was once again sitting in the apartment on rue Rampon that May evening in 1968, sensing that her beloved Jean-Louis had departed even before the police had arrived to take her to Salpêtrière Hospital to identify his body. She had caressed the tattoo on her hand like a worry stone, willing him to come through the front door, where the statue of Venus de Milo he had brought to her the night before stood vigil.

# 33 Contrition

Pierre the cat slept on the floor in front of the open doors to the balcony, a shard of sunlight bathing his fur. An early spring was setting in, and there were sounds of voices and laughter on rue Rampon as the city shook off winter. Two weeks had passed since Martin said goodbye to Christian in Berlin and Irène had finally caught up with Frederick. They were both numb. Work seemed the only respite, something to focus on and bring normalcy back to their lives, so they sat at their desks engrossed in editing manuscripts.

On the desk underneath a paperweight was the piece of paper with the name of the bar and phone number where David was working in New Orleans. Martin had folded and unfolded it dozens of times, but never picked up the phone. As the days passed, the emotional disconnect Martin felt from David continued to grow. He knew where David was and that was enough. He wished he could feel the same way about Christian, whose exile preyed on his mind continuously and left him sleepless and unable to concentrate.

Irène had gone to Père Lachaise and sat on the bench across from Jean-Louis' grave, trying to come to terms with how he died. The cleave in Jean-Louis' headstone seemed deeper; Irène traced the split with her fingertip, ran her fingers over his name. Her emotions were a tumult of anger and guilt, the nagging feeling that her agoraphobia had forced Jean-Louis into Frederick's arms. If she had been able to go out, had not been so afraid, would she have been able to prevent her husband's death? Or was Jean-Louis so caught up in the fervor of the revolution and Frederick's youth and charm that his demise was inevitable? If Jean-Louis had lived, would he have chosen to come back to her or pursue Frederick to Geneva? After the heady days of the revolution and his affair with Frederick, Irène suspected that her marriage would have ended in divorce. Still, she would rather have him alive somewhere in the world than dead by his own hand. Frederick's telling of Jean-Louis' final moments were seared into her brain, would never leave her.

After Irène and Martin had told their stories, a silence descended on rue Rampon that had not been present in months. Euan had moved out of the apartment across the hall and hired a real estate agent to sell it. He was living full-time at the Anglophile and resisted Martin's attempts to meet for lunch.

"There's nothing left to say," Euan said over the phone. "I can't see how an awkward lunch would help. I'm not angry with you, Martin. I realize now that falling in love with you was a mistake. I thought I could change you, make you forget David, but I was a fool."

Diane had called from Poland and said she and Sullivan were heading back to Berlin to check on Christian. Diane refused to acknowledge whether she was involved with Sullivan, romantically or sexually.

"Mind your own business," Diane said when Martin pressed her.

"Are you coming back to Paris? What about your job?"

"I'll email my resignation to Euan," she said. "It would be très weird working there with Mayor McBitter."

"Thank you for going back to Berlin."

"Just wait until you get Sullivan's bill."

Three weeks to the day that Irène had met Frederick, the buzzer at rue Rampon sounded. Martin and Irène were sitting at their desks eating sandwiches. Martin got up and went out onto the balcony and leaned over to see V. Hugo standing on the street.

"Monsieur Paige, please let me in. It's urgent."

V. Hugo bustled into the apartment and went to the television and switched it on. He flipped through the channels while Irène and Martin stood behind him expectantly.

"What are you doing?" Irène asked.

"I received a phone call from Frederick Dubois. He said I should come here and turn on the television at one o'clock."

On the screen, a camera was aimed at the front door of Frederick's château outside Chambéry. The scene cut to a different camera that showed heavily armed police surrounding the house, a convoy of police cars and ambulances and the roar of helicopters. Across the bottom of the screen a graphic said: *French authorities arrest drug lord.*

An anchor was trying to describe the events happening on the screen when the camera cut back to the door of the château. Two policemen emerged followed by Arnaud, who paused and turned to look back over his shoulder as Frederick was brought out on a stretcher covered by a blanket. Paramedics rolled the gurney, shadowed by armed policemen wearing bulletproof vests.

The police cleared a path to a waiting ambulance as reporters shouted questions at Frederick, who was more gaunt and pale than Irène remembered. Frederick stared straight ahead emotionless as he was rolled out of the camera shot, which panned back to Arnaud surrounded by reporters shoving microphones in his face. Arnaud held up his hand and called for quiet.

"I have a very short statement. We received information that a significant drug operation was headquartered at this château. Warrants were executed and an arrest has been made. Other arrests are being made now in Paris and across France. Further statements will be forthcoming through the usual channels."

Questions were shouted at Arnaud as he walked toward the ambulance where Frederick was being put aboard.

"What is your name, monsieur?" a reported shouted.

The camera zoomed in on Frederick, and a thin smile played across his face. "I have many names," he said. "Ask the government."

A furious Arnaud leaned down and whispered something in Frederick's ear. Frederick laughed and then started to cough.

"Get him in the ambulance," Arnaud said tersely, "and move these cameras back."

The paramedics collapsed the wheels and rolled Frederick into the back of the ambulance and Arnaud got in with him. The camera stayed with Frederick, who looked straight into the lens and blew a kiss. Then he spoke: "Time passes, and little by little everything that we have spoken in falsehood becomes true."

"Shut the doors," Arnaud yelled at the policemen, who quickly complied.

The reporters followed the ambulance as it crossed the chessboard and weaved through the topiary pieces until it reached the main drive where it was joined by police vans and a motorcycle escort.

"He turned himself in," Irène said.

"Why would he do that?" Martin asked.

"He's dying. It's a last act of contrition."

"What did he say there at the end . . . about falsehood becoming truth?"

V. Hugo cleared his throat. "It's a quote from Proust's *À la recherche du temps perdu*. Specifically, the volume called *The Fugitive*. It must be a message for you, madame."

For the next two days, Frederick's arrest and the major blow to France's drug culture was front page news and seemed to be on television round the clock. Journalists were trying to find out more about the man police called André Sarde, but whose identity could only be traced back to 1971. The pundits and experts speculated on every nuance of the case, while the police were tight-lipped, but happy to provide footage and information about the dozens of other arrests of lower-level drug dealers connected to Sarde.

Irène abandoned the manuscript she had been editing and sat in front of the television, the remote dangling from her hand, switching channels looking for more news about Frederick.

"What do you think they're going to say that you don't already know?" Martin asked, bringing dinner to her on a tray.

"I don't know," she said. "It's just a feeling that something else is coming. That this isn't quite over."

On the third day, a news anchor breathlessly reported breaking news: André Sarde was being moved from Lyon to Pitié-Salpêtrière Hospital in Paris for treatment of an undisclosed illness. The same hospital where Jean-Louis had been taken, where Irène identified his body, where the ghost of the boy Frederick used to be had manifested itself to her in the summer of 1995 as she and Martin searched for David in the aftermath of the metro bombing.

"They're taking him to Salpêtrière," Martin said. "That can't be a coincidence."

"Nothing is coincidence," Irène said.


The next day, Irène and Martin went to Salpêtrière. When they stepped out of the elevator on Frederick's floor, they saw Arnaud standing at the end of the hallway with two other uniformed officers. Arnaud did a double take as he saw them approaching.

"Madame Laureux and Monsieur Paige . . . we meet again too soon," Arnaud said, walking toward them as the officers stood in front of Frederick's door, hands not quite resting on their guns, but close enough to draw quickly.

"I've come to see Frederick Dubois," Irène said.

"There's no one here by that name," Arnaud smiled. "You must be on the wrong floor."

"I think I have a list of his aliases in my purse," Irène said, digging in her bag.

"Very funny, madame. You know it is impossible to see the prisoner."

"Is he a prisoner?" Martin asked. "Have you formally charged him?"

Arnaud cut his eyes at Martin. "How was Berlin? Cold, I imagine."

Irène put her hand lightly on Arnaud's arm, almost coquettishly. "Now, now, boys. We've come to see an old friend who is gravely ill. Surely the police won't have any objections. Feel free to search me for any nail files or weapons."

"Monsieur Sarde is allowed no visitors except for his attorneys," Arnaud said. "This is a federal case. I'm afraid it is out of my hands."

Irène looped her arm through Arnaud's and leaned toward him conspiratorially. "Walk with me." She tugged at Arnaud's arm and pulled him back down the hallway. "Inspector, the man in that room was an agent for the French government. He was complicit in my husband's death. The government has known about Frederick Dubois and let him do as he pleases for thirty years. With that horde of media outside looking for any scrap of information about the man you're calling André Sarde, I know they would be thrilled to hear my story."

Arnaud stopped short and grabbed Irène by the arm. "Do not threaten me. You and your friends have gotten off very lightly. I suggest you go home or I will have you arrested."

"You keep threatening arrest but it never happens," Irène said, pulling away from Arnaud. "Go on—arrest me. Martin will tell my story to the media. Or Diane Jacobs or V. Hugo. All I want is five minutes and then I will go home. You will never hear another word from me."

"If only I could believe that," Arnaud said.

"Five minutes, Inspector, or the media is going to be camped out at your office, your home. You won't be able to take a piss without a reporter breathing down your neck. With all the recent trouble in the banlieue and accusations of police corruption . . ."

Arnaud rocked back and forth on his heels. "Five minutes. No more."

Irène smiled. "You are a nice man at heart aren't you, Inspector?"

"Madame, you missed your calling as an interrogator. You would have had men weeping in corners."

"I've been told that before."

Arnaud walked with Irène back down the hallway and spoke to the guards. They stepped aside and Arnaud knocked once and pushed open the door.

Irène passed between the two policemen and Martin started to follow, but Arnaud blocked his way. "Just Madame Laureux."

"Don't be troublesome, Arnaud," a weak, but gruff voice, called from inside the room. "Let Monsieur Paige in. It might be my last opportunity to see a pretty boy."

A look of disgust flashed across Arnaud's face.

"Did you know that Christian was working for Frederick Dubois?" Martin asked Arnaud. "Wouldn't the press love to know that?"

"Shut up," Arnaud snarled. He grabbed Martin by the shoulder, pushed him into the room and slammed the door.

Frederick was sitting up, a stack of pillows behind his back and head. His face was sunken, almost skeletal. Monitors and IVs were clustered around the bed.

"Here we all are at last," Frederick said, clasping his hands on his chest. "I'm glad you both came. I hoped you would. I prayed."

"How long have they given you?" Irène asked.

"Minutes, hours, days."

"They won't charge you with any crime," she said.

Frederick smiled. "I've made a full confession of my crimes, which will be made public after my death. I will go down in history as a notorious, evil drug baron, André Sarde. Frederick Dubois never existed."

"And 1968 and Jean-Louis? That dies with you, as well."

Frederick drew a sharp breath and his chest rattled. "I have used that as leverage for other purposes," he said.

"What do you mean?" Irène asked.

The door opened and Arnaud stuck his head inside. "Your time is up."

Frederick shook his head. "You're worse than the bladder

watching nurses, Arnaud."

"I need just one minute more," Irène said. "Martin, I'd like to speak with Frederick alone."

Martin nodded.

"Come close to me, Monsieur Paige," Frederick said, beckoning him with a weak wave of his hand.

Martin perched on the edge of the bed so that he was face to face with Frederick, who reached out and patted him lightly on the cheek. "Try to be happy, Martin," he whispered. "People deserve second chances. Remain in light; don't dwell in darkness."

"I will," Martin said uncertainly, glancing up at Irène.

Martin went out of the room and Arnaud tapped on his watch. "One more minute."

"This is goodbye, then," Frederick said. "Jean-Louis loved you, Irène. I knew it when he took the statue of Venus and gave it to you as a gift. You believe that if Jean-Louis had lived, he would have chosen me. I don't believe that. As much as I loved your husband, he would never have left you."

Irène reached into her bag and pulled out the black leather-bound journal. "I brought this for you."

Frederick's eyes widened. "Is it?"

"Jean-Louis' journal," she said and placed it into Frederick's trembling hands. "You may not like everything you read, but you will know that Jean-Louis loved you very much. That he wanted to be with you."

"Oh, Irène . . ." Frederick clutched the book to his chest as tears slid down his cheeks.

"I must go, " Irène said, putting her hand gently on his shoulder.

Frederick looked up at her and nodded, silently saying goodbye. Then Irène turned and walked out of the room without looking back.

Frederick caressed the journal, feeling the cover's smooth surface, and then he opened it. A piece of stationery fell onto his chest. Frederick unfolded the paper and held it close to his face. Upon it, Irène had written, *Pardonne, n'oublie pas . . .*

Forgive, but do not forget . . .

# 34 Time Regained

In a back booth at Café Richard around the corner from rue Rampon, Martin poured Irène a glass of red wine. He filled half the glass, but Irène put her finger on the neck of the bottle and held it down until the glass was filled to the rim.

"I'll have to carry you home over my shoulder," Martin said, clinking his glass gently against hers.

"Good. I am beyond taste and manners tonight."

They drank in silence, the café in a lull with only a few other diners and drinkers talking quietly. There was a noisy table on the sidewalk, lots of laughter and hooting, but it was muffled by Miles Davis' trumpet coming through the speakers.

"So what are we going to do with the rest of our lives?" Martin asked.

"Sleep would be nice," Irène said. "I don't think I've slept peacefully in six months."

"Hmmm . . . that sounds like a plan. Now that we have our jobs for life, we can practically be ladies of leisure and Gerard can't say anything about it."

"Oh, he will have plenty to say," she said.

They fell silent again, steadily drinking the entire bottle of wine and ordering another. Martin was already feeling drunk.

"I feel . . ." he began.

"What?"

"I don't know what I feel. Loose ends, I guess."

"Yes. I'm happy we went to see Frederick. I feel at peace about that."

"I'm glad," Martin said. "You deserve it."

"But I also feel an emptiness that I can't quite define. It's as if Jean-Louis just died and also as if he's been dead for thirty years. Time seems to snap back and forth. I have emotional whiplash."

"What do you think Frederick meant when he said people deserve second chances? Was he talking about David?"

"Or Christian."

Martin nodded. "I thought about that, too."

"You miss him."

"Like I'm going to burn up."

Irène reached across the table, took Martin's hand and squeezed it tightly. "Then you should go back to Berlin and tell him."

"He's a drug dealer, thief and liar with multiple identities."

Irène shrugged. "That was Christian's past. He saw a different future for himself, and you were part of it."

Someone was approaching the table and without even looking up, Martin ordered another bottle of wine.

"I am not a waiter."

Frederick's assistant, Geoff, was standing next to the table dressed in a black suit as if he'd just come from a funeral.

"How did you find us?" Martin asked.

Geoff arched his brow, reached into the breast pocket of his jacket and pulled out three envelopes. He carefully put the envelopes side by side on the table as if dealing a deck of cards. Geoff put a finger on the envelope closest to Irène and pushed it toward her.

"This is a check to pay off your expenses: Monsieur Hugo, etcetera, etcetera. I am sure you will agree it's very generous."

Irène pushed the envelope back. "I don't want Frederick's money."

"Madame Laureux, this is merely a token . . . a drop in the bucket as they say. Monsieur Dubois' assets are being frozen and his fortune will wind up in the hands of the government."

Geoff put his hand on the middle envelope and pushed it to the center of the table. "These are permanent visas for Monsieur Paige and Madame Jacobs."

"What?" Martin looked up at him, incredulous. "How?"

"Part of Monsieur Dubois' negotiations for a full confession of his crimes."

Geoff put his finger on the third envelope and pushed it toward Martin. "This is for you. It is time sensitive, so you should open it now."

Martin picked up the envelope and turned it over. It felt oddly heavy and bulged in the middle. He slid his finger under the flap and pulled out a piece of Frederick's expensive stationery. Martin unfolded the paper and a locker key fell onto the table. A round tag attached with a metal ring bore the number C-17. Scribbled on the piece of paper was "Gare du Nord."

Geoff looked at his watch. "You should go right now."

"I'll come with you," Irène said, sliding out of the booth.

"No, madame. As you took a journey, Martin must also."

The taxi pulled up in front of the entrance of Gare du Nord and Martin opened the door before the car came to a full stop. People of all nationalities stood on the wide sidewalk beside piles of luggage, while others dashed through traffic to make their trains. Street vendors were selling flowers and food and volunteers were passing out pamphlets for various religious and political causes. Several tracts were shoved toward Martin as he entered the arrival hall, but he brushed them aside.

After wandering around the cavernous hall, Martin stopped a security guard who pointed him toward the lower level of the station. Martin ran down the stairs and saw the sign *Consigne Automatique* overhead. There were rows and rows of lockers of various sizes and Martin realized C was the bottom row for larger pieces of luggage. What could Frederick have possibly left in this locker that Martin had to retrieve alone? Martin realized that he had not really processed what Irène told him about how closely Frederick watched them, subtly manipulated their lives.

Martin found the locker and knelt down. His hand shook as he put the key in the lock and turned it. There was a metallic click and the door popped open. *Well, nothing exploded*, Martin said to himself, and cracked open the door. The first thing Martin saw lying just inside the door was an envelope, but there was something else pushed further back. Martin swung the locker door all the way open and gasped at what he saw: the statue of Venus de Milo that Irène had sent to him in the summer of 1995 encouraging him to return and that he had left for David in his empty Memphis apartment. The same statue Frederick had found in the streets of Paris in 1968 and Jean-Louis had given to Irène the night before he died.

Martin closed his eyes and opened them again. It was inconceivable that the statue was inside the locker, but when he opened his eyes, Venus was still there and turned at an angle so she appeared to be looking right at him. Martin picked up the envelope and ripped it open to find a single sheet of lined notebook paper. He unfolded the paper and saw messy handwriting in blue ballpoint pen. His eyes scanned down to the bottom of the letter and saw the signature: David.

Martin sat down hard on the floor and put his back against the lockers. His heart was racing and he couldn't seem to make his eyes focus. A woman working at the lost baggage counter across the hall paused and looked at Martin, but then went back to sorting paperwork without saying a word.

*Martin,*

*I can't even begin to explain how sorry I am about everything that's happened. I'm not sure about everything that's happened since I was in Paris, but I know enough to know that I've put you through hell again and that was never the plan.*

*After I got your letter, I felt bad. I seriously did. I came to Paris to talk to you, but then I thought I would just screw everything up for you and your boyfriend. I got mixed up in some weird shit with this guy and I stupidly sold him my passport and got a fake one with a new name. It sounded like a good idea at the time since my parents were looking for me and I didn't want to be found. I just wanted to disappear. I'm a coward for not coming to see you. That's what I planned to do and I got sidetracked. I was scared. I do have feelings for you and I thought I was in love with you. I still think about you, but I knew I couldn't be what you wanted. Maybe I'm bi-sexual. I was just getting so much shit from my folks and they were threatening to cut me off and never speak to me again. It was fucked up.*

*I'm in New Orleans working as a bartender at a bar in the French Quarter called the Blue Parrot. There's tons of tourists and it's open twenty-four hours a day, so I work a couple of shifts. It keeps me busy and out of trouble, I guess. It's weird writing this letter to you. This guy came in named Jeff or Geoff and basically threatened me if I didn't give him the locker key and write this to you. I don't even know how he found me because even my parents don't know where I am. He's some kind of mobster or drug dealer, I think. I brought the Venus statue to Paris to give back to you, but it was so heavy I stashed it in the locker. I left Paris pretty quickly and was going to send you the key, but then that felt like a dick move. I thought they would have opened the locker by now and thrown it away, but I guess it's still there.*

*I lost the poems you left for me. The guy who bought my passport took them out of my bag. I wish I still had them. I think about them all the time. You are an amazing writer and I know you're going to be famous one day. I guess that's all I can say right now. I am so sorry and I love you. I know you probably don't believe that, but it's true. Maybe one day when I get my shit together, I'll be able to figure out who I am and what I want. I know you probably hate me, but I hope you're happy. I'm trying to be.*

*David*

Martin turned the piece of paper over expecting to find something else written there, something more eloquent, perhaps, or another apology. Martin was overcome with the feeling that he had wasted years pining over a confused boy who would have never made him happy. He felt ridiculous suddenly, the idea of David he had built up in his mind demolished in just a few scrawled lines. David was not an enigma or unfathomable, or even a puzzle to be solved.

Martin balled up the note, crushing it hard in his fist, and tossed it back into the locker. Then he reached inside and pulled out the statue of Venus and kicked the door closed with a bang that echoed up and down the hall. He had forgotten how heavy the statue was, but he was oddly delighted to be holding her in his arms again.

"Can I carry that for you?"

Martin almost lost his grip on the statue at the sound of the familiar voice behind him. Christian was standing there, a knapsack hanging from his shoulder. Martin slowly knelt and set the statue on the floor, stood up and rushed into Christian's arms. Christian kissed him hard, lifting Martin off the floor. Over Christian's shoulder, Martin saw Diane and Sullivan sitting on the stairs.

"What are you doing here? Are you crazy?" Martin asked incredulously.

"It's okay," Christian said. "I received a phone call and was told my record was being purged and I was free to return to Paris."

"Who called?"

"Oh, for fuck's sake, don't ask so many questions," Diane called to him. "You've got your lover boy back. Less talking, more kissing."

Martin knew it was Frederick. It was all part of the bargain he had worked out with Arnaud. Leverage, he had called it.

Christian kissed Martin on the forehead, his eyes, his cheeks— the same way he did after they made love. Martin held him tighter.

Diane rolled her eyes. "Okay, homos. Get a room. I need a shower. I have serious train funk." She stood up and reached her hand down to Sullivan, who took it and pulled himself up. He pecked her on the lips and she returned the kiss. Sullivan put his arm around Diane's waist and they walked up the stairs.

"Let's start again," Christian said and held out his hand. "My name is Christian."

Martin took the offered hand and shook it. "I'm Martin."

"A pleasure to meet you. Maybe we could go out sometime?"

"I'd like that."

Christian picked up the statue of Venus and they walked up the stairs, holding hands. Diane and Sullivan were standing with a group of people looking up at TV monitors in the arrival hall. The news was on, the sound drowned out by all the noise of the station, but on the monitors was the taped footage of Frederick being brought out of his château on a stretcher. Running under the image was a crawl that France's notorious drug lord had died earlier that evening at Salpêtrière Hospital.

Irène was only half listening to Gerard, who had called her on the phone shouting that Simon Temple—the man who had bought the publishing house—had died and they were showing him on television. She was watching the news, too, and saw Arnaud standing behind a bank of microphones on the grounds of Salpêtrière Hospital.

Geoff had paid a call to Gerard with legal papers and banking account information. "I should not be so happy because this man, whoever he is, has died, but he has saved the company," Gerard said.

"His name is Frederick Dubois," Irène said.

Gerard was silent. "I am sorry," he said softly.

"No, Gerard, you are right to be happy. This is what Frederick wanted. He told me."

"I've said it before, Madame Irène, but you should write your memoir. There is so much to be said."

Maybe she would. It would keep both Jean-Louis and Frederick's memories alive, would help her ease back into whatever the rest of her life was going to be. The check Frederick had written was more than a token—it was a small fortune. She had already left a message for Euan at the Anglophile that she wanted to buy his apartment. She would present it as a gift to Martin. Maybe Diane would live there, too, if she hadn't already decided to disappear again. Irène wanted her strange little family around her, which was what Frederick had wanted, too. She had desperately wanted to hate Frederick, but that was impossible now.

Gerard was still talking, but Irène had let the receiver fall onto her shoulder. She was watching the television as Arnaud took questions from the press. The journalists were pressing him about André Sarde's real identity. Arnaud waved the question away, saying that although Sarde was dead, the investigation would continue. The truth about 1968 was going to come out, whether she wrote about it or not, Irène thought. Some enterprising reporter would dig into the past and one day would ring the buzzer at rue Rampon. Maybe Arnaud wasn't foresighted enough to realize it, perhaps he thought he could keep the past buried, but Frederick knew otherwise.

Irène looked at the tattoo on her hand, her connection across time from Jean-Louis to Martin. She felt an odd sensation come over her, an almost lightheadedness she hadn't felt in years. The balcony doors were open and she could hear voices coming down rue Rampon from Boulevard Voltaire, the narrow street acting as an echo chamber.

"I have to go, Gerard. Someone is here," she said and put down the phone.

Irène felt like she was floating onto the balcony. It was twilight; the shops and the Bel Air spilling pools of light onto rue Rampon. She saw Diane and Sullivan walking arm in arm. Then Christian and Martin turned the corner onto rue Rampon and Irène had to grip the balcony for support. Christian was carrying something under his arm and as they passed into a pool of light from the hotel, she could see it was the statue of Venus. He handed it to Martin, who took it and raised it over his head like a trophy. Martin looked up at Irène, already knowing she would be there, his reflecting hand.


There are messages humming subsonic across time, voices from the past and future calling into the void until a pattern begins to emerge. Once upon a time, Martin looked into a mirror and could see Irène on the other side, but this was not the beginning, just the middle. From the moment they were born, their lives were meant to intersect. Irène was born, her parents died, which led her to live with her aunt at the apartment on rue Rampon across from the hotel, where she met Jean-Louis, then Martin. A world away, Martin was born, met Peter, because of Peter's death met Diane, who introduced him to David and brought them to Paris, where he met Irène. And everything that came after and is still to come: call it fate, destiny, divine intervention. Nothing is random. Listen closely.

# NOTES / ACKNOWLEDGMENTS

As with *Conquering Venus*, the Paris of *Remain in Light* is a mixture of fact and fantasy. Most of the locales exist, but they've been manipulated to suit the needs of the characters and plot. The descriptions of the 1968 Paris riots are based on actual events, although some have been altered for dramatic purposes.

I had the great fortune of being able to write part of this book in Paris during the summer of 2010. I went to rue Rampon, walked along the Seine and sat in the Jardin des Plantes gazing at the Venus Genetrix. It was a magical summer made possible by my good friends Karen Head and Colin Potts and the fine folks at the Georgia Tech Office of International Education. My mentor, fellow poet and friend, Cecilia Woloch, walked me through Paris and took me for Berthillon ice cream.

I could not ask for a better editor than my longtime friend Kathy Vogeltanz, who knows more about grammar, punctuation and guns than anyone I know. Joy Borazjani knows my characters better than I do and helped keep the continuity in check. The brilliant photographer Krystyna FitzGerald-Morris made me look younger and thinner at her studio in Kent, England.

This book would not have been possible without the love, support and inspiration from these people: Joy Thomas, Tina Miller, Malory Mibab, Steven Reigns, Andrew Demcak, Kate Evans, Vanessa Daou, John Carder Bush, Kate Bush, Peter FitzGerald-Morris, Brokenkites, Jessica Handler, Christeen Snell, Jennifer and Denton Perry, Montgomery Maxton, Kodac Harrison, Lisa Allender, C. Cleo Creech, Ivy Alvarez, Ken Cloudt, Jackie Sheeler, Megan Volpert, Franklin Abbott, Tania

Rochelle, Cherryl Floyd-Miller, Rose Hall, my patient co-workers at *Atlanta INtown,* my family and the BBC Radio 2 morning crew (specifically Alex Lester and Vanessa Feltz), who sustained me in the wee hours while finishing the novel.

And, once again, to Bryan Borland and Seth Pennington at Sibling Rivalry Press for taking such good care of me and The Venus Trilogy.

# BOOK CLUB QUESTIONS

**1.** Martin and Irène define their inexplicable friendship on synchronicity—a theory posited by Carl Jung that nothing is random, but a series of connected events. What are your thoughts on Martin and Irène's platonic love for each other?

**2.** Martin's former boyfriend, David, ended their relationship because he was afraid to come out to his family. Could you identify or have you known someone with David's fear of dealing with their sexuality?

**3.** The two detectives in the novel—V. Hugo and Bernard Sullivan—are radically different in their approach to solving crime. Hugo is more gentlemanly and by-the-book, while Sullivan gets results from threats and physical force. Which detective did you like the most? Who did the better job of unraveling the mysteries?

**4.** The novel makes allusions to Proust's *Time Regained*, Lewis Carroll's *Through the Looking-Glass* and Hitchcock's *Vertigo*. What other literary, film and musical inspirations did you recognize as you read the novel?

**5.** The third book in the trilogy is set in 2005, a full 10 years after the events of *Conquering Venus*. Where do you think all the characters will be in their lives as the story moves into the 21st century?

# THE AUTHOR

Collin Kelley is the author of the novels *Conquering Venus* and *Remain In Light*, which was the runner-up for the 2013 Georgia Author of the Year Award in Fiction and a 2012 finalist for the Townsend Prize for Fiction. His poetry collections include *Better To Travel, Slow To Burn, After the Poison* and *Render*. Kelley is also the author of the eBook short story collection, *Kiss Shot*. A recipient of the Georgia Author of the Year Award, Deep South Festival of Writers Award and Goodreads Poetry Award, Kelley's poetry, essays and interviews have appeared in magazines, journals and anthologies around the world.

# THE PRESS

Founded in 2010, Sibling Rivalry Press is an independent publishing house based in Alexander, Arkansas. Our mission is publish work that disturbs and enraptures.